ON THE
SLOW LAM

By the same author:

101st Airborne Combat Medic: Transition to Duty

ON THE
SLOW LAM

LEO FLORY

ISBN: 978-1-958407-38-7 (Hardback)

ISBN: 978-1-958407-39-4 (Soft Cover)

Cover art and illustrations by Rebecca Hoekman, Elizabeth Flory and Richie Flory.

Book design by designpanache

ELM GROVE PUBLISHING
San Antonio, Texas, USA
www.elmgrovepublishing.com

Elm Grove Publishing is a legally registered trade name of Panache Communication Arts, Inc.

CONTENTS

ACKNOWLEDGMENTS...6

PART I: CONCRETE KID

1. THREE STOOGES...10
2. KNOCK! KNOCK!...23
3. WHIPPOORWILL...35

PART II: THE SLOW LAM

4. SKUNK CABBAGE...48
5. BEATERS...58
6. KING LEO...70
7. CARL BURGER...81
8. HOLY BATZ...95
9. FISH ON...108
10. STOP!...121
11. GUINNESS PRIZE!...134
12. CEASE AND DESIST!...148
13. CONCRETE KID...161
14. SOM-BITZ...173
15. HOBBITS LODGE...185
16. TWILIGHT ZONE...198
17. PEA PICKER...210
18. BLINK ME!...224
19. ROOM 21...238

PART III: REDEMPTION

20. PIKE POISONING...256
21. BIG GAME...267
22. DEFEND YOURSELF!...279
23. STILTS VILLE...293
24. FORTY-SEVEN WORDS...306
25. IGGIT!...319
26. PICAROON...333
27. ATOLL, ATOLL, ATOLL!...346

ACKNOWLEDGMENTS

First, I am thankful for the movie industry, the Spielbergs, the Cusslers, the novelists, the story tellers, the narrators, and all of the incredible sources of entertainment available today. The endless stories with infinite diversity—and the fact that there is always room for yet another.

I must thank my publishers, Mick and Diane Prodger, Elm Grove Publishing, for the wonderful job they did with my earlier book, *101st Airborne Combat Medic*. For examining the original manuscript for this novel, then accepting the task of publishing it. They are not only extremely talented and hard working people, they are wonderfully nice folks. With them, thank you to military historian and writer Ron Werneth who introduced me to Mick and Diane. He has encouraged and pushed and helped me in many ways.

I need to thank my wife Ann in a special way, as I was legally allowed to mentally torture her for nine months as I wrote the book. Ann is my first line of defense for spelling and grammar. However, the chapters come one at a time with a random number of weeks to complete each one, and each chapter ending with a cliffhanger. She was forced to wait every time, and quite forceful in encouraging me to continue!

I must thank my daughter Elizabeth who coached me through the electronic transfers from i-Pad to laptop and understanding the editing program. Her vision of the design for the leaded glass window which also became the basis for the cover art, and for her added insight, humor and traditions to several of the scenes.

I must thank my daughter Rebecca for being the first to suffer through a reading of the original manuscript and adding her many insights and art.

Thanks to cousin Richie Flory for his incredible drawing ability in illustrating the book with personal "mind pictures" of so many scenes. We also appreciate he and Carrie's wonderful and fun hospitality.

I need to thank all my siblings, June, Susan, Bonnie and John, and their spouses, as well as neighbors, Gladys Brinks and Ted Guimond, for reading the first edited copies. Your comments and critiques were so encouraging.

I would like to thank Glenn from the UPS Store in South Haven Michigan, and Laura at the UPS Store in Boulder City, Nevada, for their incredibly friendly help with so many copies of manuscript, art work, binding and shipping.

I thank all those who allowed their names to be used as personality or characters in the book.

I would thank Frank Lloyd Wright if I could, as his masterful design work has influenced the way I look at and do design and building. But, he would probably roll over in his grave if he knew that I had completely faked a home supposedly designed and built by him.

Above all, I thank the Father above for my continued health, imagination and energy.

My apologies if I have neglected to include anyone who may have helped me with this work.

L.F.

PART I:
CONCRETE KID

1. THREE STOOGES

My name is Nicholas Finn. After graduating from high school in the spring of 1964 at the age of eighteen, I knocked around town for a while and found work at a concrete mixing plant in a neighboring town. I labored around the plant for about half the summer, then was asked if I wanted to try driving a mixing truck. I did and became quite good at it. It didn't take long before the contractors were requesting I make their deliveries. But that fall, building and new construction slowed down, and there wasn't enough work to go around. I was not about to take work from the men who were supporting families, so I gave notice. I contemplated college, as my grades were quite high, but just couldn't afford it, and my heart was not yet in it.

That fall of 1964, I decided to take a long shot and join the army to the chagrin of my parents, who were religious and objected. I was sent to Fort Knox, Kentucky, for basic training. My six-foot-two-inch, 180-pound frame put me through basic in a breeze. I loved the discipline. For advanced training I was assigned to the 1st Cavalry Division at Fort Hood, Texas. I was pleased at least in the beginning since the climate was warmer there than at home. I did well in Advanced Individual Training, specializing in small arms (pistols and rifles), crew-serve automatic weapons (machine guns), and mortars (light artillery). I also excelled at map reading. Basic training, AIT, and map reading took about fourteen weeks. Upon graduating, I was promoted to private first class.

All branches of the service were gobbling up new recruits in anticipation of a conflict in Vietnam. I soon became an instructor, and with only six months in the army, I was promoted again to buck sergeant. But in the early spring of 1965, most of the 1st Cavalry, commanded by Colonel Hal Moore, received orders for Vietnam, and we shipped out with the 1st Battalion, 7th Cavalry. After a one-month journey at sea, we arrived in Vietnam and trucked to Qui Nhon, the cavalry's newly established battalion rear. We did reconnaissance patrols and day and night ambushes around the base as a regular regimen. We were all becoming accustomed to the rigors of jungle warfare in Vietnam. We made contact with the enemy only on occasion—small fire fights—but enough to teach the sort of alertness required to survive.

Orders came down from some high command, and we found ourselves given the task of establishing a forward fire base for artillery in the Ia Drang Valley, designated LZ X-Ray. This was to be the first of many major combat assaults by helicopter in the war. Colonel Hal Moore was chosen to command the mission, and he also chose to be part of the mission. In the ensuing weeks we made great preparations for the assault. The colonel and his command crew studied the best possible places for helicopters to land, drop troops, and exit quickly. Stacks of food, water, ammunition, and other supplies, proportionate for a loaded Huey helicopter, were made ready for three companies of soldiers. They were equipped with two batteries of 105mm howitzers, with four cannons each. We were ready, and the day finally came.

I was in the first sixteen bird sorties to deploy on the site, and Colonel Moore was in the first bird to land. We pushed out far enough to guard the next few sorties coming in, and as the number of men increased, we pushed out farther still. As we began to experience a bit of small arms fire, my platoon spotted an unarmed enemy soldier, and we chased after him in hopes of acquiring a prisoner for intel. As we crested a knoll in pursuit, we found ourselves in an ambush and attempted to dig in. We couldn't move from that position the remainder of the day, but we had good radio contact and plenty of ammo.

Meanwhile, as desperate as things were for us, we could hear the fighting increase at the LZ as the helos continued to bring in more and more troops along with armor and supplies. Mortar rounds were falling inside their perimeter now, but the calvary was putting it right back on them. My squad was apparently small potatoes and a small target to the enemy since they seemed to be paying far more attention to the growing threat at the LZ.

Night fell as their interest in us seemed to increase; we already had one KIA and one badly wounded, but we were ready. Foreign voices could be heard approaching as we called in artillery as close to our coordinates as possible, and we repeated this several times during the night, but we were strafed with rifle fire several times in between. I knew most of us had been hit, including myself. It was a hip shot, and I wasn't sure how bad, but I worked to stop the bleeding. Early the next morning the cavalry began making attempts to retrieve us, but it was afternoon before they were able to clear the enemy to do so.

Two of us were still alive when they found us, and we were sent to some field hospital in Vietnam then on to a major hospital in Japan. But my friend and radio operator, Jimmy Green, died on the way and was pronounced KIA at the hospital. I healed at the hospital in Japan and chose to return to Vietnam. My wound was through and through and recovery was fairly quick. It left me with a slight limp from nerve damage but still fully fit to train the new cherries for the rigors of combat, since Colonel Moore saw fit to keep me out of the field for the remainder of my tour. At the end of my one-year tour in Vietnam, I returned to the States with nearly two years remaining in my four-year hitch. I applied for truck driving school, and after being granted my request, spent the remainder of my active tour hauling troops and cargo back at Fort Hood. During that time I made two trips home on holidays to spend time with my parents. Dad and Mom both had serious questions about my tour in Vietnam, but I told them I was assigned to a large base and there was little action.

In the fall of 1968, my obligation to the US Armed Forces ended. I had spent several years in warmer climates and learned to enjoy it. Rumor had it that Atlanta, Georgia, was booming and work was plentiful, so I thought about going there. Because of the wound I received in Vietnam, I not only earned a Purple Heart, but Uncle Sam also saw fit to give me a fifty percent disability rating and a monthly check. I was eligible for the GI Bill and was also becoming interested in the idea of attending college. Going home, I found my folks in good shape. We had some fun times reminiscing, doing this and that, but I could see they were simply doing their own thing now. Adding to my decision-making process was the fact that all the kids I hung with back in school were simply gone. The few I did find were married, had kids, and were working two jobs to keep up.

I had accrued a fair amount of money when I left the service and from the disability checks coming in, so I spent some time car hunting. I first looked at all the muscle cars—nearly purchased one—but saw a beautiful 1967 Chevrolet Caprice Classic, two-door hardtop. It was already a year old, but it was perfect.

After having a couple gear-head hot rods in school, this was luxury to me and had plenty of room to pack all I needed. I headed for Atlanta in the late fall of 1968.

After finding an efficiency apartment on the east side of Atlanta toward Stone Mountain, I began hunting for work and quickly found a ready-mix concrete company that needed drivers badly. It was hard to believe just how fast six months could slip by while you're working every double shift and as many weekends as possible. But my bank account was something to be proud of, and my goal was to be able to attend college full time and work as little as possible. I didn't party much at all; dated a few girls, but nothing serious occurred. I spent some serious time figuring out what curriculum I'd want to follow if I were to start college. Math and science were my strong points, with a GPA of 3.90 in high school. After many research nights at the local library, I found that the University of California at Berkeley had an excellent math and engineering program. Plus, it sounded prestigious. I applied and was accepted (the guarantee of GI Bill money may have helped their decision). This would keep me in warmer weather, and I could see a lot more of the country.

It was late spring 1969 when I gave the Caprice a tune-up, oil change, and a new set of radial belted tires. *Popular Mechanics* said the tires were still experimental, but the good reports were solid. From Atlanta, I took I-20 west and settled in for the long haul. This car was so much nicer than anything I had owned before, and that 396 engine loved the open road. It was also the first car I'd owned that came with seat belts, both a lap belt and a shoulder harness that clipped to the headliner just above the windows. I tested the lap belt and found that it provided a strong secure feel at the wheel. I liked it and used it all the time after that. In retrospect, I suppose this sort of trip would have been much more enjoyable while traveling with a friend, especially a girlfriend. But since losing nearly all my friends in the Ia Drang Valley and a few more after that, I had become a bit more of a recluse.

I stopped at as many parks, historical sites, and tourist traps as I thought I could tolerate as the trip went on. I had already seen some of Texas while stationed at Fort Hood, but after leaving the west side of Fort Worth, the countryside became a lot more desolate. I-20 terminated into I-10 prior to El Paso, and I began to think this was the Wild West until traveling through New Mexico and Arizona. Temperatures were increasing too, and I put to use another new feature to me—this wonderful car had air conditioning.

I loved the Caverns of Sonora in Texas and Carlsbad Caverns in New Mexico, where I spent one extra night just to see the bats leave the cave and return the next morning. It would have been much shorter to just stay on I-10 on into California, but I really wanted to see the Hoover Dam, witness Lake Mead, the blue jewel in the desert, walk the streets of Boulder City, where the men and women lived while building the dam back in the early 30s, and spend a few days in the infamous Las Vegas. Being the math magician that I was and learning well the game of blackjack while in the military, I thought it could be fun.

Leaving Boulder City in the evening, I followed I-93 through Railroad Pass and then descended the mountain connecting to Boulder Highway, revealing most of the valley lit like a Christmas tree, a sea of lights twinkling into the distance. On Fremont Street I found the Golden Nugget Hotel & Casino and stayed there three nights. I won and lost at the blackjack tables and pulled the handle on the slots until my arm was sore. In the end I probably won just enough to pay for the room and food. It was all a blast, but the real fun was talking to such a diverse bunch of folks from all over the country. I-15 then took me into California, through Primm and Barstow, on to I-58 to Bakersfield, then I-5 north to Berkeley.

I did break away from I-5 early on to experience one more natural wonder, the Sequoia National Park. Even though it was late May, there were still remnants of the deep snow that falls in that high elevation. It was quite cool as well, and I needed to search the trunk for a heavier jacket. The diversion was worth it; many of those spectacular trees were there 2,000 years before our Savior Jesus was born. Being nearly alone in this spiritual place, I knelt down in a vista and prayed. I had been very neglectful about praying most of my life, and with difficulty, I reviewed the path I had been through and allowed to survive. I gave thanks beyond thanks for the experiences my God had allowed me thus far and asked for some opportunity to do better in the future.

It was around May 20 as I found my way to the university to finalize enrollment and the use of the GI Bill. I was staying in a motel but soon came to realize that I had arrived three months early and needed not only a place to stay, but something to do. Finding an efficiency apartment a long walking distance from campus, I put down roots for the summer.

My experience at driving cement trucks brought employment almost instantly. I was back doing something that I enjoyed, but for reasons I did not fully understand. Now, all my experience delivering concrete was in five-yard rear-dump mixers. This mixing truck company had begun to use ten-yard front-dump mixers that were new to the mixing business. What a blessing for drivers! With the rear dumping mixers, I had to leave the cab to extend the trough and return to maneuver the truck and trough while a crew would pull the mud. I'd have to reposition the vehicle every time the work became out of range of the trough and the mud too far away to pull, and then I had to get the truck out of the way for hosing down all the dirty parts, hang the troughs back on the holders on the truck, and finally leave the work site.

But these front dumpers only required getting out once to attach the troughs and once for cleaning and reattaching. I could see and maneuver the truck into the exact spot the finishing crew wanted instead of needing to back up by hand signals into position. However, there was one other reason for me to leave the cab and that was to pull concrete with the crew if it looked like they were short of help. It was one thing that kept me on call, since few drivers would help the finishing crew. There was one other thing that always paid dividends in this delivery business and that was having to learn every street and pig path in the area. In three months, I knew Berkeley like the back of my hand.

Aha, college at last. Classes began in early September, and I was ready in many ways. I had a bit of an awakening during my initial enrollment, since a great deal of the student types still hanging around campus were wearing long hair and sloppy clothes and actually looked drugged out. When I graduated from high school, the dress code was fairly straight forward—slacks or denims, shirt, and polo or pullover. For the girls: skirts, blouses or sweaters, and occasionally dress slacks. In the military there was no choice, just a type of dress for each occasion— clean, pressed, starched, gig-line straight, and footwear polished. I fit well into that regimen and carried it out in my civilian life prior to and after the military. I pondered this early that summer and decided that fitting in just a bit could help this "old guy" make the transition a little easier. I let my hair and beard grow.

One rule at UC was that all first-year students were required to live on campus, so I had an assigned dorm room. However, I kept the contract for the apartment, as it also provided a place of solace and a place to park the Caprice.

Dorm room 101. I arrived very early on opening day, unloaded everything I thought I would need from the Caprice, locked it in the dorm room, returned the car to the apartment, and walked back to campus. I had no apparent reason for anonymity, but letting my hair grow and keeping the apartment a secret was done through some form of instinct. I had not yet been in a position to feel any aggression toward us veterans, but I had seen a bit of that sort of thing happening on TV. I decided not to reveal my veteran status as well.

I had time to relax on my bunk before my roommate arrived, since I had already carefully reviewed my first semester books. In time he arrived, walked in, threw several duffels on the open bunk, looked at me with no particular expression, and then looked back at the door as his parents walked in carrying a myriad of stuff.

As I stood up, his parents, who appeared to be at least moderately wealthy, were the first to introduce themselves.

"Hello, my name is Thomas Reginald Mahan II, and this is my wife Susan, and my son Thomas Reginald III," the man said while offering his hand.

Susan offered a hug, which I accepted, and I offered my hand to Mr. III, who looked up to make eye contact then nonchalantly stuck out his hand. I offered to help carry anything remaining, and they took me up on my offer. After two trips, Mr. III's half of the room was quite full. There was little doubt the parents were happy with their son's roommate, even if the verdict was still out for Mr. III.

I laid back on my bunk as he went about sorting his stuff and making his bed, chatting from time to time. He was a head shorter than me and fifty pounds less in stature. He had long, unkempt black hair and a slight beard and was probably no more than nineteen. He dressed a bit unkempt as well and was wearing open-toed sandals. Thinking about his name, Thomas Reginald Mahan III, I remembered a quip I had heard in some barracks talk about Joe shit, "The Rag Man." Laughing to myself, I decided to call him Rag. I got the impression that life had probably been quite easy on him, but I would let that verdict rest until I could see him in action. Anyway, I had no idea how I, myself, would perform under a curriculum load. I had faith I could handle it, but it had been a while since my school days.

I had reconned—excuse me—explored the campus several times during the summer, so I knew all the buildings, classrooms, and especially the location of the chow hall—excuse me—the cafeteria. I knew that a lot of my classes would be orated and realized I would need my hearing aid, which was at the apartment. I needed to disappear long enough to retrieve it. After engineering a time gap, I made the one-hour round trip on foot, and as I walked, my mind slipped back to that forty-hour event in the Ia Drang Valley. Being the platoon leader, I had needed to call artillery in desperately close to our position to keep the enemy from overrunning us. My right ear sustained permanent damage, so Uncle Sam supplied me with a hearing aid. I needed it mostly for auditoriums, classrooms, or certain movies but most one-on-one conversations were no problem. My new hair growth hid it fairly well.

As the semester began, Rag wasn't very talkative, but I knew we had at least one class together, and that was math. My class load was fifteen credits. I worked really hard for about two months as I came to realize that it wasn't easy for me, but not all that hard either. I could devote more and more Saturdays to recreation and work. Concrete was being poured year-round, and the company dispatcher promised to look for Saturday morning deliveries for me. Weekend work always paid a premium, but some of the guys with families begged for a weekend off now and then. I could make $80 before noon; if it were factory work, I'd make $25, and Mickey D's would be $15. I kept my bank account in Atlanta and just wrote checks as needed, but with this Saturday work, I needed little extra cash.

After testing at the end of that first semester, I acquired a great deal more confidence since my GPA was 3.8—with math it was 3.9. I was very joyous, nearly ecstatic, when I called my parents and shared it with Rag. He congratulated me, but I could sure sense a bit of indifference. Rag studied, but he also had some sort of nightlife that involved some upperclassmen. I had to endure being awakened on many nights and was beginning to resent it. However, after our final exams, he began to talk a bit and at least acknowledged that I was sharing the room. One day not long after, I noticed his test grades in a slightly open drawer and took the liberty of having a look. He was at a 2.9, probably a reflection of his extracurricular activities and his new almost-respect for me. He also became more inquisitive about who I was, where I'd come from, and my age.

As we got deeper into the second semester, I shared more of the not too personal data. I told him I was from the southwest corner of Michigan, about halfway between Kalamazoo and Lake Michigan. I grew up on a farmette in the midst of big farms near a small town. My father was a purchasing agent for a company in a neighboring town, and my mother was a high school science teacher. I fibbed a bit about the last four years since graduating from high school in 1964 and not starting college until the fall of 1969. I told him I had worked several places in the country, settling in Atlanta for a while, and when I thought I could finally afford tuition, I chose UC Berkeley for the math program. One day Rag saw me install the hearing aid and became quite curious about it. I told him it was from a birth defect.

Depending on circumstances, I would make the hike to the apartment on Friday nights or early on Saturday mornings, poke in a load of laundry, and call dispatch. If there was work, great, if not I could kick back, listen to the radio, and rest. I hadn't bothered with a TV and was unaware of how much news and controversy Vietnam was causing. I heard snippets from time to time and was confused by it. The South Vietnamese people rejected communism and sought independence; they asked us for help, and we obliged. My experience there was horrific. I could have gone home after being wounded, but I was a soldier by choice and wanted to fulfill my duty. I did, and now I felt I had a right and an obligation to those that lost their dreams to go forward to honor them by fulfilling mine.

I was still in the service in February of 1968 when the infamous Tet Offensive broke out in Vietnam. Everyone in Fort Hood was watching when that went down, watching the revered TV anchorman Walter Cronkite crouching by a plane on an airstrip near Saigon. He proclaimed, "We are losing the war."

In five words, he effectively demoralized all America and all its current and future GIs while the GIs around him were making sure his self-righteous ass was protected. The opinion of most soldiers at the time was that he should not have made it back to the United States alive—and America would probably have been better for it.

As it turned out, the North Vietnamese Army, or NVA, and Viet Cong took only the city of Hue and held it for about ten days. They lost every single engagement in their offensive, and it decimated the Viet Cong from then on. I was of the opinion that the war shouldn't last much longer after that. But nothing ever comes to any sense or good when politicians feel they can move anything in their own direction, regardless of cost or damage to anyone or anything. Now big media was throwing in with the corruptors of American mental health. From then on news was no longer based on actual story or facts but on opinion, regardless of how distorted it was.

Rag and his friends, who now included a skinny chick that dressed mostly in black and talked way too much but needed to since every other word was four letters, started hanging out in our room on Sundays during my homework time. I began staying at the apartment until late.

Rag said, "Where have you been going so late at night?"

I replied, "I have relatives near enough to walk to, and I can do laundry and study there as well. I have a lady friend and am also spending some time with her too."

Returning early one Sunday, I was approaching the room when I heard them ranting about forming a protest rally on campus opposing the Vietnam War. I listened until I could no longer bear it, then walked back to my own place. While walking along somewhat bewildered, I gave myself credit for what I thought at the time was the intuition that caused my anonymity. I would learn in years to come that it was much more than intuition.

Things didn't change much in the dorm room. I was never involved in much of Rag's business in any way. I just didn't employ much of my friendly nature after that. Rag came in one day all bubbling and happy as he dangled the keys for his new (used) VW van that was a lookalike for his sophomore buddy Karl Hanley's car. I just thought of Karl as "Knot Head." His girlfriend's name was Ilene Chase, or "Icky Chick," who had an old VW bug convertible. They parked side by side in the limited parking lot spaces.

Posters had been showing up around campus over the last

month calling for a protest rally against the Vietnam War that was scheduled two days prior to classes ending for the summer. One was even posted on our dorm door. It was time for me to quietly move off campus, so at every opportunity I carried clothes and small things to the apartment until it was necessary to use the car. A few days prior to the campus rally, I drove to the dorm area for the first time since arriving. To my chagrin, Rag or one of the other three stooges must have seen me exiting or loading the car.

A little later Rag asked me, "What is with the Fort Hood sticker on the windshield of your car, and how did you keep that car hidden all this time?"

I felt heat at the back of my neck, my blood pressure increasing. In a slightly louder than normal but controlled voice I told him, "I completed a four-year hitch in the army, one of which was in Vietnam, and I am very proud of my service to our country." I hopped in the car and left.

Later that evening I returned, loaded the last few items, and went partway across campus to turn in a few books. Near dusk on my return, I found that someone had used aerosol paints to write all over my car. It was bad stuff, including "Baby Killer."

I went home angry to say the least, but very confused. Why were they attacking me? I didn't start that war; I was just answering the call of my country. Where was their call originating from?

As soon as our finals were complete, I made a request for my transcripts to be sent to my parents' address, as I had no intention of returning to UC. I found a body shop that could rub out the spray paint and put a new shine on the car. I closed out the apartment, gave all the extra stuff to the Salvation Army, and got a hotel room for a few days.

I filed no complaint with Rag, Knot Head, Icky Chick, or with the college. I just waited until the morning of the last day of school, knowing the three stooges would be sleeping in. About daybreak, I arrived at the campus parking lot with a loaded front-dump cement truck. All three VWs were parked side by side, so I didn't even need to exit the truck to extend the remote control trough—it had sufficient reach.

Even I was impressed at the strength of the hydraulically controlled trough as it pierced through the back window of the first van, lifting the roof a bit. I inserted about a yard and a half of mud and moved to the next van. The results were the same, so I pierced the ragtop of the bug, but it only held about a yard. I had no desire to mess up the parking lot with spilled concrete, so I shut it down and left.

I had made good friends with the dispatcher that season. He had a short load for that day, and I asked him to put on an additional four yards for me, explaining that I had a side job. He obliged without question. I then went on to the real job and completed it. I returned the truck, cleaned it, made it ready for the next driver, and paid for the extra mud at the office. I also made a generous tip to the dispatcher and asked that my name be erased from the work log that morning. I hopped into the Caprice and headed for Michigan. I had heard folklore about some jealous husband doing what I did with concrete, but it was not lore any longer.

What I had done was a crime, I know. I really couldn't get a grip on what would allow me to step so far out of my own bounds. However, I didn't have much remorse either. In fact, I would catch myself chuckling and wondering what their response may have been. I could be caught, but UC shouldn't be looking for me. I did the college no physical harm, even if they were the breeding ground for folks like Rag. My personal records would be closed to all except maybe the FBI. The fate of their vehicles would not go further than the local police. If any of the three stooges were smart enough to note my license plate, it would lead them to a defunct address in Atlanta. It would be difficult to track me down.

Again I took time crossing the country, heading back through Vegas for a bit more blackjack. I took I-15 northeast into Utah, touring Zion National Park, Bryce Canyon, Arches National Park, and Moab. Following I-70 east over the Rockies past Vale, I drove down to Denver and across the vastness of Kansas and Missouri. I-55 took me to Chicago, and I-94 was nearly home.

It felt great to be home with the folks for a while. We had a great deal to talk and reminisce about. They asked me about college, and I asked them to wait for my transcript to arrive, which it did a few days later. After we reviewed it, Dad suggested we celebrate and sponsored a stay-over in South Haven on Lake Michigan. Over a beer one evening, dad prodded me again about my tour in Vietnam. I balled up inside a bit and again told him it was mostly uneventful. They were proud of me, I could feel it, and I did not want to disappoint them or cause them concern.

During this needed respite I spent time scouting another college for my sophomore year. Hillsdale College in Hillsdale, Michigan, had great appeal, but I was now fully accustomed to warmer weather. Augusta Technical College in Augusta, Georgia, came on the beacon and I investigated, finding that it might be off the radar just enough for me to be comfortable. After forwarding my transcripts, I was accepted for the fall semester.

I stayed with the folks until we all celebrated the Fourth of July by traveling to the small town of Decatur. This town had a very active VFW and American Legion that provided the best parade in southwest Michigan. After the parade, they barbecued chicken for everyone and sold draft beer for fifty cents a cup. It was both a great celebration as well as time for setting my sights on my next goal.

2. KNOCK! KNOCK!

I REPLATED THE CAR in Michigan, using my parents' address, as it was likely I would be returning home each summer. The Caprice was packed, hugs and handshakes were given, and the 396 was ready to do her stuff. It was a long haul to Augusta, but with a couple short naps along the way, I arrived on July 6, 1969. I secured a motel long enough to find another apartment, this time in a walkout basement with access to a washer and dryer, and parking for the car. After doing the administration work at ATC, I went job hunting. The yellow pages showed me two cement mixing plants in the area, so I went to the one nearest the college first. I was hired that day and started the next. It was back to the smaller rear-dump mixers, but I knew them well.

Again, I applied for all the hours and weekends I could get, but it was a pain at times. I kept the Atlanta bank account and wired the deposits to them every few weeks. The bank was always easy to work with and answered the phone every single time I called. If I had a weekend off, I headed for Savannah, Georgia, or Myrtle Beach, South Carolina, and got a fair amount of beach time with some solid relaxation.

During that summer I experimented with a few of the top shelf alcohol mixers and found that I liked them. A good Manhattan was at the top of my list. Beer was OK on a hot day, but only one or two. I had gone overboard a few times and found that I just could not bear the feeling of not being in complete control. In fact, it was downright frightening, so I maintained my discipline always. I also purchased a small portable TV for the apartment, since it was about time I paid a little more attention to current events. The serials were funny, and PBS had some worthwhile history and nature from time to time, but national news never failed to produce something negative about America or Vietnam. It was hard to bear, but I needed to hear it.

Classes started in early September 1969 and again I put full concentration into the schoolwork for the first two months or so, finding again that I was doing well and could back off enough to work Saturday mornings and relax some. I lived off campus but found several friends pursuing goals similar to mine, and hanging out and talking with them was well worth the time. These sort of more serious conversations between classmates with varying goals and ambitions were the thing we all needed to direct us in choosing a major for the junior and senior years.

I took note of the lack of black students on campus—we were in the south, where there were many black families. It didn't make sense. During my time with Uncle Sam, their proportion seemed about normal. In Vietnam, the black GIs seemed to hang a bit to themselves in the rear areas, but on the line, we were as one. I would die for my comrade regardless of race, creed, or color, and I had full confidence that they would die for me. Time and living in the south would teach me, but being from the north and from a small town, I was insulated from what had been happening down here. My family, my church, and my school never taught anyone to be prejudice. I do not think I was just naive.

My friend and comrade, Specialist First Class Robert Butts, a black man also from Detroit, Michigan, died just a few feet from me in the Ia Drang Valley. I traveled alone to his grave one day while I was home in Michigan, but it was hard for me to do. I wondered deeply what he may have thought of the protests going on in America that vilified the GIs, black or white, brown or red. And at the same time, I was thanking our Maker that I was feeling nearly none of the prejudice at ATC.

That year my parents were heading to Florida for a month's vacation and were planning to stop and spend a few days with me during Christmas break. Prior to my parents arriving, I realized that I hadn't paid much attention to my personal appearance. I was still dressing neatly, shoes shined and so on, but my facial and head hair was out of hand. I expressed to some friends at school that I didn't trust the local barbers to give me more than a GI "high and tight" cut. And what about my beard?

These classmates of mine were probably a cut above my meager beginnings and had enjoyed life beyond the local barber. They suggested that I look for a salon that also offered hair styling for men. I decided I'd step out of my bubble and try something new. So before my folks arrived, I had found a hair stylist, who happened to be a very good looking black woman who took a liking to me and made my hair and beard look really good. Mom had expressed her pride and gratitude in my appearance over and over. At that, I was happy with the way I looked.

When my parents arrived, I gave them a twenty-five cent tour of my two-room apartment, which I might say was as spit and polished as any military barracks. We also toured the campus and some of my classrooms. They stayed in a downtown hotel for two nights as we toured the sites in Augusta and dined in great restaurants, including the famous Luigi's on Broad Street.

Once again, Dad pulled me aside and asked, "Is everything alright, do you need any money?"

I assured him, "Dad, everything is good with me. I do not need any money either, I am flush with cash."

He asked me again about my limp. I laughed, as I had really forgotten about it. My false confession to him was that it had come from a training accident and Uncle Sam had compensated me for it. "I'm good Dad, don't worry."

I met them at their hotel as they were preparing to continue their journey through Savannah and down through Jacksonville, Florida, to some destination on the Atlantic coast. We exchanged hugs, and they hopped into their car and motored south. I was so proud of them for finally using some of their precious time to simply enjoy the fruits of their work.

As for me and my frugal nature thus far, I was sitting on a nearly six-figure bank account. Trying to be wealthy was not my goal at all, it was just happening all by itself. For every time I would blow $10 on a really good cigar, $5 on a top shelf Manhattan, $25 on a needed resource book for school, I would make $100 on a full Saturday's work delivering concrete.

I celebrated New Year's 1970 at my apartment, enjoying two short glasses of Lagavulin single malt Scotch whisky along with a $10 cigar. The weather was cool but comfortable on the small porch outside. I reminisced of being with my folks in Michigan after my exit from California. They had questioned me hard about seeing news regarding a protest against Vietnam that turned into a riot at UC Berkeley about the time I left. I had explained that I knew about a pending protest rally but did not stick around to see what it was about. During that week as we were watching the national news, there was a clip from the Berkeley police announcing that they had apprehended some of the protest organizers. There on national TV was none other than the three stooges! I knew then that if they tried to file charges against me for destroying their VWs, well, good luck. My conscience was not totally clear, but any thought of a legal pursuit from them was gone.

Approaching the spring semester, I was feeling a little paunchy from too much holiday food and lounging. While in the army, I stuck with the early morning calisthenics and three-mile run prior to break-fast. It served me well, and I did my best to keep it up while in college, but it was really hard to keep a regimen. If it weren't for work and sweat-ing hard at it, I'd probably be a blimp.

I found I had access to the track at ATC and managed to start making three milers at least three evenings a week after classes. Burn-ing off that extra fuel can make you feel so much better and energized.

There were two prerequisite classes in the spring semester I was obligated to take, English and Sociology 101. Not that much interest for me, but we must be well rounded, correct? However, these classes were populated by many more girls than my other classes. Trust me now, I was very focused on my curriculum, but I was getting winks! How do you ignore that? Well, I did my best, but there was this one blond, prob-ably of Norwegian descent like me, about five foot nine, always dressed conservatively, but her physical form—OMG—showed through regard-less. Class after class went by and I made no particular move but would always attempt to make eye contact and try to share a smile of friend-ship and not of pure appreciation for what I was seeing.

Checking the roster—excuse me—the class student list, I found her name. It was Annika Bjorn. It was easy to tell that she was as serious about her education as I was about mine, with little interest in losing time in a diversion. But, she seemed to make herself visible to me and allowed eye contact. While exiting the room one day, after a particularly interesting class, I dared call her by name.

I acquired weak knees when she replied, "Well Nicholas Finn, that was an interesting class wasn't it." She had taken time to know my name too! I suppose there was never any ice to be broken, it was just the natural dance of nature, as we were finally connecting.

From that day forth, and for the next two months, it was im-possible for me to plan anything without including Annika. This also included homework, as we both had our sights set high and worked dil-igently to succeed in every class. She was still living in the dorm, but the atmosphere there wasn't always the best for study. I introduced her to my apartment, which she adopted so fast that I wasn't ready. I acted as a cabby, ferrying her back and forth to the dorm, but it improved her staying power in the classrooms.

However strange it may seem, we were still hands off but as close academically as you could get. We saw eye to eye on nearly all levels, but something was missing. We needed to share our life experiences, so we did. She was a sophomore of nearly twenty years old, had a letter in high school cheerleading, and a very high GPA. Her parents owned a dry cleaning company with outlets in several towns, and she had worked summers there for many years. She was raised as a Christian and had gone to church on a regular basis. In her sophomore year of high school she was chosen second runner up as the high school queen. She said she didn't enter the contest in her senior year for fear that she would win and just didn't want the time constraints that came with the honor. Other than that, she had little more history than what she was making day by day.

I was twenty-three, and it was so unfair of me not to share all the successes, along with the horrors that I had already experienced. I began a slow spooning, if you will, of my exploits since high school. It took a week of carefully dividing all my past into short stories. She knew of my four years in the armed service, that I was a lone survivor in a battle in Vietnam, and that I had been wounded. She knew my work delivering concrete and how it provided me with a hefty income and savings. My freshman year at UC Berkeley, my age, my last (revengeful) day at UC Berkeley, and my travels.

At the end of one of these evenings, she just looked at me, knowing that I was not lying about any of it, and said simply, "I love you, Nick."

Oh—oh—oh. I was dumbstruck—didn't realize I was hyperventilating—I must have been looking at her with my jaw on my chest. I couldn't imagine being any happier—or scared—scared to death. I hadn't taken the time to know anything about women—now, one far past my dreams just said what? I put my hands on her shoulders, massaging them gently.

As I closed my eyes, I asked her in a soft voice, "Annika, please say that again."

She said it again, adding that it had such a grip on her that she did not know how to handle it.

I hugged her and she hugged me as we stood there crying until no more tears would come. After we made our very first embrace, we looked at each other and simultaneously started chuckling.

I said, "So, this is how it's all supposed to work?" Then we laughed out loud. We kissed a few more times, my knees so weak. I offered her a chair, and we sat face to face at the dinette table. After facing one another for a short time, in absolute synchrony we both said, "What now?" We had to laugh again for we truly were like soul mates.

While taking her back to the dorm, we agreed to have a very formal talk about how to proceed. I walked her to the dorm door, where she once again allowed a wonderful hug and then planted a kiss on me that caused a tingle that went all the way to my toes. Going back to the apartment, I needed to keep slapping my own face to stay focused, nearly running two stoplights. It was Friday night, and I was obligated to work that Saturday morning. I do not think I slept that night at all, but I was totally energized when the alarm told me it was time to deliver concrete.

Both of us needed time for homework Saturday afternoon and Sunday. I was taught to be a churchgoer in my youth, but after getting my driver's license at sixteen, that ended all but Christmas and Easter for me. I attended a few universal services in the army. It was basically impossible to attend church on Sundays while in college. I did go to prayer and asked the Lord how he saw fit to send me such an angel, and promised that I would do my best for her.

We talked on the phone several times that weekend. She could call me, and I either answered or didn't—calling the dorm was nearly an impossible task. If one of the other girls answered the phone, she might make a note and pin it to a bulletin board beside the phone, but good luck after that. If one could just leave a message and a callback number—damn that would be nice.

We finally sat together during class on Monday and agreed to hammer out a deal that evening. Yeah right, hammer out things of the heart? I picked her up at the dorm, which was now a routine, and drove directly to the apartment. I kept a variety of snacks and refreshments, along with TV dinners, plus other staples. We busied ourselves getting comfortable and as she was fussing over putting some ice in her tea, I couldn't take it any longer. Moving to her, I took her glass from her hand, placed it on the table, held her close, and we kissed, caressed more, and kissed more.

"OK," I said, "let's sit and figure this out."

I started with a confession. "I think perhaps I fell in love with you back when we were playing non-contact footsies in the classroom. I have never felt so confused than I was about how hard it had hit me as you spoke those three words to me. I am still confused, but relieved, with almost a sense of peace, except that I want to touch you so badly I could slip into the netherworld." I was wondering to myself, how at my age, I had missed this wonderful feeling. I chuckled and said, "I guess I'm your slave. What is it you want?"

She had maintained a wide smile as I rambled on, while keeping continuous eye contact. She said, "I am so happy. I know what I want now...you. But at the same time, I feel so strongly about completing my education, and I love where my vocation could take me. My parents have sponsored everything for me, and I love them and can't let them down either. And at the same time, baby, I want your strong hands all over me, I want it bad."

At that point, I was picturing myself throwing her over my shoulder, throwing her on the bed, ripping her clothes off, and having my way. BLLAAAUUUUGGGHHHH!

She said, "You must be patient with me, Nick. I cannot become pregnant." I assured her that I knew and had to respect her wishes, as that would not fit in for either of us at this time.

Days passed as we continued the routine as it had been—Nick's taxi service. I worked several more Saturdays, which kept me grounded during that time at least. I had cash burning in my pocket, and there were only two weeks left in the last semester, so I asked Annika if she would care for a Friday night out. I told her of a very nice restaurant I found while my parents were in town, suggesting that it was semi-formal.

She said with a sigh, "Oh yes."

I knew dang well that she would love the idea so I had already made reservations in advance at Luigi's restaurant in downtown Augusta.

*　*　*

That Friday evening, Annika must have been watching from the dorm window for my arrival; as I was getting out of the car to go in and greet her in the dorm, she exited the building to meet me, carrying a larger purse than normal. How she came up with the attire she had on,

I cannot guess, but she looked like a dream to me. I was already out of the car, so it only felt natural to open the passenger door for her, see her appropriately seated, close the door, and assume the driving position. It was a warm Augusta afternoon, and I had prepared the car by putting all the windows down on this beautiful hardtop Caprice, so we took the slow cruise to the restaurant.

Arriving on time, we were seated very quickly, and the service followed suit. I had my heart set on a nice Henry McKenna on the rocks. Annika ordered a glass of dark port wine. As adult as Annika appeared, the waiter hesitated and looked like he was about to ask her for an ID, when I exposed a $20 bill at the edge of the table. Our order was filled.

I was quite hungry, so I ordered a medium-rare porterhouse, baked potato, and veggies, while Annika ordered roasted chicken with veggies only. It required two rounds of drinks (and another $20 bill) to complete this wonderful meal together. It was the only time thus far that we kept the chatter on any fun thing that occurred in our lives to date. It was lighthearted and wonderful.

Back in the Caprice, I so enjoyed the power windows, dropping them all down for the late-night cruise back to my apartment—not the dorm. Exiting the car, I moved quickly to see her out of her side, as she retrieved her bag from the back seat, and noticed that it was a bit heavy. Always being open with one another, I said, "So, you'll be staying here tonight?"

She looked at me with a quirky smile and said, "Dummy," then headed for the door. OK then! She had her own key by then and was waiting for me in the doorway.

Now, I had never thought of logistics as being part of my nature, but being prepared seemed to be a likely part of the way I lived. From my pocket, I showed her a small square foil package I had acquired at a local drugstore earlier in the day. The door wasn't closed yet when she planted a lip-lock on me just like the one at the dorm. I was toast!

I swear, the thought of logistics—she was so far ahead of me I couldn't catch up. I sat down on the sofa, watching as she disappeared into the bathroom with her bag. She emerged a short time later. Oh, oh, oh! What sheer cloth hides and exposes at the same time will drive you crazy! Annika was a very voluptuous, beautiful woman. She entered the bedroom, leaving the door slightly ajar. My poor feeble brain was thinking, "Now what do I do? Go in the bedroom stupid!" I took the advice and entered the room where Annika had turned down the bed, turned on a night-light, and laid propped up on the two pillows, anticipating. I was clearly a basket case. I must have fumbled around long enough for her to crawl across the bed to me, and begin unbuttoning my shirt and untucking it from my pants. She unbuckled my belt, and returned to her place on the bed.

As she lay back down, she said, "You're on your own now!"

I think I got it. I slowly removed the shirt, tossing it to the chair, dropped the trousers, stepped out from them, then pulled the white T-shirt up slowly over my head. I was no slouch either, I had abs. I heard a low guttural sigh of approval come from her as I climbed onto the bed. But then I heard what could have been a cry and saw a strange look on her face as she saw for the first time the deep scars on my hip and my leg. Bullets make terrible holes in human flesh. I had several other unnatural scars on my back and chest from shrapnel, but they were minor wounds. She had believed what I had told her, but now she was seeing it first hand, for the first time.

What took place after that is between Annika and me, but I will share that we were both quite clumsy, but nature certainly has a way of correcting what we do not know. It wasn't long before I came to realize that I had made a serious logistic mistake—I purchased only two condoms. I just didn't know. If I'd been better prepared, there would have been no sleep that night. We cuddled, her back to my chest, my arms around her, as she went to sleep making a sound like a feline purr. I'm not sure if I slept or not, but I kept guard until morning.

Reality can sure beat the crap out of you at times. Less than two weeks remaining in our second semester—well that was wonderful, but it also meant we would be separated for the summer. Annika's parents would be bringing a van to pick her up and move her things back home to Williamston, North Carolina. It was about 330 miles northeast of Augusta, a drive just long enough to make you miserable on a weekend trip, but doable. I got off the call list at work for those weeks as we supported each other through the final exams. Mental and, yes, physical!

Those days evaporated. We had made the dean's list and were exhausted. I sat on the steps of her dorm waiting for her parents to arrive and spotted their Williamston Cleaners delivery van as soon as they entered the parking lot. When they exited the van, I allowed them time to stretch from the seven-hour drive.

Annika's dad said, "Hello, we are the Bjorns. You must be Nick?"

I nodded and waved my hand, "At your service. It's nice to meet you both." Annika had advised them earlier that she had a boyfriend, which they would meet at the dorm and who would help load all her things.

Annika had everything neatly packed, so the work began immediately. It worked out well as we learned about one another in this slightly stressed condition. I found them to be wonderful, hardworking, smart people, who were also believers. They had arrived at noon, and by 1400 hours, the van was ready for travel. They debated heading straight back, but with a little persuasion from Annika, they elected to stay the night. We made plans for dinner downtown, and since it was a weeknight, we dined at Luigi's restaurant without needing reservations. Annika had hot tea this time. Mr. Bjorn insisted on paying the check, but I threatened an arm wrestle if he didn't allow me to at least make the tip—I won. He laughed.

I learned that the Bjorn family owned a dry cleaning and laundry business in Williamston and had five outlets in adjoining towns, Janesville, Plymouth, Robertsville, Beargrass, and Everetts. They also did alterations and even shoe repair. They were very hardworking people in a hard business, and they gained all my respect.

At the hotel lobby, we exchanged handshakes, hugs, and worst of all, goodbyes. Annika and I had prepared for this and wrote down all the details we needed to stay in touch. She would be working for the family business for the summer, and I would be delivering concrete, as much as the company would allow. But just like that, I was alone again, and for the first time I actually felt alone.

I dove into the summer work, and there was lots of it. I swore an oath to myself to quit at noon on Saturdays no matter what and give myself one and a half days of respite each week. I still enjoyed a Manhattan and a really good cigar on certain weekends when I felt successful from my week's work. Annika and I talked on the phone weekly, and I even sent cards in response to hers. I made the journey to Williamston about every three weeks, leaving on Friday afternoon and returning on Sunday night. Annika's parents approved of my visits, which included a lot of sleep on their living room sofa. We even managed a few day trips to the Atlantic coast, which included some private time as well.

Sometime late that August, I suppose I was feeling sorry for myself, or in an arrogant mood, or in a WTF mood, or just missing Annika, and I stopped at a VFW that I had passed a hundred times. I was a veteran of a foreign war but was never introduced to any of the fraternal organizations affiliated with the military. Not knowing how any of it worked, I walked in, sat down at the small dimly lit bar, and ordered a Manhattan. The bartender asked me for my card, and I said, "I need a card?"

She said, "Your VFW membership card."

"This is my first time in a VFW, how do I get a card?"

From the darkest end of the bar where two shadowy figures sat, a voice said, "You need to ask me, I am the commander of this post."

"Then I am in luck," I said.

He quickly replied, "Not so fast, sonny, what qualified you for the VFW?"

I proudly told him I was with the 1st Cavalry for a year in Vietnam.

He laughed at me and said, "That was no f'n war, World War II was a war. Now get the hell out of here!"

It was Saturday evening, and I had time to think about what had happened. I thought about it on Sunday as well. I don't know if I was more hurt by what he said or outrightly pissed because of this new rejection of Vietnam veterans. I was truly confused, and only time would eventually explain this mystery. On Monday I had a chat with the dispatcher and asked him to keep an eye out for an early morning short load and told him I would purchase one extra yard of concrete for that load. I purchased the yard in the office and later showed him the receipt. It took another week to find the right order, but the following Tuesday I was good to go.

During that week, I did what any respectable criminal would do, I cased the VFW, both day and night. I found that the commander used the rear of the building for some personal storage. He had a small fishing boat and a mid-60s Jeep ragtop parked in the rear of the building. Neither one was very well kept. Perfect, I thought. Now I could have just let the whole thing go, just walked away and left this jerk to his own demise, but something was holding me on this destructive course.

Tuesday morning, I was the first mixer out of the fill station, and I drove straight to the VFW, pulled around behind, exited the rig to assemble the trough, and backed up into position. It took four cycles in and out of the truck without a flag man, but I managed to put a half yard of cement in the boat and the Jeep, which was more than enough. I did a double hustle to disassemble and secure the trough and was on my way to the real job site.

About a week went by, with only a week remaining to return to my sophomore year in college, when the dispatcher advised me that the local police had been inquiring about a Dave's Concrete mixing truck seen leaving the parking lot of the VFW. He said he would be helpless when it came to the logbooks, assuming it was me they were inquiring about. He was also ex-military but served only in the States. He had a shit-eating grin on his face as he high-fived me. I had already made arrangements with the office for weekend work only, so I went home to put together whatever business I could before the police arrived.

I called the bank in Atlanta and asked for an absolute freeze on my account until I could come there in person. I had already paid for the rent on the apartment until June of the following year. Annika knew where I kept the spare keys to the Caprice, so I put my set with them. I called Annika's home several times—dang, if I could only leave a message! I called the business number, where the secretary paged her several times, but she didn't answer. I finally left a message with the secretary, asking her to tell Annika that I had done something wrong and would be detained for an unknown period of time. I also wrote a note in large print, saying, "Go to the Augusta police to find me," and placed it on the kitchen table.

That was when the knock came at the door.

3. WHIPPOORWILL

I OPENED THE DOOR, where two Augusta police officers stood, hidden grins on their faces. One asked, "Are you Nicolas Finn?"

I said, "Yes I am, and I know why you're here. I'll go with you if that's what you want."

"We're here to take you to our precinct."

"May I lock the door of the apartment?" They allowed it.

They were required to put me in handcuffs before reading me the Miranda. After, they made sure I didn't bump my head while getting in the back seat and then they closed the door.

The officer driving turned his head. "Concrete," he chuckled. "How did you come up with that?"

"I don't know, I'm innocent," and the three of us laughed.

As it was with women, I knew nothing of the law, the constabulary, or the courts. I was about to learn some hard lessons. They took me to the city jail, where they processed me into their system (booked me). They confiscated everything on my person, including my dog tags, which I did not appreciate, then escorted me to a holding cell. There were a few others in the cell, unsavory at best, sitting or trying to lay on the benches around three sides of the perimeter. I found an empty space on the bench and sat down, my brain shifting quickly back to my military life where "hurry up and wait" happened every day. It was time to wait.

My parents taught me that it is always possible to find good in the worst of times, so I spent some time assaying my current condition. I had clean clothes, clean underwear, I had showered only a few hours prior to being picked up, I was not high on anything or addicted to anything, I was strong and fit, and my staying power in tough situations had already been tested to the limit. I was good with this. I would be patient and wait. And I did.

I was put in the cell on a Thursday afternoon. A few of the unsavory individuals came and went on Friday as a new crop came in on

Friday night. I vowed to myself to just persevere as some very disturbed people joined the holding cage. Once again, trying to maintain constructive thought, I reflected on my crime as being driven by revenge, which is arbitrary; you choose to act or choose not to act. Most of the men housed with me were making their decisions based on some need, primarily drugs or alcohol. The outrageous acts that put them in jail were often driven by some girlfriend who left for another guy, or a good friend who made extra cash on their idea, or the second time they were caught selling drugs on the corner. Addiction, or simple weakness, was the primary reason for my fellow inmates.

By Monday I was beginning to look like the rest of the detainees. I was very tired, but I put my head down in solemn concentration to wait for some kind of call. It was after 1300 hours when an officer came to the holding cell to escort me to a room for questioning but not before adding the handcuffs behind my back. A man in the room, I believe was a county prosecutor, advised me that I was being charged with malicious destruction of personal property that they would be treating like grand theft auto.

"Wow, that sounds fairly bad, will I need a lawyer?"

The prosecutor asked, "How do you plead?"

"I am guilty, I can't get around that."

"You do not need a lawyer then."

"So what happens now," I asked.

"Later in the day, you will be moved to a regular cell and given prison clothing, and there you will need to wait for a court date."

"How do I put my personal business in order?"

"Good luck. You will get a couple phone calls, make them count."

Annika, oh Annika. She was no doubt already wondering about the silence. I really screwed up this time, and I didn't even know what would possess me to do such a thing. I could only hope that she received the message at work. She was smart, she would stay collected and start making inquiries. Hopefully with the police first. If she did, she would learn of my captivity and know that I couldn't reach out, so she would need to find me through the legal system.

While waiting for the court date, I was given a couple opportunities to make calls—anything out of state was cataloged and charged to some account in my name. I was fortunate on one call and made contact with my parents. That was a tough one, and they simply did not understand. I told them I would be writing to them and providing all the details. Mom was crying when I had to hang up.

One problem I just couldn't solve was the GI Bill money going for my tuition. I didn't have my records, and I hadn't committed to memory the phone numbers or addresses I would need to postpone the payments. I could only hope that the college would accrue the money for me until I could resolve it later.

A few weeks went by waiting for a court date. This was beyond military waiting (with the exception of the boat ride to South Vietnam). The food was actually quite bad, and I could tell I was losing weight. But I started an exercise regimen early on, which included push-ups, sit-ups, leg lifts, jumping jacks, squat thrusts, and torso twists. I needed pull-ups, but there was no way to do them in the cell.

It was into the third week when I was told to be ready to meet the Richmond County judge. OK, I needed a haircut and beard trim badly, but there was nothing I could do about that. I had no papers to present, and my jail coveralls were well used but almost clean—I supposed I was ready to go. I was escorted from my personal cell, this time in leg and hand chains, to the adjoining courthouse and sat in a side chamber until called. There were three others brought in to sit with me, also in chains, and we sat silent until called. I entered the courtroom first and was ordered to stand while the sentence was pronounced.

The bailiff trumpeted, "All stand! Honorable Judge Richard Stump presiding!"

Only a few people were there: the bailiff, a stenographer, an armed guard, who really looked like a tough guy, and two people in the audience, one of which looked like a reporter or something. The bailiff read, "In the case of Nicholas Finn, malicious destruction of personal property."

The judge looked at me and said, "Son, do you have anything to say for yourself?"

"Yes, sir, I do. I would be happy to purchase a replacement Jeep and boat for the VFW post commander."

My statement must have caught the judge completely off guard because as he kept staring at me as his face became more and more red, his cheeks seemed to puff up, and he held his breath. Then in what I would have thought as unbecoming of a judge, he said loudly, "It's too late for that, sonny. You are going to Richmond County Correctional Facility for the next two years!" I definitely needed a lawyer, but it was too late for that now too.

Only a few days passed before I was transferred via the short bus with four other inmates to the minimum-security correctional facility southwest of the city. Upon arrival, what appeared to be a two-sided cattle gate adorned with anti-personnel barbed wire was being opened by two guards. The bus pulled to a stop inside the perimeter as the two uniformed men closed the gate and walked up to the bus door and ordered us out. I am sure the five of us appeared as a rabble gathered outside the bus, unlike my military days. We hadn't stood long before a medium height, stocky man approached, wearing his sheriff's hat low on his forehead like a military drill instructor.

"I'm Sheriff Edward Stump. This minimum security prison is just one of my law enforcement duties, but I take particular interest in making sure all my assets stay with me until their prison time is satisfied. You will be fed equal portions of fat, carbohydrates, and protein, not only to keep you alive and healthy but able to work. And work you will."

He went through a regimen of rules, ending with this, "If you attempt to escape, or do escape and are captured, add one year to your sentence." And as a highlight, he added, "My department doesn't have tracking dogs, but Scotty Ray, just down the street, owns and trains the best bluetick coonhounds in a five-county area and loves to work them. Enjoy your stay, gentlemen, the work bus will be here and ready to leave at 0700 hours in the morning. Chow is on at 0600. Be ready!"

We were then led to our barracks, about twelve men to each of these old wood frame buildings. We were given sundries, bed clothes, fresh underwear, and three clean uniforms. It was evening by then. I made my bunk and sat on it for a while waiting for the call to the chow hall, which came at 1800 hours. We were all served equal portions of brown rice, salt pork, and boiled carrots. No condiments except for the salt in the pork. It was enough to fill my gut, and we did get the three food groups. I interacted with a few men I recognized from the barracks, but no one seemed talkative.

Early September in Augusta, and it remained very warm and humid as I laid on my bunk with only a sheet, hoping that I could sleep. As I tried to filter through the day's events and my current bewildering situation, two names came to me: Judge Richard Stump and Sheriff Edward Stump.

I must have been physically out of gas that evening because as I was thinking of the Stumps, a pounding came on the door followed by the announcement that it was 0500 hours. Time to get up and get ready. I learned quickly that it was far better to shower in the evening prior to 2100 hours (lights out), as it was a mad scramble in the morning. There was a gang shower with four shower heads, four stools with side dividers only, two urinals, and four sinks. I donned my prison ensemble of black trousers equipped with selector buttons for waist size, black and white striped cotton XL short sleeved shirt, and a pair of used, size 11 low-quarter work shoes with gray socks.

It was first come, first served at the chow hall, so getting there early was important. There was always a line of men waiting at the door that moved along at a decent pace (except when it was raining or bitter cold, then it seemed to move slowly). There were twelve barracks buildings in all, so there must have been about 150 men if the facility was full. The chow hall had a seating capacity of about forty, so it took nearly an hour to feed everyone twice a day. My first breakfast consisted of grits with butter added, link sausage, apple sauce, and orange drink. Three food groups, but no coffee.

As I finished my chow, I could hear the work buses arriving, five or six in all, which turned out to be the norm. When leaving the chow hall in the morning, we were given time to return to the barracks to do our business then get in line for the next available bus. As a bus filled, the gate would open, the bus would pull out, and the next bus would pull up to an open-sided structure where the leg-irons were put on and your name was recorded along with the bus number. Each bus had a driver armed with a revolver and a guard armed with a twelve gauge pump. The gate was reopened, and we were on our way to some work site that took about forty-five minutes to arrive at.

We were ordered out of the bus and lined up, then we filed past the rear of the bus, where there was a large metal storage box attached holding a variety of tools. The job for the day was clearing overgrowth from the sides of some rural road, along with shoveling out overgrown plugged culverts and storm drains. The work was hard and lasted until 1200 hours, when we were given a thirty minute break and an apple.

There was a large metal cooler full of water attached to the back, if you needed a drink. They supplied small cone paper cups that could not be sat down. The work ended at 1630 hours, and we took the forty-five-minute drive back to the correctional facility.

On arrival, the gate was opened and closed as each bus arrived. After exiting the bus, the shackles came off, your name was checked off, and you were free to go. On one side of the open structure there was a row of six old porcelain sinks with a powdered hand soap dispenser, which was actually quite thoughtful. Most of us used them for hand washing. That gave us a half hour or so to finish cleaning up and to get ready for 1800 chow call.

So it went for the remaining three days that week since Saturdays and Sundays were off. I think I would rather have been working in those first weeks, as I had no idea how to develop anything to occupy my time. One of the men in our barracks advised me that on Sundays there was a universal church service conducted an hour after breakfast provided by some prison ministries. I considered it an opportunity to occupy some time and sat in that first Sunday. There were three men that shared the service, taking turns with a short personal testimony of having prison time themselves, finding Jesus while in chains, and now wanting to share their stories and knowledge of the Bible. I found I actually enjoyed it and appreciated them. They did a very good job of explaining the word of God. They said they would be back about once a month, but three other groups shared in their ministry for the remaining Sundays, and they asked us to please be part of them.

I walked the perimeter of the campus several times that afternoon trying to ponder options, but there just wasn't much for me to get a grip on. I could only hope that Annika would dig deep into her intuition and just take over what needed to be done. I so needed her to assume control of the apartment, the car, and any other business that presented itself.

I went back to the barracks, sat on my bunk, and examined the area. Each bunk had three wood shelves on the wall for clothing, towels, sundries, and personal things. Alongside the shelves were three pegs, sufficient to hang your prison clothing, and in the winter, a jacket. Looking around the room, most of the shelves were full, yet mine was nearly empty. The evening passed as I reminisced about the messages of the three ministers, which were about perseverance. That is not how I felt as my mind drifted to a cartoon I once viewed, which displayed two vultures setting atop the crossbar of a telephone pole. One said to the other, "Patience, hell, I am going to kill something!" I knew that I had to persevere, but it was really hard.

Letter writing was approved of and most of my fellow inmates made it a regular practice, so I made a request for writing materials, which I was granted. Some nights I was just too beat up to try to write, but write letters I did. Letters of apology to Annika's parents, letters of apology to my parents, letters to Augusta Tech, and letters to Veterans Affairs regarding my GI Bill tuition payments.

It must have been near the second week of October when I received my first letter. It was from Annika—I was riveted in place. The letter had already been opened and was dated September 3. Why they held this from me for so long I do not know, but I shut out the sickness I felt for this part of the judicial system just to read her words.

It was as if she were speaking to me as I read her letter.

"Nick, I love you. I have assumed the use of the apartment and the Caprice, as seemed to be your wish. I am pursuing my class regimen as I need to do. But, I have also begun extracurricular activities regarding your captivity, and my parents are interested in my findings as well. Nick, I do not know your daily activities, but I have faith that you will choose wisely. Be safe, we are with you."

Many letters came after that, all opened, all inspiring or informational, but that first letter from Annika would help me persevere.

Weeks went by, and they turned into months. It was difficult to obtain information through the county legal system, even for the simplest of protocol questions. I was actually at a point where my name Finn was some kind of curse. No one should have this much trouble getting answers to such simple questions. Annika and I wanted to know what the process would be to have a personal visit. It took weeks to find out that no one could enter the compound, but instead a visitor needed to be in an automobile, approach the recessed portion of the gate at a pre-approved time, then remain in the car while the inmate was brought to the fence alongside the gate.

It was nearly Christmas before Annika was able to arrange our first visit, as nothing I did inside the system seemed to have any effect on moving any request forward. Her persistence, and perhaps her family's connection to many things in Williamston, finally persuaded some county officials to grant our first reunion.

Our visitation was to be at 1300 hours on Friday, December 23, the timing of which needed to be accomplished by mail only. I was ready shortly after noon. It was actually starting to get cold in Georgia, and I wore the winter coat provided by the prison for the first time. Constructed in heavy black cotton, with INMATE down each sleeve and PRISONER of R.C.C.F. across the back, it actually resembled a varsity jacket, but with the opposite effect of pride.

I stood in the open-air shelter where all the leg-irons were hanging to await Annika's arrival. That blue Caprice arrived one minute early, and I hurried to the fence to greet her. She had already powered the window down as she turned into park and had fixed her gaze on me. My fingers and thumbs were clenched through the fencing, forgetting entirely how cold it was. Reflecting on my stupidity for being here, I hesitated making eye contact, but when our eyes met, I knew I was forgiven.

From this point on Annika was in a very formal business mode, asking, "Are all your physical needs being met? Is there anything the county should be providing that is lacking?"

"Well having never been in this position before, I have no idea what to expect, but it seems very hard to get answers to anything."

"I agree. I've applied as much persuasion as I can muster, and only through referencing the influence of my parents in Williamston was I able to get any cooperation at all."

There was a guard assigned to all visits, watching and listening from the leg chain building, so we needed to be careful what was said, but we could express our love any way we wished and made it known aloud. The guard timed us out at fifteen minutes, and our encounter was over. Fifteen minutes in a fire fight is like a lifetime, but our first visit was over in a flash. Annika was like a rock; she was learning the legal system, and it was easy to tell she was hell-bent on understanding every aspect of my incarceration. I had shared with her that all my letters were inspected by the sheriff's secretary, so all her letters had been opened prior to my receiving them. It was a good thing for her to know, but there was little reason for us to spend time trying to create a secret way to communicate. I did the crime, I will do the time was my mindset.

She was consistent at making a visit every month that winter, and with practice, we made better use of our fifteen minutes. I told her of our near daily work that persisted through the winter. There was never much snow to shovel this far south, but lots of ice storms, which brought down trees and tree limbs. We cut them down from houses, barns, power lines, and off roadways. We used mostly axes as well as bow and crosscut saws. Some days were brutal, some just hard work. The prison ministry never failed to show up on Sundays. I had learned a few simple hymns, and when we were in the bump and grind of the work, I would start a hymn and several of the guys would chime in, and we would repeat them for hours. I knew nothing about music, but by golly I could carry a tune.

My parents tried their best to make a visit on the way down to Florida but were confused by the appointment by mail only. They had it correct on the return trip from Florida in late February after enjoying two months in the sun. I was so happy for them. Dad seemed to understand the situation. He didn't like what I did but just shook his head and grinned with the reasoning. Mom was more of a basket case. She wanted to get out of the car and come to the fence, but I said, "Mom, it's the rules. Just keep writing those letters, I love them."

We were required to stay physically clean, probably a state mandate of some sort, but one that I would agree with. Some, however, resisted in personal hygiene and were sometimes dealt with rather harshly. First by their fellow inmates, then the constabulary. We received a chance every two months to have a haircut, and by the end of that first two months I looked and felt a fright. I tried to shave around my beard, but it just didn't work. I asked the barber, who was obviously an absolute hack and probably only sobered up enough to do this job, if he would also remove my beard. He did a surprisingly good job with his hair clippers, and in minutes it was short enough to just shave. Shave I did, and in these conditions, it was something I could call a relief.

One Sunday, perhaps in late February, a preacher with the prison ministries came by himself. He was an older black man, possibly in his late seventies, small in stature but obviously well built from years of hard work, with a rugged but kind look to his face. He had an incredible no-nonsense way of going about his preaching that began with a very humble and meaningful prayer. I was captured. He gave a very brief testimony of his youth, a cheating wife, the murder of a young man trying to escape from her bedroom, and a life sentence. He was paroled after fifty years, and while incarcerated he not only found Jesus, but he also consistently read the Bible and any other related book he could get his hands on. In time he found a correspondence course in ministry and completed it. On release from prison he applied to ministerial college, was accepted, and graduated four years later.

His name was Pastor Roy Walker. He had a congregation in Blythe, Georgia, but managed to join the prison ministries once a month. I was now curious about this guy but was primarily killing time.

He began to preach in the book of Acts about Saul, a Pharisee from Tarsus and a persecutor of the very early Christians, who was on his way to Damascus with powers granted him to imprison anyone preaching in the name of Jesus. While with companions on the road, in a flash of very bright light, he was confronted by the risen Jesus. Basically, Jesus showed him that as a Pharisee, he was taught to look for the Messiah, but now he was persecuting him. Why? Saul was blinded by the light of Jesus for three days, during which he had a vision of a man named Ananias who would cure his blindness. Ananias was also visited by Jesus in a vision and told to go to Saul on Straight Street in Damascus to lay hands on him and cure his blindness. Ananias knew of Saul's history and didn't want to take on this risky task, but Jesus said "GO!" He did. Saul was then baptized, and his name changed to Paul. He became the primary evangelist for the gentiles, along with the Jews, and the founder of the church that changed the world up to this day.

I heard some of these stories in Sunday school, but Pastor Roy put real meaning to it. His point was that a change of heart, for the good or the bad, can change the outcome of your life in profound ways. Paul was proof, I was proof—he was correct. And I remembered him. I especially liked his cautious delivery of speech, with a definite southern drawl, infused with a way of pronouncing or inflicting words only black people can do. It was like music. I looked forward to seeing him again.

Doing the time was a little easier now that I had something to look forward to. Annika was working diligently on obtaining all the legal records that had anything to do with my case, but still with limited success. She was becoming concerned that she was being held back on certain inquiries, especially in regard to the VFW. The requests were simple, and it didn't make sense why she was being delayed, but she persisted. In her letters, she would allude to things I was to pay particular attention to: memories of events when I was shunned from the VFW and events the day I committed the crime. But that came to a quick end. By the first of April her letter explained that she was being denied the monthly visits, but their excuses were vague technical difficulties, and she would be notified at a future time if she would be allowed to resume. She was advised that she could also contact the county court system and file for review.

This news was depressing to say the least. And at the same time there seemed to be even more of an uptick in my work schedule. There was no doubt that I was put on work detail more than any of the other inmates. Even the guys in my barracks noticed my continuous on-call status and joked with me about it. But I was fully determined to endure, and every detail I was subjected to I did with the best of my ability. Even the sheriff's guards, who were perhaps not entirely in the know, showed some compassion.

I knew that I had lost weight, but my strength was very good and I was fully committed to tough it out no matter what. I was in the eighth month of the first year—in another four months my first year would be finished! It had actually gone by quickly. Now something in Annika's letters must have struck a bad chord with someone because when her next letter arrived, it had many words blanked out. We were no longer in good communication. I was actually, for the first time, beginning to feel a bit of anger. I did the crime, but I didn't run from the law when they came. I was completely cooperative in the county jail system, I pleaded guilty and did not request a lawyer, and I offered to purchase all new stuff for the commander. Now I was getting beat up for it and Annika was too. WHY? I would like to know why.

I went to the office of the sheriff and made a request to talk with him on his next visit, if that were possible. In only three days I was granted an audience with Sheriff Stump, but I needed to give up chow for the evening to do it. I also needed to wear the leg-irons and be handcuffed behind my back. Maneuvered into his office with a guard on each side, I was allowed to speak.

I made it brief, only asking why Annika's letters were being tampered with and, above all, why she could no longer visit. "There is nothing threatening in any way about Annika's letters or her visits. Can they be reinstated?"

The sheriff basically pleaded the fifth, only saying, "I just don't know why the letters are being tampered with, nor do I know why she is being denied visits. There are special folks back at the county level that make those decisions, and I will personally look into their reasons. Now go get some rest, son. We've got a lot of work to do this week."

Talk about being blown off! He must have granted my audience just to land the boot on my rear one more time. I was so befuddled. I was not getting the bigger picture here, nor was I understanding what drove me to do the things I did to get myself here in the first place!

At 0500 hours came the pounding on the door—the routine, the routine, the routine. Mid-April in Augusta is at least a very pleasant time of the year, frequent short rains, lots of sun, warm, and breezy. The work was hard nonetheless, and apparently the spring cleanup was in full swing. It was the third week in April, and we were getting back to the facility with only enough time to make the chow line. All the guys were dragging their chains in what seemed like slow motion to the open-air building that held all the leg-irons. I made my way to the back of the line, which extended behind the bus, and waited patiently as I always did. Most of this time I would spend with my eyes closed, stepping forward as needed. I heard the song of a whippoorwill across the street—oh, so sweet—and opened my eyes and turned to try to see the bird. I looked and looked. He reported again, then again. Oh, just for a peek at that bird!

My eyes then readjusted to what was right beside me, the gate... the unlocked gate! We were the last bus in, and someone had closed the gate but did not engage the padlock. I opened the gate slowly, stepped out, closed it, and engaged the lock.

PART II:
THE SLOW LAM

4. SKUNK CABBAGE

I WALKED BACKWARD across the gravel street, keeping the bus between me and anyone who might look my way. The view behind me was like a projector in my head, as I had viewed it many times. I stepped up off the road, through tall grass and weeds, and behind an old maple tree. I paused. I needed to control the adrenaline. I had successful control in the past, not only through rigorous military training but in real live combat.

While settling my mind, I questioned myself, "Finn, why did you just do that?"

My answer to myself was, "I don't know, it just felt right?"

"OK then, what next, happy guy?"

I stood behind that tree for at least ten minutes, examining my position and situation. If the guard alerted to my missing leg iron number, they would first need to look for me in the obvious places, which could take an hour. If he didn't alert, they wouldn't know until roll call at bedtime. Then it would take another hour to look in all the obvious places before calling for drastic measures. I could also go back to the gate and holler, "Help, I locked my stupid self out!" NOT.

Looking behind for the first time, the hedge row followed the road for at least a mile, and the spring leaves were thick enough now to obscure me quite well. I moved cautiously backward toward the hedge and turned to the west, walking carefully at first while glancing back toward the gate. At a point I felt comfortable, I began to accelerate to the limit of the chains bound around my ankles. As I began to put myself into a rhythm of fast short steps, trying to eye any obstacle that might trip me up—while focusing on any near and distant path I may take—my speed began to improve.

An hour or so went by as I began to realize that I had paid a great deal of attention to the geography of this area. While driving cement trucks, I had actually driven by the prison compound not realizing what it was. And in all the prison work bus trips that we had taken, we had traveled on nearly every road west of Augusta for some thirty miles, as well as to the ends of the county to the north and south. I cannot say that I was casing the geography of Richmond County, but for some reason I had done a good job of putting it to memory. I knew the vastness of the area that I was in and that if I kept heading west-southwest I would eventually come to Blythe.

As I continued my run, I rationalized that when they organized the hound dogs to track me, they would not stop if the dogs were on my trail, but they would go all night. As it began to get dark, I was tired, so I slowed to a meaningful walk, with just enough moonlight to show me the way. Just prior to nightfall, I had to cross over a gate between fence rows. My ankles were getting in bad shape, and the run would come to a halt soon if I didn't do something. The gate was tied shut with several feet of light rope. I stopped to rest just for a moment and had an idea. I put one foot up on a gate rung, tucked the cuff of my pant leg through the ankle ring as far as I could, then did the same to the other. It padded the raw skin of my ankles. Then I took the rope and tied it at the center of the chain and snugged the rope in my hand as I began the rhythmic run again. It not only kept the chain from dragging but it felt much better on my ankles. I just needed to stop and re-tuck every half mile or so.

My path was somewhat diagonal and took me near a crossroad. I walked to the intersection so I could read the street sign—Wells Forman Road. Yes, I knew where I was, and I was heading in the direction I intended, toward Blythe. I pulled up on the rope and began a short-stepped jog and was able to keep the pace for an hour or so, nearing the town. I was betting that the prison had not detected my absence until the nightly roll call, as it seemed that no one was chasing me yet. But that was no reason to relax.

I needed to laugh at myself—what was in Blythe for me? Perhaps I could call Annika, have her pick me up, and we could just go somewhere. Well, I didn't have a dime for a pay phone. Blythe was, however, the end of my westward journey through a lot of vacant areas of land, with only a few roads and scant population. Highway 1 turned south at that point, with many towns along the way. I would then need to keep myself hidden from everyone, especially in this black and white prison uniform. I knew I had miles ahead of me, and I knew that anyone trying to catch me who had half a brain would try to project an azimuth of my travel, revealed by the tracking dogs. They would try to predict some place I may need to cross to continue. They would alert other police to keep an eye on certain areas. The only fortunate thing in my favor was that my crime was fairly minute in the grand scheme, and even if the Richmond County sheriff pushed hard for a capture, adjoining counties probably wouldn't be that concerned. Guessing at the movements of the police kept my mind active as I trudged through the entire night.

As the sunrise slowly came to be, I could hear the traffic of Highway 1 to my right, which would be north, and I tried to keep it just within earshot as I moved west. I knew Highway 88 would eventually cross west to east, and I would need to cross it to stay parallel to Highway 1. I just didn't know how far it was. I guessed that I could have traveled some twenty miles by now, but what did that matter? I thought I heard the hounds for the first time and tried to get back into the cadence of yesterday's run. I had been on many training runs in the army, some very long runs with full field gear. They were designed to make us suffer, and suffer we did. I know now that humping that pack and an M-14 was far easier than having ankle bands chewing at every step. I think it became almost spiritual, keeping up the pace, having no food, but far worse no water, in nearly fifteen hours.

I began to see a few cars on the road ahead, still using their headlights—it had to be Highway 88. I could see enough now to look for a spot where the trees were closest to the road on both sides. Following the road for about a quarter mile, I found my spot and waited in a crouched position for the road to be completely clear of traffic. In that few minutes of silence, I could definitely hear dogs barking but still some distance away. I was relying on my one good ear and hoped that it was in a hypersensitive mode, since I sure needed it now. My opening in traffic came, and as I stood to jog across, I was made painfully aware of just how stiff I was becoming—not good. Through the thicket on the opposite side, I came to a cattle fence and had some trouble getting over it, but once on the other side, I saw a huge pastureland with interconnecting fields, wooded thickets, and some swampy lowlands. It was like a roughly mowed lawn, with the exception of an occasional burdock plant or other weed or briar that the cattle didn't want to eat.

Having re-tucked my trousers, I made fairly good time following the natural lay of the pastures, which eventually came to a narrows. This spot was a mucky bog full of skunk cabbage. I could see a farm trail to one side that was likely to be passable in summer months but was wet and soggy now. The cattle had been using it, so there were a thousand foot depressions from the cows in the black mud. That all mixed with smashed skunk cabbage and cow poop. I didn't have time to rethink anything, I just plodded through, my feet sinking in, and like suction cups, I could hardly pull them out. I fell several times, having to crawl to spots where I was able to stand again. It was only about fifty yards, but it almost did me in.

The muddy path led back to green pasture again, and just over a small hill I could see some man-made infrastructure and an old pickup truck. I stayed close to the fence to the south and could hear cowbells clanging on the opposite side of a thicket to the north. I didn't see anyone. I approached the old late-40s pickup with a million tiny dents and homemade repairs. The keys were in it, and I just laughed at the thought of a getaway vehicle. Oh, and add grand theft auto to my extending sentence? Not! The tailgate was down since it was backed up near a cattle watering tank and a working hand pump. There were several wide mouth one-gallon jars full of water in crates in the bed, along with several empty pint jars with lids. I seized a pint jar, removed the lid, dipped it in the watering tank, and slowly drank it all. I repeated that two or three more times.

I began to see Black Angus cows rounding the thicket and heading my way, so I surveyed the area quickly. About ten yards behind me, along the fence row, was an old clapboard outhouse with a walk-through tug shed built off the east side. And just to the west of that was a gate to the road. On the other side of the road was another gate that was opened to another pasture. I moved into the tug shed, which had a lot of old hand tools hanging on rusty spikes. Behind the herd of perhaps fifty Angus cattle, a farmer walked along talking to the cows. He herded them to the gate area, but it looked like the cattle knew in advance where they were going—greener pastures?

Three things were happening at the same time now, the cows and farmer were approaching, the dogs were getting much closer, perhaps crossing the big pasture, and a 1960s white Chevy Suburban was pulling up just past the gate. Faded lettering on the side said, "TRI-COUNTY TRACKING AND RESCUE" sub-titled, "Bluetick Trackers, Breeders and Trainers." I guessed quickly that the tracking team always needed a lead vehicle, a forward spotter, someone to pick them up after these cross-country runs, someone who could assist in restraining a runaway tracked down by the hounds.

The farmer went to the gate as the van driver came around the back of his vehicle and met him. I was close enough to hear the conversation.

The driver spoke first, "Mister, we have a convicted felon on the loose and he must be very close to this spot. Have you seen anyone?"

The farmer replied, "No, but you had better get that van out of the way because I am going to open the gate to get the cattle across the road before those damn dogs get any closer or we will have a stampede right here!"

The van driver, a very rugged looking middle-aged man, having what looked like a .38 revolver holstered to his belt, hopped back in his vehicle and drove to a four-way intersection just a hundred yards down the road. He started walking back toward the gate as the farmer opened it, allowing the anxious cattle to cross the road and go through the open gate on the opposite side of the road.

I was a mess mentally and physically, but turned my attention to my prison uniform, which now looked a lot like the cows, the white stripes hidden with black muck. I scraped off some of the wet mud from my shirt and trousers and rubbed it all over my head and face. I walked hunched over from behind the outhouse into the cattle. I brought two of them side by side and hung my arms around their necks. Then I lifted my feet and they carried me through the gate, across the road into the next pasture, and for the next three hundred yards. My pint jar was still in my hand.

The cattle rounded a thicket putting me just out of view. I crawled back to a vantage point and watched as the dog handlers came to the open gate. The dogs had been running in circles and kept it up. Had they lost my trail? Mud, cows, and cow poop, and oh yes, the skunk cabbage. Perhaps that fouled their noses? As the two trackers led the dogs toward the intersection where their van was parked, I could see plainly that the men and dogs were both whipped. They must have felt deeply depressed as well after an all-night run, knowing they had me cornered. They were so close when the dogs lost my trail. They were as black from the mud bog as I was, the dogs too. I knew they were not going to chase me anymore that evening, but as they were loading the dogs and themselves into the Suburban, another vehicle pulled up—a sheriff's car. However, this one was from Jefferson County. There is a county to county respect law stating simply that unless the pursuing officers are in hot pursuit, the next county is to continue a search. Richmond County had just lost their hot pursuit right there at the Jefferson County line.

The two drivers started carrying on a conversation that I could not eavesdrop on. I was out of earshot but within sight. With all the hand gestures going on, I got the idea they were giving up and someone else would need to continue. I relaxed in that position for a while but caught myself falling asleep. "No, Finn, you cannot do that, not now!"

They soon drove off, so I got up and walked over to a stump that was a good height for just sitting on. Pondering my situation again, I reckoned that a new dog team may have the same problem as the last, no fresh scent. A new team would need to circle in an ever-larger area until they picked up my trail again. I felt I had a little time. The pint jar was still in my hand, and it had a lid. I was watching the cows and the new calves moving southward in the fresh, tall grass, munching happily as they went.

Even with this short bit of respite, my mind was beginning to think more clearly—cows, calves, milk! The herd was already moving in a favorable direction, so I headed after them. In my youth, an uncle of mine maintained a cow on a one-acre plat behind his house. One of his sons, my cousin Bill, was taught to milk her, and it was one of his daily chores. Our family visited there quite often, and if it fell at chore time, I would go with Bill for the milking. Bill always goaded me into milking the cow too. I never got as good as Bill, but I had the principal technique down. Bill always had a funny bone. He trained the family farm cat to alert to a certain noise he would make, and the cat would immediately sit up and look at Bill with its mouth open. Bill could squeeze that udder and aim the milk stream directly into the cat's mouth. I would just laugh.

I began singling out the heifers that looked to have a bit of milk remaining. Some shunned me quickly, but a few didn't mind at all if I filled my pint jar. While on my knees, I slowly drank the first of the warm milk. I swear, I could feel the nourishment entering my bloodstream and traveling through my body. I repeated this at least four more times during the next forty-five minutes or so. I filled the jar one more time, screwed the lid down tight, and tried to make myself mentally ready to travel.

I wanted to stay parallel to Highway 1 since it would pass Blythe, which I thought may be less than ten miles away. I still had no plan whatsoever, but Highway 1 reminded me of the 1st Cavalry, and hopefully that would bring something to my advantage. A small town would perhaps yield some different options, maybe a slow-moving train or a chance to change clothing. It also was a great place to be spotted in prison clothes. I tried my best to pick up a tempo, even a slow one. Come on Finn, left right left, left right left, left right left. My ankles were on fire with every step and were seeping some nasty stuff, but I kept on plodding. There were many fences to cross, several secondary roads, plowed fields, fields of cotton, and young plants just emerging out of the ground.

As it began to get later in the afternoon, my body was beginning to refuse to go farther. I was in another pastureland and could see an outcrop of higher ground trailing out from a wood plot. I made my way to the spot where there was some exposed red sandy ground and a few tall weeds around the perimeter. From a kneeling or sitting position, I could see about 300 degrees of area around me, while the weeds kept me obscured. I laid down, wiggling in the sand for the most comfortable position, and the proverbial lights went out!

I awoke at the sound of voices, whispering, over here, then over there. I kept quiet, wondering how they found me. Their dogs should have alerted me. I rolled to my gut and started a slow low crawl toward the woods when all hell broke loose—these sons of bitches were shooting at me! I made it only a few feet when I was hit the first time: a hip shot again, even more painful! As my elbows dug the sand, trying to move forward, I took another hit to the side, and this one stopped me. I rolled to my back, and in the dim light I could see several figures moving in closer, speaking to one another in some unintelligible way. They began poking me with their bayonets, and as I attempted to defend myself, my hands were taking the worst of it! Bayonets? Bayonets? Bayonets? Cops don't use bayonets! I finally came to from this awful dream as I was fighting a briar bush to the side of my sleeping area. I cried and cried out, "Father, I am going to need help soon!"

The half-moon was high, so no way to tell the time. I nestled back into the sand, and in an instant, it was lights out again. I awoke this time to the faint sound of a rooster crowing, who made his report quite often for perhaps forty-five minutes. It was getting light, and I had a pint of milk cooled by the night air, ready for breakfast. I couldn't hear any hounds trying to find me—life was good!

I learned a great deal about nutrition in the army, how long the body could go without it, and especially how long we can go without water. I had pushed the limit on that one. In thinking about the trackers, they would certainly know these things as well and had probably caught a few escapees in near-death condition for that reason. Not knowing about the water I consumed at the cattle trough, and especially about the half gallon of milk I drank, they were probably betting on finding me face down by now.

As I deliberately took small drinks of the milk, I thought, "Protein, carbs, and fat, yes!" I then looked closer at my ankles, and I needed first aid badly. I tried to look forward into the day, but I couldn't plan anything. I just vowed to myself to stay diligent to the needs of this escape. I got up and started moving again; the sleep had paid great dividends, but my body was in bad shape. I was at least at a point where I could keep up a good walking pace. Within a few hours I was entering a more populated area, the outskirts of Blythe. I kept farther southeast, where there was more farmland. Moving was slow and tedious to avoid being seen. This was easier on my bones but harder on my brain. It did require sudden bursts of the best speed I could muster, then waiting completely still. It took the better part of the day to skirt Blythe and enter the farmland on the opposite side. More fences, more gates, more secondary roads.

However, while crossing a field of half-grown collard greens, I encountered a legitimate small river, flowing nicely to the west. I found a usable access and discovered that the water was about three feet deep and somewhat brown from the surrounding clay ground, but so clean to me. I rubbed and scrubbed every part of me that I could, paying a lot of attention to my raw ankles. Then, I let the river take me another mile or so downstream. It was hot as usual, and that bath was so refreshing. I filled my pint jar with river water, drank it, filled it again, and capped it. There was a downside, however. My muddied uniform of black and white stripes was once again very bright and identifiable.

I proceeded at a simple walk as my uniform dried to sweat only, and my ankles were cleaned but now so raw. I took a lot of extra time tucking the pant legs under the bands and holding the worn rope as snug as possible. I probably didn't need the pint jar any longer, but it was clutched in my hand anyway.

Meanwhile, the Jefferson County sheriff probably dispatched a dog team to pick up my trail, but not until late the next morning, so it would take several hours to find my trail again. When they did find my sandy sleeping place, the hounds probably went crazy for a while. Then they'd need to cross Highway 88 and skirt Blythe late in the day, but they'd likely lose me again at the river. By the time they could pick up my trail downstream on the opposite side of the river, it would be getting dark. Then they would have a straight run toward Highway 1; it was just a matter of timing.

My mind drifted to Annika. It was unlikely that she would know of my escape yet, and it would possibly be a week or so more before she did, unless the sheriff's office tried to notify her to contact them if I were to show up. What then, when she did find out? That could be the end of us, and it would be all my fault. My parents might disown me as well, but they probably wouldn't. I could only pray Annika would forgive me one more time and keep trying to find answers to my especially harsh treatment and hers as well. She could very well be worried sick, who knows what can happen in a prison situation. I plodded on and on, slower and slower, my head hanging lower and lower. If they could have caught up to me then, I would not have had a new burst of energy, nor any resistance. I wasn't much more than a zombie, locked in a slow forward march.

As evening began to settle in, I came along a side road, which I skirted to the north toward Highway 1. Before I reached the intersection, I crossed the road into a hedge on the opposite side and moved toward the intersection. I could see what looked like a vacant house some distance down Highway 1 in the midst of an open area. It was cloudy, not much moonlight, so it was hard to distinguish what all was going on with the structure and the vehicles parked alongside. All I knew was that once again, I was completely depleted of physical ability. I crawled under the house, which was weirdly open air. I kept bumping into obstacles until I found a place in the darkness. It smelled funky under there, like old rubber. I finally put my back against something solid, my neck on my arm, and passed out.

I awoke with the sounds of voices mumbling, first here, then there. I kept quiet, wondering how they found me. Why didn't the barking of the dogs alert me? I rolled to my gut and started a slow low crawl toward the—toward the—wait a minute, I was awake. I was not dreaming this time. People were really nearby, so I laid quiet, wondering if they had found me. But there was no concern in any of the voices, just yawns and ho-hums. There was metal clanging, chains rattling, then a diesel engine barked to life, and it went into a sustained idle. The exhaust smoke and fumes drifted under the house, nearly choking me out.

It was getting light enough now to see just a little, and I could make out the legs of men walking around the perimeter of the house. One of them then crawled under the perimeter with what looked like a mallet and began to hammer or thump on what looked to be dark round shadows. He went the full perimeter doing the same thing at each shadowy location. It looked like he was trying to flush out rats or something.

As he climbed out from under the house, he yelled out to the others, "ALL GOOD."

I was still foggy headed, drawing a blank as to what was going on. The engine revved up some, then suddenly the entire house shook and moved several inches. What the! They must be tearing this house down! I rolled onto my back in a frightened stupor, wishing I had prayed for a deliverance. I opened my eyes and as dim as it was, I could see my unspoken prayer was answered.

5. BEATERS

Above me was a two-foot-by-three-foot area of the floor joists that looked quite different from the rest of the underside of the floor—it looked like a hatch door. Straining my eyes, I could see hinge straps on one side. I painfully righted myself and pushed up on the wood, and it flipped up and opened. I stood up through the opening and climbed in, just as the house began to shake and move in earnest. I looked for a door to escape the collapse, when I realized that the house was not caving in, but moving forward and building up a little speed.

The hatch door was covered with an old but very nice hand-woven wool rug, a bit larger than the door. Closing the hatch, I tried to make my way to a window facing the direction of travel. The windows I saw had nicely fitted interior shutters or wood slat blinds. I pushed up on a blind, exposing white paper that covered them fully on the inside, so I poked my finger through the paper, making a small hole. Moving in close to the hole and peering out, I could view all I needed to see ahead. I was looking down the side of a tandem axle Mack truck, probably a 1960 B-model, set up just for pulling very heavy loads. They were moving this dang house somewhere, and now I was along for the ride, like it or not, for however long it may last!

I then moved to the rear, which actually turned out to be the front of the house. The entry door was recessed into the house several feet and had a beautiful leaded glass window with geometric shapes. A few panes were of plain glass, so I could look through them. I looked out over a small porch, nestled back into the house and covered by the roof. I looked back down the road toward the intersection as we left it behind. I saw other pieces of equipment and trucks parked in organized locations on the graveled lot. County trucks, tree service trucks, and the like. The lot was apparently used largely for this kind of thing.

I returned to my peephole and watched in the direction of travel for a very long time. I guess I was a bit dumbstruck at what was happening. They managed to get the structure up to a fast walking speed, and sometimes to a human running speed. The twin stacks on that Mack diesel were barking steadily, as it looked to me like an open road down Highway 1 for at least several miles.

The sun was getting bright now, and I finally began to look more at my surroundings. I was in a bedroom that was fully furnished, with certain exceptions, like no hanging pictures and nothing on the dresser or nightstand. The bed was completely dressed, with a wool native southwestern style bedspread on top. The floor was oak, stained a nice chocolate brown, but mostly covered with an extremely tightly woven wool rug, with geometric designs woven into very exacting patterns. This was a most delicious distraction, and I was completely absorbed in what I was observing in this house.

"Nick, Nick," I said out loud to myself. "You need to get a grip on yourself."

I turned my back against the wall under the window and tried to just breathe deep and slow for a sustained period of time. It may have helped, as I began to assess my situation in earnest. I was still completely alone. I was basically trapped, and this entrapment had upsides and downsides. First, the downsides—no food or water that I knew of yet. What would happen if I needed to use the bathroom? And that was minor to the problem of what would happen if the sheriff figured out where I was? I was very hungry and thirsty, NOW!

The upside, I supposed, was that I could actually be safe here. The sheriff's dog team had probably arrived at the truck parking site an hour or so after the movers took the house down the road, leaving no trace of them or me. Perhaps only a small oil stain on the ground from a crankcase drip of the Mack tractor. The dogs had probably gotten to the vacant lot and ran in circles again, having lost the trail. Now, the trackers too would be completely beat up from an all-night run and would need to leave empty handed. They too would have to return home with their proverbial tails between their legs.

I came to the realization that all I could do was relax and go for the ride. I laid down on the floor on my back with my arm under my neck and breathed slowly, feeling the nearly gentle movement of the house, along with the rhythmic sound of the diesel engine. I fell asleep and truly rested. I awoke some time later when the movement stopped.

Peeking out once more, I could see men with an extension ladder coming from a lead vehicle. In moments they passed my view port, and I could hear the ladder being propped against the house, then footsteps on the roof. Seconds later the house began to move again, about the length of itself, then stopped again. The ladder clanged again, footsteps stomped to the ladder, and then the men headed back toward the lead vehicle carrying the ladder. The house began forward movement again. I moved to the entry door facing the rear to see that they had apparently lifted a low hanging telephone wire above the house as it passed under.

I suppose it was rightful to feel like I was actually trespassing because I was, there just wasn't anything I could do about it now. I laid back down hoping that one day I might do something in return for the owner. Sleep escaped me for a large part of the day, as my mouth was very dry and I was no longer sweating, dehydration coming soon. My only savior now was to remain as sedentary as possible and endure until the conditions changed. It seemed like an endless day when all came to a halt again. At this there was a lot of shouting, men hustling here and there, then the house began to move slowly in reverse. There were multiple movements, forward and back, before all stopped. For the next thirty minutes or so, the men fussed with equipment associated with the two support vehicles, one lead and one bringing up the rear. I couldn't see much of what was happening, but apparently they were done for the day. One of the vehicles was parked beside the house, and its driver and crew member, along with the Mack driver, climbed in the other vehicle and headed back the way we had come.

"Holy bat crank!" I exclaimed to myself. "What a day."

From the door and the peephole I couldn't see any other vehicles or people. I waited until dusk before opening the hatch and climbing out. Crawling through the maze of tires to the perimeter, I scanned the area closely, but there was no one around. I looked for a source of water first, finding that the vehicle they'd left had a very large galvanized water cooler attached on the off-road side. Operating the spigot and tipping my head under it, I chugged for a while, then waited. After a minute, I chugged again, then waited. I thought this was BS. I hurried back under the house, through the hatch, retrieved my pint jar, and returned to the cooler. After filling it, I went to the running board of the Mack and sat down to sip and think for a while.

Now, if I could just find a bit of food. I stood on the running board and looked through the Mack's window. Quite messy in there. No passengers had sat in that seat for a long time, but in the mess, on top of a paper binder, was a bag of oatmeal cookies. The door was locked, but these old trucks had large usable vent windows, and the driver's side was ajar. I was able to stretch my arm just far enough to unlock and open the door. Climbing in and closing the door, I opened that cookie bag, which was nearly full. Knowing I had better not overdo the cookie theft, I took about five and started eating them one at a time while sipping water. Feeling somewhat content, I picked up the binder, opened it, and began to look at what appeared to be the manifest for the entire job of moving this house. Whoa, whoa. I needed to study this closely, but dusk was making it hard to read. I exited the cab, leaving everything the same, and locked the door, with the vent window ajar.

This fat spot in the road had no other vehicles, aside from the one support truck, but it was a great place to park the house for a night. Farm ground all around, and the fragrance of strawberries was in the air. Across the street was a field of them. Each row had fresh straw spread between them, ready for pickers. I ran in my chains, dismissing the pain, and fell to my knees in the first row I came to—the vines were loaded! Daylight was fading too fast as I kept stuffing my mouth and then the pint jar.

Back in the house, I laid again on the floor in contentment. Water, oatmeal cookies, and strawberries, what more could any good escapee want? Well, in reality, my want (need) list was fairly long. I needed a watch or a clock, and I wanted and needed a change of clothes to ditch this prison uniform. I needed money, a bath, a haircut, and a shave. I would love to have a radio. I needed to make phone calls, especially to Annika. And I really wanted to get these ankle chains OFF!

I reviewed what little I saw in the manifest binder in the cab of the Mack. I really needed to look at it more closely, but it appeared that the destination was near Florida, and all of its travel followed Highway 1. If that were really the case, I could plan on another ride tomorrow and possibly many days to come. That thought was intriguing, and I munched on a strawberry from my pint, wishing that I had planned better for tomorrow's ride as well, but for now I would be satisfied.

Sleep found me, and I slept extremely well. I awoke again to the sounds of the moving crew making ready for the day's travel. I could hear one of the men crawling around under the perimeter pounding on things again, when it dawned on me that he was checking the tires for full air pressure. I supposed that a flat while carrying this tremendous weight could be a big problem, and the men paid a lot of attention to it. The Mack started and went to an idle as it had yesterday, the men shouting reports, the lead vehicle moving into position, and the house making that first gentle jerk forward, then the earnest move forward.

I had slept most of the day prior and last night. I was now awake and would be for a while. I took the time to make a few more peepholes on each side of the house and then walked sentry every hour or so, looking at anything that might prove interesting. They stopped the house many times during the day to carry phone lines over or to let traffic pass at an intersection. These house movers were truly of a different breed, as they were able to stay completely calm as waylaid drivers blew their horns over and over, cursing aloud as the house passed by.

I was getting thirsty again, this time not in desperation, but the need made me think about planning for each day. For cripes cakes, how many days should I plan for? I knew nothing of the future, but having a plan, even a plan based on a hunch, was worth using. Meanwhile, I would just plan for tomorrow. I rode diligently through the day, and in the evening, probably near 1700 hours, the parking of the house started again. These parking places were probably new to the moving crew each time but apparently well-planned in advance.

Again, the house was sitting at some obscure intersection, with no one around, as I crawled out from under it, this time with a little more daylight remaining than the day before. With my pint jar in hand, I headed for the water cooler first, slowly drinking my fill. The lead vehicle had been backed into its position, so anyone passing by would not see me. I began to realize just how far I was out of my mind last night, as I had not noticed that bolted very securely onto this heavy-duty bumper was a five-inch iron worker's vice. Can this be real? I looked down both sides of the truck—it had cubbies with locked steel doors, which could hold a great many tools. In the center of the rear was a canvas tarp tied at the corners, covering the space between the cubbies. I untied the tarp and looked inside where there was a nicely organized series of various sized and shaped beaters (hammers), pinch bars, and leavers. They were not locked, as most common thieves would not have much use for any of them. BUT! I could use one of the beaters.

Everything I could possibly want to bust off these chains was right there. However, there was a physical problem that I could not raise my leg high enough to reach the vice because the length of the chain was just too short. Looking farther back in the truck storage space, I saw several buckets. I retrieved one and used it as a step stool, changing positions several times until I could tighten the vice on the leg iron and bust the lock with a junior mall. The leg-irons were built tough, but with this equipment, they were burnt toast.

Holy bats, I felt the freedom go straight to my bones. I had energy to dance around the back of that truck. I put everything back as it was, except for the bucket. I sat on the heavy bumper, bowed my head, and thanked my Maker for this good fortune. Perhaps I should be giving thanks a little more often?

Sipping my pint empty, I filled it again and started thinking about food. I went back to the Mack and was able to open the door in the same manner. The oatmeal cookie bag was nearly empty, so I did not dare take any. I looked quickly at the manifest in the binder to confirm what I had seen last night—the plan was definitely to take the house to the Florida border.

Locking the door on the Mack, I stood to survey the area. Lots of farm ground, lots of cotton just emerging out of the ground, but no truck crops. Now just at the edge of one of the fields, there stood a very old pecan tree, with just enough room between it and the road to plant four more rows of cotton. Being free of the chain, I sauntered toward the road, crossed it, and went to the tree. It had several large limbs reaching out about head height, with deep crotches in each. Gathered in each crotch were pecans, still trying to break out of the shells from last fall's fruit. I ran back to the truck, retrieved the bucket, and ran back to the tree. I took the time to remove the outer shells from all the nuts, which was easy, and filled the bucket with pecans. I went back to the truck bumper and employed the vice once again to crack the nuts. They were not as dry as they should be, but as good as gold to me.

I spread the nuts on the bumper and began cracking. I ate pecans for the next hour, throwing the shucks back in the bucket. Just before dusk, I came to my senses and ran back to the tree, dumped the shucks, then nearly filled the bucket one more time with more nuts. I also filled my pint with water before crawling back under the house and up through the hatch to make ready for another night. It was getting too dark to rummage the kitchen for something to put the nuts in, so I dumped them into the sink. I would need the bucket for other things, as I could only hold a pee for just so long, a p-u for even longer, but now that I had a bit of food, it was only a matter of time.

Tuesday night, after my second day in the house, I dared to take off my shoes and the filthy socks. I sat massaging my ankles, which were in bad shape with scabs trying to form, but they needed dressings. At least the daily damage would stop for now. I dearly wanted to crawl into that bed, but I was just too filthy to let myself do it. I lay flat on my back, on the beautiful bedroom rug, and found sleep for most of the night. Sometime in the middle of the night I awoke with an urge to do the p-u. I had placed the bucket so I could find it, so I used it and tried to sleep again. That was not going to happen. I maneuvered around to a comfortable sitting position and tried to clear my head.

OK, I knew only that this house was in the process of being moved as far as the Florida line, that I may be safe as long as I was not discovered, and that if I could find food and water each day, I would survive. But, there would be a lot more to it along the way. I tried to think beyond my immediate needs to what I would need just to be a normal person. I resolved to find a way to make a list of my most pressing needs in the morning after the moving had begun again. I did a fairly good job of memorizing the things I could think of, dozing off from time to time until the sound of a vehicle pulling up and men climbing out going through the preparations for the day's move woke me fully.

On Wednesday, as morning number three evolved and daylight slowly filtered into the house, I was becoming familiar with the drill. Because of the paper and the blinds, it was never very bright, but still more than enough light to do anything I needed to do. I stayed put until the move was at a sustained rate, then began to explore the house, actually looking closely at it. The floor layout, from room to room, was very comfortable for being a fairly small home. It was perhaps twenty-four feet wide and forty feet long, perhaps designed to fit a narrow lot. There were two bedrooms, the second a little larger than the one I had been sleeping in. The bathroom was between the two bedrooms, its door coming from a short hallway connecting the bedrooms, the kitchen, and the living area. It also had a dining room off the kitchen, which had an archway to the living room. I liked it.

The house was mostly furnished and had cotton sheets draped over most of the furniture. The rectangular oak dining room table was on a beautiful area rug, with the chairs in their places; the moving house was gentle enough that hardly anything moved out of place. I made my way slowly from room to room, trying to take it all in. Some of the furnishings were adorned with small amounts of spoon carving, but for the most part they looked more like Shaker or Mission style, and almost all of it was built out of quarter-sawn oak. My attention then turned to the woodwork, which was magnificent throughout the entire house but in a style I was not accustomed to. It all looked entirely plain, but entirely elegant at the same time. It was calmingly rich, and I liked that too.

I was walking back through every room several times, slowly absorbing and appreciating, when it hit me. My last half semester at ATC, I had one core class on architectural design. The class covered many aspects of building design, starting from the Romans to current times. However, the prof spent extra time talking about and displaying the works of Frank Lloyd Wright. For crying out loud, this had to be a Wright house! Why else would anyone go through so much trouble to move a house from outside Atlanta to the Florida border? I was happy with myself, thinking I may have solved a mystery that existed in my own head. I looked at the full-length leaded glass window in the walnut entry door—it was similar to his famous Wheat Straw pattern, but it looked like geometric flowers. A brass nameplate at the top of the door said "Rosa Laevigata." A lovely name, I thought.

I had tried to show respect for someone else's house from the first time I climbed through the hatch, but now I had a resolve to respect it even more.

I found a container to put all the pecans in and put them in a cabinet. Then I brushed down and cleaned the chaff from the sink. I put my dirty socks into my dirty shoes and put them under the bed. There, everything was neat and tidy. The house had stopped moving several times that day, and I would peek out to assess the problem, then continue to study the structure.

I continued the tour, observing that there were many built-in furnishings in the bathroom, the master bedroom, and the dining room. I focused on the dining room cabinetry, as it included a writing desk. I turned a dining chair to sit while examining the writing area. All the glass or wood doors had solid brass hardware that latched, and the normal contents were still on the shelves. I snooped, yes snooped, and found several things I needed. A tablet for taking notes, writing paper, envelopes, pencils, and pens. This changed my thought pattern. Last night I vowed to myself to try and decide what things were the most important that I needed to try to do. Now I could write them down, erase, and write again!

Pondering my immediate needs was a tough challenge. I needed three different columns. First were things that were life sustaining: water, food, and money. I listed them under the column titled "Crapshoot." Second, things I really needed: different clothing, different shoes, a haircut, a shave, and a bath. I really needed to communicate with Annika and my parents, SOON. I could write letters, but where would I acquire a stamp? Oh yes, and money. I also listed these under "Crapshoot." Third, I listed what I wanted: a flashlight, a wristwatch, a battery powered radio, pajama trousers, a legal ID, and MONEY! I listed these, again, under "Crapshoot." It was all a crapshoot. I have always been a successful strategic planner (except for my unexplained criminal actions), but I needed to plan for the now.

Then I thought more about the money part. I had over $48,000 in my Atlanta account but was unable to touch one penny. Thinking about that more, without legitimate identification, I couldn't even make a withdrawal. I needed to remove my thoughts from that ongoing frustration for a while.

I had always been able to look at my circumstances and determine an outcome or a direction to follow. It was true even in my youth, playing with friends, playing games, later playing sports, and even later yet, playing war. If you didn't know a possible outcome, you could at least imagine one and go for it. In my current circumstance, I could not even guess what was going to happen next. I tucked the tablet back into the drawer under the writing desk, retrieved my pint of water, and sat down on one of the covered living room chairs to sip.

I debated whether I should be trying to sleep during the day or during the night. I really needed the early evenings to scrounge for food and water, but without light I was helpless. Each of the stops were planned since they needed a place to park this unusual load, and someone took great time and skill to find each parking spot. If I could get into the Mack tonight, I would look carefully at the stopping sites and write them down. That could give me an advantage. During the travels so far, I thought I had glimpsed signs for Wrens city limits and also Louisville. We were definitely following Highway 1, but geographically I couldn't put that in miles.

Planning the next stop, I would need more water first, then hopefully add something additional to my diet, aside from year-old pecans, which were actually quite tasty. I snooped through all the kitchen cabinets and found a good two-quart water container, other useful bowls, and two cast iron skillets.

It was slowly getting darker in the house, and I was thinking that the crew was working a little later, when it began to rain. It rained hard, and the forward movement continued, but at a noticeably slower pace. The rain stopped after about an hour, but we traveled at least another hour after that.

The sun came out again, and the Mack added a little more speed, so I sat down for another hour. Finally all the signs of stopping for the night were being revealed. The driver of this rig truly knew what he was doing as he pulled past the parking site, allowing him to back the house into its resting place for the night. The crew worked, hardly speaking to one another during their thirty-minute procedure to secure everything, folding in the WIDE LOAD bumper signs on their crew truck. As they finished, they all climbed in and drove back north.

I waited patiently for a period of time, just to make sure there was no one around, but the place was desolate for sure. An old wood-framed abandoned service station was the only structure around. Down through the hatch, out under the house, and to the back of the Mack. I brought my pint, the two-quart jug, and the pan full of pecans. After filling the pint only, I tore into the pecans, eating about half. Satisfied for the moment, I went for the driver door, and since the truck now facing the road, caution was required to not be seen. Oh, praise be, I was once again able to unlock the door. Climbing inside, I found a full bag of oatmeal cookies and the manifest binder for the journey.

Thinking that the binder was just as important as food, I went back to the house to retrieve the tablet and began to note all of what looked like pertinent information. It was all here, including contingencies for unscheduled delays. Every stop, including mileage, and the driver's notes showing the actual odometer readings thus far. Yes, now I knew not only our exact plan of travel, but the projected times of arrivals. But, I was still hungry.

Stealing four cookies and exiting the cab, I took my first look at the surroundings. I had plenty of daylight remaining, so I ventured into the old gas station, empty for the most part. There were a few things that could be useful to some junk collector, but nothing that I could use. Oh, except for another nice galvanized bucket, which I added to my possessions. This was still farming ground, and across the road was a large field of potatoes, already in blossom. In stealth as usual, I crossed the road into the field. Digging my hand under the plants in the soft soil, I could feel lots of new potatoes. I pulled these egg-sized spuds from under the plants until the bowl was overrunning.

In the contentment of holding my potato clutch, I slowed my return enough to notice the water flowing under a bridge I'd crossed to get to the potato patch. It was flowing quite hard from the day's rain. Working my way down, I wanted to wash the potatoes, which I did, then a much grander thought came to mind—why not wash me? Forgetting about being hungry, I hurried back to the house. In the bathroom cabinets there were bars of body soap and large bath towels. Are you kidding me? Returning to the bridge and the access area to the water, which was completely out of sight of the road, I stripped down. That was the first time those grimy pants were taken off since my exit from the prison. Previously I could not take them off with the leg-irons on.

Buck naked, I washed every part of my body, twice, then once again, really concentrating on my ankles. The stream was about four feet across and two feet deep, just enough to stretch out and let the cold water massage my entire body. I still had daylight, so I began washing my pants, shirt, and underwear using the body soap. I washed my socks, which were getting a bit threadbare, and finally the leather shoes.

I squeezed all the water I could from the clothes, including the prison-issued boxer shorts, bunched all of it together, and made my way naked and barefoot back to the house. Going to the rear of the rig, which was actually the front of the house, I put the wet clothes and bowl of potatoes on the porch. Then, wrapped only in the towel, I crawled underneath to access the hatch. Once inside, I wrapped myself in one of the cover sheets from a living room chair and headed back to the porch. The door had a very handsome deadbolt with a worn thumb turn that easily unlocked the door. I tried wringing more water out again and hung each piece, including the towel, over the wrought iron railings to dry. I put the potatoes in the refrigerator, as they fit well there.

Going to what I considered my bedroom, I indulged myself with the idea of sleeping in a real bed, but there was still light coming in the windows. So, I went back to the kitchen, looked in the fridge like a sleepless teenager on any given night, and grabbed several new potatoes. Condiments would be great at this time, like salt, but with all the furnishings that remained in the house, there were no food products of any kind. So, I chewed on raw potatoes.

Near dusk that Wednesday night, I heard a car pull in near the house. There was enough light remaining to peek out and see a county sheriff's car. An officer exited the car, looked all around, stretched his arms, pulled out a flashlight that he didn't need yet, and began a slow walk toward the rear of the rig. I was barefoot and should not have been sneaking from peephole to peephole, but I did anyway. He was headed back toward the washed prison clothes.

6. KING LEO

I FROZE IN PLACE as the officer walked within a few feet of the window I was peeking through. Wrapped only in a furniture sheet, my knees started knocking uncontrollably—what if the officer could hear it? I waited, paralyzed, except for my knocking knees, for what was about the same amount of time it would take a man to relieve himself. He walked back past the window again, got back into the squad car, and sat for a while with the dome light on. I tried to see if he was using the radio for backup, but all I saw was the motions of his arm writing on a small clipboard. After about five minutes, he drove off. He probably did take a leak but never saw the clothing.

For me, I was shaken to the core. After feeling so wonderful with the bath, a supply of fresh carbohydrates, and a good supply of water, this was the yin and yang of mental highs and lows at the same time. Feeling weak, I went to the desk chair and just sat for the longest time. I finally decided to try the bed in my bedroom, there being just enough moonlight to make my way to the room. I pulled the wool bedcover back and extracted the pillow, replacing the bedcover. I crawled onto the bed, wrapped my naked body in the furniture sheet, found a comfy spot for my head on the pillow, and savored the comfort for about...

I awoke, having to pee, so I found the bucket under the bed and used it. It was very dark, so I made myself comfortable again. As my mind drifted back to the deputy, I had really thought I was caught. All I could think of was not wanting to go back to that jail. I thought that I had been reckless in putting the clothes on the porch, even though it seemed so safe. I left the bed, feeling my way through the kitchen to the back door, and with just a trickle of moonlight, I gathered the drying clothes, towel, and shoes and put them on the ceramic tiled kitchen floor. I found my way back to the bed, rolled up in the sheet, and went back to sleep.

I awoke to sunlight sneaking through the bedroom blinds, just prior to the arrival of the movers. I was losing track of what day it was,

Thursday or Friday? Not that it mattered to me, but I didn't know if the moving continued on weekends or not. It was definitely a Friday when I walked out of the compound, and I spent two days, or two nights, staying ahead of the dogs. I must have found the house on Sunday night, and three nights in the Wright house put me at Wednesday night, so today would be Thursday.

I couldn't dress, as the clothes were still quite wet. I found the boxer shorts and put them on anyway, then wrapped back up in the sheet. I went to the chair in the living room that the sheet belonged on and sat down in it. I stretched out and listened to the workers prepping for the day's move. I was becoming accustomed to their regimen, including the thumping of the tires for air pressure. I was content with the stash of new potatoes, a few remaining pecans, and enough water for several days.

I really needed something to do. I went to the writing desk, retrieved my list of wants and needs, turned to a fresh page, and started a letter to Annika.

Dear Annika,

By now I am sure that you know I am on the missing-in-action list. I simply have had no way of contacting you, and I am so sorry for that. Yes, I am on the lam from the law. I am in what I will describe as a very unusual circumstance, but fairly safe considering. I have lost some weight, but I'm healthy and making the best of each day.

You have probably been very afraid for me, and no doubt very angry too. I agree with you, what I did was so foolish, and a negative outcome surely seems inevitable.

The gate at the prison was left unlocked and all I needed to do was walk out. I could see a clear path for escape, and I took it. Something inside just said, "GO."

I love you with all my heart, and I know that I have hurt you deeply. I can only hope that you will choose to stick with me for a while longer and keep looking for answers in the court system. I have now even tried praying for a good, or reasonable, outcome. I am desperately looking for an opportunity to call you. When I can, I will call the office at the laundry and send mail there too, as I did with this letter. Please do not do anything for me that would cause you to be aiding and abet-

ting a felon. Please stick with me, you are in my thoughts every minute.
Nick

I sealed the letter in an envelope, created a bogus return address, and was thankful that I remembered the address for the laundry. It was ready to mail. Then I did the same for my parents, with similar wording. I then added that I really needed my driver's license, asking Mom to try and renew it. She knew the manager at the Secretary of State, and the manager knew I had been in college and out of town. Mom knew how to write my name. If it was done prior to any news of my escape, she would likely not be held for aiding and abetting. My parents were probably in contact with Annika, but I asked them to stay in touch with her anyway. Even though I had no way to mail the letters yet, it at least gave me a bit of hope.

I had sat for a long time and needed to stretch. I walked sentry, looking out each of the windows with the peepholes. The lead truck a hundred yards ahead and the truck bringing up the rear a hundred yards behind were all just chugging along as the scenery slowly crept by. We were in some small but impactful hills, which caused the Mack to go into a much deeper guttural report. Then on the downhills, the many breaks on all the axles would squeak and squeal as the driver applied the brakes and the Jake break to the diesel engine, helping to hold back the forward motion and barking loudly to the bottom of each hill.

Earlier, I had hung the clothes over furniture that I knew the moisture would not hurt, and they were finally dried out. I dressed again, and the socks actually felt good against my very raw ankles. I sure hated to put that striped shirt back on. Then, I decided to go through all the bathroom cabinets, which revealed more nice surprises. The body soap was a good one, and now I had a shaving kit, complete with a shaving mug, a brush, and shaving soap. In my early years, I'd seen my father brush on shaving soap mixed in a mug, so I knew how to use it. The kit also had a very nicely built gold plated double-edged safety razor—NICE. The next thing was a tin of petro-carbo antiseptic salve—YES. I immediately sat down on the commode and applied the salve to my ankles. The stuff actually had an odd smell of petroleum. The drawer also yielded a comb! I should be giving thanks.

I had returned the chair cover sheet and sat down just to enjoy the ride for a while. I thought about the logbook in the cab of the Mack and decided it would be prudent if I could examine it further. It had pages of side notes of obstacles like uncrossable bridges that required detours and the like. Once I examined those, I would then be able to think like the crew thinks, which could give me some kind of advantage. As we chugged through the rolling hills, I thought about the shave kit. If I waited much longer to shave, I would need clippers to shorten the whiskers first. It occurred to me that it really didn't take much water to shave. While in Vietnam I shaved many times using only enough canteen water to fill the cap of an aerosol shave cream can. Having several days' worth of water now, why couldn't I pour a cup or two into the sink, make some soap in the mug, wet my face, brush on some soap, and shave?

While climbing in and out under the house, I noticed that the plumbing had been simply sawed off. If I were to open the sink drain a tiny bit and let it drain out over a half mile, no one would ever notice it. So I shaved, taking my time and enjoying every minute. I performed the regimen for draining the sink, added a few more cups of water to rinse off my face, and then rinsed the cup, brush, and razor. I gapped the drain plug slightly again until the rinse water was gone. There were washcloths in one of the cabinets along with the towels, so I took one to wipe out the sink, then stored it separately. Everything went back in its place, except the comb. I smiled into the mirror as I made my growing hair look decent again.

Feeling energetic, I did more house exploring. I went through the chest of drawers in my room, then through the chest of drawers and the built-in closet in the master bedroom. I was hoping for clothing but there was none. However, in one of the drawers there was a nice sized tin of King Leo mints. The pink ones the size of a nickel but four times thicker. It was full, so I put one in my mouth and savored it. The jail simply didn't provide any niceties like this, so it had been a long time since I enjoyed such a treat.

I sat on the master bed and enjoyed another mint, thinking back on the first time I tried to eat one. As a kid, we were fortunate to have Jake and Edith Fritz as neighbors, who were lifelong farmers and getting elderly at the time. Edith raised laying chickens, as many as two or three hundred. She spent a great deal of her days washing and candling eggs. She would grade them for size and pack them appropriately. Many times, Mom would take me for the ten-minute walk to their house to purchase eggs. Mom and Edith would usually strike up a conversation, while I was to wait patiently. One time we were there and in the center of the table was a small bowl of the same mints. I just pointed to the bowl, and Mrs. Fritz handed me a mint. I put it in my mouth immediately.

Now, Mr. Fritz was a cigar smoker, and in those days he thought nothing of smoking in the house, and the house smelled strongly of it. I had just begun to savor the mint when the real flavor made itself known—stale cigar smoke! I stood up, milled around for a while, and gestured to Mom that I was going outside. I ran to the nearest bush and spit that thing out, nearly gagging. Now this mint was the real thing. I returned the tin to the drawer, but it was on my radar now.

Examining the house more, the living room had an area on an outer wall and floor that had been tightly and neatly boarded up. So I examined it more closely, thinking it was most likely an opening left from the removal of a fireplace. No doubt, the movers rejected trying to move it with the house. I think all the Frank Lloyd Wright homes we viewed in class had fireplaces, but there in the wall was yet another clue. An electrical box that would service the fireplace was fastened to steel pipe electrical conduit. Conduit was nothing new in the 30s, but was only used on commercial buildings, never for housing. However, Mr. Wright insisted on only the very best.

Even though the nights were fairly cool and cooled the house, the sun in the day would heat it up again to the point that I would sweat. However, with my recent bath in the creek, and today's shave, I was feeling as good as I could feel in this unusual style of prison. We didn't have many long stops that day, as the movers pulled into a roadside picnic area on the east side of the road. We must have made good time, even in the hills, as it seemed earlier and the sun was higher than other evenings. The usual half hour of shutdown, lockdown, fold up, and put away took place, and the crew headed north again.

Looking out the peep to the east, I saw a neatly kept little roadside park with several picnic tables, a charcoal grill by each one, two trash barrels, and a small gazebo with a hand operated water pump at the center. YES! I looked to the west at a farm field growing something I could not identify at the distance. I was concerned about leaving the house so early since cars were speeding by from time to time, but no one stopped at the park. I waited for at least another hour, trying to plan what little I could, before venturing out. I unlocked the front door, which now faced north, and looked for any traffic that might be headed south. It was much quicker and easier to jump from the porch than crawl out from under, so with great caution I used the porch. I took both buckets, one for clean water, one for p-u, then went to the hand pump. It took a few dry pumps to get it primed up, but then it gave a steady flow of water. I rinsed out the p-u bucket, dumped it over a nearby fence, filled it again, and let it set to soak while I filled the other bucket. I ran back to the porch, setting the freshwater bucket up first, then climbing up. I carried the bucket carefully to the bathroom and poured the water into the tub, where I had inserted the plug. I repeated the trips until the tub was half full. Then I rinsed the p-u bucket one more time, placed it back under the bed, and refilled the drinking water containers.

I was laughing at myself as I finished my new chores and decided to see what was in the field across the street. Dusk was just beginning, and traffic had nearly ceased. I waited for a good opening and dashed across through some tall weeds that would help block the view of a passerby. I had gone to the field completely unprepared and needed to go back and retrieve the water bucket. I then filled the bucket with the most beautiful red radishes I had ever seen, stripping as much of the greens off by hand that I could.

I carried them to a picnic table, which was blocked from view for the most part, and dumped them on the table, then went back into the house and retrieved a bowl of new potatoes, the large skillet, a fork, and a paring knife. I remembered that the Mack driver was a smoker from the evidence he left, so I went to the door, but the vent was closed! Crap. I looked closer at the vent to see that the latch was not pulled down, so I bumped the opposite side, and it opened! A quick unlocking procedure, and I was inside. I looked at the rusted vent latch and tried to lock it, but it was rusted in place. Haha, good for me! Now I knew I could always rely on getting in the cab. It only took a minute to find plenty of matchbooks, enough that I privileged myself in taking two books along with me. I closed and locked the door without bothering to look at the manifest this time.

I dashed about the park, picking up a bunch of tiny tree branches, and put the pile at the base of the charcoal grill. I broke the sticks into small pieces, filling the grill, but I needed paper to start the sticks. Searching the trash barrels revealed that an entire family must have used the park to eat their McDonald's meal. The barrel was half full of discarded sacks and such. I unloaded the contents of the barrel onto a picnic table and sorted it all out, finding a small pile of salt and pepper packets. YES! There were also multiple packets of ketchup, mustard, and relish. YES! I was actually looking for good dry paper, but there was plastic tableware and lots of unused napkins. YES! I also found one complete hamburger, unopened. I smelled it carefully, along with all the uneaten french fries. They all smelled very fresh, possibly only a few hours old. I stacked all the usable fire starter paper neatly, except what I would need to start my grill fire. I saved the usable items, and the remainder went back in the trash barrel.

I made short work of cutting out the greens and roots from the radishes and gave them a quick wash, then sliced them into the fry pan. I did the same with several potatoes. By then my fire was going nicely as I added fuel, keeping the fire as small and concentrated as I could. In about half an hour there were enough coals to set the fry pan on the grill. I removed the untouched burger meat from the bun and put it in the pan. I needed at least a little grease to cook my meal, but I still needed to add some water from time to time.

When the potatoes and radishes were soft enough, I put the pan on the table. While it cooled, I put the fire out and sat down to a hot meal, topped off with a pint of fresh water. With the addition of salt and pepper, the concoction was quite good. The radishes put some zest into the spuds. Dry sand was along the sidewalks, so using a few of the papers, I scrubbed the skillet aggressively with the sand, inside and out. Rinsing at the pump finished the job. I looked carefully for any remaining evidence and retired to the house via the porch, locking the door behind me.

The dark house was somewhat hard to navigate, and I thought of lighting a match, but I ruled it out. Placing everything on the floor near the kitchen, I found my way to bed, removed my shoes, rolled up once again in the chair sheet, and felt content and comfortable.

I tried to think strategically, bringing to mind the itinerary in the Mack—we were past the town of Wadley and the city of Swainsboro, with the city of Lyons next in line. That would put me at about 130 miles away from Augusta, for what that was worth. Knowing where I was geographically was of rudimentary importance to me, but at least I could rest that frustration. I was planning out places to put my newfound possessions but fell asleep first.

I awoke from an uninterrupted night's sleep and stretched every muscle I could stretch then laid on the bed for a while. I slept in my T-shirt, pants, and socks, so getting dressed wasn't necessary. After just sitting for a minute, I got busy putting everything away to my satisfaction.

I returned to the living room, replacing the cover sheet on the chair, and sat in wait for the moving crew. They arrived as usual and got to business, and within a half hour we were under way. I continued to just sit, but it was driving me crazy. I went to the dining room desk, pulled up a chair, retrieved my notes of the manifest, and studied the route. We skirted one of the towns and went straight through two. It appeared that we would go straight through Lyons, but there was a problem noted about a stoplight at the main intersection of town. Well, we would see what that was, but it was Friday, and the manifest stated that the move would continue on Monday. So, they were taking the weekend off! YES!

As I sat at the desk, I began looking at the books so neatly shelved. There were some great titles in this library, including reference, law, and how-to books, and even a small book entitled *Frank Lloyd Wright*, but the majority were suspense novels. Oh, and there was a very nice King James Version of the Bible. I thought about reading *A Tale of Two Cities*, but it lost out to the Bible. Through the years, I had been introduced to the Bible—I knew the basics, had heard many of the Old Testament stories and the Gospels, but I had never succeeded in reading it for myself. If I were actually able to continue traveling in this house, it would last about ten more days. I couldn't possibly read it all in that time, but what else would I be doing during the day?

I resolved to read the Bible while traveling, and it finally gave me a mental purpose during the day. I began to read Genesis right then. As the move continued, and my rear end began to get sore from the oak chair, I moved to the living room chair. Genesis, in itself, is a large book, relative to the Bible. From the creation, to the flood, to the Tower of Babel, the story of Abraham, the twelve sons of Jacob, and Joseph and his final words. I was mesmerized at reading these words and stories at a time when there was very little distraction.

I laid the good book down about every hour or so to walk sentry, looking through the peeps, then returned to the reading. I kept this up all day, as the sun began to heat up the house to a point that I was perspiring. I thought about the bathtub with enough water in it to lounge in. Laying down the good book, I indulged my thoughts. Stripping down, I climbed into that claw foot tub, the water at room temperature, which felt great, and relaxed. Ah, life on the lam isn't all bad. The gentle vibration of the house traveling down the road felt so good as well, and I was totally relaxed. I was thankful for a personal truck driver, as he drove my motorized home farther south. I must have lain in that water for a half hour, pondering whether I should drain the water out slowly or save it for more use. The water was far cleaner with only one use than I was when this house found me. Yes, I think it found me.

Exiting the tub, I used the towel that I used for my bath in the creek. I dressed again and hung the towel on the rim of the tub near the wall, leaving the almost clean water in the tub. Then I returned to reading while sitting on the living room chair with a refreshed attitude. I continued reading intently to the end of the amazing book of Genesis and felt grateful for my reading experience. I turned to the book of Exodus and moved the page locating ribbon there, as I hoped that I would be reading the second book tomorrow.

Say what you want about the Bible, say that there is no redemption, but I care to differ, as there between the two books was a $100 bill. I was shocked. After food and water, money was the thing I needed the most. I got up, went back to the desk, sat down again, laid my head on that Bible, and this time gave thanks to my Maker. Then, of course, I gave thanks to whoever put that bill in there. Then a riveting thought came to me. There are sixty-six books in the Bible. I turned next to Leviticus, another $100, then to the book of Numbers. There was $6,600 in this Bible!

I simply didn't know what to think. I fondled that first bill, while thinking that I already had a great debt of thanks that would need to be paid back to the owner of this house one day, but now I would literally be stealing from them. I knew as long as I could access my own money, I could pay it back. I was already in deep shit, but would using some of this money put me even deeper? Yes, it would. I returned the bill to the Exodus page and put the Bible back in the cabinet.

I went back to the living room chair and sat with my legs straight out, almost laying prone. I was trying to get a grip on this possible good fortune. If a circumstance were to arise, I would indeed use some of this sanctified money to acquire things that I really needed. I resolved that if I did have an opportunity to use some of the cash, I would create a ledger to account for every penny.

I was trying to keep an eye on the sun, as the day was starting to grow long. While peeking out toward the west, I was looking at vast fields of agricultural land, so I moved to the east window and the view was the same thing. The ground looked a rich dark red and very flat. Almost all of it was planted so neatly, with dark green wisps sticking out of the ground in perfect long rows for miles. I recognized them as onions, millions of them. Then I realized, duh, everyone had heard of the wonderful Vidalia sweet onion. This must be the place where they were all grown. The city of Vidalia was only a few miles to the west of Lyons. I almost thirsted for one of those sweet softball-sized onions.

For the movers, it must have been a very good day, with only a few stops, hills, and phone lines. The road was very good now as well, smooth as silk as we moved through this flat land. I indulged in some of the remaining potatoes, sprinkled with a packet of McDonald's salt, and topped that off with more of the remaining radishes.

I could tell that we were coming to a more populated area since the traffic was more intense and less forgiving. This moving house totally blocked the road, but only temporarily in any one place. Just a little patience, and a traveler could be on his way. I related their anxiousness to mine with months in captivity, not just a few minutes of delay. I could hate them, but I chose to laugh at them instead.

All the signs of stopping were starting to accrue when a tremendous explosion occurred! I hit the deck and started a low crawl. I was instantly transported back to Vietnam, and we had incoming! I was on the floor, on my elbows, looking left and right with sweat already appearing on my forehead.

The truck driver slowed the house to a stop, and within a minute I could hear voices shouting, "BLOWN TIRE."

I laid my head down and breathed deep a few times, and thought,

"Well, you sure handled that like a real trooper."

I was continually impressed with this crew—they may have appeared on the surface to be somewhat of a rabble, but they knew this business. The truck in the rear pulled forward. I could hear a gas-powered air compressor fire up as the crew busied themselves like ants carrying tools and a serious jack to the site. I could hear the clanging of tools under the house, along with a pneumatic lug wrench zipping lug nuts from a hub. The house never seemed to move when the axle was lifted enough to swap tires. Not much more than twenty minutes and we were rolling again.

There was still a little adrenaline seeping into my system, so I walked sentry, peeking from every window. It appeared we were entering the beginnings of a suburb, and I knew from the ledger that the parking site would be on the north side of town. Shortly after, we came to a stop, then began a slow turn to the left and began moving alongside large piles of gravel, higher than the house. We were driving on a huge gravel lot, and at the end of the piles the rig made a right turn, continuing until we were headed back toward the road. Then all came to a stop, and the shutdown procedure began.

As I moved about surveying the area, a late model Cadillac pulled up near the house and a man dressed in very nice khaki pants and a white *guayabera* shirt designed to wear outside the pants stepped out of the car. He also wore a Panama hat and had what looked like a 35mm camera hanging around his neck. The hat hid his face as he moved about and took several photos of the house. He talked to the Mack driver for a period of time, making gestures and pointing to the house. The driver beckoned one of the crew to his side, making gestures to him. He left in a hustle towards one of the crew trucks, which were both in view. He retrieved a four-foot ladder and hustled to the porch area, out of my sight. I moved with stealth to the stained glass door to witness what he was doing, as I could hear the aluminum ladder clang against the porch.

I found a tiny piece of the leaded glass window, in the center of a flower, that allowed me to see out to the porch, and I watched Mr. Khaki Man approach the ladder. Oh, not good! He was up that ladder in seconds, followed by footsteps across the short porch and a key rattling in the dead bolt.

7. CARL BURGER

As I saw Mr. Khaki Man approaching the ladder, I did an about-face. Taking giant tiptoe steps to the hallway, I scooped up the hatch door and slithered down as quickly as I possibly could. The hatch closed silently as the front door opened. I sat on my butt, arms around my legs trying to present as small a figure as possible. All I could do was wait. I could hear the footsteps go from room to room, all through the house, hesitating from time to time.

I was going nuts—did I leave anything out, did I replace the sheet on the chair? What if the p-u bucket smelled? What if he looked in the fridge, or the kitchen cabinets, or smells the petro-carbo salve I had just reapplied to my ankles? And, oh my God, what about the water in the tub! I waited and waited. Finally I could hear his footsteps heading for the porch and the door close and lock. The crew member made short work of the ladder, while the driver and the man began to chat.

The man said, "I am pleased with the progress and the expertise that has been shown in the move. The only thing out of place was a dining room chair near the desk, but other than that, things looked perfect. I will be in town on Monday to watch the house being moved through, and I will be taking a few photos as it goes by certain notable sites. Being a reporter, I informed both the Swainsboro and the Waycross newspapers of the move through Lyons, with the expected dates of arrival. They made a front-page article about it, so you men should expect a few spectators."

Now, I was thinking that this was the man that I would eventually need to show gratitude and to repay. But as their conversation went on, he said, "I will be giving a full report to my boss, so please keep up the excellent work." There was something about his voice quality that seemed so familiar.

I stayed put, tucked in beside a set of dual tires until the man and crew left. Entering back through the hatch, I laid out on the living room floor for a very long time, nearly in tears some of the time. The emotion eventually became controllable, and I sat in my favorite chair to organize my thoughts. While under the house, I had no chance of surveying the area, so making a good effort at the peepholes seemed a reasonable next move. I did so and could see what looked like a church to the south, about two hundred yards away. It looked like it had a good-sized pavilion on its north side, with lots of people busying themselves in and around it. I would need to wait until dusk to venture out. I was getting hungry.

I went to the dining room and put my chair back in position to use the desk, retrieved the Bible, and opened it. I turned to the book of Exodus and vocalized that title several times. I read about how the Israelites made their escape from slavery in Egypt. After all the plagues, the Egyptian people gave them nearly everything they had just to see them go. I supposed I was in some sort of exodus, and now I had found all the financial means I could ever want for escape right here in this Bible.

I began to read the book of Exodus, slowly and meaningfully. But a very gracious gift had been put into my hands. Now, what should I use it for? I could buy a bus ticket, a train ticket, possibly an airline ticket, whatever didn't require an ID. I tried but could not concentrate on the Father's word at that time. Leaving that $100 bill at the beginning of Exodus, I closed the Bible, put it back in its place, and waited for dusk.

At a point when I felt that there was enough darkness to conceal my moves, I ventured out. Standing behind the house, I did the usual 360. Nothing to the north but the gravel and dirt piles, to the west was Highway 1, and to the south was the now vacated pavilion beside the church. There was an ancient fence row of Osage orange trees to the east that went past the rear of the church and on into the city limits. I moved out to the east, finding a path through the fence row that hid my intended travel path quite well. I walked the distance to the church and found another opening through the tangle that allowed access to the church yard. A small light was burning in the center of the pavilion, so I kept a low profile as I entered what looked like a rather large rummage sale.

Holy bats, there was a lot of stuff there, including many neatly stacked articles of clothing. Again, I was nearly to tears as I sifted through piles of trousers and shirts. The light was dim, but I found denim trousers, T-shirts, flannel shirts, short sleeves, and casual shirts, all that would fit me. I included an Alabama Crimson Tide Football hat. I fully buttoned one of the long sleeve shirts and stuffed it with all the clothes I thought I could use, then tied the arms together. With further observation, I could see tables covered with sheets, revealing the shapes of plates or bowls. I abandoned my duffel bag of clothing and pulled back the sheets to reveal a treasure trove of cookies, cakes, and pies.

I was so hungry, I ate several pieces of fruit pie, finding the first to be fresh strawberry and rhubarb. It was so good I ate another, slowing down enough to truly enjoy it. Then on to a Dutch apple, which was astounding, and finally the most wonderful southern pecan pie I had ever tasted. They were all on individual cellophane-covered paper plates. I removed the covering from two small plates of cookies, wrapped them in the cellophane, and slid them carefully into my shirt pocket. I stacked the paper plates and found a trash barrel, shoving them to the bottom. Then I tried to arrange the table so their loss would not be noticed.

With my hunger momentarily appeased, I began to look through the rummage tables, thinking of my greatest needs. What did I truly need for this leg of my vacation? I came across an Eagle Scout backpack, the kind a seasoned Boy Scout would wear for extended camping treks. Yes, I would need this. Searching, I then found a military or Boy Scout style flashlight, with the lens facing ninety degrees to the battery barrel. Yes, I would need this. As I hit the button, the light came on very dim, proving that at least it worked. I was satisfied for the moment that I had fared well, and that gave me faith and new ideas for tomorrow. I was about to carry off my booty when I spied a fishing rod and reel, with a small tackle box. Did I want it or need it, flashed through my head. I really wanted it, but it could prove very useful in the remainder of this ride. Being one more thing to carry, it caused me to stuff everything else into the backpack.

Now I knew that I was absconding with the slim profits of this good church, but thinking of the words of Jesus telling us to pay mind to the imprisoned, I felt he was watching over me. I mounted the backpack of new possessions and headed for my mobile home. The last streetlight north of town was near Highway 1, just beyond the center of the quarried piles of earth and gravel, and it was a beacon for my path of return. I was listening and watching cars go by as they accelerated up to speed while leaving the city limits. However, I heard one slowing down and the gravel drive making that familiar grinding sound against the tires. I had gone squat behind the trash barrel and did not look up as the head-lights swept across the pavilion. The lights were now aimed between the pavilion and the church, and the driver skidded to a stop. I took a quick peek from the side of the barrel to see the shadow of a police cruiser, its roof light coming on, flashing red. My heart started pounding hard again as the vehicle settled, but only for a second and then the tires be-gan spinning in reverse, throwing stones as the car sped backward onto the road. The tires squealed as it headed back toward town.

I reached up, grabbing the barrel rim for support to steady my knocking knees, then immediately made my way back to and through the fence row, heading north at the edge of some cultivated field. The streetlight twinkling through the trees provided just enough light to travel quickly back to the rear of the house. I put the ruck, pole, and tackle box on the porch, entered the house through the hatch, opened the porch door, and moved it all inside. With it being too dark to do a proper job of sorting the clothes and putting them in my dresser, I just removed them all from the rucksack, unbuttoned the shirt, and tried to roughly arrange them under the bed.

It seemed too early to go to bed, and with the adrenaline rush, I just wasn't tired. Remembering a yard hydrant at the corner of the pavil-ion, I took the water and p-u buckets for a return trip. I had been using the pages from a Sears Roebuck catalog for the sanitary work, so I need-ed to edge back into the fence row for dumping and hopefully conceal-ing the waste. Arriving at the hydrant, I rinsed the p-u bucket several times, then walked back to the trees to dump it. I added about an inch of water to it while I filled the clean bucket about three-fourths full.

When I finished, I went over to the tables in the pavilion again. Among all the treasures, there were many pots, pans, and the like. I sift-ed through the kitchen wares, hunting for a possible lid for the p-u buck-et, and eventually found one with a metal lifting ring at the center that fit nicely inside the rim of the bucket. I was more worried about smell causing curiosity than sanitation. But a lid would also keep flies out of it.

I was finally tired enough to turn in, feeling quite safe, so I stripped off the prison uniform, prayerfully hoping that I would never wear it or any other again. Exposing the feather pillow and wrapping up in the furniture sheet, I breathed slowly and deeply while reminiscing of the evening's good fortune. I must have gone into an uninterrupted deep sleep all night. In the early morning I jerked awake, seeing the early morning sun peeking through the shutters again. I stretched, putting my hands behind my head, savoring the moment, and of course, thinking about the newfound possibilities for my logistics plan.

It felt as though I had worked all week, earning a weekend off, so I lounged until there was plenty of light to work by. I first went to the desk to retrieve the tablet and pencil, since I needed to list all the purchases I would love to make. Then I stopped, turned to the prison uniform, folded the uniform as tightly as possible, and placed it in a drawer. What should I do with it? How should I dispose of it? Pulling out the casual clothes and organizing them for color, sleeve length, and such, I set one ensemble aside for the day. I folded all the others and placed them neatly in the drawers. Before dressing, I put some water in the bathroom sink, soaked a washcloth, and did what my mom called a spit bath. I let the water just drain out, so it would be dry before we pulled out on Monday. I put more water in the sink and gave myself a nice shave, letting the water go down the drain, then rinsed the sink clean.

Dressing in clean clothes felt so good—a pair of denim pants, a white T-shirt, and a short-sleeved dark blue casual shirt. I had two problems, the pants were nearly a size too big, and I didn't have a belt. The prison shoes were in really tough shape and looked bad, but having a plan for both, I let it go for the moment. The fishing pole and tackle box needed a home, so I went to the back door of the house, which led to a small, enclosed back porch. It housed a clothes washer and dryer, several cabinets, a small highboy table with two chairs, and a broom closet, which the pole and box fit nicely in. I fetched the rucksack and looked it over carefully. It was fairly old but in very good shape, strong enough for a heavy load. Noticing a lump in one of the many pouches, I discovered a very nicely preserved Boy Scout style pocketknife. YES! And the two primary blades were quite sharp. I hung the ruck on a chair back and returned to making the list.

My plan was to go into town, purchase new clothing, belt, socks, and, oh yes, underwear! I needed to go to the post office and a grocery store. I was also hoping for a barber and a drugstore. I completed my list, making breakfast out of the delicious cookies I'd carried home last night. I exited the house through the front door. I thought I could not lock the door, but remembering keys that were in the desk drawer, I retrieved and tried them, finding that one worked perfectly. YES! I locked the porch door behind me and jumped to the ground. I went to the back of the escort truck and found some cord to use as a temporary belt, leaving the shirt hanging out to conceal it. There were plenty of shop towels and a can of axle grease I substituted for shoe polish. With some work, I had the prison issue shoes looking quite good.

I joyfully said to myself, "Well, Finn, isn't this shopping day?" The front porch was facing directly toward the fence row, my path completely hidden. Finding my previous path through the trees, I headed toward town, passing the church. I had folded up the ruck, carrying it under my arm, as the hedge went another two hundred yards and then turned directly east. At the corner there was a well-worn path leading to a country road that led into town. The road also made an intersection at that point, with a southbound back city street lined with clapboard houses in disrepair. So I just walked on the edge of the backstreet one block away to the north end of the town. The business district went five or six blocks south from there.

I just refused to worry much about being spotted, but I kept the cap just a little low over my eyes anyway. The last house on the south end was no doubt abandoned, grown mostly into a thicket with an old mailbox protruding from a bush. I looked around as I wadded the backpack tight enough to fit into the mailbox. I had three $100 bills in my shirt pocket as I walked south into the business area. Most of the stores offered little use to me, until a five-and-dime store came along. Going in to browse, I gathered up a toothbrush and tube of toothpaste. This was needed since I hadn't brushed since I had walked out of jail. I added a gel aftershave and a four-pack of D-cell batteries. The clerk bagged them up while operating the cash register and voiced the total. I handed her a $100 bill, but she said she could not break it. I asked if I could leave the bag on the counter and come back later with change, and she agreed.

Strolling on down the street another half block produced a barber shop. The barber, sporting a rather large handlebar mustache and reading the Swainsboro newspaper, looked up with a smile.

I asked him before he could stand, "Can you break a $100?" He just nodded, so I sat in his very old and elaborately decorated barber chair. I said, "I could use a military style high and tight."

"You betcha, I've done a thousand of them." He draped me with a cloth and started the clippers buzzing. As he cut, he talked about what he just read in the paper. He said, "In order to move some famous house through the main street, the stoplight had to be taken down and traffic is being routed around a temporary detour until the move is complete. It said townsfolk may want to set out portable chairs and just enjoy the oversized load being moved through town." I was enlightened as he performed a perfect cut.

He finished the job after whipping up shaving cream in a cup and brushing it around my ears and the back of my neck. He then stropped a straight razor several times and carefully cut a perfect line around my ears and across the back of my neck. He topped it off with a hot towel cleanup and a splash of very fragrant aftershave. Removing the sheet and whipping it in the air briskly enough to make it pop, he invited me to leave the chair. I handed him the bill, and he returned $97. I thought for a second then I handed him an additional two dollars. He was startled, but I told him sincerely, "Thank you, Mike," as I noticed his name, Mike Siver, printed on a business card on his counter. I left his shop and continued down the street.

My next stop was a corner grocery. Now this took some careful thought. Protein was no doubt the hardest thing to come by so far. We would be stopping near at least two more towns, but whether I could venture out like this was unknown. I went for the canned meat and put five cans of spam and five cans of corned beef hash in my cart. The condiment aisle yielded little since everything needed refrigeration, except some hot sauce, so I added a small jar of hot sauce and a camping-style salt and pepper. I added another fifteen cans of assorted soups and Dinty Moore beef stew. Passing the fresh veggies, I spotted a small bundle of celery, which made my mouth water so bad that I added it to the cart. Then I added a plastic bag with about twelve small apples, which would hold up for weeks.

At this point I knew this load would be at the limit of the ruck and resolved to make more than one trip to town. At checkout, I asked the clerk for double bagging, and she did. It was all I wanted to carry arm in arm. I headed for the ruck, passing the five-and-dime along the way. The clerk recognized me and smiled as I sat the bags on her counter. I paid the bill, she tossed the small sack into one of my big sacks, and I hurried to the old mailbox. Approaching the old house, I pushed through the overgrowth to a broken down set of steps that thankfully worked nicely as a place to set the grocery bags, as my arms were tiring. I retrieved the ruck and promptly sorted all the contents into it, pulling the cords to the opening and tightly bunching it all in a big ball. I closed the canvas lid over the opening, then using the cross-arm swing, I mounted the heavy pack on my shoulders and headed for home.

I made the hike with ease, trying not to break out into a real sweat. I sat the ruck on the porch, jumped up to unlock the door, went to the kitchen, and proceeded to store all the supplies in the cabinets. I went to my favorite chair and just sat for a few minutes, pondering what I just accomplished and planning the next excursion into town. It was time to stop for the moment and give thanks to our Maker. I did.

I locked the house as I left again, following the same route as in the morning, and placed the ruck back into the mailbox. It didn't take long to pass the corner grocery, going deeper into the main part of the town. As I came to a Woolworth's store, I knew that I could outfit myself with some nice clothes.

I went for the genuine Levi boot cut denims first, a pair of Dan Post western boots, and two very nice Van Heusen short sleeve shirts to go with the pants. I added two white V-neck tees and two pairs of brightly colored boxer shorts. (One to wear, one to wash.) Now for the nice stuff. I found the slacks that I really wanted, but they all needed to be tailored to length—not good. I needed to accept the lower class at this time. I finally found a very nice pair of tan dress slacks and two dress shirts, one long and one short sleeve. There was a bonus of a loose fit off-white cotton shirt, what I would call a Panama sports jacket, and a Panama hat. Now I would need another pair of shoes and dress socks.

I had to pause. What was I doing? Was I out of control again, or was there a possibility of using this stuff? The future was so unknown at this point, so I just kept shopping for shoes. I bought a pair of cordovan wingtip shoes and splurged for a can of polish, an applicator, and a buffing brush. The store had other men's items including watches, and I added to the pile a battery powered Timex watch that displayed the day and date. It was similar to the Seiko self-winding watch I had purchased in Yokota, Japan, on the way back home from Vietnam but at three times the cost.

Believing I had what I needed and wanted, and being mindful of just how much the ruck would hold, I headed back to the house. I found homes for all the new items, stripped off all the tags, and either hung them in the closet or placed them in my dresser.

As afternoon crept faster into the equation, I headed back into town for the third time, placing the ruck in the old mailbox again. This time with a more hurried pace, I headed south looking for the post office. Passing the Woolworth store, I stopped someone on the street to ask where I could find the post office.

The local responded with a finger point south and said, "Three more blocks sonny."

Arriving, I walked in cautiously, looking at the bulletin board. There were definitely wanted posters tacked to it, but my mug shot was not one of them. I purchased a roll of stamps, pulled the two letters from my shirt pocket, licked and applied a stamp to each, and then shoved them through the outgoing mail slot. That was a really good feeling, but next, I asked the teller where I could find a payphone.

It was just around the corner, under a canopy attached to the post office building. I had a pocket full of change, which I had saved during the day, and dialed the office phone at Annika's workplace. The receptionist answered the phone promptly with the preloaded biz about the laundry, and I answered boldly with, "This is Nick, I need to talk to Annika please."

She knew who I was, and said, "I will try to find her."

The pause was disturbingly long before Annika's voice said, "I hate you! No, no, I hate what you did! I do not understand this! I have been going crazy, so worried!"

I heard crying for several moments, then a complete change of tone in her voice.

"Are you alright, do you need anything, where are you?"

I said, "The ankle chains really caused me a lot of damage, but I now have them cleaned and dressed. I will not tell you where I am, and the only thing I really need is you. Annika, I am residing in a most wonderful place. It lacks certain personal requirements at times but is providing a most unconventional path to freedom."

"Look asshole, I am so pissed at you. I am barely in control, but I am not only willing to follow you one more time, but I have also been actively looking into the entire case against you."

I expressed my deepest thanks and trust, and that I didn't know when I would have an opportunity to call again, but if she were willing, opportunities in the future may provide a chance to meet.

She was hesitant, stuttering a bit, then said, "I will need to hear your plan, Nick."

"That would be fair," I replied. "I mailed a letter today too and will probably be able to send more, but I will have no return address. I can't even say what state I am in, but, if you were with me, I know in my heart that you would be pleased with my position and my place."

"OK, OK, for the moment, my heart is back in it. But Nick, my heart cannot take another big blow like this last one. I need to hear something positive from here on out."

"I can certainly agree with that." I went on to say, "I believe now that most people never have a single opportunity to simply step out of their lives long enough to even take a fresh breath. To truly think about what they are doing, where they are going, or what is truly important. But, Annika, I think that is happening to me now, and it is not over. I know I have hidden issues within me—I do not know what they are— but there's something about all of this solitude and freedom at the same time that just tastes like an answer."

Annika switched the subject and explained that she had done very well in her classes and had made the dean's list again, despite her extracurricular activities digging into my legal case.

"Nick, I have been fascinated with all aspects of the law. I cannot believe how I have been stonewalled at every attempt I have made trying to get even the simplest of information in your case. I am considering changing my major for my junior year. I think I want to study law."

"Well baby, you have the beans for it. What I know of your parents, they would be so proud, and I would too. Go for it girl, go for it!"

We ended the call with, "I love you's," and I promised I would call again soon and send letters. With a determined satisfaction, I was so happy with the connection to Annika that I needed to just sit for a while before calling my parents.

Since it was Saturday afternoon, I had no idea where Mom and Dad might be, but I plugged in the change and dialed. Mother answered the phone—dang.

"Don't go nuts Mom, it's Nick." She went nuts! I waited for her to collect herself a bit and asked, "When did you find out that I went on the missing list?"

"Wednesday a sheriff's officer came by and informed us that you were a fugitive, and that we had better notify them if you showed up. We haven't slept since."

"Mom, I screwed up for sure, and I don't really understand why I did what I did. The opportunity came to just walk out of that awful place. I could see an opportunity to run and my head said 'Go,' so I did. Now, I have found myself in a very unusual situation, a way to live quite comfortably as I move slowly toward a way to solve my problem. Mom, I have been in touch with Annika, and she stands beside me. She is working on my legal case too, at least for a while. Please stay in contact with her."

I asked her about renewing my driver's license, the details of which would be coming to her in a letter very soon. I said, "I think you can pull it off without really breaking the law. It's simply time for renewal, and I am out of town.

"Tell Dad I love him, that I am safe and comfortable, and that I am pondering my future with all seriousness. Tell him that I have begun to read the Bible from the beginning, and that I am truly finding redemption between the pages of each and every book. I love you Mom, goodbye."

I put more change into the phone and called my bank in Atlanta. I was put on hold, and my call changed hands several times. Finally a clerk came on that was familiar with my account and explained that I would need to appear there in person to alter anything on the frozen account. I thanked her and said that no changes would be necessary at this time. Although there was no legal requirement, she added that a county sheriff from Augusta had recently inquired about my account and that he was acquiring the legal means to seize the account.

I thanked her in earnest and said, "Keep it frozen, I will look into the law." I then put the last of my change back into the phone and dialed the laundry one more time. The receptionist answered again, so I asked for Annika, and she put me on hold.

Only a moment had passed when Annika answered, "Now what, asshole?"

Chuckling from her comment, I said, "Annika, I just talked to my bank in Atlanta. They shared with me that a Sheriff Stump was trying to access my accounts. I am certain that they are safe, but that may just provide you some legal questioning to work on."

"I agree Nick, I will add it to my list." We said our goodbyes again.

I hung up the phone and sat on the bench for the longest time, trying to get a real grip on just where I was and what I was doing. Basically I was completely free. But yet, in complete bondage. If I didn't follow a strict regimen of behavior, I would be behind bars in short order.

I stood up, still very confident that my identity was quite safe here in Lyons, Georgia. I walked south many more blocks looking into store windows and enjoying the evening. I crossed the main drag and walked back toward home soaking up this pleasant southern town. Just before I crossed back east, at the corner of Phelps Street and Delaware, I saw a restaurant with a billboard that said, "Carl's Lunch." For cripes cakes, I was hungry. I entered the restaurant and sat at a long curved bar that allowed a view of the cook working at a big flat griddle. A waitress was working the tables in the room behind me, but the cook, presumably Carl, took my order at the counter. Oh, the smell was off the charts. I ordered a cheeseburger, with a full slab of fresh Vidalia onion, ketchup and mayo, an order of fries, and coleslaw. My order was complete. If a king ever dined on a Carl burger, fries, and coleslaw, he would fire the royal chefs. I savored every bite, every fry dipped in ketchup, and sipped slowly on their draft root beer. Before leaving I took note that they were open on Sunday morning for breakfast—ohhhh, breakfast.

It was time to head back, walking slowly with my head up, my eyes nearly closed. I nearly walked past my corner but corrected and walked east to the path that led through the hedge. I walked slowly along the field that brought me back to my Frank Lloyd Wright oasis.

I took a chair from the dining table and moved it to the porch. I sat for the longest time looking toward the old hedge and pondered the last two days. I did not know how this was happening or why, but I fully intended to follow this adventure wherever it led.

Aside from the jail ministries, I hadn't been to church in quite some time. Tomorrow was the Sabbath day, so why not experience the Baptist church next door? I retired myself to the porch until it was nearly too dark to see, then thought about the D-cell batteries I had purchased. I was such a jughead, I could have been sorting out all the essentials I purchased today. It was too late to find the new batteries and the flashlight, so I resolved to sort it all out on Sunday after church.

I gathered the sheet from my favorite chair and fumbled my way to my bedroom, collapsing on the bed. I thanked our Father briefly, and it became Sunday in an instant. Taking time to just stretch, I laid on the bed not knowing the time. Thinking about that reminded me that I needed to retrieve the watch I purchased yesterday, read the directions, put the battery in, and start using it. So that was my first task of the day, but, on the day of rest, I took my time. After reading the directions for the watch, everything was set but the hour.

Now, the church marque said that Sunday services would start at 1000 hours. All I needed to do was wait until cars began to show up, then mosey on over. In the morning light, I sorted out the dress slacks, a short-sleeved shirt, the Panama shirt jacket, and hat. Dressed to the nines, I walked through the hedge on down to the path at the back of the church. I waited in the shadows of the trees as folks arrived. It didn't take long to see that I was over dressed for this service.

The people attending this church were truly the salt of the earth. I returned to my house and changed clothes to try and match the people I was seeing. It was a Baptist church that had a mix of black and white people attending. I changed back into used denims, a plain short sleeved shirt, and greased prison shoes. I returned to the church and sat in the back row, feeling quite obscure, but still like a snowflake in a coal bin.

I was totally comfortable until Pastor Roy Walker entered the sanctuary from a side door and stepped up to the podium. I was looking at someone who had seen me in prison. He could know that I was an escapee from one of the prisons that he visited. When I saw him at the correctional facility, he had said he tried to come visit the prison once a month. His last visit was three weeks ago. Would he remember me or not?

He introduced Chirl Bontreager to do the worship songs, with the help of the Brenneman sisters. They chose three songs of the old favorites known by everyone in the church. There were at least two of the black brothers that knew the baritone parts of harmony in these songs, and it sent chills down my body to hear them sing so well. Then, a man named Bob Graham did a worship in tithes offering for the general fund, said a prayer, and passed the offering plate.

It was time for the morning message from Pastor Roy. The pastor based his message on the Old Testament story of Joseph, who was sold into bondage as a young man, was falsely accused, and was imprisoned for many years. He faithfully endured his prison time and was exonerated in the end for interpreting the Pharaoh's dreams. He elaborated on the high position that Joseph eventually received and how he was reunited with his family. He did a wonderful job of adding many personal takes on the story, a lot about owning your own trials and doing the time necessary to be justified. It was a wonderful story, wonderfully executed, but it was the opposite of what I was doing. It hit hard.

I had put a $10 bill in the plate as it passed, but there was also a donation box near the main exit door. I planned in advance to donate to the church for all that I had taken from the rummage sale. I walked out quickly after the final song and stuffed $500 into the locked box. Hopefully more than they could have earned with the entire rummage sale.

I rounded the front of the church, to the north side, and hoofed quickly east toward the hedge. I was nearly passing the church when the pastor opened a side door and shouted, "WAIT SON!"

8. HOLY BATZ

My flight instinct was very high at that point, but I liked Pastor Roy and obeyed his command. I stopped, grinding my teeth, my eyes squeezed tightly shut, then turned around and faced the preacher with a toothy smile.

He said, "Son, I just want to thank you for joining us today, will you be visiting us again?" Before I could answer, he narrowed his eyes, turned his head a bit, and looked at me closer. Then after a few seconds, he shook his head, as if he had forgotten something, and looked at me again.

With hesitation, I answered, "No, sir, I will be moving on tomorrow, hopefully to live in Florida one day."

He thanked me again and went back into the church. I headed straight through the hedge and back home.

I went to my chair and sat down, bending forward with my head in my hands. I allowed some time to pass as I pondered how close I had come to being identified. I even recalled that he had told our group back in prison that he was the pastor of a church in Blythe. I should have remembered that and was beating up myself for the error. I said to myself, "OK, get a grip, Nick. You promised yourself a breakfast at Carl's Lunch, and you are definitely hungry."

I checked my new watch and saw there was only about forty-five minutes left until closing time. I went into a light jog toward town, turned west on the first street, and then south down the main drag. I slowed to a casual walk for the last block approaching Carl's Lunch. Entering, I chose the bar counter seat viewing the action of the cook. If it was Carl, I didn't know, but it was the same guy that was working the grill yesterday. Within a few minutes, he took my order, constantly looking back at the grill as he wrote.

The restaurant was only half full since it was nearly closing time. I watched the cook working the grill like a true artist, like a conductor directing an orchestra. He cracked eggs with one hand, while the other hand wielded a spatula flipping a large pile of hash browns. The orders were held with oil-soaked cloth pins sliding on a tight wire that was strung from one side of the grill to the other. I watched as he clipped mine to the far left and charged at the grill. He filled plate after plate as his waitress delivered the hot food to each table.

As he pulled my ticket up for a read, he said, "I remember you from yesterday, you new in town?"

"No, just passing through."

With quick artistry, he produced my order of three eggs scrambled with Swiss cheese, three pieces of bacon, and hash browns with onions. That, complete with two pieces of whole wheat toast, and, oh yes, coffee!

I took my time, adding a little salt and pepper as I enjoyed every bite. I added ketchup to the hash browns and strawberry jelly to the toast and thought of it as dessert, sipping the black coffee as I finished. I paid for the food and tipped the cook generously. I continued to walk south for many blocks, arriving at a city park. Finding a comfortable bench and stretching my legs, I just watched as the local folks took advantage of the simple pleasures they found there. Finding myself about to nod out, I walked across the street and headed back north toward home.

After several blocks, I encountered two men in front of a VFW post. They were in deep conversation, and both were sporting hats with military insignia. They were about my same age. I stopped and eavesdropped for a short second, since they spoke of running for positions in the governing body. I moved in a bit closer, but they took notice and said, "Can we help you?"

I said, "Yes, I am a Vietnam veteran and am guessing that you were too." They were indeed. I explained, "I had a rather bad experience with a VFW in Augusta a year ago, and I am wondering if the atmosphere is the same here."

They answered, "No, in fact, old Commander Bruno really likes us Vietnam veterans and worked hard to get us to sign up."

One of them held his hand to his chin, squinted in thought, then told a story he had heard about a rather cranky commander up that way. He said, "The guy doesn't care much for Vietnam vets and would make them leave the post. One of the vets he threw out apparently took serious offense and wrecked some of the commander's stuff by pouring concrete into them."

As they laughed, I laughed and said, "Well I don't know about that, but I too was put out of a VFW by a cranky old vet up there."

They were headed back into the post and asked if I wanted a beer. That sounded so good, so I hesitated a moment, then declined. I told them I would be moving south tomorrow and needed to stay straight.

As I took my time walking back north, and as I passed a Piggly Wiggly store, it occurred to me that I hadn't purchased any toilet paper. Not good. I entered the store and purchased a four pack. I felt better carrying something, since perhaps it may be more normal looking.

As the afternoon slipped by, I really didn't want to go back to the house, but that was all that was left. And, well, I needed to do more sorting and put fresh batteries in my flashlight. Yes! That alone was worth going home for, and as I walked, I realized the flashlight showing through the windows at night would not be good. But, it gave me an idea.

I took the route home from the last street to the fence row behind the church. Keying my way in and locking the door behind, I put the toilet paper in a bathroom cabinet and wished I could keep the p-u bucket in the bathroom, but it just would not fit between any of the shelves. Finding the flashlight and the new batteries, I went to the desk and swapped the old batteries for the new. The light worked great! Then a new problem came to me—trash. I now had trash. I retrieved one of the neatly folded paper grocery bags and commissioned it as a trash bag. I would now need to find a cabinet space to hide it too.

I really wanted to deal with the bright light from the flashlight, and so I went on a hunt for the tools to fix it. Among the many items usually found in a kitchen drawer, there was a pair of scissors and scotch tape. From the back of a small tablet, I cut a piece of gray cardboard large enough to cover the lens of the light. Putting the lens down on the thick paper, I traced around it and cut out the circle. After punching a small hole in the center of the disk, I taped it tightly to the lens bezel. Proud of my work, I tried the light, even though it was still daylight, and it worked great. My thinking was that it would give off just enough light to navigate through the house, and it should work perfectly for night reading without shedding too much light to be noticeable from the outside. YES!

As I was climbing onto the porch this last time, I had noticed a pile of discarded equipment in the northeast corner of the large gravel lot. It looked like it was primarily things made of steel. I waited a little longer until dusk was setting in, and then I went to the pile to see if there was anything of value to me. Looking in and through the pile as I walked around it, I spied yet another galvanized pail. This one was beat up badly and had a few rust holes—ah, perfect. I extracted it from the heap and took it home. Possibly tomorrow night I could render it into something I badly needed.

When I got back to the house, I stripped to my new shorts, took an extra pillow from the master bed, rolled up in the chair sheet, and leaned back on the two pillows for some Bible reading. First, stepping out of my norm, I gave thanks and confessed that all of us seemed to put ourselves into some sort of prison, sometimes more than one prison. I also proclaimed that I would do my best to remain content with this prison, for as long as it took. I read in Exodus for about two hours. I declared lights out at 2300 hours and turned in.

I awoke to the sounds of the movers. Checking my watch, I saw it was 0530 hours. It seemed earlier than normal, and there was only a little sunlight coming in. Once I remembered that there could be delays getting through town, I understood. All the usual work was being done, including the thumping of the tires. The Mack fired up, then went to idle. Then the sound of a different engine, just outside the house, vibrated through. I investigated to find a Standard Oil delivery tanker parked beside the Mack. It took until 0600 hours to fill the big saddle bag tanks with fresh diesel fuel.

When the fuel truck left, the lead truck maneuvered into position. Shortly after, a sheriff's cruiser pulled in front of the lead truck. All the drivers and men gathered for a short counsel, then dispersed to their respective positions. After a few minutes the sheriff pulled out slowly with his red lights spinning. With a reasonable gap between, our lead truck began rolling, and with another reasonable gap between the Mack and the lead truck, that familiar first tug at the house occurred, then forward motion. I dressed myself in the used denims and shirt and walked around in the new socks. I redressed my ankles with the petro-carbo salve, as I had done every day since I found it. My ankles were getting better.

Like an unusual parade, the formation moved slowly toward the center of town until all came to a stop. Looking forward proved somewhat difficult, but I could see utility trucks stationed at opposite sides of the stoplight intersection. One had a heavy boom being maneuvered above the stoplight, and the other was a man-lift maneuvering beside the light. The light was hooked to the lift as other workers disconnected the support cable that held it over the street corner. Again, like Carl the cook, these workers were well versed in their business, and soon the light was lifted high above the level of the house roof. The wave of a hand sent the police cruiser slowly forward, then the lead truck, and then the Mack.

There were actually quite a few spectators watching as the house moved through the center of town. I even saw Mr. Khaki Man taking photos as we headed steadily south. The sheriff's deputy pulled off at an intersection outside town, got out, and waved at the trucks as they passed. The driver of the Mack blew the air horns several long reports, then added just a little more acceleration than usual. A human would need to run hard to keep up with us now. From the map in the ledger, the road toward Baxley seemed to be flat and straight, but it would take two very long hauls to get there. That could be part of the reason for the early start and the extra speed. Crap, I realized I could have gotten my own Georgia state map at the Sinclair station in Lyons—my bad.

The morning excitement over, I settled in to continue reading the book of Exodus. Ah, Exodus, a fitting book for what we had just gone through, and who knew if there would be a promised land in the future for me? Well I possessed no promises whatsoever, but I still maintained hope that perseverance would yield something better in the end.

I sat at the table reading until my rear end was so sore that I had to move to my favorite chair. I continued reading through the entire morning and into the afternoon. Exodus, like Genesis, was about fifty pages of fairly small type, but I finished it. I wondered if this was an appropriate time to express thanks.

Resting my eyes for a long moment, I thought, "Dang, I sure am getting hungry." Going to the fridge, I grabbed a nice warm apple and cut off two sticks of celery. I grabbed my third bucket to use as a trash can, removed the packaging from the salt and pepper shakers, and disposed of it in the bucket. I licked the celery troughs so the salt would stick and held them over the bucket as I sprinkled a generous amount of salt on both sticks. I leaned against the kitchen counter crunching away slowly on each stick. When I finished with the apple, I tossed the core in the bucket and returned to my chair. Wow was that nice!

Reclining as much as I could, I tried to go into strategic planning mode. Again, I now was fairly certain where we were going, but I had no idea what might happen or present itself at each stop. I went to my dresser, pulled out the new Levi denims, put them on, and thought that they were like cardboard! I decided to wear them as much as possible while in the house to try and break them in. I put on the Dan Post boots also, as they needed some break-in time too. I needed to suffer with this and decided to also restart an exercise regimen in the denims and boots.

I had stripped off the T-shirt and tore into the exercises for the next two hours, going through every military calisthenics I could think of. I reminisced about some army drill instructors, prior to calisthenics, shouting out, "I'll count the cadence, you count the exercise." I chuckled as I counted both.

I could feel that I was still in some recovery from the desperate run from the dogs. However, the daily labor from the chain gang work had actually kept me in quite good shape. Good exercise always pumps the good endorphins into your system, sometimes nearly creating a bit of euphoria. In my high, I resolved to stick to a daily exercise regimen as long as I could.

The day was getting long in the tooth, and there was little doubt that this day's haul was going past normal hours. The sun was not setting yet, but it was getting close. It remained daylight until after 2100 hours this far south in late July. Shortly after my observations, the driver slowed and began to maneuver into a roadside park nearly identical to the first one, except this one was on the west side of Highway 1. This routine exit and stop only took the crew about twenty minutes to wrap things up, leaving me with about forty-five minutes of usable daylight. Oddly, this time as the crew truck left, it went south instead of north.

I was ready, and when there was no traffic on the highway, I jumped off the porch with the third bucket and headed for the crew truck. Looking through the beaters and pinch bars, I found what I needed to punch holes through the top and bottom rims of the bucket. I wanted the pail to remain functional, but I wanted its rings to be laid flat so I could set the big fry pan on the top without obstruction. I was not a blacksmith, but with a few repeated efforts, the bucket became a portable camp grill.

Like the last park, there were grills, picnic tables, trash barrels, a water pump, and—oh yes—toilets. I repeated many of the tasks from the first park, gathering a supply of sticks and paper, and placing them near the grill. It took two trips into the house to retrieve the food and tableware. Spam was the entrée this evening.

With enough light remaining, and prior to lighting the fire, I took the bucket with me as I climbed over a fence into a field of onions. The bulbs were not full sized yet, but they were still the size of a baseball. Using my Boy Scout knife, I field stripped a bucket full of fresh onions and headed back to camp. Night was closing in as I pumped water and cleaned the onions. I chuckled as the holes in the bucket worked great as a strainer for cleaning my new food source. Multipurpose bucket. Then I loaded the bucket with some wadded paper, put sticks on top, and lit the paper through one of the holes in the base. While kindling my tiny fire, I noticed the light illuminating the advertisement on the door of the Mack: "TRUE'S HEAVY MOVING AND TOWING," with a phone number. I had observed it many times, but now I saw it as a way to contact the owner of the house. That, however, would require some thought. I concentrated on cooking supper.

Sitting on the very end of a picnic table, I fed sticks into the bucket until there was about a half inch of red glowing coals. Time for the fry pan, which sat over the edge of the pail far enough that it could not fall in. I put a generous amount of oil in the pan first, then sliced and diced two onions into the hot oil, stirring occasionally as I opened the can of Spam. I was sipping water from my quart jar and splashed just a little water into the pan to create some steam to speed the cooking. As the onions approached the finish, I added three slices of Spam, about half the can. The meat was very salty, so I didn't add any salt to the onions, but smothered the meat with them. The aromas were really quite something.

There were occasional cars and trucks traveling in both directions through the evening, but I was quite out of sight as I fully enjoyed my homemade supper. I added a salad of two more sticks of salted celery.

Now, there was work to be done. I dumped the remaining coals into the park grill, rinsed the bucket with water, and put the onions back in it. I scrubbed the fry pan with sand, rinsed with it water, and gathered everything back into the house. The flashlight was really earning its keep now, as I could find the proper homes for everything. Next, I added a great deal more physical activity to the day by doing a one-man bucket brigade. I put about fifteen pails of water back into the tub, one bucket at a time. Then I refreshed my drinking water containers.

With the anticipation of an earlier start tomorrow, I prepared for bed. My bucket of onions needed to dry, and there just wasn't much air moving in the house. I wanted to set them on the porch, but if I overslept, the crew would spot them. Hmmm, I tried something different. I opened the hatch and set the bucket near the opening for the night. A little fresh air would be a blessing anyway.

"I love this flashlight," I thought, placing it on the dresser. It provided just enough light to do all that I needed to make ready for my bunk. I thought perhaps the Levis had softened up just a little too. Getting comfortable and taking slow breaths, I reminisced about the day, then concentrated on the advertisement on the door of the Mack. It wouldn't do any good for me to call the company, at least not for the foreseeable future. I had no return phone or address, no way to carry on a conversation. Would it be possible to ask Annika to make contact, without it being involved with me?

Whoosh—whoosh—whoosh—whoosh. Waking up in the middle of the night was hard, but I was hearing something unusual. Whoosh—whoosh. I found the flashlight to look at my watch, now at 0300 hours. I saw something flash by the light, so I turned the light upward. Whoosh! Crap, it was a brown bat, racing from room to room, passing over me every five seconds. I hated bats; I wasn't afraid of them, I just hated them. So much for leaving the hatch open. I got out of bed and made my way to the front door and opened it wide. Then I jogged through the house waving the light back and forth. It took a few laps, but that ugly thing finally left. I closed the hatch! I hadn't had many bad dreams lately. I wondered if this diversion would add to that problem. Only one way to find out—get back in bed and try to sleep.

My thoughts went back to the moving company, as I was absolutely resolved to repay the money I was using. The movers were the source to the owners. It seemed strangely necessary to one day thank the owner for the privilege of using the house in this way. I would work for free, volunteer for whatever they may need, but if I were caught and sent back to prison, I might never have a chance to demonstrate my appreciation. My thoughts turned to Annika. I missed her so, especially now when everything was uncertain. I so hoped that our next stop near Baxley would have access to a phone.

The noise of a crewman thumping the tires woke me. I just laid in bed until long after the move began. It was 0600 hours, probably an hour earlier than normal, so another long haul was likely to follow. But, I got out of my bed, made it neatly, dressed my wounded ankles, and changed into the Levis and boots. By then I was getting hungry again, so I opened a can of corned beef hash and ate it cold. An apple was a nice finish, but also more trash to deal with.

Leviticus was next in my Bible reading, but I had skipped most of it, since I had found it to be a very complicated and boring book. I sat down at the table and dug in to read. As it happened yesterday, after a few hours, my sore rear sent me to my chair for the remainder of the book. Once I finished it was time for exercise, and again I spent at least two hours doing calisthenics. By now, my brain and my body were pooped out, so I stretched out on my chair, laying my arms over the chair arms. Wow, I came to my senses—I had a tub half full of water! I quickly stripped down and climbed in, breathing very deep and slow. I was soon relaxed and cooled down in the tub. But suddenly the Mack geared down, adding the Jake break, and came to a stop.

Getting out reluctantly, naked and dripping, I checked the rear first but could see nothing wrong. Going to the front, I saw the driver was already out of the cab pointing at a low hanging limb. These guys were prepared for nearly anything. As the extension ladders came out, I could hear a chainsaw fire up and rev several times before shutting off again. Like a blip on the TV screen, the limb fell to the ground, chopped into movable pieces and hauled to the ditch. Giddy-up!

The farmland slowly gave way to more housing as we moved south late that afternoon. Baxley couldn't be too far ahead now, so I dressed and hoped for tonight's parking to be somewhere near town. The exhaust from the Mack changed to a slightly lower tone but kept moving steadily forward. It was Tuesday, only eleven days since I had become a fugitive, but it seemed much longer at times. If my guess was correct, we were about a hundred miles farther south. That didn't seem like much either, with somewhere near a hundred miles yet to go. I needed to look at the logbook in the Mack again, as some of the upcoming details were getting foggy in my memory. There was a problem with the city of Waycross, and I needed to look at it closely. Acquiring a Georgia map should probably also be high on my list.

The Mack slowed again as we were passing commercial businesses. We slowed again and began a right hand turn onto a side street. I just glimpsed the Troupe Street Road sign as we passed. We traveled a few hundred yards and made another right into the very large parking lot of a warehouse of sorts. There were docked semi-trailers along the sides, some with truck tractors attached. With more than enough room to pull around, we continued around the back and halfway up the opposite side, where the truck stopped. I couldn't see the front of the building, but I could see a sign on the side that said, "Baxley Beverage, Budweiser Distributors." Ah, I thought, I'm finally home!

When the crew left, I was ready, rucksack under my arm. I didn't want to wait until dusk, so I used the hatch and crawled out near a fence alongside the house. There were overhead lights around the fenced compound that hadn't come on yet, but I could see the one at the center of the house would put a shadow on my entry door. There were lights near all the doors on the warehouse so truckers could navigate any time of night. The place was active, but not bustling, and I walked unnoticed out to the street.

The sidewalk along Highway 1 led past all sorts of commercial businesses, but I was looking for a pay phone. My route took me past a McDonald's, and the aroma was nearly too much, but I held the pace. In another two blocks there was a corner grocery with a pay phone in the front. I needed change, so shopping came first. I gathered a dozen cans of various fruit and another full head of celery. I asked the young clerk if the store had Georgia maps, and she said it didn't. I asked for an extra two dollars' worth of quarters, and she obliged.

Going to the phone, I dialed Annika's parents' number. When we talked that first time, she had added that with her study of the law, it would be nearly impossible for a judge to allow a wiretap on her parent's phone in a case like mine. That had been good news. The operator asked for seventy-five cents, so I shoved in the coins. I tried to prepare myself for whoever might answer the phone, but when her father answered, I froze for a second.

"Sir," I said, "please do not hang up the phone, this is Nick. I want to talk to Annika, but I need to talk to you too, if you will, sir?"

Mr. Bjorn said, "Yes, I will talk. Nick, we are worried sick about you. We are hoping that you are safe, but Nick, we are so confused about why you did something so bizarre!"

"Mr. Bjorn, there are two bizarre things I cannot account for—destroying a car and a boat and escaping prison because of it. Sir, I am working very hard on that answer."

"Here is Annika, please spend some time with her."

As Annika took the phone, I thought about Mr. Bjorn. He hadn't given up on me either. I was swallowing hard when she said, "Nick, I still love you."

I broke down, and I broke down hard. It took a full minute for this ex-cavalryman to regain control, but when I did, I was concise. We talked about many things, including her legal work, and if she would care to research one more thing for me. She agreed, and I gave her the name and phone number of the towing company. I asked her to simply familiarize herself with the company. I explained I had no idea when I could call again, day or evening, but I would try to send a letter again. When the money ran out, the receiver went to the dial tone.

I went back into the store and traded for more quarters, returned to the phone, and dialed my parents. Mom answered, and things went to shit for a while again, but then she composed herself. I reassured her that I was actually doing quite well, considering, and asked how everything was there at home. After some small talk and "I love you's," I asked her about the driver's license. She explained that she knew so-and-so down at the DMV, and that they knew that I was in college and they would put my license renewal on the fast lane. YES! All I needed to do was figure out how she could send it to me. Dad was at his bowling league, so we said our goodbyes, and I promised I would write as soon as I could.

With a small load in my backpack, I continued south, since I could see a Sinclair gas station sign about three more blocks down the road. Arriving at the station, I was able to acquire a Georgia state map.

I had some change remaining as I spied a coke machine in the corner. It was an old one, the type where you needed to hold the lid up, grab the cap of the bottle you wanted, and slide it through a series of slots to a door that could only be opened if you put in a dime. I chose a Vernors ginger ale, pulled it out, popped the top in the built-in opener, and thought about my childhood. I always chose Vernors because when you took about two quick swigs, the carbonation in that pop was so high that it would immediately blast out through your nose! What a rush! I took sips and enjoyed the memories.

As daylight was closing, I hoofed back toward the house, which brought me back past the McDonald's restaurant, which I could not pass. Again the aroma seemed like an oasis, and I floated to my place in line. I studied the menu and settled on a Big Mac, large fries, and a coke. I moved my treasure to a table after gathering packets of ketchup and a few napkins. It had been at least a year since I had eaten anything from McDonald's. I wasn't a big fan, but they always maintained clean bathrooms. In my travels, I often stopped just to use the facilities. But this burger was really good, and the fries were perfect when smothered with ketchup. YUM.

Carrying the ruck over one shoulder, I approached the beverage company parking lot. From there I could see the steeple of a church farther north. I was in a very satisfied mood, but so not ready to shut down for the night. Continuing on toward the church, I could see the activity of automobile traffic. When in range of the marque, I could read that the church sponsored a Tuesday night Bible study from 1930 until 2100 hours. Perfect, I thought as I entered the sanctuary with about twenty-five other folks and sat down in the back.

Pastor Bud Holmes took the pulpit, only to announce that he had a family emergency earlier in the day and that Pastor Roy Walker had graciously agreed to teach the Bible study in his place. Pastor Roy joined him at the pulpit as the two men shook hands and hugged, then Pastor Bud left.

Pastor Roy introduced himself again and said that he had studied the Bible school program for the evening and would continue where Pastor Bud had left off. "We will be studying the arrival of the True King. We will be looking at the words of Zachariah 9:9–13."

He then read from the study pamphlet, *Peace to the Nations,* which was a primer to the words of Zachariah. Pastor Roy then invited someone to begin reading the verses of Zachariah, pointing to the first person in the front row. That person read and looked at the one next to them, who read, and so on, until the appointed reading was finished. Great discussion then occurred, guided by Pastor Roy, who did a masterful job of explaining the text.

The Bible study came to an end, with a very meaningful prayer and a dismissal from the Bible study, along with many thanks for the participation. Pastor Walker then said in a very clear and concise voice, "Brother Nicholas, I would care very much to have a word with you before you leave."

9. FISH ON

I COWERED IN THAT back row. I had been marked, I had been had, I was toast. As before, the flight instinct was so high that my body was shaking as the assembly left the church. Pastor Roy walked slowly toward me as the last person left the church. He moved past me to the doors and locked them, returning to the pew in front of me. He rubbed his wrinkled, stubbled chin for a minute, then focused his aged dark brown eyes on me.

After an extended time, he said, "Nicholas, do I need to be worried?"

My head fell to my hands as I said, "No, sir."

"I didn't think so." Again an extended silence followed. "You had time to run, but you didn't?"

"I wanted to, but Pastor Roy, I have enjoyed every word you've spoken, even those at Richmond County Correctional Facility. I thank you for that, but, sir, how did you identify me?"

This wonderful old black man, now relaxed in his pew, began to explain. He traveled Highway 1 every week from Richmond County southward. He had seen that house many times on his travels since it kept a steady path south.

"I really didn't remember you from Richmond County, and you had escaped between my monthly visits. I was unaware until my last visit there just four days ago. Then, when I welcomed you to the church in Lyons, you looked familiar, but I passed it off as an old age thing. When I learned of your escape and where the dogs lost the trail near Blythe, I remembered that was the first time I'd seen the house. Then, days later it was parked just north of our church. Now it's parked just south of this church, and here you are again.

"By the way, when we counted the money from the rummage sale, we discovered the largest donation that had ever come to the church. Son, did you have anything to do with that? And where on earth would you acquire that kind of cash just a week after escaping prison?

Are we looking at robbery as well? You look healthy and fit—how can this be?"

The questions continued for a while longer, since he was surprised that I was clean shaven, had a haircut, and wore nice clothes. He finally said, "Son, you are obviously a Christian, or trying to be one, so you know that as a man of the cloth, I am duty bound to turn you in. I need you to start talking now, and it better be good!"

I breathed deep, knowing that the truth was the only thing I could tell him. I replied, "How much time do we have?"

"All night, if that is what it takes." He asked to pray before beginning and then did so. At his amen, I breathed deep again and began to tell him of my youth. Then, up to my army days. I told him of the Ia Drang Valley and of being a lone survivor but finishing my tour even though I could have been sent home after being shot. I described how I completed my four-year obligation and finally had my chance at college. I shared my good grades and success at UC Berkeley, and for the second time, I confessed my sin against the three stooges. Pastor Roy was diligent about his serious demeanor, but I could see that he sure wanted to laugh. That brought us to Augusta and my second year at Augusta Tech, meeting Annika, falling in love, and then my random visit to a VFW, where I thought I would find comrades.

At this point I choked up and admitted that my actions were indeed premeditated, but I didn't think at all about the possibility of getting caught. I told him I never caused any trouble to the legal system. I plead guilty and offered complete remittance to the commander for what I had done. But that didn't matter because they gave me the maximum sentence. I further explained that at the correctional facility, I tried to be a model citizen and just do my time. It seemed, however, that they worked me far more than the other inmates. On the one hand, I didn't care, as it made the time pass faster, but on the other, I wondered why it was happening. I finally told him about the day I found the gate left unlocked and just walked out.

I needed to pause for a while, so he took over. The pastor said, "So, I honestly believe that you are telling the truth, since you don't seem to have any reason to lie about anything you have said so far. Now tell me about the house."

I proceeded with the two-day run from the dogs and that crossing a county line must have saved me with a delay in the hunt. I explained my complete exhaustion when I crawled under what I thought was a house being torn down, finding the trapdoor, and the house being my moving prison ever since.

Then he said, "I get, I get it. Yes, I get it! But the money, that is the big one for me. How did you get the money?"

I had to laugh at that point, but he scowled when I did. "That's an easy one, Pastor. It came directly from the Father's word," I said in a woebegone way.

He scowled even harder at me, as if I were a blasphemer. I further explained that when I found the King James Version of the Bible, I committed to reading it for as long as the ride lasted. I told him about finding the logbook in the Mack, so I had a very good idea when the arrival time would be. I told him what happened when I finished Genesis and turned to Exodus, and his eyes got big. I told him all sixty-six books had a $100 bill in between. For the first time during that conversation we both laughed, looked at each other, and laughed again.

I shared with him the money I had frozen in Atlanta, that I could easily pay back all that I had used, and that I had made a ledger for accounting every penny. I told him that the bank said the sheriff in Augusta was trying to access the account, and that Annika had been made aware of it. I explained Annika's dedication in looking at my case through the legal system and her trouble in trying to do it. I told him she might even change her major to law because of the stonewalling she had received.

After settling from the laugh, Pastor Roy went into a long silence, his elbow on his knee, hand massaging his chin, and eyes closed. His verdict was far from what I expected when he said, "Son, what can I do to help you? I am still duty bound to alert the authorities, but I am duty bound to my own convictions to choose when."

I broke down for a minute, and he handed me a tissue from his suit pocket. He sat with one leg over the other, a hand on either side gripping the edge of the pew, looking at me. I could see his compassion plainly.

I told him I simply didn't know what drove me to seek revenge in the way that I did, or what possessed me to walk out of prison. That was a mystery to me.

He thought for a minute and then began to explain that with so many Vietnam veterans returning these days, through the churches, he had attended a non-denominational seminar on an old phenomenon known as shell shock, a syndrome that seemed to occur when people were subject to horrific conditions or fear for long periods of time.

"As a preacher, I must be prepared to counsel on all kinds of personal problems. All the southern states have had a distinctly higher per capita number of men in the armed services, and we should be prepared for problems resulting from it. I believe I'm now witnessing this syndrome in you."

Well, that was new to me, I had been going about thinking that I was just fine. Now this preacher was telling me I likely had a mental problem? I could not refute, could not deny, as what I had done was not in my norm. I asked the pastor if he could share more information on the subject. He posed the problem of connecting in the future if I didn't turn myself in and asked what my plan was.

"Annika is working on it," I explained. "She thinks that I should turn myself in after crossing the Florida line because the time that it takes to extradite me may be enough time to produce new evidence and maybe a new trial. She, however, has no idea of my mode of travel in the house. Now, I may be able to make a call from time to time, depending on where they park the house, but only at random. Please take Annika's business number and give me the best number for you where someone is likely to answer and take a message." We traded numbers.

"Pastor Roy," I said, "there is one more thing to consider in this equation, and that is the house itself." I asked if he knew anything about it, and he didn't. I added the question for him to consider. "Why would anyone go through so much trouble to move a house so dang far?"

His eyes perked in question. I asked if he had ever heard of Frank Lloyd Wright, and he said no. I explained briefly of the man's famous history as an architect, and that this house was very likely one of his early works.

"Who knows," I said, "we may possibly use that information as a tool down the proverbial road. Someone could pose as a historian or something. I do hope to know who owns it."

It was time to part ways. Pastor Roy looked at the floor for a moment, then looked at me, smiled, and said in his southern black drawl, "You on the lam, son. On the slooooooow lam." Then he laughed, shaking his head, as he opened the door for me to walk out.

I hustled back to the parking lot of the Budweiser distributor and walked casually along the fence to the rear of house, where I jumped unnoticed onto the shadowed porch. I keyed in, put the backpack on the dining table, and went to my chair to just sit and chill for a while. What had just happened?

Getting up, I took a dining room chair out on the porch and sat in the shadows, watching while an occasional truck would arrive and another would go on its way. I spied some warehouse worker sitting outside on the steps of the building, smoking a cigarette. It gave me an idea. I jumped down from the porch and headed straight for the worker. He spotted me at the halfway point and watched as I approached.

He looked at me curiously and said, "What are you doing in that house?"

I answered sternly, "I am a Pinkerton detective, and I am a night guard," dangling the key for him to see. He bought it. I explained that it was going to be a long night since I was having some family problems, and it would be of extra value to me if he could produce a case of long necks.

I asked, "Now, what would a case of long necks cost me?" As he hesitated, I said, "The house and I will be gone in the morning, and I will leave no evidence."

He said, "$20!"

"Go get it." He returned with the case, looking left and right as if someone was watching. I gave him $30, and said, "That's your tip."

I sauntered back to the house with a case dangling in hand, placed it on the porch, jumped up, and carried it into the house. Just enough light from the parking lot came through to see my way to prepare for the night. The beer was unfortunately very warm, and it reminded me of my time in Vietnam when the supply helicopters would bring us canned beer for a treat. First it was stuffed into canvas duffel bags, then put on a PSP steel helicopter pad to bake in the sun. It was flown in an undulating helicopter, many miles, and thrown out onto our LZ to be distributed among the troops. If you opened a can, it would blow to the top of the trees.

After stowing the case in the last of the cabinet space, I went back to the porch chair and opened one bottle, very slowly. I nursed that beer for a half hour and thought deeply about my experience with Pastor Roy. In the short time I knew him, it was as if he had become my best friend. Now I would trust him to the end.

I was about to pull off the boots and make ready for bed, when I thought about the ledger in the cab of the Mack. I took the flashlight, a notepad, and pencil. I moved off the porch with no one in sight but stayed to the south side of the house along the fence to the passenger side of the Mack. I stepped up on the running board and tested the vent window and had to laugh, as it was in the same condition as the driver's side. Reaching through, I unlocked the door, trying to keep the clutter inside the cab. I couldn't sit, so I stood on the running board, grabbed an oatmeal cookie, and chewed slowly as I opened the binder to look at the intended route. It was going to be a two-day trek to the little town of Alma, with the first stop near the Big Satilla Creek. After Alma, it was another two days to the south branch of the Satilla River, just past the town of Dixie Union. As I noted this down, I nearly choked on my cookie when I read that the house could not pass through Waycross and needed to be put on a barge on the Satilla and moved by waterway to a landing just north of Hoboken.

I had hoped to be somewhere near Folkston, Georgia, just a few miles from the Florida line in about a week, but this changed things. The manifest said the barge time would be undetermined but planned on at least seven to ten days. I quit reading, as my brain was already on over-drive. Locking the truck door, I returned to the house, found my Georgia map, folded it to show only the portion that was of concern to me, and followed Highway 1. I took a small piece of paper and folded it a few times to make it stiff. I found the mileage scale on the map and put dots on the edge of my paper so I could scale the mileage from point to point at the ten- and twenty-mile marks. Now I could not only read what was to happen next, I could see and scale it on the map. This didn't change a thing, except for my ability to anticipate my own needs.

The barge thing bothered me, since I would most likely be to-tally disconnected from the grid for more than a week. I needed to get messages or calls to Annika and Pastor Roy before that happened. I put the map in the desk drawer, turned off the flashlight, and just rested my forehead on the desktop for a long period. I thought for a minute that just walking to the nearest police station would be a lot easier. I stripped and turned in to my bunk without reading.

I awoke to the pounding of the tires, which now was almost like an alarm clock to me, but at least now I could squint at the hands on my watch to verify the time. It was nearly 0715 hours, and the crew was back to normal travel for the day. I chose to lay in bed as the work took place and the Mack fired up and went to idle. I had seen these guys many times now and had begun in some unconscious way to name them.

My favorite, of course, was the Mack driver. He looked to be about 10 to 15 years older than myself, and he sported a very worn marine style baseball cap with military insignia on it. He was likely a marine. Too old for Vietnam, but perfect age for the Korean War. He really was in charge of this field crew and executed his job well. He was also an accomplished driver. I pictured him as Old Sarge.

The driver of the lead vehicle was different. He was normally the driver of the crew on departure and arrival. He never wore a hat, unless it was a hard hat, as his slightly graying hair was combed perfectly, the natural waves following the shape of his head. He was always neat, even with his agility. If it came to stopping traffic or producing a chainsaw or ladder, he was on it quickly, running to each post. He reminded me of Tonto.

Then the driver of the following truck. Quite different again and as wiry as an orangutan. Probably six foot two, always wearing a deeply curled-in baseball cap, with a ball of chew bulging from his right cheek. This was the guy that was willing to go through the mud, blood, and the beer to fix anything that was broken. He was the guy that always checked the tires. He made me think of Harold, my best friend from high school. Harold would die on his sword to fight for whatever cause we were fighting for, or against!

Old Sarge, Tonto, and Harold. I knew them, but I didn't know them. I wanted to know them, as I hoped that they were carrying me to freedom.

That familiar tug came, and we began to move, making the right hand turn back onto Highway 1 and heading south. I had slept well, and so I got my lazy bones out of bed, dressed in the Levis, boots, and a T-shirt. Time for calisthenics. I went through the drill for the next two hours, then stripped and climbed into the tub to cool off. The water didn't really look all that bad, and I had no idea when I might be able to fill it again, but it was time to set the drain to the dribble mode and let it go. After redressing, I felt like I could whip my weight in wildcats but had no way to expel the energy. It was so hard to repress pent up energy, but that was exactly what I needed to do. I went to the desk, sat in the dining chair, breathed deeply for several minutes, and tried to think in a rational manner.

When we reached Alma, I could very likely send mail, but I so hoped for a pay phone. I pulled out the stationary and began to pen letters. First to Annika, then to my parents, and finally to Pastor Roy. I was very much afraid to involve Annika in my mode of transportation or my exact whereabouts, as it kept her innocent. I did the same with my parents but instructed Mom to send the driver's license, if she could get it, to Annika. I advised them both that there could be a silent time coming up, that could last up to ten days, and to be ready for that if I could not call prior. My letter to the pastor was different. I explained the exact route, with tonight's stop likely in the middle of nowhere, and tomorrow's likely near Alma. One or two more days to the Satilla River then onto a barge for up to ten days. I also told him that the barge trip would end just north of Hoboken, off load, then head south toward Racepond.

The letter writing was an excellent diversion, even if sending them could be untimely or even worthless. I hadn't thought of eating and was getting hungry as it was nearly noon. I opened another can of corned beef hash and a box of Ritz crackers. Finding one of the fresh onions nearly the size of a Ritz cracker, I made medium slices for each cracker. I must have eaten fifteen onion-smothered crackers before twisting the Ritz wrapper tightly closed and putting it back in the box. The hash can was only half gone, so I would need to have it back on the menu very soon. I sipped my pint of water dry and filled it again. I wasn't worried a bit about my very real bad breath.

It was time to read again and dig deep into Leviticus. The word means, "pertaining to the Levites." The Levites were a people, or family, within the twelve tribes of the Israelites who were designated to be priests for all the tribes. If it weren't for the foreshadowing of a coming Messiah, one could dismiss all the rules and regulations cited for these priests. This was hard going for a reader who was having great trouble just sitting in one place for an extended period of time, but it still captured my imagination and deep thought in the reading process.

Today's pull was nearly uninterrupted, as it seemed like we were preparing for a night parking spot. It was only 1600 hours, but that was indeed what was happening. I hustled to every view port to watch the driver back this big rig into a graveled area that approached a rather large electrical distribution site. A sign on the surrounding fencing said, "Consumers Energy of Georgia." Other than a few houses in the distance, there were no commercial businesses. It wasn't desolate, but it was seriously rural.

Waiting for the crew to leave, which they eventually did by heading south again, I felt just how alone I was. I had been totally alone in the past, awaiting death in the Ia Drang Valley, which never came. This was different. Not a catastrophic fear, just a sadness. A simple sadness that resided in my bones.

I told myself, "Wake up, Finn, we may have opportunities, even in this nowhere place."

I loved it when they backed the house up to park for the night because then using the porch was fairly safe. I moved a dining room chair to the porch and sat, looking back into the jungle-like foliage that surrounded this fenced area. Defoliant spray must have been used to keep this crushed white limestone area so devoid of even the smallest weed. Off to the south of the crushed stone parking area was a trail, a slightly used two-track, possibly a good place to walk.

My western boots needed a great deal of breaking in, so I locked the door, jumped down from the porch, and headed down the path. Walking with haste at first, I came to my senses and just slowed down to try and enjoy this botanical wonderland. After a few minutes, I did relax as the sounds of so many birds became evident. I stopped, listened, and looked carefully around and in front of me. An anole scurried from a stump up a tree. Then it occurred to me that if we were far enough south to see anole lizards, we may also encounter rattlesnakes! I proceeded with an open mind to nature—all of it. The path continued winding for what I would guess was a quarter mile, when it came to the most beautiful clearing beside a river.

I could see that some local folks thought enough of this place to keep the trees pruned back and to maintain a small structure along the riverbank. It was made of planks laid flat on chunks of sawed logs, nailed and roped in place, to form a place to stand at the river's edge.

Judging from some of the trash left behind, this was a place to fish.

I had daylight remaining, so I headed back to the house at a fast pace. On arrival, I keyed back in, went to the back porch, and retrieved the fishing pole and tackle box. Bait! What would I use for bait? I grabbed the half can of spam, left from two days ago, and also grabbed two long neck bottles of warm Budweiser, then hustled back to the river. I fumbled with the tackle for the longest time, needing to remember how to tie a hook to a line. I finally ended up with a spam bated hook about a foot up from a large sinker. I wasn't sure what fish would be in these southern rivers, but catfish would probably be a sure bet. Catfish are bottom feeders, I thought, as I cast the line to mid-river and let the sinker take it to the bottom.

I had put the bottles of Bud in my back pants pockets for the hike. I pulled one out, retrieved my trusty Boy Scout knife, flipped out the bottle opener, and opened one of the warm beers.

At this point I needed to breathe deep, "Nicolas, this is freedom, enjoy it."

There was nothing to sit on, but the post driven into the riverbed that supported the walking planks served as a good place to set my beer. I kept the line just snug enough to feel if something nibbled on my bait. I waited for about half a beer before the line went taunt.

"FISH ON," I exclaimed to myself as I jerked the pole in an attempt to set the hook. Holy bats, the pole bent like I had hooked a log. I pulled again, barely a budge, and pulled once more and the line went loose! Oh no, what happened? I reeled the line back in to find my bait was gone, dang. OK, I was excited now, shaking with the adrenaline rush while I applied another chunk of spam to the hook and cast it back in mid river.

I finished my first beer, tested the line over and over, and finally opened the second Bud. Time passed, and dusk was beginning to threaten my fun. The second Bud was nearly empty when the line went taunt again. This time, I waited, then waited a little longer, finally jerking the line to set the hook. It didn't feel like a log this time, but it was still substantial. It ran downstream, the drag on the reel being set to light. Finding the adjusting wheel, I quickly added a lot more drag, and the catch slowed down. It held a steady pull for a short time, then turned and headed back upstream. I cranked the reel as fast as I could to keep the line taunt as it turned and went back downstream, but it was losing its pull. Two more attempts at escape, and I was able to reel in this river cat. I didn't have a net to scoop it out of the water, so I needed to get on my knees on the planks and grab the fish by the mouth, taking him from the water to the bank of the river.

Oh, this was a nice river cat—the live weight would be at least two pounds, maybe three. It swallowed the hook, so I cut the line to make it easier to carry, left the Bud on the pier post, grabbed the pole and fish, and headed back to the house at nearly a run. I put the fish on the rear bumper of the lead truck, which was backed in alongside the house. I ran a little water from the drinking can onto my hands to rinse off a bit of fish slime, then put the pole on the porch. I needed the water pail in order to clean the fish, so I keyed back into the house, put the pole away, grabbed the water bucket and the p-u bucket, and made for the river. I flung the contents of the p-u bucket back into a thicket along the way, then rinsed it out with river water a couple of times, dumping the rinse water back into the woods. I chugged the remainder of the Bud, filled the water bucket about three-fourths full, and tried not to spill too much on the jog back home as the two Bud bottles rattled in the p-u bucket.

I figured I had about a half hour of good daylight remaining, so I made haste in the job of cleaning the fish. I really needed a pair of pliers for skinning the catfish and remembered an old pair in the cargo area of the lead truck. YES, there they were. I locked the bottom jaw of the cat into the vice and cut the skin all the way around the catfish, just behind the gills. It took several tugs, and then the skin came off. I went back inside and retrieved one of the grocery bags and used it to contain the discarded fish parts. After severing the head and dumping the innards, I rolled up the bag and headed back down the trail. Just fifty yards or so down the trail, I flung the bag as far back into the woods as I could and then pulled out a dry dead bush that would have plenty of fuel to provide a cooking fire. I was in such a hurry that I wasn't thinking fast enough. Jumping back onto the porch, I bagged up everything I would need to prepare a meal, including the bucket grill and fry pan.

The menu included two potatoes, two onions, and a can of peaches. I broke branches from the bush in a frenzy and got my fire started, then cleaned the spuds and onions and diced them directly into the well-oiled pan. While the fire was settling into a bed of coals, I washed the fish thoroughly in the river water, knowing the heat would kill any bacteria. The Boy Scout knife was sharp, but it wasn't a filet knife, so I needed to fry the cat bone-in. As the sun finally set, leaving me struggling to see, just the right amount of moonlight kept a vigil. The coals were hot, the pan went on, and in a minute the taters and onions were sizzling. When the taters tested soft, the coals were down to a medium heat, so I pushed everything in the pan to one side, added more oil, and laid the fish in the pan. Wow, that was a lot of fish.

I tended the fish carefully for about five minutes, then when the white meat began to flake with my fork, I took it out and put everything on my plate. I had used the big rear bumper of the truck as the preparation table for everything, leaving me with nowhere to sit. I hadn't had a meal at the dining table yet, so I hoisted my plate up onto the porch, went back into the house, sat at the dining table, and fully enjoyed my fresh catfish dinner by flashlight. I could not eat all the fish, which was as good as any I had ever tasted, and hoped that I could finish it during the pull tomorrow. Now, I need to clean up my mess.

There wasn't any sand nearby to clean the fry pan, but there were still a few coals in the grill bucket. There were plenty of sticks remaining from the bush, so I broke them up and rekindled the fire. While the grill was building heat, I put everything else away in the house. The bucket was blazing fairly high at this point, so I inverted the frying pan and placed it over the bucket. The oil caught fire, and a nice blaze rolled out from under the pan as I sat on the truck bumper until the fire began to subside. I used a rag from the truck to insulate the pan's handle and moved it to the ground to cool. I then used the water in the fish cleaning bucket to extinguish the remainder of the coals in the grill bucket, which essentially washed everything out of it. I brought the two buckets into the house and sat them on a grocery bag for the night.

It was early evening, too early to hit the sack but too dark for anything without the flashlight. I really didn't feel like reading, so I sat in my favorite living room chair, leaned my head on the overstuffed back of the chair, and tried to ponder just where I was in life. It struck me that I really needed to be thankful at this very moment. I submitted a prayer of thanks through our Prophet, Priest, and King, Christ Jesus, trusting that he would deliver it to the Father.

I sat in that chair, with the cover sheet over it, the same sheet that I had been sleeping with for over a week. It was supple from use but really needed cleaning. How was I going to do that?

I must have drifted off, when suddenly all hell broke loose, headlights flashing through the windows, the sounds of trucks—big ones—on all sides! Gravel crunched under big tires so close that I was afraid to look out. I heard a booming voice say, "What the hell is this thing doing here?"

10. STOP!

"WHAT THE HELL is that thing doing in the way? We'll all have to back out onto the street tomorrow!"

Another booming voice said, "Shut up, Butch. You must have missed the memo—the boss told us a house would be in the lot tonight. It will be gone tomorrow! Don't worry about it!"

At first I was afraid to look, but after a few minutes I started going from peep to peep. There were six big trucks, some hauling trailers with telephone poles on them, some with huge spools of wire. Three of the trucks had folding man-lift buckets mounted on top. They had signs on the doors that matched the sign on the fence, "Consumers Energy." They had a right to be here. These men worked as the moving crew did, securing everything for the night, then they all left in a passenger van.

I would be an old man before I was thirty! I mean this was nothing compared to the Ia Drang, but it was one more gray hair on my head for sure. I may have been ready to nap before, but I was wide awake now. These lineman, I thought they were called lineman, had a long day. They were typically brutally tough men, but smart too, and they handled high voltage every day. That kind of work takes a sense of discipline for safety many levels above us common folk.

I advised myself, "OK, Finn, you have two more towns with possible stops, Alma and Dixie Union. You need to take any possible opportunity to stock up for the barge trip. Take inventory, make a list of necessities, and pray for a pay phone." I vowed to do the work tomorrow and turned in just prior to 2200 hours.

I had been so busy through the evening, I hadn't noticed just how quiet it was here. There were some sounds of frogs and crickets coming through the walls of the house, but it was tranquil. I couldn't escape the fact that I was so alone, yet there were people out there that were pulling for me, even with my full-fledged shithead status. I think my dreams that night were of trying to land an unlandable catfish.

Once again I awoke to tire pounding—it was Tonto doing his first job of the day. I got up, having slept really well, and was already hungry. I rinsed my face, brushed my teeth, and dressed for the day, sporting a T-shirt from the church sale that displayed "GO CARDINALS" and their high school logo. I suppose I could have just laid in bed, but for the eternal optimist, there is always something that can be accomplished. I opened the can of corned beef hash from yesterday, sat at the dining room table, and spooned slowly to the bottom.

I grabbed the notepad from across the table and tried to think about things as if I had some control, but I was back to a wish list. If this barge trip was going to take ten days, I needed some fresh fruit, or at least canned fruit, or both. I was eating the last apple as I made the notes. I had half a bucket of fresh onions, which were keeping well, but the potatoes were nearly gone.

These one-night stops were tough, objectively fun for me, but tough. Barely enough time to complete what I needed for the day. It was tiring and exciting at the same time. I knew the basics of what I needed, if I only had another chance to make the purchases.

Old Sarge pulled the house out from in between the Consumers trucks with ease, turned south on Highway 1, and brought it all up to a good walking speed. The point, or lead truck, was leading the house, with the slack truck bringing up the rear. *Point* and *slack* were terms from my days in Nam. *Point* was the first man in line—the first to face the enemy. Last in line was the *slack* man, who had to continually look to the rear for the approaching enemy, and look forward to stay with the group. He also needed to scan the flanks, left and right, to the rear, and back to the forward movement, over and over, all day long. I thought perhaps it was somewhat the same for these drivers.

So, our next destination was to be the town of Alma. Looking at my map and using the scale for mileage, I guessed this would be a very short haul. However, for me, it was always a long day in this strange prison. The manifest in the Mack just didn't have much detail about the night parking spots, so it was always a surprise. I just wanted to be somewhere near town and tried to be positive about the next stop.

I settled in to read the good book, finishing the book of Leviticus and moving on to the book of Numbers, which was a tough book to read, but I took my time. The Israelites had been wandering in the desert for some thirty-eight years, and they were at the plains of Moab. Basically, all the elders that made the exodus from Egypt, who had continuously rejected the miracles that brought them out of the bondage of slavery, had died off. The new generation needed to be counted in a census, prior to entering the Promised Land. Then they were made to listen to the laws of the Father, through Moses once again.

I read until my eyes gave out. It was mid-afternoon, and it was getting really hot in the house. We were passing by a great field of farmland without many trees along the road for shade. I opened the hatch door in hopes of some circulation. It worked, but it also brought in the exhaust from the Mack. I stretched out on my favorite chair, having soaked a washcloth in water, and laid the cool cloth over my face. I repeated this many times that day and smiled to myself, thinking that a bit of suffering was just fine in trade for my deliverance. While stretched out on my chair, we passed the town of Alma, but I didn't realize it until I did a recon and peeped a "Leaving Alma" sign.

I needed to do something, even if it was wrong. I went to the desk and retrieved the map and my notes from the manifest. It looked like the barge would be on the Satilla River, just a mile or so south of Dixie Union, according to the map. I just couldn't tell from my notes whether we would be parking north or south of town. What if we went directly onto the barge? Tomorrow was Friday, would we have another weekend off? Finn, get a grip! We would see what we got and make the best of it.

Now, my watch had a calendar, but it only showed the day. We were coming up on Thursday night, May 25. While in prison, we were given most holidays off, since the guards that conducted the work details were on holiday. Easter had been a very long weekend, so we inmates had been looking forward to Memorial Day. I was thinking that this just may be a holiday weekend coming up. YES, Memorial Day. I flipped the pages in the notebook to my grocery and necessities list and added the need for a calendar.

Six to ten days on the river—how would I plan for that? I made my best guess, planning primarily for canned food. Snacks could be useful and fun too; munchies of all kinds would be so nice. As I daydreamed about a wonderful shopping experience, the house began to slow down. I went to the peepholes and could see that we were passing through the town of Dixie Union. We traveled south, past the part of town where the sidewalks ended, and turned into a large graveled lot for what appeared to be a marina. An Evinrude sales and service sign fastened to a post at the entrance solved any question.

As the crew did their shutdown procedure, I looked at my notes from the ledger and could not determine if they would be back on Friday or not. I would need to go to the cab of the Mack tonight to see what was in their plan. Meanwhile, I sorted out my cash on hand and borrowed another $100 from the book of 1 Samuel, which I noted in my ledger as $800 owed so far. I still had quarters for a pay phone but would probably need several dollars' worth. I dressed casual, wearing the prison-issued shoes since they were much more comfortable on a long walk than the western boots. I waited patiently until the crew left, heading south toward Waycross once again, then I ventured out onto the porch to stand and survey my environment.

I was anxious to see what the town had to offer, but I needed to look carefully at the manifest in the cab of the Mack first. The cab was facing the road, about a hundred yards back, and there wasn't much for traffic. I just walked to the cab, as a workman does, hopped on the running board, put my arm through the vent, and unlocked the door. Sitting in the driver's seat, I opened the manifest, which had an obvious marker added in for today. The extra notes made it clear that the house would not move to the barge until Tuesday, May 30, after Memorial Day. YES!

Checking my watch at 1630 hours, I knew I had nearly five hours of daylight remaining. I could fully walk the town to find just what it had to offer prior to carrying in the backpack and making any purchases.

I breathed deep and started in on a brisk walk toward town, which turned out to be about a mile. Arriving at the place where the sidewalks started, I moved off the road and onto the sidewalks. I was about to pass the fourth or fifth house, when I spotted a boy's bicycle with a for-sale sign leaning up against it. It was a Schwinn bike, with a large wire basket on the front and metal bench seat on the back. It was very neatly done and in very good shape, the paint perfect. I went to the door and knocked. A man about my age came to the door using crutches and made his way to the porch to sit down in one of a nice pair of wicker porch chairs. He waved an invitation for me to sit down too.

I started the conversation with, "Nice bike, how much do you want for it?"

He said, "You know, I ordered it from the local hardware store and paid $25 for it in 1969, just prior to being drafted into the army. I had the only full paper route in town, and I had made good money doing it my last years in high school. When the bike finally arrived, I had to join the army and never delivered a paper with it. I was assigned duty with the 101st Airborne Division in Vietnam. We were trying to make our way up Hill 937, when I lost my lower right leg." He then described some of the action that took place on Hill 937, which was subsequently nicknamed Hamburger Hill by a medic.

My heart was in my throat, and I was trying to hold back tears, but it didn't work. I went to my knees in front of him and confessed that I was with the 1st Cavalry in the Ia Drang Valley, and my survival was a miracle. I sputtered, "Welcome home, my brother, welcome home. By the way, my name is Nicholas Finn."

"And mine is Danny Wakefield." We shook hands.

He knew, as only a brother would know, that I was for real. We went on to talk seriously for a while, confessing our gratitude for survival, and then on to the lighter things, such as girlfriends. He was a good looking, well-built man, and said that his high school girlfriend had waited for him to come home. He said they were planning a wedding in the fall, and they needed to wait until he was healed enough for the final fitting for a prosthetic leg. He bragged a bit about the VA taking such good care of him. His new leg would be state of the art.

I explained to him about Annika, who was about to finish her sophomore year in college. I told him that I was on a very unexpected trip to Florida and was not sure when I might see her next. We swapped addresses and phone numbers (my parents' number). We vowed to stay in touch, but I would only be in town for the holiday weekend, prior to heading on south. I paid him $25 for the bike, knowing that I now had another true friend as I rode it toward town.

Dixie Union was a small town, but it appeared to have pride, with well-kept, nice lawns and lots of flowers. Some of the houses were large and resembled plantation homes. The bike was nice as I cruised four or five blocks north through the suburbs into town. Arriving in the business section, I walked the bike through town, taking into account each store and what they offered. I was also looking for pay phones. Reaching the north end of town, I crossed the street, heading back south, and stopped about midway at a hardware store. The Schwinn was equipped with a very nice kickstand, so I parked the bike and entered the store. I asked where I could find D-cell batteries and was directed to aisle three, where I picked up a ten pack. Oh my! Across the aisle was an entire selection of the newest transistor radios, from pocket size to tabletop. I splurged. I bought the biggest portable they offered, with FM, stereo, and two built-in speakers. It used D-cell batteries too or a 110-V plug in. I added another six pack of batteries to my cart. The bill was just over $30, and I begged the cashier for change in quarters.

Continuing my walk back south, I passed a decent clothing and shoe store as well as a bustling grocery store. There were two restaurants in town, both sporting breakfast, lunch, and dinner. There was also a bar at the far southeast end of town that had the windows blacked out just a little too much for me. Just past the bar was a coin laundry. YES! I made plans for the laundry.

Mounting the bike with my treasures, I peddled south past the houses to the river. On the opposite side of the road, just past the marina where the house was parked, was a tourist motel by the name of River View Lodge, which had cabins for overnight or weekly stays. It also had a restaurant near the road, open to the public all day long, and a pay phone near the parking lot. I was definitely getting hungry again, so I rode to the rear of my house and offloaded my new radio and batteries. I hoisted the bike onto the porch and then walked to the pay phone at the restaurant. I first dialed the campus dorm phone, which no one answered. That didn't surprise me. I dialed my old apartment, and the phone had a ring but no answer. I dialed Annika's parents' house, and there was no answer either. Dang, if I could only leave a message.

I then dialed the number that Pastor Roy gave me, and the phone picked up. It was a woman on the other end, who gracefully asked if she could help. I told her I was Nicholas, and that I would like to talk with the pastor. She explained his absence and asked for a message. I asked if there was a good time in the next three days when I might catch him at this number. She explained that Sundays after seven in the evening could be best. I thanked her and asked her to let him know that Nicholas called and would try calling again Sunday night, and then I hung up.

I really wanted to have a sit-down supper right then, but I walked back to my house, went in and gathered all the clothes, towels, chair sheet, and pillowcase, put them in the bike basket, and went to the coin laundry. The place was surprisingly unoccupied, so I used two washers for all my stuff, then took note of the finish time. With thirty minutes left in the wash, I went back to the restaurant.

Entering the dining area, and waiting for a maître d', I subconsciously scanned for a table with a seat facing the door. When my eyes spotted the best possible position in the room, there was Danny Wakefield. His girlfriend was on the opposite side, and as he marked me, he motioned for me to join them. This was an uplifting experience that almost brought me to tears as I joined them, sitting on Danny's side of the table.

Danny's girlfriend, Pam, was a very good looking and distinguished young woman, who happened to be quite smart as well. We talked about everything as they worked on their rib-eye steaks with asparagus and me my lesser chicken fried steak with a side of grits. The highlight of my meal was two glasses of very good, very cold milk, which still paled in flavor to the warm milk directly from the cow just two weeks ago. I excused myself, expressing a date at the laundromat, and promised I would stop by to see them soon. I peddled the bike back to the laundry, where the washing machines had both finished their cycles, so I loaded everything into two dryers and coined them into the start cycle.

I had two hours of remaining daylight, with forty-five minutes remaining on the drying time, so what to do? Well, mounting the bike, I went south toward the Satilla River. Highway 1 crossed the Satilla with a very nice but old steel suspension bridge, wide enough for the house to pass, but that would not happen. I rode across the bridge just to get a look at the river. Most of the creeks and rivers down here were cloudy, and this one was too, but not as bad as most. I crossed to the northbound lane and started back. About halfway across, I could see a marina of sorts on the east bank. It looked like a natural relief in the river that allowed docks to be built without interrupting the main body of the river. I stopped riding at the center of the bridge and took a good visual recon of the mooring area. I could see the large steel barge at the far east end. It was near the launching site, so I rode down to the road that led to the marina area.

There were more pontoons than boats, some with cabins, as well as fishing boats and speed boats. Several people were fussing with equipment on their watercraft but were very quiet otherwise. My map showed that there was likely more than a hundred miles of navigable river that led to Saint Andrews Sound on the Atlantic coast. Folks could camp on the river for days. I rode on down to the barge, parked the bike, and walked a plank onto the large flat steel deck. I was sure that it had been painted at one time, but now it had a nicely aged patina of rust orange. It had enough room for the house and the Mack tractor, but only time would tell if the workers would keep the truck coupled or not. The barge had an enclosed pilot house on the rear starboard side and a host of equipment along both sides. If all went well, I would have time to explore it more closely soon.

I still had fifteen minutes remaining before the dryer would time out, so I pedaled harder and arrived just in time. I flattened and folded all the clothes as neatly as possible and filled the front basket of the bike. The furniture sheet I folded to fit the rear bench and used a discarded plastic bag to tie it down. The ride back to the house was leisurely, as it was slightly downhill from town to the marina. I stacked the clothes and sheet on the porch, then hoisted the bike on board as well, out of sight.

Some days were average, some were bad, some were horrible, some spectacular. I would call this a very good day. I didn't need to scrounge to eat, I found a new friend, I had lots of batteries for my flashlight, and I could read and listen to the radio. The FM on this radio was working better than any radio I had ever heard, so I tuned to a station playing rock music, which I was about a year behind on. Several new songs that I hadn't heard were my favorites. I read, using the modified flashlight, until about 2200 hours, when I finished the book of Numbers and moved on to the book of Deuteronomy, the fifth book of the Pentateuch, which were all written by Moses. Joshua was about to become the new leader, and Moses needed to re-instill God's law into the people before Joshua would lead them to the Promised Land.

I still refused to open the covers on my bed, but I put the clean pillowcase on the feather pillow, laid out the nice clean and supple furniture sheet onto the bed, and climbed in after stripping down to my shorts. I awoke with my body jerking to some stupid dream. Squinting at my watch, I saw it was 0700 hours Friday morning. Putting both arms behind my head, I tried to decide whether I should get up or just laze out a while. After another fifteen minutes, I could tell that I had slept well, since I was wide awake and might as well get the day started. I took a spit bath, dried with a freshly washed towel, and noted that I would need to look seriously at a fresh water supply that could last ten days on the river. Today, I would wear the newly washed denims—wow, what a difference. They were much softer, but still somewhat starchy feeling. Depending on whether the laundromat would be open on this holiday weekend, I would put them through the cycle again.

Fully dressed, with a light pullover and the baseball cap, I peddled toward town, headed for the Omelet House restaurant for breakfast. Once again, as I waited to be seated, I scanned the dining area for the best seat facing the door, and again there was Danny. We marked each other and both shook our heads with a silent chuckle as he motioned to come sit. Danny sported a black baseball cap with the 101st Eagle patch embroidered front and center. He was no doubt recognized and respected by the local folks, and I found solace in that. I ordered a cup of black coffee, my second cup in nearly a year. I savored the aroma first then took gentle sips—oh so good. Danny was having a rather large homemade cinnamon bun, but I ordered a Cajun seafood omelet, with onion-covered hash browns.

As I waited for my food, the two of us traded stories of our youth, leading up to our time in the service and how we got there. He told me more about Hamburger Hill, and I told him more about the Ia Drang.

"How about that little limp you have?" He asked directly.

"You have me. I had a through and through bullet wound in my right hip, and it must have messed up some nerves. Ahhhhaaa, my order arrives!"

I was consuming the absolute best omelet I had ever tasted as the waitress refilled my cup of black bean. Danny and I talked as the brothers we were, and he shared a story about one of his best friends in Nam.

"His name was Leo Flory, a medic who arrived about a month after me. He was from Michigan, but otherwise we had many things in common. Just prior to Hamburger Hill, our company, B-Co 2/501 Airborne Infantry, had traded places with A-Co 2/501 to pull perimeter guard on a newly constructed fire support base named Airborne, which was on the east side of the A Shau Valley. We then did a combat assault to the opposite side of the A Shau Valley to the base of Hill 937. During the night of the last day of that five-day mission, Firebase Airborne, the one we had just left, was overrun by the NVA. B-Co was flown back to FB Airborne early that next morning, where we spent two days cleaning up the aftermath and sending the twenty-six killed in action back to the rear in body bags. We also needed to clear the base of all the dead NVA soldiers, about a hundred of them.

"After that, B-Co was temporarily broken up and sent to guard different Fire Support Bases for about a week. During that time, Doc Flory, after ten months on line, finally received orders for an R&R and left the company to go to Japan for a week. The next day, B-Co mustered back together on FB Airborne and made another combat assault back to the base of Hill 937. Doc Flory was replaced by a new medic by the name of Carl Michal Sneed. The two only met briefly as they traded places in a logistics helicopter, Sneed joining B-Co and Flory heading to R&R. Flory gave Sneed what he called a 'catastrophe bag' to carry on light missions but told Sneed that he wanted it back upon his return. They shook hands and the chopper lifted off as Doc Sneed disappeared from Flory's view in the rotor wash."

Danny continued, "So, Doc Flory arrived back at LZ Sally, the 101st rear base just north of Hue City. Shortly after arriving, he learned that he would not need to return to the field. He learned that B-Co had gone up what was now called Hamburger Hill, and that his replacement, Carl Sneed, had been killed in action. The new company commander Captain Franzinger and two others in B-Co were also killed in action.

"Doc Flory visited me in the 325th Danang field hospital just prior to my being sent to the US military hospital in Japan. The Sneed thing had truly hit him hard, but he was looking forward to returning home within thirty-five days."

Danny explained that he only had phone contact with Doc Flory since then, but one day soon they planned to reunite. I turned deeply inward for a moment, absorbing Danny's story, and thought about how nearly all the friends I had made in the 1st Cavalry were dead. Danny had comrades to look forward to seeing again, and I was so thankful for that.

Prior to parting, Danny chiseled for more information as to why I was in their town for the Memorial Day weekend. I just rolled my eyes and said, "You know, sometimes you just need to escape." I told him that I would stop at his house over the weekend, gave him a salute, and left.

My brain was derailed with the up-close stories resembling my recent past, but shaking my head to clear my thoughts, I mounted the bike and headed toward the stores. I decided to go for the food first and plan for ten days. Even if the barge trip ended in six days, it would take another several days to make the Florida line.

At the grocery store, I concentrated on anything canned—fruit, vegetables, stew, and meat. I added a quart of dill pickles, and since bread would spoil after a day, I bought two boxes of saltine crackers instead. Eggs hold up for seven or eight days without refrigeration, so one dozen went into the cart. I was about to add canned juice when I came to my senses—the bike basket would be full. I cashed out at the register and took the first load home. After putting the goods away, I immediately returned to the store, thinking that drinking water could be very hard to get on the river. I bought as much fruit juice in half gallon jugs as the bike basket would hold and delivered them home too.

Peddling back into town, I laughed as I likened myself to a pack rat preparing for winter. At the north end of town, there was a second-hand store that looked interesting, so I stopped in. They were blessed with clothing, so I looked for a pair of shorts. The proprietors, a group named North Wayne Mennonite Church, conducted well-organized sales displays with sizes posted and separation of male and female goods. I found three different pairs of short pants, two with extra cargo pockets. I added two more tees with breast pockets, then looked at their shoes. I fitted in a pair of flip-flop sandals and a pair of low-cut white sneakers. While checking out, I spied in their glass cabinet, a Zippo lighter I felt I needed, and bought it too.

Having room remaining in the basket, I went back to the hardware store and bought a ten-pound bag of Kingsford charcoal, a quart of charcoal lighting fluid, and a small squeeze container of Zippo lighter fluid. Upon leaving the hardware, I checked out a display near the door, advertising a new product called "duct tape." It showed graphics of all the uses—good tape, very sticky. You never know, I thought, and purchased a roll. There was a small store in the center of town named the Stationers Store, which sold anything a business or individual may need for business, mostly relative to paper and clerical goods. They had a simple, flip-able calendar, with space to write notes in each day. The basket loaded again, I returned to my house to put it all away neatly.

It seemed a good time to play phone detail again, so I headed to the River View Lodge. It was nearly 1100 hours as I dialed Annika's family business first, and the secretary answered. I told her who I was and asked for Annika.

She said, "Hello Nicholas, I will find her."

The phone went to music for a minute, then Annika answered, "Oh Nick, I have been waiting for a call. I received the letter and was so thankful for it. Is your condition better or worse?"

"Annika, I'm actually doing quite well. I am eating properly and sleeping well too. I was enjoying some freedom for the holiday weekend, but I'm being cautious about it."

She chattered away some, which I enjoyed hearing, and ended with her delight with her final grades for sophomore year.

"Annika, have you made contact with Pastor Roy?"

"Yes, I have, and I really like him. I think he could be a true advocate for you. Does the pastor know where to find you?"

"Not actually, and there are more important events coming that you need to know. I believe that I will be out of contact for up to ten days. I may send a letter, but I am not sure."

"OK, Nick. I will be ready for that, meanwhile I want you to know that I will be switching my curriculum to law for my junior year, and I have made some discoveries in regards to the VFW commander and the sheriff, but I will tell you about that later."

I told her that I loved her deeply and missed her so badly, but I believed this would all be worth it. She all but parroted my words, and we said goodbye. We had talked for quite some time, and I had used a lot of quarters, but enough remained in my pocket, so I dialed the pastor. Again his wife answered and said he could come to the phone.

Pastor Roy answered, "Finn, how are you, and where are you? I'm guessing only about sixty miles farther south?"

As he chuckled, I explained the upcoming barge trip, and that the house was to arrive in Hoboken around June 8–10.

He laughed again and said, "Son, you're going slower yet!"

I laughed too. "Thank you for contacting Annika. She likes you and will work with you in any way to help."

The good pastor ended the conversation with a prayer for safety, and we shared goodbyes.

I called my parents, and Mom answered again, but this time she spared the drama. She was probably desensitized by now. She told the story of actually obtaining my driver's license, and that she should receive it in the mail within a week. I couldn't thank her enough. I told her I loved her, that I was doing great, to tell Dad hello, and to forward the license to Annika.

It all felt so good. I was still full from the omelet and didn't need lunch, so I rode the bike toward the house, thinking about reading the good book and taking a nice nap. So I did. I awoke with a big yawn, climbed out of my favorite chair, and went to the kitchen for a snack. Dill pickles were nearly the only item on that menu. OK then, it's time to stock up on junk food. I took the bike down from the porch and pushed it to a nice public restroom at the side of the marina. Nice, for the time being, to not use the p-u bucket. As I emerged from the men's room, there were people busying about at the marina, and one caught my eye. A small-framed man, wearing a blue plaid shirt, and a light blue baseball cap. He looked nappy, with a nappy reddish beard. He was in a hurry, fussing with a small aluminum boat that had faded red trim. Among the vacationers, he looked to be just a fisherman in a big hurry with a large tackle box.

I hopped on the bike and headed into town one more time. I went to the grocery store, walked the isles, and tried to think of anything I might not have planned for. After getting many bags of various chips, caramel corn, and nuts, I spotted another full head of celery, and that was it. I still needed water, but the marina probably had a water supply for that.

As I returned toward the marina, the road went down a slight grade prior to flattening out near the entrance to the River View Lodge, so no peddling required for a minute, just silence—except for a car coming up fast and hitting the brakes hard enough to make the tires squeal. Stopping alongside me was a Georgia State Police patrol car with two troopers in the front seat. The passenger had his window open and shouted, "STOP!"

11. GUINNESS PRIZE!

I STOPPED—THAT'S WHAT people paralyzed with fear do! I don't know what that officer may have seen on my face as he barked, "WE'RE IN PURSUIT OF A MAN WHO JUST ROBBED THE BAXLEY BANK AND THE ALMA BANK! A little guy wearing a blue plaid shirt, blue baseball cap, and bib overalls—scruffy looking—have you seen him?"

I hesitated far too long before saying, "Sorry officer, the squealing tires scared the crap out of me, but yes, I did see a man like that." I pointed and said, "He was on the dock just a minute ago, fussing with a boat. He was carrying a large tackle box." The tires on the patrol car spun on the pavement as they blasted toward the marina.

Snack? Hell, I'm following these guys. I pursued, pedaling that Schwinn as fast as I could toward the marina. The patrol car had made a big cloud of dust in the gravel parking lot as it side-slid toward the dock entrance, and both officers bailed out on a run, guns drawn. I spotted the suspect as he put his green Johnson outboard motor to full throttle, gaining speed fast as he went east past the moorings holding the barge. The troopers ran in that direction, but it was too late. They ran back to the patrol car and started shouting on the radio. I turned and left for town promptly, hoping to avoid any other questions.

Riding up to Danny's house, I went to the door and knocked, but there was no answer. I was hoping to just sit with a friend and describe what had just happened. So, I rode to the business area and walked the bike to the grocery store. I studied the junk food aisle again carefully, trying to add things that were tasty but also nutritious. That was hard to do, but I did add a quart jar of peanut butter since it would keep for a very long time.

I really wanted to stop wearing the prison shoes, even though they were very comfortable. I went back to the used store to see what they had. Rummaging through the rack, I found a pair of penny loafers that fit. I also found a well-used yellow hard hat and vest, the type that road workers or construction workers might use. I had a thought about a possible use for them and added them to my shoes. The bill was $3, and I gave them $10. The Mennonite women were dressed like anyone you may encounter on the street, with the exception of the prayer cap pinned to their hair.

The town had a small Rexall Drug store that had a soda fountain in the front corner. I went in and ordered a classic root beer float and sat for the longest time sipping away. My mind drifted off on this and that, and settled on the time Annika and I were at Luigi's restaurant in Augusta for our first real dinner out. The maître d' sat us in such a way that I was facing a wall. There was a window facing out to my right that helped, but I was so uncomfortable, I was on the verge of vomiting. I had no clue what the problem was, so I finally stood up, tried to just breathe, and as I turned to view the room, the sensation disappeared. I asked Annika if she would mind trading places, and she obliged. I sat facing the room and the door, and the problem was gone. I wondered what made me think of that now, even as I unconsciously sat in the best spot to view the door and room.

It was almost 1900 hours on Friday evening, and I was brain drained. I walked the bike to the end of the business district and rode back to the house with my stash of goods. At the house, I hoisted everything onto the porch and brought it all inside. I slept well that night. Even though I'd had a short nap during the day, I was burned out. I held out enough strength to put everything away neatly and concealed. Mr. Khaki Man was very likely to be back on the scene when they put the house on the barge. So, I was prepared.

I took off my shirt and denims, pulled on a T-shirt, and sat in my living room chair. Pretzels, yes pretzels, and beer came to mind. Jumping up quickly, I retrieved a bag of pretzels to munch on and a beer to sip, as I dialed the radio to a good rock and roll station. As I munched, I listened to the songs "I Can See Clearly Now," "Schools Out," and "Burning Love," all on the top ten for the year. I laughed, as I could relate to all of them. After a little time, the song by Eric Burton and the Animals "We Gotta Get Out of This Place" came on, and it brought chills. It was not only relevant while in Nam, but it was relevant now. Then the song "Lean on Me" came on, and a warm feeling drifted in because I knew there were people out there right now pulling for me and worried sick about me. I was leaning on them.

I made it my rule to use the flashlight in the manner I set it up for earlier. A tiny hole in the center, push the button for just a second, and be careful about observing what you see during that one second. Then move forward as far as you can before blinking the light again. In only a few nights, I was surprised just how much I could do and how far I could go with just one blink.

Just after 2100 hours I needed to give up for the night, and, using the blinks, I made my way to bed, got comfortable, and was out until 0400 hours, when I needed to pee. I pulled out the p-u bucket, which was empty and cleaned, but chose not to use it. I slipped on the denims and tried the penny loafers for the first time. Blinking my way to the door, I let myself off the porch and headed for the public restrooms, blinking my way across the twenty yards of parking lot to the structure. It was fun, but I was about to pee my pants when I finally arrived. Inside the john, it only took one blink to do my business and get back out of the door, three blinks to get back to the porch, and three to get back in bed.

Refreshed by the night air and the excursion, I laid happily awake for a while, staring into the darkness. I thought about Danny and what he went through, what he was going through now, and how he had risen above it all, tackling life as we all should and pursuing his dreams. Danny had told me earlier that after he had graduated in 1967, he kept up his paper route but also went to work at a company that specialized in what the concrete business called flatwork,—garage floors, sidewalks, driveways, and the like. He had seen some imprinting of concrete with designs that looked like stone or brick, some like leather. Colors could even be added to the concrete mix. He was so excited to get started in the business of decorative concrete work.

Whoa, I awoke at 0700 hours confused for a few seconds. Breathing deep for a minute, I gathered my thoughts. It was Saturday morning, May 27. I had been on the lam since May 12. That was only fifteen days, but it felt so much longer. I would like to think that I was in some kind of time warp, but reality was forcing me out of bed and into clothing. In a T-shirt, pants, and bare feet, I did calisthenics for an hour, not having missed a day since I started. I sat and panted for several minutes and thought that I could smell bacon frying somewhere.

I donned a colorful shirt, shorts, and sneakers, mounted the bike, and headed into town to see who was doing breakfast. I didn't get far, as the aroma was obviously coming from the River View Restaurant, and the bike steered itself to the front door. I parked the bike, went in, and was seated quickly, as it was still quite early. I ordered black coffee as I studied the menu. I loved omelets and spied one that boasted spinach and seafood, which included lobster and crab, with mozzarella cheese. It was pricey but sounded so good, so I ordered it with rye toast.

As I waited, I sniffed my coffee cup every time before taking a sip; it was just so enjoyable. As I sat, I picked up on some of the chatter in the restaurant. Some of the folks were talking about the bank robbery yesterday. They were dumbfounded that such a thing could happen so close to Dixie Union. They were saying that the state troopers were shooting at the guy as he fled from the docks.

"Some guy in the parking lot spotted the robber and informed the troopers, but no one knows who he was yet."

Another guy said he was at the marina at the time and had seen that old fisherman that showed up a few times every year.

"What do they call him? Catfish Jack, Rag Man Jack, or something?"

Another said it took the sheriff an hour to get a patrol boat in the water to look for him, but they'd had a constant group of boats on the river since then. I had just witnessed the rumor mill in action, and I was not about to correct anything.

Ahh, my steaming seafood omelet arrived along with the rye toast and a refill of the coffee. Sitting alone, I spent the entire time simply enjoying the tasty concoction of southern cooking. It was finally time to leave the restaurant, but I did not have any place to go. As I moved through the exit door, I noticed a poster that advertised a parade in town on Memorial Day Monday, starting at 1100 hours. I thought that may be an enjoyable thing to watch and wondered if it would pass by Danny's house. Well, sometime today I would just ask him.

Meanwhile, I had serious thoughts of running out of drinking water while on the barge. I had only emptied one of the canned juice jars, but I would have liked to have at least a half gallon a day in reserve. Juice was the same as water, but I had only enough for about six days. I rode the bike into town to resolve that problem. Back at the grocery store, I purchased six half-gallon bottles of white grape juice, the cheapest that they had. I love the stuff, so it didn't matter to me. It filled the bike basket perfectly, and I took it home.

The marina was busy as the weekend progressed, but no one seemed to notice the guy on the bike going to the back of the house parked in the large marina lot. I unloaded the bike and stored the juice in the last remaining cupboard space. Knowing that the day was not done, I sat with my legs dangling from the porch, wondering what to do. As I sat, I had to laugh, as there was a water hose, at least fifty feet long, hanging on a nice holder just twenty feet from the house. It was for anyone who needed to clean their watercraft prior to leaving the marina. I assumed it was also to fill my bathtub. I uncoiled the hose, pulled it to the porch and into the house, and filled the tub in broad daylight. I thought perhaps I could make this happen again prior to Monday evening.

It was late morning by then, so I hopped on the bike and rode up to Danny's house to knock on the door. I could hear movement in the house, but it took several minutes for him to make it to the door. He was pleased to see me and once again made the invitation to sit on the porch. We chatted about a great many things, laughed, cried, and wondered why. He explained that most of his rehab was done in Jacksonville, Florida, a long drive, but worth it. He said the facility, doctors, and therapist were great, and he had gotten to know many other veterans going through similar physical problems. Then he excitedly explained that his first prosthetic leg should be ready for fitting within the next two weeks. Yes, this was good news.

I asked him if Monday's parade was going to pass by his house, and he assured me that it would. He invited me to join him, his family, and his girlfriend. I agreed.

Then he said, "But, on one condition, that you join us for church tomorrow at 1000 hours."

I said, "You bet."

Then he explained that they would be at the First Baptist Church, at the north end of town. We shook hands, and I said, "Airborne all the way."

"First in, 1st Cavalry. Gary Owen."

Now it was early afternoon, and I had a lot of day remaining, so I thought of making calls. I also thought of putting my denims through the wash again. I went back to the house, got the denims, and found a few other items that could be washed, including the yellow vest. The laundromat had coin changers, so I put in a $20 bill, and then I had quarters to last a month. I poked my laundry in a machine and headed back to the River View pay phone.

I dialed Annika first, thinking she should be home on Saturday afternoon. Her father answered, and for a second I felt concerned, but it faded to being thankful. I announced, "It's Nick. How are you doing, sir?"

"Don't worry about me, how are you?"

I shared, "Except for my stupidity, I'm actually doing quite well and even making new friends. I'm eating well and getting plenty of exercise, fresh air, and sun. I am as safe as I could hope to be under the circumstances, and if all goes as planned, I should cross the Florida line in about fifteen or sixteen days."

He started laughing and said, "For crying out loud, Nick, I can walk from North Carolina to Florida in fifteen days, by what means are you traveling?"

"That's a legitimate question." I laughed, "Sir, I cannot wait to tell you."

"Well Annika is out until about 5:00, so you should call back again after that."

I agreed, then told him to give my regards to Mrs. Bjorn. Then out of nowhere, I said, "You know I love Annika, and I miss her badly."

He replied, "I know Nick, and she loves you too. We will stick with you. Please don't let us down."

"I am determined to never let that happen again," I replied.

As soon as we hung up, I dialed Pastor Roy, and he answered the phone. I filled him in on the events of the long weekend and the planned launch of the barge on Tuesday, May 30. I told him about my newfound friend Danny, and that I would be meeting him at the First Baptist Church in Dixie Union tomorrow.

He was quiet for a minute and explained that he knew the church. "I actually had planned a weekend off. That's somewhat of a long drive, but what if I were to meet you there?"

I was delighted at the idea and said his mileage could be easily compensated, plus a tithe for his church. It was agreed on.

It was a beautiful Saturday afternoon, and with some time to use before calling Annika, I started riding north. Going past Danny's house a block or two, I turned east on a side street and back north after one block. This way I didn't need to walk the bike. After about five blocks of beautiful old homes, so well kept, I was mesmerized. Another thing so different here was the huge, old live oak trees covered with Spanish moss. Some shaded four or five homes each and actually created a peaceful or tranquil look. I turned back west to intersect with Highway 1 and traveled north several more blocks to the church. The church and grounds were well kept also, with a paved and striped parking lot. Riding to the back of the lot revealed a small but very nice pavilion with a brick grill that looked like a fireplace. It had six picnic tables—very nice.

After sitting in the shade of the pavilion for a while, just looking around, I then headed back south, this time riding a block west to inspect the homes on that side of town. I pedaled slowly and coasted, as most of the town was sloped slightly toward the river. About halfway, was a small city park. At its center was the largest live oak that I had seen yet, and it shaded the entire park. Wow! Then it dawned on me, like getting hit on the head with a brick, I needed a camera! Not much chance of purchasing one prior to launch, but I had an idea. On the ride back, I stopped at the laundromat to move the clothes from the washer to the dryer.

As my watch ticked toward 1700 hours, I coasted slowly back down toward the River View. It was a little early, but I couldn't wait. After dialing and coining the phone, I was relieved when Annika answered on the first ring. I exhaled, "Oh, I feel better already." We traded "I love you's" and made some small talk for a minute. I told her I was so thankful to have talked to her dad earlier.

"His first impression of you must have been really good because he is in your corner. He is supporting me with anything I need to help you."

"Annika, how will I ever be able to thank you enough? Especially now that I need to tell you that I will be out of touch for some ten days, but I'll only be a few days from the Florida line after that. Baby, I can only ask for patience."

She replied, "Well, I will just ignore the ten day thing for now and talk about my work. I felt helpless at first, but I got a toehold here and there that gave me a little more confidence. I also want you to know that I have switched my major to law, and that my professors are in full agreement.

"I discovered a law passed in 1967, called the Freedom of Information Act, FOIA for short. I have been using it and hitting roadblocks with the county that should not be happening. I have written requests for FOIA's of all sorts in my case, but they took time. The few that had returned seemed to have some discrepancies about the licensing of the Jeep and boat behind the VFW.

"I also inquired about Trues Towing but didn't understand what they had to do with anything."

I said, "Please just be very familiar with them because questions will be coming for them, hopefully soon. I met a new friend named Danny, and he is likely to become a lifelong friend. That is, if I can keep my head straight long enough. Annika, I am living well, eating well, and have excellent digs."

"How can this be? How could you be moving south toward Florida, hiding as a fugitive, and living comfortably?"

"Well, along the way, I found a can of fu-fu-dust and used it! You will hopefully know soon enough." We ended the call with the idea that I could possibly call again Monday evening.

We had talked through about four dollars' worth of quarters, maybe an hour and a half. I loved it when I could leave church after a good sermon and actually feel fed with God's word. Well, it was the same feeling with Annika—I felt fed.

The River View was still open but would be closed for Memorial Day. I was very hungry again, as I could smell something cooking that I couldn't identify. It was early enough that the table choices were still open. The maître d' began to guide me to a table, but I shook my head and pointed to the table that Danny had chosen before. She smiled and led me to it. They had beer on tap, and when the waitress arrived, I ordered a Miller High Life Draft (as advertised, the champagne of beers) and sipped as I studied the menu.

The waitress returned, and I asked, "What smelled so good outside?"

"Our Saturday evening special is always lasagna, so that must be what you were smelling."

I ordered the Saturday special and was not disappointed. It was seriously good Italian food, complete with the best garlic toast I had ever had. It took two more Miller Draft beers to finish it.

Now, I had been exercising, doing military calisthenics, for close to two hours every day for over two weeks and had worked hard on the chain gang for the past year. But tonight, I felt like a fat cat! At 1830 hours it was time to go home, but I had forgotten not only to call Pastor Roy again, but also the laundry! So I hurried to the pay phone and dialed his number. I was nearly surprised when he answered, and I said, "It's Nick."

He answered quickly, "That wasn't you robbing those banks down there, was it?"

I laughed, "No, but I became involved, as I had spotted a man at the docks that fit the description and told the state police." I heard a low grumble in his voice, but otherwise silence. I reminded Pastor Roy of the Baptist church service on Sunday, and he thought he could probably make it. Then I peddled that bike as hard as I could to the laundromat, catching the owner just locking the door. A $20 tip reopened the door with a smile, and I headed back home with my laundry.

At around 1900 hours I coasted the bike back down to the marina and directly to the bathrooms, as the three beers wanted out badly. I didn't pay much attention to the sheriff's officers trailering their boats at the launch, apparently finished with their bank robber hunt for the day. I positioned myself at one of the two urinals and began the long-awaited relief, when one of the officers entered the john, going directly to the other urinal. He was obviously in pain too. As we both maintained a steady flow, my alcohol induced mouth said, "Did you have any luck?"

He just answered, "No, but we are not giving up." He sighed in relief and turned to leave, when I farted. He turned, with a strange questioning look on his face.

I looked back at him and said, "Ahhhh, bonus." He laughed out loud and left.

I needed to laugh at myself as I finished and then rode the bike back toward the River View to wait until the cops left. When they did, I returned to the house and hoisted the bike onto the porch. With the small amount of light remaining, I worked quickly to get comfortable. I had finished the Pentateuch, the first five books of the Bible, and was ready to start Joshua and the next twelve books of the history and plight of God's chosen people, the Israelites. Joshua was on his own now to lead the people into the Promised Land. I jerked awake. It was 2300 hours, so I took the chair sheet with me and blinked my way to my bedroom.

I must have slept hard, as I awoke at 0715 feeling great. I cracked four eggs into a glass and whipped them good with a fork and drank them down, then opened a can of peaches and ate them with great delight. I went directly into calisthenics for the next hour, and when I finished in a full sweat, I shaved and climbed into the room temperature water in the bathtub. After using soap on my pits and other important parts, I soaked for another fifteen minutes. I thought if I was going to church in this nice town, I may as well dress up.

I put on the khaki cotton loose fit trousers, the loose fit khaki shirt that was not to be tucked in, and the khaki Panama hat. I put a small wad of cash in my pocket, checked to see if anyone could see me, and jumped from the porch. I took the bike down and walked it to the bathroom, as there was one more task to be done prior to heading to the church.

I rode to Danny's house, arriving a half hour early, and he had already pulled his car out of the garage and had put the top down on a 1972 Chevelle Super Sport convertible. Yes! His girlfriend was just coming out, so he did a quick reintroduction and invited me to the back seat. Pam drove us to the church, giving the engine a little rev at each stop and grinning at Danny. As we made our way to the church, I explained that I had invited a friend to join us, but I wasn't sure if he would make it.

Danny said, "No problem."

As Pam parked the car, the lot was filling up. Danny exited the car, hopping on one foot as he retrieved his crutches from beside me in the back seat, then I climbed out. I scanned the lot for Pastor Roy but didn't see him, so we proceeded to the front doors of the church, where there were two greeters. A lady and a gentleman both shook our hands and made us welcome. As we entered the sanctuary, I spied Pastor Roy sitting with his wife near the back row. I had already removed my cover and tapped Danny on the shoulder, pointing to the couple. I whispered, "These are my friends."

Danny looked at them then looked back and forth, saying, "We really want to sit up there with our parents."

I smiled, "We will be here when the service ends."

The service was well attended, primarily with white folks. The building was well appointed and well kept. After the beginning announcements, the choir director did a very professional job of bringing the congregation to a standing position and announcing the song titles and page numbers. In lieu of an organ, they were using a piano and six people in their choir. I was impressed with the harmony that they produced on several of the old traditional hymns.

The preacher started us in prayer, then did a short recap on the first three elements of his ten-part series on the Ten Commandments. "Number three, 'You shall not misuse the name of the Lord your God.' None of us care to have our name misused, maligned, or dragged thru the mud, so how much more for the father of us all!" His entire sermon made very good sense, and Pastor Roy gave a head nod and smile at the end.

We were near the back of the church and made our exit first, standing on the sidewalk in front as folks left. We were smiling and greeting as they passed, but I noticed that many were simply ignoring the Walkers. I eventually turned to Pastor Roy with a questioning look on my face.

He looked back, did his chuckle, and whispered, "Trust me, I'm used to it." They both looked great—Pastor Roy with a black suit, white shirt, and tie, and Mrs. Rose Walker with a beautiful but modest full-length dress, light blue with large floral print. She was carrying a small Japanese style fan. I was proud to be with them.

Danny, his girlfriend Pam, and their parents eventually came out, and we all stood and talked while making introductions. There was a plan for all to meet at Pam's parents for a Sunday dinner, and they extended the invitation to us as well. Pastor shook his head no, and I said I would pass as well.

Danny looked at me with curious eyes and said, "Finn, we need to talk, alone."

"Oh thank God, I need to talk to you too. However, Pastor Roy and his wife will be with us." I nodded toward the small pavilion at the rear of the church, and we strolled in that direction. Pam headed off to her parents' home, and Pastor Roy volunteered to take Danny to whatever address he needed when we were finished. The four of us gathered at a picnic table, and I said to Danny, "You first."

Dan collected his thoughts for a moment, then began with the day I purchased his bicycle. He reminisced about finding a true brother, nearly in tears. He reminded me that I had said I was staying at the River View Lodge for a long weekend and I was interested in the bike for touring everything in the area.

I nodded.

He continued, "I have a lot of time to watch out my front window, and I have watched you time after time, riding past with that basket loaded. On Saturday, I called down to the River View and asked if they could connect me to your room. They said that there was no Nicholas Finn registered with them. I was sitting on that thought when I invited you to church, but now I want to know what is going on with you!"

I breathed out all the air in my lungs, with my head down, then raised my head and inhaled. I put my hand on Dan's shoulder, speaking directly to him, and advised him that what I was about to tell him was going to be a great burden to him, but a great relief to me. From this point he could be accused of aiding and abetting a known felon.

I told him that Pastor Roy and his wife already knew my situation and were pulling for me. I did my best to use brevity in explaining my last years with the cavalry, working for the concrete companies, and entering college at Berkeley. I told him of the three stooges, their VWs, and why I did what I did. I explained the VFW in Augusta and why I did the deed there as well. I shared the story of Annika and how she was pulling for me too. Then I told him about my escape, ending up in the Frank Lloyd Wright house, and how it was about to take a barge trip on the Satilla River.

Danny wondered how Pastor Roy fit into this strange story, and I nodded to the pastor to share. Pastor Roy then explained his connection with the jail ministries, traveling Highway 1 on a regular basis, seeing the house, and seeing me twice. He explained to Danny that I had shared the truth of my escape and my plight to cross the Florida border. He also said that he was duty bound to tell the authorities, but meanwhile, his focus was to see me cross that border.

Danny just stared into space for a while, trying to absorb it all. I added that I had no idea what made me do the things I did, but they were not the kind of thing I would ever do again.

He switched subjects so fast, I struggled to catch up. He said, "I know a lot about the river, tell me what you think the program is."

"Based on assumptions, the house is to be loaded on Tuesday, May 30. It could take anywhere from six to ten days to complete the trip to the dock near Hoboken."

He said, "This trip should be fairly routine, but there have been reports of pirates on the river for many years and lots of things stolen, mostly at night. However, I have fished the river for years and never had a problem."

"Danny, I have a fishing pole. I made a great catch on a river north of here, and I intend to try and have a fresh catch every evening while on the river."

He shared great advice about baits and lures.

Before we got up to go, Mrs. Walker cleared her throat a bit and said in her southern drawl, "Mr. Finn, I have been thinking about your story. Now, whether you end up free or back in that jail, you need to contact the Guinness book, cuz you must be setting a record for the slowest escape ever recorded. Why, son, you may even win a prize!" We all had a good laugh, but it was true.

We walked Pastor Roy and his wife to their light blue four-door '63 Plymouth, and I assisted Dan at the back door first as he put his crutches in the center. I hopped in on the opposite side as Pastor Roy took Danny to Pam's parents' home. I exited the car in haste to open the door for Danny, who was already poking his crutches out of the car door. When he was upright and in grip with his condition, we did a healthy man hug and vowed to watch the parade on Monday.

Then the pastor took me to the River View. We sat and chatted for a while, and I could attest that Mrs. Rose Walker was the most wonderful, reserved, polite, and intelligent woman. It was a privilege for me just to know her. Pastor Roy spoke about a few more calls with Annika and how impressed he was with her determination in understanding the law. He said they would probably meet soon. I thanked him again for coming and passed an envelope to him with the proceeds of Joshua and Judges inside.

After walking back to the house, I took the bike back down from the porch. It was early afternoon, and perhaps Pam's parents had not served dinner yet. I rode the three-mile distance to their place and was greeted by all of them on the front porch. We all chatted, laughed, and carried on as Pam, her mother, and would-be mother-in-law put on a first-class Sunday dinner. For a guy on the lam, this wasn't all bad. I really wanted to chat with the men, but I helped with dishes instead. It didn't take long anyway, and I was back on the porch.

It a wonderful afternoon, and as evening approached, I excused myself, hopped on the bike, and coasted slowly to the dock. I was happy with the day and my amazing friends—I was content. I was anticipating a trip down the big river and the new encounters that may result. Riding to the rear of the house, I hoisted the bike onto the porch as a very loud and commanding voice from the marina bathroom area said, "FREEZE—PUT YOUR HANDS ABOVE YOUR HEAD!"

12. CEASE AND DESIST!

I DID FREEZE AFTER letting go of the bike, which bounced on the kickstand. I spun in shock into the face of a police officer. All the day's wonderful experiences evaporated with those few words. I moved my arms up slowly and waited for further instructions. He had not drawn his gun, but his hand was at the ready. The adrenaline was coursing through my system, but I had been in worse places than this. I calmed myself and said, "What's the problem officer?"

He said, "We are watching this place carefully, as a bank robber was spotted here Friday. What are you doing here, and show me an ID."

"My name is Harry Layman, and I was sent here by the Vandoorne Agency to act as an undercover guard for this historic house that is to be barged down the river. Its owners became aware of trouble on the river and hired us to protect it." I borrowed the name of a policeman in my hometown in Michigan to avoid giving the officer my real name.

"How about that ID?"

I said, "It's inside the house with the rest of my stuff, including about eight days of canned food."

"Go get it."

I made the leap onto the porch, turned toward him, and asked if I could put my hand in my pocket. He agreed as the light was fading toward night. I put my hand in my right front pocket as he watched and slowly pulled out a shiny brass key to the house. Seeing the reassurance in his face, and a tiny grin, I put the bike aside and keyed my way into the house, leaving the door wide open. I made sure to make noises as I retrieved the hard hat and vest, then returned to the door.

"It's boogie dark in there! Curse me for not returning earlier and sorting my stuff." I showed the officer my hard hat and vest and explained I was to wear it on the trip. "I can't find my flashlight either, can I borrow yours?"

He said, "Forget it, I'll see you on Tuesday morning."

"No, you won't. I'm supposed to hide inside the house until the barge stops each night."

"Sounds damn boring to me."

"Yes, it's the cost of being the new guy," I answered as he headed across the parking lot to his squad car.

It really was dark in the house, but I had placed my flashlight near the door, so I blinked my way to my favorite chair and fell in. The emotions festered for a while, then began to boil out, first in damning myself for being so careless, then into tears of thanks for being delivered one more time. I just did not feel like reading that night, so I reminisced on the events of the day. I was still wearing the khakis and thought how nice it was to be dressed up and to join friends at church. I thought about how I had come to love and trust Pastor Roy. Despite the adrenaline shock I had just endured, it was a good day. I focused on Memorial Day as I blinked my way to the bedroom and hung up the dress clothes in the closet. I was looking forward to another day with Danny as I crawled onto the bed and wrapped up in the chair sheet. Soon it became Monday morning, Memorial Day.

Waking at 0715 hours, I couldn't believe I had slept that hard. I couldn't even remember any stupid dreams. In the dim light, I put the sheet back on my favorite chair, then went to the kitchen in search of breakfast. I yearned to go back to the River View, but the restaurant was closed. I cracked four eggs into a glass and whipped them thoroughly, then drank them down. I opened a can of pears and ate them all, drinking the sweet juice left in the can. It was time for calisthenics, so I worked out for the next two hours. After sitting and catching my breath, I slid into the tub of room temperature water. I thought about how much nicer a hot shower would feel, but in my current situation, this was excellent!

I dressed for the day in a nice button-down shirt, cargo shorts, and sandals. It was still early, so I walked down to the docks. Many vacationers were prepping their boats for an excursion that day, and others were apparently sleeping in. It was so peaceful that morning there on the river, the water so full of reddish tannin that it looked almost black. Yet, you could see down through it quite a distance. The air smelled of fish, and I hoped that I would have my chance to catch a few.

I milled around until about 1000 hours then rode the bike to Danny's. He was already on the porch and waved me in with a big smile.

I turned the bike toward the road, in the exact spot it was when I bought it. I walked to the porch and told Dan that he ought to keep the bike since he would be able to ride it again in only a few weeks. He smiled, nodded his head, and agreed. I said, "Trust me. I do not need the $25 for the bike, as I used $100 worth of it."

Danny said that he could drive his Chevelle if I trusted him, and that he wanted to see a friend—another Vietnam veteran—back in Alma.

I said, "Game on, let's go."

He tossed me the keys and asked if I would get the car out of the garage and drive it towards the road. I, of course, was pleased with the idea, as this convertible was at the top of its class in muscle cars. It boasted a 396-cubic-inch engine, a Holley four-barrel carburetor, dual exhaust, and a four-speed transmission. Oh yes, this was a hot rod. I got out of the car, circled around, and got into the passenger seat as Danny crutched his way to the driver's seat and tossed the crutches to the back.

"Pam may have a big problem with this," he said as he sat in the driver's bucket seat and fastened a factory lap seat belt. "I hadn't ever used seat belts before, but it seems to help my effort with only one foot." He shifted into first gear and alternated between the clutch and accelerator, his right hand jumping back and forth between the floor shifter and some gizmo on his dash, as the tires threw a bit of driveway gravel and launched onto the street.

Danny was so gifted. He eased the car north through town, then opened it up gradually as we cruised into the country. I felt so free—the top down, wind blowing through our hair, the destination a comrade in arms. As we came into Alma, Danny had some problems shifting down as he slowed to the speed limit in town, but he compensated well. He drove confidently through several city blocks to his friend's house, and on arrival, he asked if I would go knock on the door.

A young woman answered the door, leaving the screen door closed, and said, "Hello?"

"Hi, I'm Nicholas, I'm with Danny." By then she had spotted Danny in the car and waved him in. I went back to the car to help, but Dan was quick and efficient, not needing help.

We went to the large veranda porch that seemed to wrap all around the very beautiful and extremely well-kept house. Dan's friend had joined his wife on the porch by then, and we went through introductions. David and Pam Krautshield. I turned to Danny and smiled as he said, "Yes, two Pams."

They invited us to sit in overstuffed porch furniture since the temperature was very comfortable outside. After a few minutes of chatter, Pam excused herself, saying, "You men need your time."

Danny explained that he and David met during rehab appointments in Jacksonville. David was also in the 101st Airborne in Vietnam and was wounded during an ambush, shot through the upper right arm, the bullet making a huge hole through his arm and into his chest. It was not very noticeable, except for certain movements in his right hand that he just couldn't do.

David was an only child who lost his dad shortly after returning from the service. His mother had passed away some years earlier, and now he was the owner of their successful fuel delivery business, which was located next door. After an hour or so, David asked us to follow him into the house, as he wanted to show off his trophy room. It was actually his office, and it was filled with everything! Every space on the walls was filled. Gas pump fill valves, old hood ornaments, dozens and dozens of model cars, a six-foot wooden airplane propeller, and photos of delivery trucks, family, and friends holding a catch of fish. There was of course an area dedicated to his military service, centered on a shadow box holding all his medals, awards, and patches.

It came time to head back home, and David saw us to the car. Danny successfully backed the car out of the drive, shifted gears, and headed back toward home. Danny had made his own alteration to the car that made it a lot easier for him to drive. He couldn't use the clutch and the accelerator at the same time, so he installed a throttle cable to the carburetor. He could add just enough gas to make good forward motion as he shifted. His hand jumped quickly from the shifter to the throttle, adding or subtracting engine RPMs as needed, just like the accelerator. Once in top gear, he would pull it out just far enough to maintain a nice even speed. He called it his cruise control.

Arriving back in town, we saw that the city had blocked the street out of town several blocks north in preparation for the parade at 1400 hours. We followed the detour south to Danny's street and pulled into his drive. He climbed out, asking if I would return the car to the garage, which I did. He then asked me to help him put several lawn chairs in the front yard near the sidewalk. We added a folding table, which Pam quickly filled with snacks and drinks, and all sat down in preparation for the parade.

This far south, you needed to be ready for very sweet iced tea. While not to my taste, I still enjoyed it and indulged in all the snacks, including the pralines, to the full. The parade started with the city police sounding the sirens as they set the pace for the parade. Several other police cars followed, the drivers' faces looking familiar (imagine that), then came the VFW and the American Legion marchers. Their color guard marched first.

As they were passing, the one marching alongside acting as a drill instructor, or cadence caller, ordered them all, "Halt!" He ordered, "Left face, ten hut!" With all the guards facing Danny at attention, the drill instructor then ordered, "Hand salute!"

They held that salute as Danny rose in shock and saluted back. As Danny rose, I rose too and moved several steps toward the road, turned, and saluted him as well. The instructor then commanded, "Right face! Forward march! Your left, your left, your left, right, left."

Danny was of course dumbstruck and moved to tears. I was nearly there myself, but I was so thankful that this small town would do the right things for its veterans. We watched as a good part of the town's population marched past the house, several school bands, fire departments from around the area, horses and riders, old tractors, floats of all kinds, and finally hot rods—lots of them. The parade ended at the marina, and we just sat in the yard chatting for the hour or so that it took for all the participants to find their way back to the start point and on their way home.

We sat in the yard a while longer and relaxed, then Pam went back to the house with an armload. Danny reminisced about our visit to his friend David. He asked if I had seen the butt of a handgun on the lower shelf of David's desk, and I answered, "The 1911 with pearl grips?"

"Yes, the .45, ready for a right-handed person." We agreed that it was odd that both of us would notice something quite obscure in the midst of a thousand other things. We laughed and agreed that David's trigger finger must still work!

We talked about the next few weeks, and I promised to call the first chance I got. He warned me to stay sharp while on the river. He added that gators on the river generally avoid humans, but in an encounter, a blow to the very tip of the nose could send them away quickly. I helped put everything back in storage as Danny settled into a porch chair, so content with the day. We made our final goodbye complete with man hugs and some military hoorahs, and I headed for the marina. I was alone again, and I knew I would be alone for quite some time. However, I still had quarters in my pocket and could call Annika one more time.

Punching in the required quarters, I dialed Annika's home phone. After a few rings, a voice came on the phone and said, "Hello, this is Katherine, may I help you?"

Now, Annika's parents were at a point where they could keep a full-time maid at the house and provide living quarters for her. She recognized my voice, and said, "Oh, Mr. Finn, the family will all be out for several more hours, can I leave a message for Annika?"

Yes, just to leave a message would be great! Aloud I said, "Hello, Katherine. Yes, please take this message for Annika. Please contact my new veteran friend Danny Wakefield and stay close with him. I will call at my first chance, if all goes well in the next six to ten days." I thanked Katherine and hung up.

Danny had become a true friend to whom I had confessed that I had kept Annika in the dark about where I was and how I was traveling, since she could be accused of aiding and abetting me. He understood and had agreed to keep that trust.

I needed to use the remaining daylight to be doubly sure the house was in perfect order for Khaki Man, should he do an inspection. Pam had provided a constant supply of munchies during the afternoon, so I wasn't a bit hungry. Coming and going from the house with caution now, I went down to the docks at dusk, found a place to sit, and just watched. At near dark, a sheriff patrol boat came into the launch with two uniformed men. They went through the drill of backing their trailer into the launch, loading and securing the boat, and leaving. They may have been on patrol for water safety reasons, but I would bet they were also looking for a bank robber.

There were night lights on the docks and one at the end of the parking area, so I could see to make my way back to the house, but I wished I had brought my flashlight as I was trying to jump up on the porch. Dang, it was boogie dark. I fumbled my way in, found the light, and blinked my way into comfort, ready for bed. To read, I just hit the on switch, since the tiny light was perfect for reading, and I returned to the book of Joshua. He had rallied the Israelites and parted the Jordan River at flood stage, and they had all passed through to the Promised Land on dry ground. Now they had a problem—they needed to defeat all the people who were already occupying it. The first big one was the city of Jericho.

I gave up reading at 2100 hours and got comfortable for sleep. I was a bit restless for a while, trying to anticipate the morning, but I calmed as I concentrated on thoughts of being with Annika. Again, I slept so well that I was awakened by my old friend Tonto, pounding on all the tires. I put my hands behind my head, awakening slowly. It didn't last long, as I needed relief quickly, so I peeled out of bed and found the p-u bucket to make its first deposit, liquid only.

I really needed to get a grip, get dressed, put the chair sheet back in place, and be ready to exit, or hide, with very short notice if Khaki Man showed. I was also starting to get hungry. Well, the earlier the better, so I opened a can of hash and ate it slowly as I moved from peep to peep watching and waiting for any action. 0700 moved on to 0800 hours. As a few more players arrived and some loudmouthed directives were being ordered around the area, I circled the interior perimeter of the house, peeking out of every hole that I had made every few minutes.

The barge was loosed from its mooring and moved a short distance into position for a loading ramp and secured again. Then the Mack fired up. I went to the back porch of the house, which overlooked the backside of the Mack. I could see Ole Sarge at the wheel, preparing to drive this powerful pulling machine. He needed to correct the angle of approach to the dock as he engaged the lowest forward gear, nursing a little forward movement into a turn toward the dock. In only seconds of movement, he stopped and reversed the motion, jacking the entire house into a new position, the gravel grinding under the tires as he then headed directly toward the barge.

I was fully ready for Ole Sarge to just drive the house onto the barge, when the Cadillac driven by Khaki Man arrived. However, I must admit that all was poised perfectly for photo opportunities.

A gathering of the players began just outside of the dining room peephole. I could see all the hand motions and animated speech going on but couldn't hear much of anything. Khaki Man never entered the house this time, but he was shooting many photos. The Mack fired up again and began inching toward the ramps. The barge had its own crew for loading, so Tonto and Harold didn't have much to do. I couldn't see how the leveling devices worked on the ramps, but as we moved ever so slowly onto the barge, all seemed to remain quite level. The Mack alone, with the big block of concrete across the axles, had to be over eight tons. But the house, who knew, possibly sixty or eighty tons? The barge had to be about eighty feet long since the house and Mack alone totaled sixty to sixty-five feet. The house was about twenty-four feet wide, and the barge about thirty-two feet, making for a good walkway all around.

I was taken in by it all and lost track of time, but by 1000 hours, the barge crew had everything chained down and ready for travel. Everyone left except the barge—not sure what to call him, a pilot, a barge master, or a captain? I will call him the pilot. So, the paunchy pilot, wearing a very weathered baseball cap, bib overalls, and a flannel shirt with the arms cut off, pulled off the rope tethers from the moorings and went to the pilot's house at the rear starboard side of the barge. As I heard a diesel engine start, I wished that I had paid more attention to the mechanics of this vessel, but I would have time to do that soon.

Unfortunately, I did not have a straight-on view of the pilot house and could not make one. The windows were in just the wrong place. I was surprised, at first, that there were no other crew on board, since this thing seemed quite large for one man to operate. But what did I know, I was just along for the ride—a very slow, but very safe, ride. I heard what sounded like a stick shift transmission changing gears, then the diesel engine added RPMs, and our floating mass began to move. The pilot took the loaded barge out to mid-river and added just a little more fuel to the diesel. I was moving from peephole to peephole for half an hour or so, finally realizing that this was it. I was on the river, moving closer to my goal.

I went to the dining room table, pulled out my chair, and sat down to think. I reckoned that there was a good reason to continue my daily regimen. I did calisthenics for the next two hours, then rested in my living room chair. But prior to continuing with the book of Joshua, I looked more carefully at the book selections in the glass door cabinets. A great deal of these books were of the whodunit, mystery, or action thriller variety. Quite the collection, but most of the authors were unknown to me, except a booklet on Frank Lloyd Wright. I finally settled on the good book. Joshua had success at Jericho and had many battles to come. The Promised Land was for the most part subdued, and the land was divided between the twelve tribes of Israel.

It was amazing how stable the house was while traveling down the road, but this ride was leaps and bounds above that—I barely felt any movement! I moved to my living room chair, stretched out, and went to sleep in short order. I awoke in a start at 1300 hundred hours, anxious about the day, but slowly realizing that there was nothing to be in a hurry about. I made my way to the back porch of the house. It was a small area containing the cabinet I had put the fishing pole in. It also had a tall chair with arms and a backrest.

Now, the door from the kitchen to the back porch was substantial, but the exit door from the porch to the exterior was a lightweight door with twelve glass panels and a push button lock that worked from the inside only. I took a dare with myself and opened the door, which swung inside. I thought about removing the paper, but just opening the door was easier. I moved the tall chair against the kitchen door to hold it open. I sat in the chair facing the river in the direction of travel. It proved to be an unobstructed view.

It was like a king's seat! Full view of the river ahead, boats passing downstream, boats passing upstream, many pontoons and houseboats with vacationers yet to head home. From my perch, I was in the shadows, and I doubted that any of the passersby could even see me. However, many people pointed at the house and watched curiously as we floated by. I only left the spot to acquire snacks and canned food for the remainder of the day. The shadows were beginning to grow long when I began to hear changes in the engine speed and the direction of travel. The pilot eased the barge into the moorings, which had no infrastructure around them. This mooring had walking planks about the perimeter but no bridge access to land. The engine went silent as the pilot left his cabin and tied off at three places along the side and rear of the barge.

The pilot did a walk around the barge, looking at this and that, then climbed down onto a small screen metal deck at the port side rear of the barge. I had not seen the aluminum boat, with a fifteen horse

Evinrude motor, floating along behind us. The pilot pull started the motor and sped back the way we had come at ten times our speed downstream.

Wonderful! It was 1900 hours, with plenty of sunlight remaining. I put on the orange vest and hard hat, got the fishing pole and tackle box, then jumped down onto the steel deck of the barge. Danny had given me a few pointers on baits, so I began the cast and reel, hoping for bass. I worked my way around most of the perimeter. I then climbed down onto the plank walkways affixed to the moorings. I tried several baits, but no luck. I switched to hook and bobber, using small chunks of spam again. It worked, and within thirty minutes, I caught three nice eight-inch sunfish, perfect for supper.

I gathered up my cooking bucket, a handful of charcoal, the charcoal lighter, the fry pan, and anything else I needed. I fired up the charcoal and let it preheat while I filleted the three fish. I just chummed the water with innards and bones. There were several plastic five-gallon pails sitting here and there on the deck, so I turned two of them upside down near my charcoal oven–one for a table, one for my butt. Nice. I also opened a can of string beans, drained off the water, and poured them into the fry pan. I had already added a generous amount of corn oil, and that began to sizzle. I added the six filets after the beans had a minute to cook. All was ready in just four minutes, and I slid it all onto a plate. Just a little salt and pepper, and I was eating in high style.

Time to clean up. Everything that I had went back on the porch first, then I took the charcoal bucket and stepped down onto the heavy screen deck at the base of the stern, just six inches above the water, and quenched the fire. When everything was secured in the house, I got comfortable and ready for bed with the last of the daylight. It was time to read, but I had to recount everything I had observed on the barge as I was fishing. First, the pilot's house, a small rectangular cabin made of steel and glass with rounded corners. Black rubber glazing held all the glass in place. The front and two sides were made like awnings, so the pilot could open them in the heat of the day. It was only three feet wide and six feet long, full of controls and gauges. It was locked.

Behind the pilot house was the power plant, which looked like a huge outboard boat motor, but without all the cutesy coverings. All the wiring, cables, hoses, and gadgets were exposed, like all the old tractors.

It was all on a turret, which could rotate 180 degrees to the left or to the right. In front of the pilot house was a ten-kilowatt generator and welding cables locked in a storage cage alongside it. In front of the generator was the diesel fuel tank, which probably held a thousand gallons of fuel. Both the starboard and port side of the barge had steel pipe posts, eight feet tall, every ten feet with lights on top. Three cables, each gaining a foot in altitude, were stretched tightly down each side to form a safety fence.

I had noticed other things as I fished, like the four corners of the barge held what I would call a pike. Each was a seven-foot pole, or shaft of wood, probably ash or hickory, with a steel hook on the end. They looked like a handheld tool for mooring the barge or for launching. I could only hope to look more carefully tomorrow. On the port side was a small rectangular box with a door and louvers instead of windows, all made of steel. It had the word "HEAD" stenciled on the door. It looked locked, but when I had gone to inspect, I had found it was open. YES. Farther down toward the bow from the head was another container about the same size, with a steel screen door that was unlocked. It contained heavy tools for dealing with objects the barge may be hauling, along with chains, turnbuckles, binders, and the like.

Enough thought of the barge for tonight. I would look closer at my mode of escape tomorrow. Pulling my sheet from the living room chair, I rolled up in bed with double pillows to read for a while. The book of Joshua was action packed as the Israelites conquered the Promised Land. I woke up, the Bible still in my hands, as daylight peeked through any place that would allow it. I rested in bed thinking about Tonto thumping the tires like an alarm clock. What would happen today that I could mark as a time to get my butt out of bed?

At around 0700 hours I could hear the sound of an outboard motor nearing the barge. I went to the leaded glass entry door at the porch and peeked through the prism glass to see the pilot of the barge. He tied off his aluminum boat to the stern of the barge and climbed onboard. He went to three places on the barge that were tied and pulled the ropes onboard. But on number three, the rope was apparently too tight, so he went to the nearest corner of the vessel and grabbed a pike. Returning to the mooring rope, he quickly maneuvered the pike through the rope, pulled hard on the wood shaft, and made enough slack to set the mooring rope free. The pilot then replaced the pike and entered his tiny house. He soon started the engine of his giant outboard motor and let it idle for a few minutes.

The pilot used caution while leaving the moorings, as the engine of this barge was very powerful. It could probably cause damage to the moorings if misused. But we were on our way again, as I was beginning to get hungry. I decided to eat something different this morning—canned hash. Well, the thought was nice. I added a can of sweet cherries to the morning menu, and they were really good. As it was still a little cool, I decided to do my regimen of calisthenics and charged hard into them for the next two hours. I had thrown the sheet back onto my chair and sat long enough to do a good cool down. I did a spit bath, using the bathroom sink, but didn't drain the water yet.

I gathered up the good book and made my way to the back porch, where I set up the tall chair and plopped in my king's seat facing upriver as we slowly floated toward Hoboken. Like most rivers, we were either turning toward the starboard or toward the port, rarely in a straight line.

I do not remember a time of being so relaxed. This was forced relaxation, but it was working since I could all but forget that I was on the lam. I finished reading about Joshua and all the conquered land, along with his farewell exhortation to the leaders of the Israelites. I then moved on to Judges, an interesting time in the history of the Israelites since they had no central government. Judges arose as God saw fit to keep them out of trouble.

After resting my eyes and eating some munchies, I decided to read the pamphlet about Frank Lloyd Wright. He was an amazing architect, far ahead of his time, or just with an idea about architecture far different from any designer of the time. His insistence on absolute quality and perfection drove suppliers and contractors crazy, but he paid good money for the work—or his customers did! He spent a lot of time on the job sites nit-picking the managers of the work. By the time he was finished with the interior design, there wasn't much space for the home-owners to put their own collections of photos or art. But the interiors of these homes were extremely beautiful. On one occasion, he showed up several years after the wealthy owners of one of his houses had moved in. He presented them with a vase that he had been hunting for. It was to be displayed on their fireplace mantle. He removed their personal decorations and placed the vase at the center, and of course, it looked perfect. Interesting man.

I greatly enjoyed reading as we passed boats of endless variety, mostly vacationers. Occasionally there was a boat with serious fishermen onboard. Somewhere in my relaxed stupor, time passed and the pilot began the maneuvers for mooring. Again, there was infrastructure for tying off the vessel, but no connection to land. At the pilot's satisfaction, he hopped down into his boat, started the motor, and sped back upstream.

I was ready for bass fishing and started casting as soon as he was out of sight. It was a replay of last night—no bass, and only two redear sunfish, but they were a bit bigger than the first. I cooked the redear in the same way, cleaned all that I could clean, put everything away, and prepared to go in and relax.

I was still wearing the orange vest and hard hat, ready to jump up on the porch, when I heard a boat approaching at a great speed. I looked up to see a sheriff officer shouting into an electric megaphone, "Stop! Cease and desist! We will be boarding your vessel!"

13: CONCRETE KID

OH, THIS BEAUTIFUL DAY, reduced to a sour ball in my gut in a matter of seconds. The two-man crew in the sheriff's boat nearly crashed into the steel landing deck, as one of them nimbly negotiated the steel screen and jumped up onto the main deck just in front of me. I instinctively put my hands up and stared at him like a deer in the headlights. It was nearing dusk, but there was still plenty of light to see as he came face to face, his right hand on the strap of his pistol holster. He looked closer at my face, blinked a few times, and said, "Oh, it's you."

I recognized him too. "You're the officer who challenged me back at the Dixie Union dock." I looked at his badge, "Hello, Officer Bradley, how are you?"

He laughed a bit, "We thought we may have caught the river thief. And you were correct in that you would not be seen at the launch, but you would have a presence around the house while on the river."

I said, "Rules of the Vandoorne Agency." I added, "I'm a young, new agent so I get the shit jobs, but hopefully it will be worth it. Have you had any success with leads for Catfish John, or whatever they called him?"

"We've been looking for him for nearly thirty years, but he is real, not a myth. After the bank robberies, we became very determined to catch him."

The sheriff wished me well, got back into his boat, and left, never asking me for an ID. I breathed many sighs of relief.

I made ready for the evening, turning on the radio and turning the volume up so I could hear the top songs as I moved through the house preparing for night. It was a pain, but I took my good bucket down through the hatch and placed it under the bath sink drainpipe, went back up, washed my hands, took a spit bath, and let the sink drain down into the bucket. Again climbing back down, I dumped it over the side, and then filled it with fresh river water, putting it back into the bathroom. It was getting dark enough by then that I needed to employ my blinking flashlight to prepare for night number two on the river, June 1.

As I positioned my head just right for reading, I started the book of Judges. Joshua had passed away, and he was laid to rest with his forefathers. Again, without a central government, our Father put in place judges, sometimes warriors, to bail out the Israelites from their backsliding. The first was Othniel, then Ehud, then Shamgar, then Deborah and Barack, and then Gideon. Gideon was a farm boy who resisted his commission from God to fight the Midian army. He had a weird way of selecting his fighting men, but he won all the battles.

As the batteries in the flashlight began to dim, it was a sign for me to catch a little shut-eye. It was so calm on the river that I didn't remember anything, until the pilot's outboard motor came sputtering up to the rear of the barge. I remained in bed, listening to his activities of unhitching the barge. The power plant started and idled for a while. Then gentle movement ensued, with wide sweeping turns, as he put the barge in line with the river. Then with more RPMs to the diesel engine, we were on our way into day three.

It was a replay of day two: one can of cold hash, and one can of fruit. I was already jonesing for the River View Restaurant, but oh well. Next, two hours of calisthenics and a rest period. I had fresh water in jugs for brushing teeth and to drink, but I used river water with a bit of soap to wash my pits. It was only 1000 hours, and I had the entire day ahead of me, so I went to my king's chair on the back porch, opened the in-swing door, put the tall chair against it, and sat down high on the chair, looking downrange in the direction of travel.

For achievers, it is so desperately hard to just let time pass. I was an achiever, and this was as tough as it gets. But, having absolutely no choice in the matter at this time, I was gaining tolerance for it. A person can actually go much deeper into their thoughts, and I did. I went back to the most traumatic time of my life, when I knew that I was probably going to die. Hours passed then, as they are now; I didn't die then, and with patience, I could survive this strangest of prison vacations too.

I think I was in a self-induced trance, when I shook my head and just looked at the surroundings. Looking to port, I observed an old wood yacht, mostly buried in the riverbank, and almost completely sunk. It had been there for years. Scanning slowly to the right, back into the cypress swamp, my eye glimpsed what looked like a man-made structure many yards back into the tag alders. It was old and rotten, covered with moss and dried algae. If it weren't for my elevated position above the river, I may never have seen it. I caught the slightest glimpse of the bow of a small aluminum boat trimmed with worn red paint, on the opposite side of the horizontally positioned old planks, forming a low parapet wall.

I was absolutely positive that it was the boat I saw when Catfish John made his getaway back at the Dixie Union Marina. I wanted to jump out, run back to the pilot and yell for him to stop, but I couldn't. I marked the position in my mind—the old boat on the north side, cypress on the south. But behind the cypress, the swamp must have had a little high ground, as a hundred yards back in, I could see the top of a moss-covered live oak nearly obscured by cypress trees.

At a point when I was so close to total relaxation, my mind was set on edge, and there was nothing I could do about it but ponder. My thoughts were racing, wondering if it was possible that I might have just discovered the whereabouts of the infamous river pirate Catfish John. My entire future was a blank, but I knew I would never forget this location. I surmised that even the tallest boat in the sheriff's fleet would never be high enough to see what I was able to see. It's no wonder that even with all the searching over all the years, Catfish John had never been found.

I had jumped out of the chair and was standing in the doorway, leaning out as far as I could to absorb every detail that I could in the passing view. I finally sat back down, a half shit eating grin on my face, wondering how I might use this information to my advantage. The possibilities were befuddling, so I encouraged myself to just enjoy the moment, as I now had a new tool in my bag. I must have sat there for several hours, just watching the river go by, but the old wooden highboy chair finally got the best of my butt, so I went back into the house and looked for a snack. Animal crackers looked pretty good, and I ate several packets. I got out the fishing pole and the tackle box, and mounted a bass lure I had not tried yet. I would be ready to fish when the barge was moored. Time to read, and my living room chair looked dang good.

Continuing the reading in Judges, I learned many temporary leaders were put in charge, good ones and bad ones, up to the time of Samson. He was a great leader and warrior, but weak-headed when it came to women. Even after being blinded, he managed to bring down 3,000 of the primary leaders of the Philistines, including Delilah. I might need to read about Samson again.

I found myself able to nap for a short while that afternoon, then sat down and wrote letters to Annika, my parents, Pastor Roy, and finally to Danny. I addressed and licked stamps for all four envelopes, and as a return address, I used:

Concrete Kid
J. Bird Blvd.
Freedom, Florida 22711

Hopefully they would all have a laugh with that, especially 22711, my inmate number, if I could ever get them to a mailbox. I kept the radio tuned to the rock and roll station in Jacksonville most of the time. A new song was being played entitled, "Tired of Being Alone" by Al Green. Oh, how I could relate to that. So many new people in my life, but all at a distance. So many other songs were introduced, it was hard to keep up, like, "A Horse With No Name" by America, "Wild Horses" by The Rolling Stones, or, get this, "Take Me Home, Country Roads" by John Denver. The songs were fantastic! And how about this while you are on the river, "I Feel the Earth Move" by Carole King? Yup. I can relate!

I returned to the back porch, sat in the high chair to watch as the river went by and the pilot would maneuver us to a new mooring site. All was quiet for an hour or so, when I heard a boat motor slowly passing on the port side. Soon enough an old wood speed boat pulled slowly by, with three young men as passengers, one as the pilot. All three appeared to be barefoot, wearing bib overalls and very worn T-shirts. They were pointing at this and that on the house, then accelerated and moved on. As I sat in the shadows of the porch, I knew they couldn't see me. Other boats and pontoons passed as well, all looking at this strange sight moving down the river. But, there were many more passing in the opposite direction, some slowing for a better look as well.

As the day began to grow gray hair and we approached 1800 hours, I watched as the next mooring site came into view. I held my position until the pilot had the barge squared away into the moorings. I stayed put in the house as he exited the pilot house and headed for the three primary corners to tie off. Only minutes had passed when I heard the outboard motor start on his boat, throttle engage, and the boat head fast back upriver. Time to fish!

I donned the hard hat and vest again, jumped down on the deck, breathed in a lung full of the southern Georgia hot fresh air, and looked for the first place to cast my newly mounted bait. Working my way counterclockwise around the perimeter of the barge, I made countless casts and reels. As I approached the moorings on the opposite side, where the cattails and lily pads began to get in the way—FISH ON! Holy bats—the drag was set too tight!

I loosened it quickly as the fish headed for open water. I thought for a second that I had given it too much slack, so I added back more drag and finally began to crank him in. The fish had a slower and steady hard pull, but this guy was going nuts. I kept up the slow reeling in as the fish was tiring out. I had no landing net, so I laid down on the steel deck, raising the pole as high as possible with my right hand and reaching down as far as I could with my left, and caught a finger in his gill.

I had the biggest bass I had ever caught, at least four pounds. All other thoughts went out the window, but I had plenty of daylight remaining to figure out what to do. I went back into the house and got the Instamatic camera, took a couple of photos of the catch, put the camera back, and came out with tools to filet it. With a half dozen trips back and forth into the house, I had charcoal burning in the bucket, oil deep in the fry pan, and fish bubbling in the oil. I couldn't possibly eat all the fish, but it would all be cooked. I had never had bass for breakfast, but perhaps tomorrow would be a first.

I was out of ideas for adding to the meal, so I sliced and diced an onion, and put it all into the bubbling oil. The filets came out first and had time to cool as I let the onions become nearly crisp. I ate half the bass, all the onions, and a can of pears. All I needed was a couple of good burps and all would be right with the world.

While sitting on one of my inverted buckets, I could see under the house and noticed something that I hadn't seen yet. There was a very heavy grating deck, possibly ten feet wide, through the center of at least two-thirds of the entire deck. I shimmied under the house and could see through the grating to the water below. At either end, the first twenty feet or so were steel plate. I then jumped down on one of the heavy mesh platforms at the stern and could see that the barge was actually built like a catamaran. There was a ten-foot gap between the starboard and port side steel flotation tanks, with this grating covering some two-thirds through the center of the deck. I no longer needed to worry about draining the sinks or the bathtub, as all would go straight through the grating into the river. YES!

I joyfully washed all the dishes, using plenty of soap, and pulled the drain plugs. I always took about a dozen trips with a two-gallon bucket to adequately fill the bathtub, and I did this time as well. I counted it as part of my daily exercise regimen. However, I would leave the water in the tub until some future time when it had gained another ten or fifteen degrees of daytime temperature.

As day three on the river was coming to a close, I tidied the house in the last of the daylight, brushed my teeth, and crawled into bed with the good book. Picking up on Judges 13, I read again how God granted an unlikely elderly couple the ability to conceive a child, which they name Samson. Now it seems that everyone has heard of the story of Samson, whether they were taught biblically or not. Unlike the superheroes of today, Samson was truly a brutally tough man. His strength was sanctioned by the Father. His entire story consists of slightly more than three pages in the Bible. But from birth to death in those short pages, he bent the history of the Israelites and is remembered three thousand years later. Try that!

It was an easy day, and I was getting sleepy anyway. I sat the book down on the nightstand and turned off the tiny light coming from the flashlight. Adjusting the pillow to sleeping mode and breathing deep and slow for a while, I thought about how utterly peaceful and quiet it was out here on the river. I reminisced about things in my childhood back home in Michigan. I gave personal thanks for having a stable and safe home to grow up in. There was a rhythm in my brain that at first was putting me to sleep but slowly gained authority. I realized I was hearing an outboard boat motor moving slowly past the barge, and then it stopped at the stern.

I heard voices, low but squeaky, then foot movement on the steel deck. My denims were on the floor at my feet, and I slipped into them in a short second, the same with my T-shirt. I needed to blink the flashlight to locate the old prison shoes, put them on, and head to the hatch.

As I moved my way toward it, I could see flashlights moving past the windows. I opened the hatch quietly and descended under the house. Now, all the axles and tires supporting the house were in two rows, one to the left and one to the right. There was a gap of some five or six feet in between the two rows, making an open path the full length of the house. Then, each side had two tandem axles, parallel to each other. Each tandem set had eight tires. I think there were at least six tandem sets on each side of the house. I could not crawl in the midst of the tandems, but between each set was a four-foot gap that anyone could crouch down and maneuver through.

I hardly needed to use my light, as there were three people waving flashlights as they made their way around the house. As I was trying to get a grip on some sort of strategy, they converged on the opposite side of the barge. It gave me a moment to blink my way to the opposite corner of the barge and slip out one of the pikes, then move back under the axle carriages. Having no clue what might happen next, I waited near the midpoint of the house. The three individuals separated again and began to return around each side of the house, their flashlights flailing about as if they were not concentrating on anything. Two went to starboard, one went port, so I went to port and made ready between axle sets. I waited as number three worked his way toward the stern, flashing his light on everything. Just as he was about to pass my axle set, I quickly shoved the pike out between his feet and held tight. It worked! It tripped him in a most magnificent way, and he splattered face first onto the steel deck.

It was all I could do to keep from laughing out loud. It took him longer than I would have expected to right himself, stand back up, and stagger to the stern sputtering, "This damn house is haunted. This damn house is haunted."

The other two were headed down the starboard side toward the stern, their flashlights zooming in every direction too. I moved one axle set toward the stern on their side and waited. I let the first guy go by then put into play the exact same move as before, slipping the blunt end of the pike in front of the next step of second guy. Blam! He hit the deck hard, just behind his friend. Again, it took a while for him to recover and stand back up. Then he started pushing on the other guy, saying, "This damn house is haunted! This damn house is haunted!"

At that point, I should have sat still, but I waddled my way down through the center to the stern. I stayed well behind the shadows of the tires as the three joined forces.

"I put my dang light back on the place where I tripped. Weren't nothin' there!"

Another said, "Same for me, this place is haunted!" They jumped back into their boat, hollering, "Start that motor, Billy, get the hell out of here!" It was the same three redneck brats that had cruised slowly by the barge earlier in the day. I could only hope they found what they were looking for, some form of adventure!

I blinked my way back to bed, chuckling as I fell asleep. Again, my brain was sensing a rhythmic beat that continued to get louder and louder, my eyes opening to dim light coming through the blinds. It was day four, and the sound was the pilot, tying off and boarding. I was seriously considering sleeping in for a while, since I could do that if I wished. But what would Annika do? I put my feet on the floor and sat for a minute, realizing that I needed to pee really bad. After taking care of business, brushing my teeth, and partially dressing, I waited until the barge was on its way downriver, then started a two-hour regimen of exercise.

It was difficult to get a good cardio rhythm going, but jumping jacks and squat thrusts came quite close. I also found that the oak trim above the opening from the dining area to the living room supported my weight for pull-ups. YES!

I had kept several plastic bags, just in case of a need, and had used one to cover the leftover fish. I pulled the plate from the bag and sat at the dining table for a breakfast of cold bass, canned applesauce, and a glass of fruit juice. I ate a little more than half the fish and saved the rest for a snack later in the day. After cleaning up, I went to the desk and checked the calendar. Memorial Day was May 28. This was day four on the river, putting me at June 1 and nineteen days on the lam. For crying out crosswise, it sure seemed longer than that. My ankles were completely healed, only the scars remaining, but you know, I bet it was still quite fresh on the mind of Sheriff Stump!

I had been fully enjoying the forward view, high in the tall chair. I gathered a few snacks, water, and the Bible, then put the doors in position and sat down in comfort. It was a gorgeous day, somewhat warmer than normal. In the back of my mind I was thinking the bath water may acquire a more desirable temperature today for a bath this evening.

I started the book of Ruth, the eighth book of the Bible and the third of twelve books on the history of the Jewish tribes. It's basically a love story, the love of Ruth for her widowed mother-in-law, Naomi. Ruth, a gentile, later married Boaz, a Jew, and their offspring were among the ancestors of Jesus, a thousand years before his birth.

At about 1300 hours, I ate the remainder of the bass, along with a half sleeve of saltine crackers and a glass of juice. It was time for a short nap in my living room chair. About forty minutes later, I woke up full of energy but no way to burn it off. I pondered the idea of doing the calisthenics all over again. At least in prison, there was something to do every day. It really was a strange form of solitude, my own mental punishment for walking out of Richmond County Jail. However, I was thinking that those anxious feelings were always temporary as I went back to the tall chair for the late afternoon scenic cruise.

As we made our way slowly down the river, I occasionally noticed live oaks on the higher ground and thought about Catfish John. Could that have really been the front deck of his boat that I saw? Is it possible that his hideout was back among the oaks somewhere? Will I ever have a chance to go looking for him or his hideout? Will I be able to give the location to the sheriff of that county some day? Could I use the information as a plea bargain? My imagination and thoughts lasted long enough to see another mooring coming up in the distance, and the changing sounds of the barge were evidence of a landing soon.

As we approached the mooring docks, I could see several fishermen at work, which was different, as there were no boats. Once the mooring was complete and the pilot took off in his boat, I donned my hard hat and vest, walked out on the porch, and shut the door just hard enough to draw a little attention. I got down off the porch, walked across the barge to the dock, and stepped on to it, hopefully looking like I owned the place. I walked to the fishermen, who were sitting on folding chairs and said, "Hello, gentlemen, what is biting this evening?"

One ole fart looked at the other and said, "Shucks, Willie, you see any gentlemen round here?"

Willie said, "Nope, don't see none, but the sunfish is bitin' fine! Teehee, haha!"

I laughed too, then asked them how they had gotten there, since

I saw no boats. They turned their heads toward a thicket of trees behind the moorings and explained that there was a dirt path back there and room for several cars. I asked how far it was to the next town, and if it had a pay phone. They explained it was about six miles to Sunnyside, but there wasn't much there. I thanked them, knowing the walk would be too far and possibly held nothing I needed, and went for my tackle box and rod. Baiting the hook for sunfish, I sat on a plastic pail and began to fish.

One of the fishermen hollered over, "What is the deal with that house? We see a lot of strange stuff a floatin' down this river, but that's the first time for a house."

I took my best guess, explaining that it was built by a very famous designer back in the 1920s and was being moved to a new site to be preserved as a historical monument. They nodded their heads as if they understood me and kept on fishing.

I had a few nibbles and needed to add new bait, but the bobber suddenly went nearly out of sight! A sunfish with plenty of fight, so I let him work until he was tired then reeled him in. He was at least ten inches long, maybe eleven, so he went into the bucket. I baited and cast back in, while the other fishermen had caught at least three more. A few minutes later I caught another, this one about a nine-incher, which was enough for supper. The bucket and utensil drill began. Lighting the charcoal first, I set up my dining area and supplied it. This evening I added canned sweet corn to the fry pan along with the four filets. I could have eaten all four, but I saved one for tomorrow, since this morning's bass was definitely good.

The fishermen watched occasionally as I cooked and ate my meal. To them, it probably looked normal. Then they left with their catch. With daylight remaining I grabbed the fry pan and headed up the path toward the parking area, hoping for some sand to scrub out the pan. I was in luck and cleaned it thoroughly. Back at the house I washed it with soap and water. When everything was cleaned up, I went to the tub of almost lukewarm water, stripped, and climbed in. A bit of soap here and there, and then I just soaked. I called it quits as the house began to go dark, and I got ready for bed. I turned on the radio for a while, scanning the ban, and found a bluegrass station, not the kind of music to rest by, but it really spiked my interest. The only bluegrass music

I had heard was the intro to the *Beverly Hillbillies*. Now I heard names like Earl Scruggs, Doc Watson, Lester Flatt, and Ricky Skaggs; it was foot stomping. I noted the channel and moved on, finding a good southern gospel station, which was much better for preparing for sleep.

I finally gave up and got into bed, rolled up in my sheet, stacked the pillows for some reading, and finished the short book of Ruth. Marking the page for the book of 1 Samuel, I placed the Bible back on the night shelf. Pushing the second pillow out of the way, I snuggled in for sleep, which must have happened quickly. At the point of slipping into the land of Nod, my brain was recording a rhythmic beat once again. I wanted so bad to let it go, but my senses put me at alert. Opening my eyes in the dark, I listened, and again I could hear the sound of a boat motor moving slowly alongside, then to the stern. The brats were back, and this time they would get clobbered!

I dressed the same way again, dropping down through the hatch with my flashlight. I waited for quite a while, then saw a very tiny light, like mine but on full time, its movements slow and purposeful, making its way around the house. It took several minutes for the tiny light to go completely around the barge, then it went to the tool cage, where I could hear some metal clanging. I worked my way closer to the stern through the center bay of tires. Then I heard a loud thud, enough to break steel. I didn't think it was the brats anymore, and I got a bit of a cold chill, but now my senses are where they should be—on high alert. I could hear one of the metal cage doors open, a rustling of things, then the tiny light and footsteps went back to the stern, where something flopped onto the deck. Someone was there to steal whatever they could get.

I had been stationary, but now I needed to take some form of action, so I moved close enough to the stern to make a blink or two as the footsteps headed back to the cage. It was welding cables in a pile. There was a lot of that sort of thing in that cage, and soon enough the footsteps were returning. As the tiny light appeared near the cables, I could see a pair of very worn sneakers and totally worn-out trouser legs. As soon as he went for another load, I blinked my way straight out the back and to the port corner to get a pike. I was quick about it, but silent. I thought that what this thief was taking was only the valuable things he could get, except for empty plastic buckets and the pikes.

I moved to the port side rear corner of the house, but not under it. He returned with what must have been his last load, then went to his boat with it. The guy was holding the tiny flashlight in his mouth, so as the light turned to the boat, I gave my light one flash, which for a half second, lit him like a Christmas tree. He couldn't have noticed, and didn't, but what I saw was the guy that had been fussing with his boat back at the marina. It was Catfish John! My brain first sent a wave of fear down my spine, as this man used a gun in the bank robberies. But it quickly changed to one of anger. This piece of shit was on my barge! I watched as he loaded all the copper cables onto his boat; they were heavy, and his boat sunk down several inches.

With a junior mall beater in his hand, he shined his light toward the back door of the house. It looked like he chewed on the light for a while, pondering. Then in a flash, he was up on the porch, concentrating the tiny light on the door. I knew the deck was unobstructed and moved silently in behind him, not even needing to blink my light, so I slipped it in my back pocket, then held both hands on the pike.

He had no idea that I was right behind him as he raised the beater to bust out the stained glass window. I had placed the pike directly between his legs, which were spread wide in preparation of his hammer blow. At the twitch of the light that would have indicated the start of his swing, I heaved up on the pike with snapping strength.

14. SOM-BITZ

THE CRY OF TRUE pain was ear-piercing as he dropped the beater directly onto his right foot. The tiny light he held in his mouth immediately went out; he must have bitten on it too hard. I backed up a step or two as his agony continued, retrieved my flashlight from my back pocket, and blinked to see Catfish, laying on his side, completely out of his mind. I placed the pike against the back of the house and blinked again to see him now struggling to move from the porch.

Now what the hell should I do with this guy? My mind was racing as I thought to tie him up! He was already trying to escape, when he fell from the porch to the steel deck, which made him go limp. Thinking I had a minute, I turned the flashlight peep on full and raced around the barge looking for something to tie him up with. I didn't find a darn thing, and as I rounded the opposite side, I saw him struggling to find his way in the dark toward his boat. The guy wasn't much more than a midget, but tough as nails.

I blinked him several times as he fought for consciousness and again tried to move toward his boat, fighting the pain as he went. I wanted to feel sorry for him, but instead, I retrieved the pike, blinked him for accuracy, and thumped him hard on the side of his hairy head. There was groaning, but no more movement. In the interim of deciding what to do, I took all the cables he intended to steal and piled them on top of him; they were heavy enough to buy me time to think. Then it came to me—duct tape.

I had to return to the house through the hatch, found my new roll of duct tape, and exited through the front door onto the porch and down onto the deck. The duct tape came with a tough plastic wrapper that needed to be removed first! Should I curse the manufacturer, or myself for not being prepared? The wrapper needed to be cut with my Boy Scout knife just to be able to use the tape! I suppose I was a bit frantic at this point but controlled enough to start with his hands first. I moved the cables off him, tossing them to the side, rolled him on his belly and taped his wrists tight. As an extra measure, I pulled tape around his gut two times. His hands and arms were totally bound.

As I looked at his legs, I grabbed them and pulled them together for the tape, but then, having a much better thought, I went back into the house to the bottom drawer of my dresser. I returned with the leg-irons that scared me so badly. Looking at the clasps that I bent off nearly a month ago, I placed them on his ankles, then went to the porch and picked up the beater that Catfish dropped on his foot and proceeded to pound the clasps back tight on each leg.

Checking my watch, I saw it was nearly 2300 hours. I sat my butt up on the porch, just to ponder about Catfish. What in the heck do I do now? While he was seemingly unconscious, I searched all his pockets. He had a wallet snapped into his bib pocket, which I removed and looked at. There was no identification, only cash of all denominations, including a $100 bill. My sixth sense told me to record the serial number on that bill, so I jumped back into the house and wrote it down, then snapped the wallet back into his bib.

Adrenaline was remaining at a high level—think, Nick, think! As he moaned a little, I thought it best to put the cables back into the cage, and while doing so, I looked at the lock mechanism to see if any repair was possible. I grabbed the beater and bent things back in order; at a glance it looked normal, but it didn't work completely. I noticed several canvas sacks in the bottom, and it gave me an idea. They held chains, so I dumped one out and took the bag with me back to Catfish. The bag had a drawstring and was just the right size to pull over the man's head. He had not seen me, nor heard my voice, so why not keep it that way? I pulled it over his head, as he began to come to a bit, and drew the strings together. As bad as the man smelled, he probably had lice, and the bag may help keep them in.

I finally sat back down on the edge of the porch and just breathed easy for a while. What were my options? I could just dump him over the side, and a gator would find him soon enough. I could put him in the house and tape him to the kitchen floor. I could put him in his boat and just push it out into the river, and someone would find him tomorrow but may let him go. I was not going to hand-feed and water this piece of shit for the remainder of the trip, while he peed and pooped himself.

I'd put him in the boat, start the motor, leave it running slowly, and point it down the river.

OK, time for the help of King Leo, a big pink mint. I got two, in case one wasn't enough, and sat back down on the porch. Halfway through the first mint, I realized I didn't need the tiny hole on the light for a while and removed my pinhole lens carefully. Then I thought about seeing what he had in his boat, which looked about fifteen feet long and beat up. It was a clutter of miscellaneous junk, including all kinds of rope that I could have tied him up with! In the back near the outboard motor were two five-gallon fuel tanks, and they were both full. There were also two one-gallon tin cans full of fuel. He had a ten-horse motor on this thing, which should make it fairly fast. I took the second mint from my shirt pocket and went back to think for a little longer.

It was nearly midnight, but what I really needed to do was get him to a place with a pay phone nearby and call the sheriff's office. The only one I knew of was back in Dixie Union. If the barge pilot could make it back there each night and farther downstream each day, perhaps I could too. I had just finished the second mint, realizing I had a plan. I thanked King Leo for the calming assistance but then thought that this was probably a time when I should be asking the Father above for safety and success on this next mission. I did.

I didn't care much to touch the guy, but I needed to muscle him into the boat and lay him mid-deck between the two seats. He was slowly coming around. I went back in the house and got another pair of batteries for the flashlight and filled my trusty pint full of water. I boarded the boat, untied the bow, pushed off, and stepped around Catfish to the stern seat to start the motor. I examined it, read the worn instruction labels, flipped the choke, pulled the start rope, and fired it straight off. It didn't have a reverse lever, so I rotated the motor about three-quarters of the way around and gave it a little gas. We moved gently away from the moorings and the barge. When the distance was about right, I rotated the motor back, gave it more gas to move out toward the main body of the river, then opened the throttle slowly to become accustomed to the feel.

The boat began to plane off nicely at about three-fourths throttle, so I went full throttle. It was about quarter moon on a very calm night, so I could see what I needed to see as we seemed to nearly skim across the top of the water. I could negotiate the twists and turns in the river in seconds, where the barge would take a half an hour. I shined the light on my cargo about every half hour, and at about 0130 hours he started thrashing around. Just before 0200 hours I spotted the old sunken yacht and slowed to a stop, letting the motor just idle.

Catfish was now groaning and trying to sit up. I crouched over him and began to maneuver him onto the front bench seat.

He was feeling the pain and started cussing at me, "Yo som-bitz, yo som-bitz!" He sobbed, "Yo som-bitz, yo hurt me! My hind parts is throbbin', my head is too, yo som-bitz. Why can't I see, yo som-bitz, talk to me, who yo is?"

Remaining silent, I wrapped my left hand around the back of his neck, squeezing tight, then I loosened the sack tether with my right hand and pulled the sack to his forehead. I shined the light on the old yacht, aiming his head at it, and gave him a few seconds to take it in. I knew when it hit home, as he stiffened up, inhaled, and held his breath. I pulled the bag back down, snugged the strings, then went to the motor, added some gas, and moved toward the opposite side of the river. I knew I could never find his secret entrance at night, but I may get close enough to cast light on the live oaks.

Catfish was squirming and sobbing but didn't speak as we crossed the river. I put the bow of the boat up to the lily pads and tag alders, as near to the spot I saw his boat as I could guess. I could see the tops of the live oaks, YES! I once again squeezed his neck, loosened the tethers on the bag, and slid it up on his head. I had no trouble maneuvering his head to view the light shining on the oaks.

He stiffened again and broke his silence, "How in Hal yo know wheres I live? Yo da FBI? No som-bitz know where I live!" He groaned out, "Talk to me, who you is? Yo hurt me bad, my hine-parts is swellin' up, my head is too. Yo still alive, so I knows yo didn't try da get back to my place, haha."

Then he mumbled, "Ol' Catfish gotta surprise for some dodo what tries to get back in there. Oh Lordy, I is hurtin' so bad."

I did pay attention to that, as I replaced the bag on his head.

He responded, "This sack stinks bad, my hind parts is killin' me," as I spun the motor around to back away from the lily pads and headed down the river once again.

I was pleasantly surprised at 0300 hours when I could see the night lights from the Dixie Union harbor. I idled down, maneuvering into the harbor and as close as possible for the walk to the pay phone at the River View. Now, what should I do with Catfish? If I tied him to a mooring, the sheriff may deduce he was brought here by water, so I needed to take him to the pay phone. I tied the boat fore and aft against a pier, which made it easier to get Catfish out of the boat. He groaned in pain as I slung him over my shoulder and made a steady pace to the phone. There were some wooden posts painted white near the door of the restaurant. I put him down there and tied him to one with a bit of rope from the boat.

Catfish began yelling, as best as he could, "Where yo got me? I can see light a-comin' tru dis bag. Who is you? Yo som-bitz! I don't gets ta talk too much ta any-body, septin' for the man at the scrap yard down in Woodbine. He makes me stand six feet away cuz he says I stink. Now yo got me good, at least talks to me, damn it, talks to me!"

I still had four quarters in my pocket, so this had better work. It only took one quarter to make the dial, so I looked in the phone book for the Ware County Sheriff's Office instead of the Dixie Union City Police. It could take the dispatcher an extra minute or two to call Dixie Union, giving me time to get back to the boat. I dialed the sheriff's office, and they picked up on the second ring.

After a curt hello from the dispatch, I said, "You have a fugitive, a bank robber, your river pirate, Catfish John, or whatever you call him. I tied him to a post at the River View Restaurant in Dixie Union. You need to dispatch some officers down here to get him—this is not a prank!" I hung up the phone.

Now ole Catfish was some thirty feet from the phone, but he heard my report. He sobbed out, "Yo som-bits, yo som blitz, who is yo? Who is yo?"

I had to pass him as I ran toward the docks but stopped behind him. I pulled my trusty pint of water from my shirt pocket; it was still half full. I loosened the strings on the bag and pulled it up to his nose, then placed the jar to his lips while pouring a bit of water out. He got the idea and drank the remainder.

"I thanks ya misser, yo a G-Man ain't ya? It took a dang G-Man to find me, dint it?"

I gave a couple of reassuring pats on the shoulder and ran back down to the marina. Aside from the phone call from thirty feet away, he probably could not identify my voice or my face.

It was 0350 hours when I began to hear the sound of sirens in the distance. I untied the boat, pushed off hard, started the motor, and eased out of the marina. I headed downstream just far enough to watch as the patrol car skidded to a stop in the restaurant parking lot, then I cranked the throttle back to full. I was thinking the pilot surely had not arrived yet, and that I had a good chance to get back to the barge and deal with Catfish's boat. I was also thinking about Catfish and what the sheriff's officers would hear when they pulled the sack off his head. I had a hunch he would not tell them anything that could convict himself. But, what about when they asked him who tied him up, who tied him to the post, and who made the call? He may say something like, "Haha, it was a gol-dang G-Man, not one of you all! You ain't never found me, it was a true life G-Man what did!"

It seemed the old boat was cruising just a little faster with the weight loss. It was stunning out there on that glass smooth river so early in the morning. There was light enough just from the stars that mirrored on the water. After an hour and a half, the engine suddenly sputtered and conked out. NOT GOOD. I lifted the port side fuel can, which was empty. I needed to take tank exchange class 101 quickly; I engaged the choke and pulled again, and the motor came to life.

I think I needed the adrenaline rush, as I was really getting tired. I passed the old yacht, which gave me an idea of the distance I could go on one fuel tank. Catfish probably had all that committed to memory. At around 0600 hours I was almost nodding out, but a crumb of daylight began silhouetting the river. Soon enough, the profile of the house became visible, so I slowed and pulled alongside. I was so tired but needed to think strategically. I was sure I wanted to keep the boat, as it could mean freedom or pleasure. The sound of another boat motor was coming in the distance, probably the pilot. NOT GOOD!

So how could I keep the boat, and where could I keep it? I idled the motor to take me to the front of the barge, which was against part of the moorings, my thought being that I could tie the boat back underneath the barge in the space between the two flotation tanks. I shut the motor down and climbed onto the planking, pushing the boat under the planks and into the gap beneath the deck. I quickly climbed back into the boat on the opposite side of the walking planks to maneuver the boat into the space.

I found the best of the old rope and tied it to the bow and under-side of the barge with about four feet of slack. Then I tied another piece to the stern, which was below the start of the heavy deck grating above, poking a loop through, so I could retrieve it from above. I also tilted the motor up out of the water and latched it. Crouching down between each of the steel cross beams, I made my way back to the bow, pulling the boat just far enough to use up the slack in the rope and allow me to climb out of the boat onto the deck. Looking under the chassis of the Mack, I found the stern rope, and pulling the boat back out of sight, I snugged and tied it. The boat was secured and very much out of sight. I crawled back out from under the Mack and sat on its running board, hung my head for a while, then made my way to the hatch and to my bedroom, the sheet still spread out as I left it. I took off the prison shoes and collapsed on the bed.

In my delirium, I had thought the approaching boat could be the pilot, except it was now Saturday. The boat came alongside with a couple of curious onlookers then continued on its way. I was physically and mentally tired, but not like running from the dogs. Then, I'd had the satisfaction of a continued escape, but now I had the satisfaction of a successful capture of a known criminal. With those thoughts, I passed out, not waking until early afternoon.

I awoke with a start, swinging my feet to the floor, bracing my arms on the edge of the bed. I hung my head with my eyes closed, just gathering it all in. It didn't take long to think about how hungry I was and when I could get started fishing. Choosing to not do calisthenics and instead walk the perimeter casting and reeling, I bated up for sunfish.

With my hard hat and bright orange vest, I sat out on the river side of the barge on a bucket and tossed in the line. I sat so I could lean back against a tire and just watch the bobber. As I sat, I noticed some-thing I hadn't paid attention to previously. At the end of the row of infra-structure on the barge, the welding cable cage's lock and clasp needed more repair. There was a gas-powered water pump bolted to the deck. It had plenty of hose wrapped tight on a hanger. YES!

I reeled in and propped the fishing pole against the cable railing. Checking the little engine for fuel, I sat the choke and gave it a couple of pulls; it started, YES! I shut it back off. It had an intake pipe with a screening device that I dropped over the side into the water. I connected the coiled hose to the output end of the pump, and then I shimmied under the house to the hatch and climbed in, dragging the hose with me. The bathtub was just around the corner, and I fixed the hose securely, aiming it into the tub. I went back out to the pump, started the engine, and then went back to the bathroom to watch the tub fill. At the right moment, I folded the hose, squeezed it tight to stop the flow, shoved it back through the hatch, and let it blow.

After replacing the water pump hose and intake piping, I went back to fishing, with the thought of an evening bath. I sat for at least two hours, watching boats go up and down the river, and caught three nice sunfish. During that time, I munched away on a sleeve of gingersnap cookies and chased them with apple juice. I sat longer yet, pondering my situation and all that had been happening, all that I had been allowed to pass through. Once again, I thought this was probably another time I should be thanking the higher source. So I did.

I set up the cooking gear near the back of the porch, cleaned the fish in the kitchen sink, and then rinsed it by bailing a pan or two of river water out of the tub, which was quite handy. At the rate I was going, I only had about three days of cooking oil remaining, but I was not ready to conserve it yet. I emptied a can of hominy corn into the pan first, my favorite, and placed the filets in the bubbling oil. In four minutes, it was done, and I slid it all onto a plate—I ate well.

As I cleaned up my mess, putting everything back in its place and out of sight, my mind drifted back to Catfish and what might be happening to him. I was certain that the Dixie Union police would have been first on the scene, and if they had a jail house, he would have been brought there. But, before the day would end, he would probably be in the custody of the Ware County Sheriff's Office. I laughed to myself, thinking that the sheriff's deputies would have one heck of a time just getting Catfish untied, then they would need to clean him up. Good luck with that.

* * *

My new friend Danny spent a lot of time with a friend of his who was the day shift dispatcher at the Ware County Sheriff's Office, and he was there when they brought the suspect in. Danny later told me that when they had taken Catfish John to the county jail, the only difference in him physically was that the sack had been removed from his head. He remained in a great deal of pain and resisted being moved.

Every time the officers would attempt to move him, he would make blood curdling groans, saying, "My hind parts, my hind parts, they's swollen, hurtin' bad!"

It was late in the afternoon before they had him untaped, untied, and the ankle shackles off, which took the employment of a black smith, and then they put him into a jail uniform. They laid him on a jail bunk and let him sleep for several hours. All the men that handled him chose to wear rubber gloves.

Catfish John woke up, intently complaining of the same pain, so a sheriff's EMT had looked at him and recommended a doctor be summoned to look at him as well before they handled him much more. Another hour later a local doctor had arrived and examined the lump on the side of his head, then the size of his scrotum, as Catfish obliged and cooperated. The doctor had agreed that the man had undergone an exacting trauma, but there was no reason they couldn't ask him questions. However, he had added, "This man is as filthy as anyone I have ever seen, so I would advise a detox cleaning, if that is possible. Buzz cut his hair too, as he may be carrying lice or fleas."

After the initial booking, the sheriff's officers had taken photos of him as he was and as they removed the tape and ropes. They had also asked ole Catfish many questions as they proceeded. Like, "What did you do with the money from robbing the Alma and Dixie Union banks?"

Catfish had replied, "I didn't rob no banks." But the sheriff had good photos of him at each bank and had showed them to him. He'd said, "Taint me, taint me!"

As they were preparing him for a thorough cleaning, they had continued to ask him questions, "So, Catfish, where do you live?"

He had explained that he lived on an old yacht and that he had lived in it for many years, floating up and down the river. He had told them he had lived on every inch of the river at one time or another.

A detective had asked him, "So, where is your yacht now?"

Catfish replied, "I don't know, that G-Man musta took it, and where he went is unbeknownst to me."

The detective had continued, "Catfish, tell us about this G-Man that captured you. What did he look like, what government agency did he work for?"

Catfish had gone into an extended story about how this mysterious G-Man had been tracking him for many years, and how he had evaded the G-Man in breathtaking close encounters, but finally, on his own yacht, the G-Man had caught him by surprise.

Danny said it had gone on like that the remainder of the day, until they eventually had Catfish fully cleaned up, hair and beard cut, de-loused, de-flead, and ready for a cell. Catfish had explained that the few times he glimpsed the G-Man, he had a tan suit on, a white shirt, and a black tie. He always had a tan fedora on and sunglasses. Catfish said he was a big man, six foot six or bigger. He had a big square jaw and deep-set eyes. The officers had listened, knowing Catfish was their man, however, they had no history on him, nor any direction to head from anything that he had said.

The deputies and detectives had left him alone for a while as they conferred among themselves. The consensus had been unanimous—Catfish was spinning a yarn about everything. But what else did they have to go on? Someone had in fact subdued him and made full-faith contact with the sheriff's office. One of the detectives had noted that it was curious that the good Samaritan didn't contact the Dixie Union police, and wondered if he had wanted—or expected—a delay? They had concurred that if Catfish did have a yacht, they wanted to know more about it, so one of the detectives had continued to question him. "Mr. Catfish, do you have a real first name?"

Catfish had replied, "Yes I do, sir. It's Catfish."

"OK then Catfish, I have a few more questions for you, then you may rest in your cell," one of the detectives had promised.

The detectives had asked what color his yacht was, and the answer was white. They asked the make of the yacht, and the answer was a 1958 Owens, the first with a fiberglass hull. The detectives had asked him if the money from the bank robberies was on the yacht.

Catfish had answered, "I din't rob no banks! But everything else I owns is on dat boat. If dat G-Man outsmarted me, he sure as hell gonna out smart yous. That boy's probably steerin' my boat to Florida by now."

As he had said that, he had gotten a strange questioning look on his face and asked in a most assertive way, "Well, ain't that G-Man one of you all? Why in hell don't you all know where he is? I heard him call you all and tell yas where to find me, then he gave me a drink of water. I ainta goin' to be doin' a damn thing for yous men unless the G-Man tells me it's OK. He is da one what brought me in, not you clowns." As he had sat in his cell, he had crossed his arms in determination.

*   *   *

When all my chores were done, I took a dining room chair out onto the front porch, sat down as a free man, and relaxed as I watched the river flow slowly toward the west. As I sat there, I needed a small project, so I put the peephole lens back onto the flashlight, since it worked so well for night reading. The sun began to set far to my left, as the mooring had the rear of the barge facing northeast. As I sat there resting, my brain began to work properly and formed an entirely new thought. I was in possession of a boat, and I had enough fuel to negotiate the river back to the site where I believed Catfish had his boat hidden and enough fuel to return, plus two spare cans. Tomorrow would be Sunday, the day of rest. I construed that to also mean a day of relaxation on the river, or a possible expedition. But what I was thinking of was reconnaissance of the possible hiding place of a known bank robber. All my thoughts became consumed with the idea, and I began the strategic planning for an early morning journey back up the river.

I sat in that chair until the daylight faded into dusk, imagining everything that I would need to prepare for a simple Sunday morning outing on the Satilla River. I planned for a quick breakfast, a snack while on the river, water, and some canned juice, as the fresh water was getting low. I put everything I thought I'd need into the Boy Scout backpack and placed it near my living room chair. As darkness caused the use of the flashlight, I prepared what I may want to eat in the morning prior to the adventure. I snacked on some cookies, then brushed my teeth and went to bed, preparing to read the good book for a while. The book of Ruth was amazing, and I needed to reflect on it first before moving forward into the book of 1 Samuel.

I was just starting to read, when my thoughts reflected back on something Catfish said as he was jabbering. It was something to the effect of, "Yo ain't been to my hideout, cuz yours still alive!"

I put my feet back on the floor and thought about that. Basically, only two people knew where I was, but neither of them knew what I would be doing in the morning. If something happened to me, I would probably never be found. Now if my name was written on the shit house wall, then so be it. But, Annika and my family should know. Also, what about Catfish's hideout? It might never be found. Was the bank money there? Were there other treasures there, and could there be buried bodies?

I went to the dining room desk, got out the tablet, and drafted a letter. In it I thanked the owner for the use of their house and hoped they found everything in good order. I asked that they looked closely at each book in the Bible, which I laid on the note when I finished it. I wrote part of it like a last will and testament, giving the car and bank account to Annika. Then I wrote a farewell to all and that I loved them. I printed my name first, then signed it.

Then I wrote a brief story about Catfish John and how I felt totally obligated to find his hideout. I then drew a crude map of the river where the old yacht was sunk and the direction to go on the opposite side. I left it in the center of the table.

I went back to bed but opened the louver covering the window in hopes that the morning sun would wake me. Then I rolled up in the sheet and breathed long slow breaths. I felt content with the message and my preparations.

I slept soundly, and the window light did work because I was up before the sun rose. After eating a cold can of Dinty Moore stew, I worked the boat out from under the deck, brought it around to the stern, and loaded it. I also took the beater, and for good measure, I took one of the pikes. At 0645 hours, I started the motor and set off upriver.

* * *

At Ware County Sheriff's Department, a detective following protocol ran the serial numbers on the inside ring of the very well-polished leg irons. He found that they were issued to the Richmond County Correctional Facility and immediately called them. They confirmed that an inmate went missing over a month ago and they would inform the Sheriff. Several days passed before Stump got the message, and he declared that he personally would deliver mug shots of the fugitive and pick up the irons himself.

15. HOBBITS LODGE

THE RIVER WAS AGAIN like glass as I added more throttle, but not full throttle, hoping to conserve the fuel. I may need the boat for other reasons in the next few days. The trip took nearly two hours, and I was happy that the full sun was mostly behind me. I had only seen two other fishing boats so far, and there was no one in sight as I slowed at the location of the sunken yacht. I idled the boat slowly a distance upriver from the live oaks, which I could only see just the tops of. I poked the bow of the boat into anything that looked like a used path through the lily pads and reeds and tag alders.

After many probes, I found one that seemed to travel back some distance. Not far in, I noticed an upright tree limb about two feet out of the water, which probably didn't get there by itself. It could have been pounded in there as a marker. The path meandered its way back to where small brushy trees grew out of the water, with one opening between them. It opened up into a small body of water just large enough to turn the boat around. There on the riverside was a low wall of old boards fastened to posts. The wall would have easily blocked the view of a small boat, unless it was ten feet above the water, which made me chuckle. There was barely a need to tether the boat, as it couldn't get out of this corral on its own.

Posts had been driven into the riverbed that supported a narrow but strong planking system that went another fifty feet or so to the river's edge, but not much more than the soggy riverbank. The walkway had signs of continuous wear. As I climbed from the boat, I left the rucksack but took the beater and pike. I worked my way very slowly along the planking to the path that led back into the cypress trees. As I stepped onto land, there were bird feathers all over the ground, some very old ones and some very fresh ones. They were colored like chicken feathers. I wondered what the heck that was about but kept going along the path. Not far in, the path came to a pinch point between two trees that were covered with vines, without a good way to go around in either direction.

Vietnam 101 kicked in, and I froze and began to look very carefully at everything there. Then I saw it: a black tripwire, stretched taut across the opening at the base of the trees. Wow. I then did recon as far as I could to the right and left to look for evidence of a device. Everything was covered with Spanish moss, so much so that it couldn't have gotten there naturally. Moving with absolute caution, I put the large hammer in the path and used the pike to lift moss from the structure behind the tree on the right. I could make out a rusted steel frame. So now what? I pondered for a short minute then thought to just trip the dang thing! I took the hook end of the pike and placed it over the tripwire, working my way to the far end, and then pulled.

There was only a slight hesitation prior to a substantial slamming of old steel framework onto the tree to the left. I watched the framework shake or bounce several times then stop. The action threw most of the Spanish moss and other camouflage off what looked like an old piece of farm machinery. It had a great many steel tines that were crudely sharpened. Dang, Catfish, this thing could kill a person or injure someone badly. NOT GOOD. It looked like it was only half of the original farm tool, and several of the bottom tines were bent or broken off. I braced myself against the left tree and pushed on the framework, taking considerable strength to swing it open. I moved past it, and let it slam back.

Once on the opposite side, I looked for its source of power and a way to disable it. A quick hunt revealed a cable-driven counterweight fastened to a tree some twenty feet away. The counterweight was hanging only two feet from the ground and consisted of bricks stacked neatly on a metal pallet. I just threw the bricks to the ground, then I opened the deadly framework, and it stayed put. I then retrieved the beater and the pike, moving up the grade toward the live oak area. Again, another pinch point in the trail, just like the last one. Come on Catfish, give it a break! I held respect nonetheless and looked it over very carefully, finding the tripwire and tripping it. Dang, that thing hit hard, and I needed to give credit to ole Catfish for his ingenuity in this desolate place. I forced my way through the framework and disarmed its counterweight. The device looked like the other half of the farm tool.

I needed to stay alert as I moved forward into the shaded shelter of a huge live oak tree. The limbs of the tree encircled nearly two hundred feet in circumference. At first glance it looked like mounds of earth in many piles under the outer edge of the canopy. It was so shaded that I needed to let my eyes adjust. As I stood, ever so slowly scanning this large, subdued space under this tree, I came to the realization that all but the tree was actually man made. It was the most phenomenal camouflage I had ever witnessed. I was dumbstruck and stood in the same place for a very long time, mentally mapping what I was seeing. The crow of a rooster broke the silence. I shook my head, but it didn't seem to help. What was I looking at? If I could imagine a hobbit, his home, and place of work, this would be it!

There were several openings into this skillfully covered structure, with layers of Spanish moss, vines, and pine straw collected for mulch. But there were no pines around here, so he would have needed to import it. In the deep center of what I would call a courtyard stood an old cast iron furnace, with only the big cast iron fire pot and its door remaining. It had stove pipes connected together, reaching up to the limbs, and suspended beneath them; the pipe went all the way to the opposite side of the canopy. It had small holes made every foot or so as it went. I assumed it was to spread the smoke from the fires so thin throughout the tree canopy that it would not be detected from the river or by airplane.

There were small piles of coated electrical wire lying in front of the furnace area, obviously awaiting their turn to be burned and cleaned of impurities for the recycler. Cleaned copper brought a much higher price. There were several piles of steel parts, also disassembled and prepped for recycling. Then there were many piles of miscellaneous metal junk that would need to be disassembled, sorted for the metal type, steel, copper, brass, or aluminum, and burned if it was coated copper.

I was standing in the same place as I make these observations and could deduce that Catfish's operation was based on what his boat could hold, about five hundred pounds. Had he been stealing all these items from the residents on the river, or was he known as a junk collector? Thievery must definitely be part of his operation, as he had gone for the copper welding cables on the barge. Burned clean, they would have brought several hundred dollars.

As I began to understand his operation, I looked farther to the outskirts of the live oak. Many smaller camouflaged piles, about the size of a human body, dotted the perimeter. I took a breath, telling myself to relax; I had seen plenty of dead bodies in Nam. Leaving my fixed position for the first time, I went to one of the grave-like piles and just kicked the camouflage up and away with my foot. What I saw was all the parts of the junk that were not recyclable by ordinary means. Plastic, Bakelite, Lexan, fiberglass, and the like. On first observation, it looked like he was trying to appear as a legitimate recycling business.

The rooster crowed again, waking me from the hobbit's trance. I skirted the central structure in a counterclockwise direction toward the crow of the rooster. I was still carrying the beater and the pike as I crossed what seemed to be the central path to the main structure, house, or hut. I dropped the hammer there but kept the pike. Working my way around the west side of the tree's canopy, there were many chicken coops, with some of the chickens running loose, including the grandest red rooster, who was very friendly. They all looked healthy and fed well, with lots of eggs in the cages. An additional source of food and cash? As I continued my reconnaissance around the abode and the outer edge of the canopy, I saw many of the piles of non-recyclable junk. Catfish had been at his business for a very long time.

I was mesmerized by the amount of Spanish moss hanging from the limbs of the live oak and all the trees in the area. Looking up and following one of the limbs, I had to do a double take, as I was looking at a moss-covered boat motor tethered to the limb. As soon as I identified that one, I began to see boat motors hanging from all the limbs. I needed to laugh, as now they began to remind me of rather large Christmas tree ornaments. Many of them were very old antique motors, some looked like new, but all were covered with this natural camouflage. I guessed a hundred of them in all. Perhaps this was his retirement savings?

At the outer perimeter, where other small trees were trying to grow, I was jolted when I realized a thousand eyes were looking at me—the hollow eye sockets of dried fish heads. There were hundreds of them, nailed to the smaller tree trunks. There was a nail through each gill flap so the heads stuck straight out. Some had a stick still stuck in the mouth to hold it wide open until it dried. Morbid-looking fishing trophies. I laughed again, thinking that most were bass, including some big ones too.

While I was looking up, I was also observing the central structure of the hobbit lodge, which looked like it could have an upper floor. Three-fourths of the way around stood another structure with an opening big enough to walk into, so I leaned through the opening, and my nose told me it was an outhouse. Nearly back into the main courtyard, I found a steel cage, about the size of a clothes dryer and partially buried in the ground. Water flowed out from the cage continually, forming a small creek a foot wide. It was an artesian boil or well! Looking into the cage, there were eggs in a basket, hanging just above the water. It was a refrigerator! The water flowing out was quite cool and perfect for drinking. Catfish definitely had it going on!

I eventually arrived back at the place I dropped the beater, so I turned to the hobbit house and prepared to go inside. I took one step forward and stopped. I brought the Instamatic camera along, but it was in the rucksack, and I might need the flashlight as well. I did an about-face and began the march back to the boat, passing through trap number two, on down through trap number one, and through the lowland trail to the boat. But as I broke through the opening to the mooring area, I froze in stark fear. There alongside the very end of the walking planks was an alligator, ten or twelve feet long! He could eat me!

He was mostly hauled out of the water onto the bank, his mouth wide open and eyes closed. I waited and waited, afraid to move, as I was only ten feet away. Curiously enough, it almost looked like it was waiting for something, as his bottom jaw laid on the bed of chicken feathers, his top jaw arched up. He had some war scars on the side of his head, so he might have followed the path too far one day and found the trip wire? What had Catfish done now? He had a trained guard at the entrance of his hideout, and it probably alerted to the sound of the boat motor coming in and then chicken treats. I backed up several paces, and the gator stayed put. I needed to think. Do I feed it a chicken? How many chickens? I couldn't bring myself to do that, but the day was marching on, and I needed to do something to get that thing out of there.

I thought about what Danny said just prior to my heading downriver that the very tip of a gator's nose was tender, and a whack to the nose may send them away. I had played baseball in school and was a fair batter as well. I had the pike, and without enough forethought I moved into position, some seven feet from the reptile. The thing didn't flinch as I moved into the batting stance. I gauged my distance, focused the steel hook of the pole dead on his nose, and swung with all I had. The steel hook hit just above the line of his teeth, and I saw flesh flying back toward the water.

Holy bats, all hell broke loose. I had no chance to run, as it spontaneously began wild death rolls, as if it had prey. It made noises that I didn't know gators could make and made a cartwheel, gnashing its teeth wildly as it flew through the air. It bounced as it landed, its head now toward the water, its arms and feet going like spinning paddle wheels, throwing mud and water, as it dove for the river. It looked like a motorboat as it crossed the mooring pond and crashed a new path through the thicket and into the lily pads and reeds beyond.

If I were a druggie, I would be popping a downer about now. What a rush! I put the end of the pike on the ground and leaned it on my shoulder so I could bend down with my hands on my knees. I hung my head for a while, breathing slowly. OK, I was now good, so I went to the boat and gathered up the ruck, walked the planks back to shore, and proceeded back up the path using the pike as a walking stick. I was beginning to take a shine to that wood pole.

Near the old furnace was a six-foot-long work bench with a back board loaded with quite well-organized tools. It also had a four-inch Wilton vice bolted to an outside corner. Under the bench were trays of various wrenches and sockets. Catfish could dismantle almost anything, and if that didn't work, he could pinch it in two with bolt cutters, chop it with an axe, bust it with a big beater, or hacksaw it in two. I placed my ruck on the bench, got the beater from the path, and placed it at the base of the bench. It was his anyway.

On the opposite side of the work bench was another bench the same size built for cleaning fish and the like. It had a large, old porcelain basin set down in an opening in the work surface cut just for it. There were assorted knives and a pair of pliers for skinning catfish or opening mussels. In between the grave-like piles of unusable scrap, there were smaller piles of dried fish skeletons missing the heads, crawdad carcasses, and shells from mussels. Ole Catfish ate well, mostly protein, which would explain his lack of weight, and also how he was dang tough.

Time to go inside. The opening to the interior had no actual door, but a framework I needed to step around to enter. It would block some wind, but my bet would be that it would block light at night. I needed my light at once, as it was fairly dark inside; however, I immediately found a host of flashlights on an old lampstand close to the opening, and I experimented with all of them. One of them had a big six-volt battery and lit most of the interior. With the light, I could see he had plenty of spare batteries as well.

Again, I needed to just stand in one place and try to take it all in. As I looked through this space and at that space, I used one of his larger flashlights to focus on this or that as I went along. The sheer volume of collectible things hanging from every possible open area was mind-boggling in itself. There were crates and crates of everything that you could think of stacked on boards around the perimeter, the boards keeping the crates off the dirt floor. It was all surprisingly neat and well-kept. He placed pieces of various types of plastic sheets on top of all the crates for additional protection from a leak in the roof or other falling debris.

I began looking at the structure, which was built from native wood poles and beams, with the remainder built from every possible board he could have collected over the years. All assembled with nails, but structurally sound, the building and its unusual shapes looked strong. I couldn't find much evidence of roof leaks either. A small table, with one chair at the center of the space, had a single plate, a cup, and a glass, along with a silver fork, spoon, and a sharp knife, though none of them matched. I sat down in his chair and studied the room from there. Along one side was a bench that resembled the tool benches outside. I concluded that he probably built all of them. This one was designed for preparing food and had canned goods on shelves above, fresh eggs in a basket, and a wash pan placed in a hole, cut just for it, like the one outside.

Alongside the bench was a small cast iron camp stove and a pile of dry kindling to fire it. There was a cast iron fry pan on top with a large cast aluminum tea kettle for heating water. Its chimney went out through the roof and connected to the piping from the furnace. Closer to the entrance opening stood a narrow wood box, leaning back slightly against the wall. It had a clasp but no lock. I opened it to find his firearms. I examined them one at a time: first, a Henry pump 22 caliber rifle, the best small game rifle you would ever want. Second, a Harrington & Richardson single shot .410 shotgun, the best varmint gun you could ever want. Third, a Remington double barrel twelve-gauge shotgun, the best game shooter you could ever want. Fourth, a very old Henry lever action 44, good for fairly big game. Then unwrapping an oil cloth revealed a 1911 Colt, military .45 ACP, the best possible sidearm you could want. Catfish probably used it to rob the banks. All were well-oiled, and ready for use. He had several boxes of ammunition stacked in the bottom, slugs, bird shot, buck shot, and ball ammo for the 1911. I used his oil cloth to wipe off any place I might have touched the guns, just in case they were checked for fingerprints.

Near the trunk of the old live oak tree was a steep stairway, almost a ladder, leading up to an upper room. I was so entranced in what I was witnessing that I was no longer thinking about why I had come in the first place.

"Finn, refocus. Refocus, dude, you still have work to do!" I said aloud.

As I shone the light into the darker places, I saw there were marine gas cans under several shelves of junk, at least six or eight of them. I left the chair and went to the cans to check if they had fuel, and they did. YES! While bending down to pull out the cans, my eyes focused on a most beautiful green jade vase on the next shelf up. It was very exquisite but dirty. I was so drawn to it, but I didn't have time to deal with it now. I took two of the gas cans out of the hut and sat them on the ground near the workbench. Back in the hut, the stairway and upper room were the only things left to explore. I climbed slowly, looking for anything unusual, but there was nothing. The stair ended with a small landing and a door, the first door on the campus so far. I opened it carefully to peek in, shining the light ahead. It was slightly lighter in this room, as it had actual windows with dormers over them extending farther than normal. The windows were open and had screens. There was a single bed with a very worn mattress and a few dirty blankets folded neatly at one end.

This was Catfish's inner sanctum; no collectibles up here, save a few pieces of Florida memorabilia. I sat on the bed and pondered again. I didn't see any books, any literature of any kind, no calendar, nor a written list. But there was a Bible on his nightstand. I opened the first page of the King James Version to the ledger of ownership. The last date entered was the birth of a son named John in 1912. I was certain of two things: he was illiterate (but smart), and this Bible may be the only heirloom or memory of his past that he possessed. Beside the Bible was a pair of binoculars in a worn old leatherette case. They must have been important to him.

I put the Bible down on his nightstand and sat there for a while longer. The only cash I had seen was in the top pocket of Catfish's bib overalls. I hadn't seen anything on the grounds that looked like a place this careful man would put his profits. I stood up to go to the stairway and the heel of my prison shoe caught something. It made me mad at first, and I shined the light back to curse whatever it was. But tucked back under the bed frame were six tackle boxes, not the cheap ones, but the heavy ones with rubber seals. The ones that were advertised to never leak. I pulled the one to the left out first, and it looked familiar; Catfish was carrying it to his boat back in Dixie Union. I opened the unlocked clasp and tilted the lid back. Two bait trays folded out first, but they were empty. I opened it all the way to see a great deal of cash in all denominations, but mostly $100 bills.

My heart was pounding as I relatched the box, placed it back under the bed, and opened the next. It was the same only the bills were sorted, banded, and stacked neatly. The next four tackle boxes were basically the same, with one exception—they became more and more stinky of old money. How long had this man been doing this, living in this way? He was on a continuous mission and would have continued for years to come if he hadn't robbed those banks on that particular day. He must have not known that he was already far richer than most people could ever dream of.

I didn't know how much money was in those tackle boxes, possibly a million. I thought about Joshua leading the Israelites into the Promised Land, where they were not allowed to plunder the cities they captured, but instead everything was to be killed, destroyed, and left. But, I was thinking this was different; I was merely exploring, not conquering. But again, I could live very comfortably as a fugitive or get caught with it all trying to get off the barge in Hoboken.

My brain was burning with indecision, as I thought about what Annika would do—take the high road on this, Nick, just take the high road. I also wondered how much of this would become plundered by the authorities before it ever got to an evidence file, as my full intent would be to turn in the location of this hideout to the sheriff. I settled on this: I had gone through great risk by bringing in a known bank robber, and now I could turn in nearly everything he had stolen. I had at least earned a right to some of this money. I went to the second tackle box and took out five stacks of $100 bills, probably ten thousand in each, then put the box back. One stack to replace the money in the house Bible, with extra to give to the owner for my rent and transportation. Another for Pastor Roy because he needs a new car. One for Danny as a wedding present. One for Annika's parents for their trust and help. And one for my parents, so hopefully they would go on an extended vacation. All I needed to do was get it to them.

Then the old Finn took over my goodie-two-shoes new thought process. I placed the five bundles of bills back in the tackle box, closed and latched it, grabbed the box by the handle, and taking it all along with Catfish's Bible and his binoculars, headed back down. I put the small items in the ruck, along with my flashlight. As I did, I saw the camera and realized I hadn't taken any photos. I went back upstairs first. I opened all five remaining tackle boxes, placing them so I could get several good shots of all the cash. Then I placed them back under the bed again and took another photo of them, thankful that this camera had a battery-powered flash. Going back down, I took photos of the interior and the green vase. I took photos of the work area, the furnace, the inside of the house, and the house itself. I took a photo of the chicken coops also.

As I prepared to leave, I mounted the ruck and leaned on the pike, which I would call my staff. I took another slow look around but felt that I had missed something. Then, slapping myself on the forehead, I thought, "The chickens!"

I needed to let them all out, since it would probably be weeks before I could alert the authorities on how to find this place. Chickens do well in the wild. Then I thought, "Eggs." I went to the water cooler and snatched the basket with about a dozen eggs already in it, then went to the coops, pushing many hens out onto the ground and gathering another two dozen eggs. As the hens began running around scratching the ground everywhere, the red rooster began crowing like a bugler over and over. I swear, that rooster came over and stood looking directly at me, making a full cock-a-doodle-do, then headed into his newly released flock, as he had a lot of work to do!

I was chuckling as I made my way back down the path to the boat, stopping short to look slowly into the mooring area—no gator! I climbed into the boat, preparing for the launch, when my brain began to work correctly again. Fuel for the boat! I jogged back to the bench, where I had placed the two marine gas cans, and hustled back to the boat with them, placing them in front of my rear seat. I pull started the boat motor and made the maneuvers to leave the mooring, and in minutes, I was in the main body of the river.

It was much later in the day than what my head was telling me it was at 1800 hours. Even with a two-hour trip home, there would still be plenty of light. The summer solstice was not until June 21, so the days were still getting longer. But, I was getting hungry. I hadn't even thought of food while exploring John's hideout. However, I did use the tin cup at the artesian boil to drink my fill of truly fresh water.

The boat cruised best at about eighty percent throttle, skimming comfortably downstream. I opened the ruck and found that I had only packed cookies for a snack, so I indulged, eating nearly all of them, and washed them down with the jar of apple juice I'd also brought. Aside from that, I must have gone into a hobbit's trance, thinking about what Catfish accomplished over several decades. I wondered what his childhood must have been like, what happened to him, how he ended up at the live oak hideout, and what sent him on this lifelong quest.

Pontoons went by, yachts went by, fishing boats went by, canoes went by, but no one paid any attention to the old aluminum boat with the old boat motor carrying a small load in the mid-deck and a single pilot looking forward. I began to understand how Catfish cruised this river a thousand times never being noticed by anyone.

Toward the end of an hour on the river, the cookies were wearing off and I was getting anxious to get back to the house. I had a mix of thoughts about the day and how I could absorb what happened. I just couldn't form a conclusion, so now, what was next? I was collecting mental baggage that I didn't need. I surely didn't want it, but it was reality.

My hunger grew as I felt the familiarity of the sights on the river—I was getting close to home. Rounding another bend in the river, revealed the outline of my house, which I steamed toward in anxious anticipation. But wait, there was a Brantley County sheriff's patrol boat just pulling up to the barge. I swallowed hard as I turned the boat downriver, trying to pay no attention to what was happening at my house. I cruised on downriver to a place I could not be seen and shut the motor off. I just anguished for a while. It had been a strange and fascinating day, but I needed time out, and I needed it badly. I sat for a while then thought of the binoculars and chuckled to myself. Was it really possible to use them this soon?

It took a minute to figure out the focusing devices on this pair of Bushnell binoculars, but in time, I could see what was happening on the barge. There was another boat, alongside the sheriff's boat, that I had not seen. There were people on the barge that looked like vacationers in shorts and flowered shirts. I could see the deputies' hand gestures and the people getting back into their boat. One of the deputies jumped up on the porch, moved forward, and checked the doorknob. It looked like he was satisfied that the door was locked. He jumped down from the porch and started walking around the full perimeter of the house, eventually arriving back at their boat. Apparently satisfied at sending the house gapers on their way, the Brantley County sheriff's deputies got back into their boat and motored upriver.

I waited until they were completely out of sight, then started my motor and moved cautiously toward the barge. I was tired and hungry as I did the due diligence of putting the boat back under the barge and unloading the tackle box and the few things that I took with me. The fuel tanks remained in the boat.

Making my way to the porch, I jumped up and keyed my way into the house, with just enough light to put things back in their places. I was so tired that I laid in bed with my clothes on and without the sheet. My poor brain was spinning. It was a love-hate relationship with Catfish. I could commend him for his independent way of life, but it was mostly by thievery, and he had booby traps that could kill someone.

Later, well after dark, I heard another boat pulling up that sounded like a much larger craft. In only seconds, I could hear the footsteps of many men going around both sides of the house and see flashes of light coming through the shutters. They were on the porch just as fast. I rolled off the bed onto the floor, putting my hands behind my back with no resistance. A horrible crash came at the door as glass flew through the house. Another second and their lights found me as their guns opened fire. I'm hit—all went black.

16. TWILIGHT ZONE

IT WAS REALLY BLACK, and I couldn't see a thing. I hit my head on the floor and thought I saw stars. There I was on the floor, still fully dressed, with sweat dripping off my face. That dream was a bad one, and I had thought it seemed so real. I laid there on my gut for a while, trying to remember where I left the rucksack. I finally crawled to the living room, found my chair, and sat down. I took off my prison shoes in the blind, found the sides of the sheet, and pulled it over me. I pondered the dreams. I'd had bad dreams as a kid but nothing like these; they made me exhausted and sometimes sick.

The chair offered a familiar comfort, but it just wasn't the same as my bed. I slept, but woke up far too often. Eventually, light began to creep in, so I made the sheet neat on the chair, found the ruck, and laid the contents on the table. I turned the flashlight on, which helped me put everything away. I took the wire egg basket to the kitchen, wondering if I could really eat four dozen eggs before they spoiled. But, I thought they were probably quite fresh and just might last. The fridge had metal racks, and I adjusted one to the bottom to make room for the basket. It worked, and they were out of sight.

My brain fog was leaving as I felt the first hunger pangs. My last actual meal was the can of cold Dinty Moore stew. The eggs really looked good, so I washed up five of them, cracked them into a tumbler, and whipped them with a fork. I added salt, pepper, and a nice shot of hot sauce. I drank down the mixture and thought about exercise, when I heard the pilot's boat approaching. I would need to wait until we were under way. I sat in my chair and listened to his moves, wondering if he would notice the missing pike, which I left in the boat. All went as normal, and when we were streaming down river, I started my two-hour workout.

I rested for an extended period of time, snacked on some gingersnap cookies, and chased them with white grape juice. The weather was amazingly nice, and the thought of sitting on the highboy chair, looking down river, and reading 1 Samuel was looking good. However, I needed to find a home for the tackle box, so I just put it in the back porch cabinet with my box and pole. It looked like it was supposed to be there. I also needed to find a place for Catfish's Bible and binoculars. I added some space beside the house Bible by just pushing on the row of books to make room. The two Bibles looked normal side by side. I reset several other books to make room for the leatherette case for the binoculars and sat them in place. They looked natural as well.

I took the first bundle of bills and replaced the bills that I had taken from the Bible. I took three more $100 bills and put them in my wallet. The rest went into the drawer, under other papers. I wondered what Catfish would do to hide it and had to chuckle as I put the remaining four bundles of bills in the bottom hold of my own tackle box.

My chores complete, I grabbed the house Bible and made ready the forward observation cabin. I sat on the highboy and relaxed for a reading session. 1 Samuel is a very interesting book. Samuel was a priest and judge, but he was also the first prophet. He negotiated with God the Father over the wishes of the people to have a king rather than judges. He anointed Saul as the first king, but the Father later rejected Saul for good reason and appointed David to replace him. David slayed Goliath. Saul liked him at first but then became jealous and tried repeatedly to kill David. But David survived and spared Saul's life several times, until Saul was killed with his sons in a battle.

I put the good book down and went into a meditation of thanks and prayer. I had been delivered many ways and many times. Wasn't it right to be thankful for that, and to express it to our Maker? Yes, it was. I even asked the Lord to be with Catfish, a man now completely confined, who lived a life of complete freedom. Catfish John was in the wrong, but his mental anguish would be desperate at this time. I asked the Father to be with that sinner and ease his mind.

As we went deep into the afternoon, I was so relaxed, just watching the river moving slowly past, the scenery slowly changing. I thought about using the bathwater in the tub, which should be at its warmest peak. As the thought was beckoning me, I spied a great number of painter turtles sunning themselves on a log barely afloat. It was a large log, and its trajectory was headed toward the center of the barge! What would it do to my boat? I jumped off the porch, onto the back of the

Mack, and down onto the main deck. I knew the pilot couldn't see me from his cabin. I went for the pike on the forward port side but quickly realized that it was the one I had in the boat. If I went to starboard, the pilot could see me! I grabbed for my wallet, putting it on the running board of the Mack. Then I jumped down onto one of the heavy grated platforms as the log was being swallowed up between the flotation tanks. The turtles were scattering as I jumped in on top of the slippery log in hopes of guiding it past my boat.

The space closed in, so I rode the log past the boat then grabbed the transom of the boat as I went by, pulling myself off the log and floating in the water behind the boat. The barge wasn't going very fast, but as a swimmer, I had no chance of stroking fast enough to reach the platforms. I finally started a hand over hand, moving to the front of the boat, then working my way up the tether, where I could grab the main frame. I let myself drag along for a few moments to catch my breath. Then I traversed across to one of the heavy grated frames and climbed on. I was nearly exhausted as I heard the log banging its way between the flotation tanks. It must have alerted the pilot because the engine slowed. I peeked toward the rear of the barge, through the maze of tires, and could see the feet and legs of the pilot walking back and forth at the rear of the barge. He must have seen the log, as I could hear radio traffic warning others of the dangers of the floating log. Shortly after, the engine resumed its normal rhythm.

Ok, well that was unexpected. I made my way back to the porch, grabbing my wallet as I went. I decided to strip down there on the porch, as the floor was tile. I first closed the door and stood back out of sight, then stripped down to my underwear. Leaving the clothes in a pile, I went to the bathroom, where getting wet again seemed much more enjoyable. I bailed water out of the tub for shaving, then climbed in to soak and soap. When you only have one bathtub of water, where do you draw the line between wash and rinse? I wanted to be clean, but I didn't want to itch from soap residue either.

In the mid-afternoon, I was redressed, had washed the wet clothes in the bathtub, squeezed them as hard as I could, and laid them back on the porch floor until evening. We would be mooring soon, so I went to the dining room table to sit. The tablet lay in the center of the table, my last will and testament and a map to the hideout of Catfish

John written on it in detail. The expedition to Catfish's hideout was over, but what would happen to me was still out for debate. I put it into the drawer, as someone might eventually find it there.

The calendar showed that it was Monday, June 4. I just didn't know how many days would be remaining on the river, but from what I knew so far, it just couldn't be very much farther to Hoboken. What if I were to make a reconnaissance run this afternoon to see just how far it was? The decision was unanimous between me, myself, and I. However, the five eggs for breakfast were totally worn off, so I needed to eat. I savored the taste of fresh gills, but the boat trip was far more important. Fishing could take too much time. I settled for my last can of Dinty Moore stew, cold.

It wasn't long before I could hear the pilot start the mooring maneuvers to dock the barge. Again this mooring site was desolate, with walking planks all around but no access to land. The pilot did his walk about and tie down, then headed back upriver toward Dixie Union, a two-and-a-half-hour trip. That amazed me, but it also meant we must certainly be close to the final destination of the barge trip.

Having plenty of daylight remaining, I gathered anything I may need for a boat trip to Hoboken. Going to the boat, I couldn't get it out from the front, as the mooring planks were too low. I made a precarious climb into the boat, then I needed to push hand over hand from above, girder to girder, to the rear of the barge. Once in the open, I loaded the things I might need, started the motor, turned down the river, and applied the gas full throttle. There was definitely a sense of freedom in doing this, and ole Catfish had been doing it for years. For him, it wasn't a sense of freedom, but rather it was true freedom, and he lived it. I admired how he was, but I was completely happy with bringing him down, as one day, he would have hurt someone.

As this river continued to get bigger, so did some of the boats. Yachts—nice ones—with sunbathing women up on the decks. YES! The scenery was quite enjoyable out here! I dressed as casual as I could: denim pants, which are fairly acceptable everywhere, with a light plaid short sleeved shirt and slip on shoes. I also wore the baseball cap, as I just didn't know how some of these small southern towns may take to strangers. It seemed likely, being a town with a mooring site and a boating harbor, that it should be somewhat up to date. I was also hoping for a mom-and-pop restaurant, but most of all, a pay phone.

At about an hour into the trip, I passed one of the mooring sites, like the ones we had been staying at. There was a large barge similar to ours, which was stacked with shipping containers three deep. The load must have been heavy, as the flotation tanks were deep into the water. Another half hour passed, and the river opened up wider yet, where buoys with signs advised the larger craft to stay in the main canal. Another ten minutes, and I could see a boat harbor on the south side of the river. I made my way into the marina and found ample space to dock this small boat.

I thought it funny, as I had brought the rucksack but didn't really need anything. I wanted a phone, and that was it. I tied off Catfish's boat and headed for civilization. This facility looked a great deal like the Dixie Union marina, with one exception, no River View Restaurant. Highway 203 headed south from the long river bridge, so I started hoofing it toward town.

Hoboken was only a half mile away, a six-minute walk for me. It was a town without much for suburbs, just a few houses and then the main street. Talk about a flash from the past, this place was trapped in the 1930s or earlier. Main Street was a gravel road, only five or six buildings in all. A gas station with only one pump, and a wood frame and wood sided building with a roof projection that went out over the pump bay. A small bait and tackle store, a small bar, a very small bakery, which I needed to visit, and a general store. This general store seemed to be the mainstay for the town, with "Drake's Little Super" hand-painted on a sign above the porch roof.

There were no sidewalks, but each building had a porch roof and a wood deck along the full length of each building. It was like the western movies on TV. Drake's porch was at least sixty feet long and ten feet wide. It was facing north, so it would be in the shade most of the day. There were benches and chairs along the wall, including rockers. Near the main entry, four men sat at a table playing checkers, old timers, and all wearing tattered bib overalls. Two black men and two white men concentrating on their game. I walked up to enter the store and stood to just look at what they were doing.

All four turned up and looked at me, a bit of a question in their eyes, then went back to the board game. All four men had a rather large bulge protruding from their cheeks, and my first thought was a possible common deformity. Then I noticed all the old brass spittoons near all the tables and chairs. Oh yes, this was Mail Pouch chewing tobacco territory. The act of chewing the tobacco must mess with a person's ability to accurately judge where the mouth of the spittoon was, as most of these vessels were glued to the deck from all the missed spit. I also noticed that the handrail that went from post to post at the edge of the deck must be used a great deal by chewers as well. The dirt street in front looked as though it was strewn with horse poop the first three feet out, and dried spit balls of chewed tobacco.

This building must have had five or six additions over the years and looked like a somewhat unified patchwork quilt. I entered the store, stepping back in time, except for the merchandise, which was the normal shelf items. The large railroad cast iron pot-belly stove in the center of the store was a distraction, however, along with the rocking chairs that surrounded it. In a desolate place like this, diversification was very important, but the proprietor of this place took that strategy to another level.

As I made my way to the checkout counter, hoping to acquire quarters since there was a pay phone beside the bakery, I passed a glass front display cooler, which had assorted fresh cut meats. The meat included alligator steaks, fresh catfish and bass, frog legs, along with the normal meat cuts of pork, beef, and chicken. I could see through a viewing window toward the rear of the store and watched a butcher dissecting an alligator. I read that the store had a butcher shop that would contract with anyone who wanted to have an alligator or a wild boar butchered. They also accepted any fresh fish that they may be able to sell. If it didn't sell the first day, they smoked it, and they were very good at it. The butcher had that deformed bulge in his cheek too.

The display cooler was vertical and six feet tall, with full length doors and glass. The frame was made of white porcelain. Between two of the doors, was a mounted beer tap, a sign above it that advertised Miller Draft twenty-five cents a glass. Seemed like a good idea to me, as the glasses were at arm's length on the opposite side of the aisle. I made my way to the counter with a half-pound alligator steak and one glass of draft beer with a few sips missing. I asked the young man at the counter for quarters and handed him a $100 bill. He accepted the bill and gave me the change, along with a $10 roll of quarters.

I went to the porch, found a seat, and rested with my legs crossed as I sipped my beer. It was quite cold and tasted so good, it reminded me of another, so I went back to draw another glass. Sitting back down and sipping a little slower, I had a small chill run down my spine, thinking of the *Twilight Zone*. When the beer was gone, I returned the glass to the counter, then crossed the street to the bakery. But before using the phone, I was totally drawn into the store by the most wonderful aromas of baking confections and bread. I bought a loaf of marbled rye bread, thinking that I could eat the entire loaf in one sitting. I just needed to apply butter. The teller was a short portly woman in her early sixties wearing a very modest dress with tiny flowers all over it.

As she made change, she said, "You going to be here Saturday night? Many of the boys gather on the porch of the Little Super and make music and sing, it's a good time." She continued, "Old Sandy Hankins is a fiddle player, and he can play 'Foggy Mountain Breakdown' all by himself, as there ain't no one can keep up with him." She was the nicest woman, but then she smiled, exposing many missing teeth. Not the best presentation for serving food!

It was now about 1700 hours, and I was sure Annika would be home as I dialed her number. The housekeeper answered, so I told her who I was and thanked her for answering, as she said excitedly that she would find Annika.

I didn't wait long, when Annika came on, saying, "Oh Nick, I have so much to tell you!" She was almost sobbing in excitement.

I answered, "Girl, I also have so much to share with you that it must be in person," and that nearly put me to tears. I told her that she should go first, as what I had to share couldn't be done over the phone. Her reply was that there was far too much for her to share over the phone as well, but she would share what she could for now.

To my absolute surprise, she said, "Nick, I know where you are and how you are traveling." She explained that she didn't expect a call until June 5 or 6, when we would arrive in Hoboken and leave the barge. She wanted to know how I was able to call from somewhere in the wilds of the Satilla River. She also explained that I was the one that gave her all the clues and phone numbers, and that she had just followed them.

She said, "No more bullshit about protecting me from aiding

and abetting, I am in all the way."

Well, she was about a light-year ahead of me, so I just said, "Oh thank God that you know. And yes, the house should arrive in Hoboken tomorrow, June 5. As for me, I have acquired some transportation of my own, and I am enjoying the extremely rural hospitality of this desolate town of Hoboken in advance. Oh Annika, I will love to explain my diet on this expedition so far, but you most likely wouldn't enjoy it. Tonight it will be grilled alligator steak and scrambled eggs."

She laughed, but said quickly, "You know I could be in Hoboken by tomorrow night?"

I answered, "Oh, what a wonderful thought, but Hoboken isn't the best place, not much for facilities and a bit rustic. However, the next stop will be near Racepond on June 6, which looks like a bigger town. I never know what the conditions of the parking site might be, the moving process is very slow, and it could be June 7 before we arrive, I just don't know."

She said, "Nick, what I would really like is to stay with you in the house."

I nearly dropped the phone. I replied, "Baby I couldn't imagine anything nicer. You know, there were times that I have been free as a bird, like right now. But most of the time has been a very strict regimen of staying completely hidden and inside the house. Each stop is a crapshoot, but on average, I have gotten everything I have needed, and as you know, we now have four new extraordinary friends. I love your idea. Would it be possible to travel to Racepond in advance, even if you needed to stay there an extra day?"

She replied, "I could do that, and I can get extra intel as to the conditions of the parking site for the house."

I said, "Girl, you are a light-year ahead of me! All I will need to do is wait for the knock on the door!" We exchanged some extended "I love you's" and hung up. I was so excited!

I shoved more quarters into the phone and dialed Pastor Roy, but no one picked up. Dang, if I could just leave a message. I punched in more quarters and dialed Danny, and Pam answered immediately. She recognized my voice, and said Danny was on the porch and would take the phone to him because they had gotten a very long cord.

Danny answered and said, "Your girlfriend Annika is quite a persistent young woman."

"I know, isn't it wonderful?"

Danny went into some details about their first conversations and how she had contacted the heavy movers, posing as a historian. She knew almost everything, and he had no choice but to share how we met and how I was living. He went on to explain that she had already talked with Pastor Roy, and that he could not lie in answer to her questions.

I explained to Danny that he and Pastor Roy acted in complete respect to me, and I loved them for it. I begged him to listen carefully to what I was about to share with him now.

"Annika does not yet know. Danny, did you recently hear of a bank robber being found tied up at the River View Restaurant?"

"Yes, that is big news here, how do you know about it?"

"It was me that put him there."

There was silence for a minute, and then he said, "You are shitting me, Finn."

"No, and there is a lot more you will not believe." I went on to tell him that there was a lot at stake, aside from my hope to turn myself in on arrival in Florida. I told him I had also found the hideout of Catfish John, and what I found there could cause serious governmental corruption if it was not handled carefully.

"Finn, what the hell are you talking about?"

"Danny, this man Catfish has been in the business of stealing, robbing, and recycling for forty years. He lived mostly off the land and has kept all the money."

Danny, still not believing what he was hearing, said, "How in the hell do you know this?"

I told him that I had been there and that all his money was in tackle boxes on the second floor of his hobbit house. I told him that the directions to the hideout were written down on a tablet in the drawer in the dining room cabinets of the house I was living in. I ended it with, "Danny, if anything happens to me, find this house and read where his treasure is."

Needless to say, Danny was dumbstruck with what I told him, but he knew I was serious about every word. I shared the idea that Annika may want to meet me at Racepond on the 6th or the 7th. And he was pleased with the idea. He had never met Annika but had talked with her on the phone several times. That, and my soulful approval of her was enough for him.

Danny said, "Finn, I need to think about this for a minute." And the phone went silent for more than a minute. Then Danny said, "Nicholas Finn, what is your intent for this treasure?"

I felt bad that Danny was testing my character, but he needed to do it. I answered him, "Danny, it is a treasure. I have seen his accumulation, and I have smelled the old cash. It's real." Then I explained that my hope was to use it as a tool, along with the fact that I single-handedly captured a known bank robber and turned him in, to perhaps reduce my jail sentence.

I could hear a sigh of relief in Danny's voice as he said, "My comrade, I am with you all the way, and I am in position to be of help."

I continued explaining that there were many antiques in the hobbit house and outside the house that it will take a crew weeks to sort through it all. But cash was cash, and it could disappear in seconds. I just did not know who to reveal the map to first. It must be someone beyond reproach.

Danny replied, "I see the dilemma you are facing, and right now I have no idea who could truly be trusted with a large amount of cash, especially if you are back in jail."

I said, "I couldn't ask for anything more, my friend," and hung up the phone.

I punched in another quarter and dialed Pastor Roy one more time.

"Praise the Father," he answered.

I told him it was Nick and hoped that he was doing well.

He responded, "I feel I could whip my weight in wildcats."

"Me too."

Pastor Roy asked, "Are you in Hoboken?"

I explained that I was, but the house would not arrive until tomorrow, and I had use of a fishing boat for the day. I also shared with him that I had stories he would have trouble believing, and I knew that he was praying for my success, as it was working so far. I told him that I had just talked to Annika and Danny, and that I was glad that she knew where I was. I asked him if he could contact them again soon, as there was a great deal of new information they would share.

Pastor Roy said, "Nick, I have been doing more research on shell shock and have found several good articles." He then explained that one of the articles had a list of twenty markers to look for in shell shock patients, and it had four categories for the twenty markers. "I am having them copied at the library and will bring them to you, if you ever arrive anywhere!"

Pastor Roy went on to say "Nick, I really do not know much about you, but what I do know has many aspects that fit the twenty markers, so you should seek help."

I said, "Pastor Roy, I really do not know a lot about you either, but I do have full faith and trust in anything you say. I swear an oath between you and God that I will seek help at the VA at my earliest opportunity."

We rattled on about whatever for a while, and I told him that I was now reading the book of 1 Samuel in what I hoped would be a complete Bible read through. He remarked that I may find prefigures of Christ in many of the Old Testament books, including 1 and 2 Samuel.

The pastor wanted to close us out with a prayer, and I submitted and said amen along with him when he finished.

It was now 1830 hours, and I had about two and a half hours of good daylight remaining, so I headed back to the boat at a good brisk walk. I was jonesing about the idea of fishing again, but I had 'gator steak and a fresh loaf of marbled rye bread. The dirt road was dusty, and as I made the hike back, at about the halfway way point, a young black kid around thirteen, was headed toward Hoboken. We were about to pass, but I stopped. He had a stringer with about six nice-sized catfish slung over his shoulder, and I commented, "Nice catch!"

He said, "Shucks, mister, this ain't nothin, I usually have ten or more, my arms just got too tired from rowing that old boat. But I'm sure glad I have it."

I asked him what he did with the fish.

He replied, "Well, I see Old Catfish's boat at the marina. He gives me the best price, but if I can't find him, Drake's gives me twenty cents each."

I left him saying, "Good luck my friend!"

When I arrived at the marina, there was no one around. I hopped into the boat, fired it up, and headed back upriver at full throttle. Two hours later, arriving at the barge, I unloaded everything onto the rear mesh platform. I found that I could motor my way back between the flotation tanks to the front, tie the boat, and climb out.

I got to work quickly, setting the radio on the porch with the volume turned up on a rock station. Then I started a charcoal fire in the bucket and gathered what seemed right to go with grilled gator. I put the gator steak in a bowl and poured out a warm Budweiser beer over it as a marinade—what did I know? I opened a can of sweet corn and made the fry pan ready with plenty of oil. It was time, so I put the fry pan on the bucket first, then got the contents hot, the oil bubbling, and gave the corn one minute to heat. I then sat the fry pan on the head of a big bolt in the deck, so it was somewhat airborne to conserve the heat longer. I put a wire rack on the bucket and flopped the gator steak on it. My experience with beef steak was four minutes, flip... three minutes, flip... two minutes, flip... two more minutes, serve!

I didn't know what to expect with this piece of meat; it was white and semitransparent like fish, but solid like beef or pork. As the first four minutes passed, it went from semitransparent to white, like fish. At the fourth minute I flipped it and watched the cooking process closely. It smelled like fish.

I followed the beef regimen with the gator, probing it with a fork. It didn't flake like fish, making it harder to determine when it was done. I pulled it off the grill, put it into the fry pan, and put the fry pan back on the hot bucket. It came back to bubbling in short order, and I waited one more minute. Tonight, I added a warm Budweiser beer to my menu, as I indulged in a delicious alligator steak. I wanted to just sit and veg for a while, but then I thought about the possibility of a long day tomorrow and how lounging in the tub would feel really good. I ran the hose back under the house, up through the hatch, and into the tub, then started the pump. Three minutes went by quickly, and I dared not let the tub overflow.

With everything cleaned and put away, I sat on the porch and watched the sun set, fully content with the day. I made ready for bed and had a reading session in 2 Samuel. I turned the flashlight off at 2200 hours and went to sleep, only to be awakened by a rumble that became louder and louder. Then the entire house and barge began undulating in larger and larger waves, and light began to flash through the louvers.

17. PEA PICKER

I WAS SO GROGGY, but the adrenaline began to take over. In my fog, I grabbed my flashlight, which I didn't need, headed for the porch door, holding on to anything along the way to steady myself from the movement. I got to the door, opened it, and went outside; it was nearly as light as day. Passing by was a barge ten times the size of this one, with giant lights beaming up the river and lights alongside. It was loaded with steel Conex containers stacked four high. It was moving slowly, but faster than we had been traveling. This thing must have been very heavy, as the water rose and lifted our barge several feet up. It was like the tide coming in fast. I marveled at the thing, not knowing that shipping goods by inland water was still alive and well. I didn't know if manatees were in these waters or not, but if there were, they may not have much chance when those monsters traveled through.

The excitement was over, so I sat in the living room chair until the movement calmed down. Blinking my way in the dark had actually become fun, as I made my way back to bed. How far could I go in just one blink? And in three, I was in bed again. My thoughts sent me down many rabbit holes as I attempted to sleep. One was the possibility of staying in the house until it was taken off the barge, then hitchhiking through Folkston and across St. Mary's River into Florida. Even if I had to walk all the way, I could be there in less than two days. But then came the 'but.' If I were picked up for anything, it would mean facing the Georgia law. I rested my mind firmly with the idea that I would stay with the house until we crossed that bridge into Florida.

I awoke to that wonderful sound of the pilot's boat arriving. The man I now thought of as Popeye was doing his business of making ready our vessel to head down river. The footsteps sounded around the barge, stopping to remove the mooring ropes, and then engine idled for the warm-up. It was nearly like music, but I sure wanted to be back on land!

I got out of bed and put the sheet back on my favorite chair, while thinking that it would be nice to find another laundromat. I sat in that chair for a while and decided that the five-egg mixture would be a good fit for the morning breakfast, and so I sallied forth to make it happen. As the barge turned and headed down river, I went into my two-hour session of calisthenics, finishing with chin-ups from the hallway door trim. I went to my chair again, just to rest for a while, then got dressed for the day.

I adorned myself with the same clothes I wore yesterday while visiting Hoboken, then went to the back porch to sit in the highboy and read the good book while watching the panorama of the river. Next was 2 Samuel, which is an astounding story of David finally being fully recognized as king and bringing the Israelites into complete union. In the zenith of the Israelite nation, David committed a horrible sin with Bathsheba, which included murder. David ultimately confessed his sins to God, and his union with Bathsheba resulted in the royal ancestry to Jesus Christ.

For the first time, I was recognizing some of the scenery as it went by, and we were getting closer to the marina. I began to wonder if the crew would unload the house today or wait until tomorrow. I decided to just take it as it came because worry only gains you ulcers. I breathed deep and just enjoyed the ride.

At about 1400 hours, the Hoboken Marina came into sight, and even before the pilot began the maneuvers toward the dock, I placed the highboy chair where it belonged, closed and locked the back porch door, and moved to the living room chair to await the docking. I didn't wait long, as within thirty minutes we were tied to the dock that would allow the Mack to pull the house off the barge, heading forward. The pilot went to the rear of the barge, climbed down onto the grating, untied his boat, started the motor, and moved to the boat ramp. He loaded the boat onto a trailer and headed north over the bridge on Highway 203, toward Blackshear.

Well, I could now assume that the moving crew would not show up until tomorrow, and that gave me a delicious amount of time to do whatever. I wanted to fish again, and the catfish that the young boy had on his stringer yesterday really looked good, so I baited for catfish and sat on an overturned bucket. I played catch and release for an hour before hooking a big one, which would feed me well. I fought it for fifteen minutes before it gave up. I pulled it on deck and prepared to skin it. I dressed the fish, and in the process, I chummed the water with the car-cass. At 1500 hours it was far too early to have supper, so I put the fish on a plate and covered it with another plate, then decided on a walkabout.

I realized I hadn't called my parents last night, so I had better do that soon. But first thing first, I needed to get the boat out from under the barge. The barge was again pulled up quite close to the bulkhead of the loading dock, but with enough room for me to climb down and pull the boat close enough to get in. Just like the last time, I needed to kneel down low to grab the deck framing and push the boat hand over hand to the rear. Once in the open, I started the motor and maneuvered to an open bay within the dock walkways and tied it off.

I hoofed on into Hoboken and straight to the Little Super, as I needed a few more quarters and a cold draft beer or two. Apparently it was a time of day when none of the tobacco chewers were sitting on the porch, so I just enjoyed the quiet, sipping the brew. I thought about the remainder of the trip, down Highway 203 to Racepond, then back on Highway 1 toward Folkston. Judging from the map, it looked like a day's travel for each. I didn't need food, but another half gallon of juice may be in order, and I needed to fill at least two jugs of fresh water. I could fill the water at this marina. Returning the pilsner glass to the store, I grabbed a jug of Welch's white grape juice, paid at the counter, and head-ed for the phone.

Dad would be working at this hour, but I may catch Mom, so I pushed in the quarters and dialed. It took six rings, but she answered, sounding out of breath. "Hello, hello," she said.

I replied, "It's Nick. Are you OK?"

"Yes," she replied. "I was hanging laundry on the line outside and heard the phone ring through the open window. It's a beautiful day." She carried on about how thankful she was that I called, and she won-dered where I was and how I was.

I explained that mentally and physically I was doing fantastic; however, I would still have several days remaining before reaching my destination. I told her that I had several wonderful stories that I just couldn't wait to share with her and Dad. I also asked if she had been in contact with Annika. She had, but Annika had been somewhat vague about what she knew of the situation. I begged her not to worry because Annika was a brilliant woman. "By the way," I asked, "has there been any progress with the application for my driver's license?"

"Yes, it was mailed out a few days ago."

"Fantastic. OK Mom, gotta go— and tell Dad I love him too."

*　*　*

At Brantley County Sheriff's Department, Sheriff Stump arrived to take possession of the leg-irons. Walking boldly into the building and going directly to the dispatcher's counter, he announced loudly that he was Sheriff Stump from Richmond County and needed to pick up the leg-irons found on the bank robber. He also informed the dispatcher that he was also here to question the bank robber. He demanded the dispatcher pull out all stops to make that interview with the prisoner as soon as possible.

The dispatcher said, "Sheriff Stump, your request is above my pay grade, so I will be connecting you with Sheriff Joe Leary of Ware County. Please have a seat in the lounge."

The Sheriff's blood pressure went high, as his face got red, but Stump knew he was at the mercy of the dispatcher, so he went to sit. He waited, very impatiently, for about a half hour, until the dispatcher announced with a loud voice that Sheriff Leary would arrive in fifteen minutes.

Sheriff Leary walked in and addressed himself to Sheriff Stump, applying a few pleasantries. He said, "Your pair of shackles will be on the counter, and I will accompany you to visit our prisoner Catfish John, who is temporarily housed in our jail, awaiting state charges." Leary went on to say, "We are not sure what you need to question him about since every word he has spoken is in the depositions we sent to you."

Stump said, "It's that gut thing, you know." As they walked, they crossed the street to the jail facility.

The two entered the twelve-cell block, which was empty, except for John. Sheriff Stump approached John, and with a very stern voice said, "John, I have some questions for you."

John, taken by surprise, spun on his cot, putting his feet on the floor, and looked at the intruder and said, "Who da hell is you?!"

The sheriff shouted back, "I'm Sheriff Stump, and I want to know who put those leg-irons on you since they belong to me!"

John replied, "Well where da hell you been? I done told every officer and detective in this county it was one of yawl, it was a G-Man, he told me so."

Stump snapped back, "Well, what did he look like?"

Catfish crashed back onto his bunk, saying, "I already described him as best as I could, now leave me alone." John made one last comment, "I'll talk to the G-Man, that's it, yous know who he is."

Sheriff Leary explained to Sheriff Stump that what he experienced was what they were all getting from Old Catfish, but if he gave them anything new, he would share it immediately.

Stump asked Leary if he would mind if he went down to the site where he was captured.

Leary explained that he wasn't captured but picked up completely bound. Sheriff Leary directed him to go to the north end of the River View Restaurant, over in Dixie Union, to see the pay phone he was laying by.

Stump did exactly that. He got out of his squad car and walked to the phone booth. From there he could see the moorings, where the sighting of the robber was reported. He walked down to the docks, trying to get a sense of it all. Walking down onto the docks themselves, he inquired of a fisherman, if he was at the docks when the bank robber made his escape or saw anything unusual that day.

The fisherman replied that he was on the river at the time, but the only thing unusual to him was a house on a barge. It was on a frame with many tires holding it up and a truck hooked up ready to pull it.

The fisherman laughed and said, "It looked so funny, like a giant houseboat."

Sheriff Stump walked back toward the River View, pondering as he went. There was something about a moving house that was tickling his brain, but what? He then went to the River View and reserved a room for the night of June 6.

* * *

After talking to mom, I still had quarters, so I called Annika again. She could still be at work, so I called the laundry, and the receptionist, recognizing me, put me through to Annika's extension immediately. She answered, and said, "Nick, did you make it to land?"

I answered, "Yes, the barge is docked at the Hoboken Marina, I expect to be moving on land again tomorrow in the morning." I went on to say that the ride down to Racepond could be a long day, but it looked like open country.

Annika informed me that the crew would be arriving early, and their destination would be Racepond, on the south end of the city, and the parking place would be at a pecan processing plant. It would be off season, not many people there.

I said, "Annika, I do not know how you know that, but I am glad you do. So, Annika, is there a motel in Racepond?"

"There is, and the pecan farm has a large parking lot behind the plant, so it will hold the house and my car at the same time."

"Well shut my mouth, baby, you come on down!"

We ended the conversation with the "I love you's," and I dialed the phone for Danny. Again, Pam, a woman normally in complete self-control, answered the phone but began shouting, "Danny, Danny, it's Nicolas!"

And in seconds, I heard Danny say, "Dude, where are you?"

I explained that I was at the Hoboken Marina, that the house was to start moving again tomorrow, and that I would be happy to be on land again.

Danny replied curtly, "You need to shut up and listen for a minute my friend. You definitely screwed up by putting the leg-irons on Old Catfish, as they had serial numbers on them. They were traced to the Richmond County Correctional Facility, the one you walked out of."

"Oops, I didn't see any serial numbers on them, how bad is the problem?"

"Do you know this guy named Sheriff Stump? Well, he was at the county sheriff's facility today, and I was sitting with the dispatcher when he walked in. He is quite the bull in the woods. He came to pick up the leg-irons, but demanded to talk to Catfish as well, and his request was granted. The report we received from the jail was that Catfish was not cooperative, but demanded to talk with the G-Man that brought him in."

Danny continued, "He wanted to know the exact spot where Catfish was found, and he was told of the River View Restaurant. Later, when I went home, his Richmond County patrol car was parked at the restaurant, and it still is. It looks like he is staying for the night."

I told Danny that I knew the sheriff because he was the one that saw to it I went to jail, and the one that made sure I was worked harder than any of the other inmates. I took the time to explain to Danny that I never spoke a word to Catfish and that he never saw my face, so he could not identify me. I shared with Danny that Catfish kept calling me a G-Man when I left him to be collected by the police.

I said "Danny, the guy believes in his head that it took a real government agent, tracking him for years, to bring him down. You know Danny, that man lived his entire life as free as a man can live, and now, overnight, he is totally confined. He is also free to tell his story any way he pleases. A G-Man caught him."

Danny agreed with me and explained that he would call Annika at least twice a day until the house crossed over the St. Mary's River into Florida.

I told him that I too would call at any opportunity I had during that time, and that his warnings had been well received. Then I shared with him the possibility of seeing Annika at the night parking spot for the house, slated for Racepond tomorrow night.

"Well, for a man on the lam..." He coughed, "...on the *slow* lam, you're not living an all-bad life. Tell Annika hello from Pam and I." We then shared our goodbyes and ended the conversation.

All business finished in Hoboken, I walked back toward the marina. I kicked the dirt road along the way, thinking about Sheriff Stump. He was a determined man. The leg-irons were recovered in Dixie Union, but how could he connect me to the moving house?

As I arrived at the marina, the young black boy that I spoke with yesterday was maneuvering his old wood boat into the mooring site, looking for an open slip. His boat had a pair of eccentric oar locks. They really looked crazy, but the pilot could sit in the boat facing toward the bow and pull back on the oar handles, but the eccentric pushes the boat forward, YES! You could see where you were going.

The boy landed the boat, collected a stringer of catfish, and headed quickly toward land. As his bare feet headed up the dirt path in my direction, we made eye contact, and I smiled. He stopped, grabbed the stringer off his shoulder, and showed me his day's catch, which was all he could do to hold it up.

He pointed, "That is the boat that belongs to Catfish John, have you seen him? He always gives me five cents more for each fish than Drake's."

"Son, you take your fish up to Drake's, then come back here to me, as I have something to tell you."

The boy came back a half hour later, and I directed him to sit on the bench beside me. So, I asked him directly, "How do you know Old Catfish?"

"I don't know. He's always been on the river, for as long as I can remember."

I asked him if he was friends with Catfish, and he said, "Yes, we's good friends."

I asked him, "What does Catfish call you?"

"He calls me 'Pea Picker.' I don't like it, but that is what he calls me."

"Well then, you are the one Catfish talked about. You are the one he wanted me to give his boat to."

The boy's eyes got big as dinner plates, then he turned his head a bit, squinted at me with great question, and said, "You joshing me? Where is Catfish?"

I waved my hand through the air and said, "Catfish John has gone to the sweet by and by."

The boy didn't know whether to be happy or sad, and asked with his bottom lip shaking, "What happened to him?"

"First, what is your real name, and where do you live?"

He replied that his name was Larry Harris, and that his family lived downriver toward Raybon, but only a mile or so. He went on to say that they were all poor folk, and his poppa and momma worked mostly on the farm land as sharecroppers.

I went on to ask Larry what grade he was in school, and he really couldn't say. He replied that the truant officer couldn't find them way back on that farm, so he never went to school much. He helped his folks the best by spending his time on the river catching cats.

He asked again about Catfish, so I spun a yarn. "He became very sick, his hind parts you know, so he took his boat to Dixie Union to find help. He got to the marina there and made his way up to a restaurant called the River View, as he knew there was a pay phone outside. He had no quarters and laid there until a stranger paid for a call. All Catfish could do was call the police, as he had never been to a clinic or a hospital. The police found him all tied up in a bad sickness, so they put him in the squad car and took him to the most proper facility he deserved.

"Once there, they put him in a private room, by himself, with his own bed. They cleaned him up and asked him many questions about how he ended up there. He was weak and couldn't tell them much, but he said all he had was that boat, and if he were to die, he wanted them to find a boy named Pea Picker down by Hoboken Marina and give him his boat. Then his life was locked away. I am a federal agent, what you folks call a G-Man, and I was hired by the Ware County Sheriff's Office to find you. Now I have done my job."

Larry's jaw had dropped from the beginning and was still that way when I finished. I told Larry he needed to hear more, bumping his arm to wake his mind. I opened my wallet and took out five $20 bills, which was more money than he had ever seen. Then I added to it, four $100 bills. I told Larry that the money had belonged to Catfish, and that he would want him to have it. I advised him to give the big bills to his parents, and they would know what to do with them, but he was to take the $20 bills and use them to buy the thing he needed to catch more catfish, and that would include gas mix for his new boat motor.

I felt sorry for Larry, as he was completely beside himself. I broke the ice by inviting him to learn how to operate the motor and maneuver the boat. He just nodded his head and stood up, so we walked together to the old boat and climbed in. I had him sit so he could see me work the controls to start the motor. I showed him the kill switch and went through the start procedure again. I had him untie the boat and showed him how to turn the motor around to reverse the thrust to back out of a tight spot. He was all eyes and ears now!

I maneuvered the boat down river a short distance, exaggerating turns, then opened the throttle to about half, as Larry leaned forward into the wind. I advanced the throttle to three-quarters, as he leaned farther forward, then I opened it up, and the boat went into a flat plain at about fifteen or eighteen knots. Larry's smile was a sight to see as I slowed, made a big turn back toward the marina, and put it back to full throttle.

I slowed and idled back into the slip, where Larry tied us off. I then invited Larry to sit in my place and do the same thing. At first he shook his head, but I scolded him a bit, explaining that this was it, and he had no choice. If he wanted the boat, he had to learn it now! He relented and moved to the stern. I showed him that the motor had a fuel tank of its own, but he had four extra five-gallon fuel tanks, with two full, and I showed him how to switch them out on the motor.

He picked it up quickly, as we began the start procedure, and he started the motor with the first pull. That big smile was back, and this time I could see teeth. I untied the boat and motioned to back out and go. He went forth with confidence, maneuvering the boat back out of the slip, turning, and zigzagging out of the marina to the open water.

Every time I looked back, all I could see was big pie plate eyes and a big toothy smile, as Larry dared to add throttle to the motor. I motioned Larry to cut the motor, so he did, and I told him to take me to his parents. He grinned again and gave it the gas.

His parents' house was beside the river, along with eight other sharecropper homes. Larry was correct—these were poor folks. I met his parents in the yard in between the homes and the water, and they were very leery of me, and I couldn't blame them. But Larry was the bridge between the white and the black in this meeting. I did the best that I could to explain to them that what their son was given was the gift of a man who was no longer able to live. The man knew Larry and liked him, and this was what he would want. I also explained that the boat, having a gas motor, would need to be registered with the state as having new owners, but that the current registration would be good until the birthday of Catfish John. However, we did not know when that would be.

I told them that I was not able to give them the proper paperwork for ownership at that time, but that I would return and provide them with it. Meanwhile, I asked them to allow Larry to use the boat to do his fishing. I shook hands with them both and beckoned Larry to take me back, and that is what he did. Larry performed as if the boat was his all along, and I had a toothy smile all the way back to the marina. Larry maneuvered into the slip, and I tied off the boat. I turned around on my seat to face Larry and spoke to him again.

I said "Larry, as I told you, I am a G-Man. I will be on another mission starting tomorrow, and I never know how long a new mission may last, or even if I will live through it. I promise that I will return to help you register your boat in the correct way and get you a legal title to it.

"But meanwhile, Larry, no one can know of me or where I have been, or that I have been here. Not even if the police or the sheriff ask about me—you are to say nothing. Larry, do I have your promise?"

Larry said, "Mr. G-Man, you have my promise! But sir, how are you going to go anywhere from here?"

I answered his question by telling him that another agent would pick me up in Hoboken later tonight.

Then, I was alone again. It was about 1800 hours, and I was suffering somewhat from brain drain, but so happy about the outcome with Larry. I swore an oath to myself that I would return to this place, find Larry, and see to it that he went to school. He was smart and was deserving of the chance to succeed further.

I went back to the house to prepare the catfish I'd caught earlier. The starboard side of the barge was near the cypress swamp and hidden, so I set up the charcoal bucket there, allowing time for the coals to become fervent. Then, first simmering a full can of hominy corn in the oil, I added the filets for about four minutes. As I savored that meal, I knew I would miss the fishing and fish dinners, but being off the river would make up for it. The charcoal was still hot, and it gave me an idea. I wasn't sure how long eggs would last at room temperature, but boiling some would sure make them handy to eat. I added more charcoal, a stainless steel bowl with water, and a dozen eggs. In only twenty minutes, they were done.

After I cleaned up from dinner, I went through the house very carefully, just in case Mr. Khaki Man showed up for the offloading. I had one last thought about that pike that I used to clobber the gator I call Old Scarface and to subdue Old Catfish, so I went promptly to the deck and retrieved the same one that I had used. I stood it up behind the back porch inside door, hoping the pilot wouldn't miss it. Then it was bath time, perhaps the last one for this leg of the journey. As I soaked in the tub, I was listening to the rock station on the radio, and the second song was, "Bridge Over Troubled Water." The tub water was not warm, but that song really gave me chills. Crossing the bridge was my only hope! But then the song "I Think I Love You" came on, and I felt better, as the possibility of seeing Annika tomorrow night was a real possibility. After that "Up Around the Bend" by Credence Clearwater Revival came on. It reminded me of where I was headed tomorrow. I pulled the tub plug, and dried myself, then the tub.

As the light dimmed, I rolled up in the chair sheet on my bed, using a double neck pillow so I could start on 1 Kings. Now King David, an amazing man and King of Israel, wanted to build a permanent temple for God, but God advised him that he had too much blood on his hands. He was allowed to gather what would be needed to build it and provide the construction plans, but his son Solomon would be the king to do the actual construction. I awoke when the flashlight hit the floor, so I shut down for the night.

Then, like music to my ears, I could hear Tonto pounding on all the tires. He had his way of moving quickly between all the axles, reaching every tire under the house on the inboard sides, then even faster, going down each outboard axle. At nearly the same time, I could hear the members of the barge crew removing chains that held everything to the deck of the barge. Then Old Sarge fired up the Mack and put it into the warm-up stage. I wanted to see as much of this as possible. I got dressed, brushed my teeth, and had three slices of marbled rye bread with butter and peanut butter for breakfast, chased with a tumbler of juice. YUM.

In less than an hour, the gears of the Mack ground into low, and that first gentle pull took place. Then a steady slow move from the barge to land, then into a slow left hand turn toward Highway 203, and then onto the road where a slightly faster pace began. We were on our way to Racepond! We quickly were in vast flatlands of agricultural ground, the road heading dead south with nothing to see. It seemed as though Old Sarge was adding just a little more acceleration than normal, so I would need to run at full speed instead of a fast walk to keep up now.

I thought, "You go Sarge!"

I took my shirt off again and started my two-hour regimen of exercise. The radio was again set for rock, which was nice during a workout, and the song "The Long and Winding Road" by the Beatles was playing. It was June 7, and it was twenty-seven days on the lam, but in my mind, it seemed like twenty-seven months. I was at a full sweat and wishing I had not drained the tub because Mr. Khaki Man never showed. I sat in my chair to cool down.

*   *   *

At the River View Restaurant in Dixie Union, Sheriff Stump was enjoying an early breakfast. He had inquired the night before of the local police if anything had changed since the apprehension of Catfish. They informed him that several days later they investigated a car that had not moved since the apprehension. After running the VIN, they discovered that it was stolen and did an extensive fingerprint search. They found John's prints and the owner's.

The sheriff had a legitimate question bouncing around in his head—how did John get to the restaurant?

His thoughts led to another question, "Delivered by a G-Man?" He went back into the restaurant, which was somewhat crowded, and tapped his baton loudly on the floor to get everyone's attention. He announced in a loud voice, "I am Sheriff Stump. On Friday June 2, a subdued bank robber was picked up here at this restaurant. We do not know how he got here already tied up. Did anyone here see anything? I mean anything UNUSUAL around here that day or the day before?"

The announcement got everyone's attention, including a couple seated at a table near the back, who almost choked on their coffee at the sound of his name. Danny and Pam felt the sheriff's gaze fall on them, when a local man who fished the river stood up and said in jest, "Yes, Sheriff, the biggest houseboat any one of us had ever seen was at the loading dock."

The sheriff looked away from Danny and Pam, and moved to the man's table as the man's grin faded. Stump said, "Tell me more."

The cowered man said, "I saw a barge with a house and a big truck sitting on it. The barge was gone the next day."

The sheriff immediately left the restaurant and went to his patrol car. House movers haunted his thoughts as he remembered a solitary note on his desk that a house was being moved at the very place the Jefferson County Sheriff dogs lost the trail. He was lost as to who may be moving a house, but then the detective in him thought the mover would need permits, lots of them. He radioed his dispatch to call the state of Georgia, but his radio would not transmit the distance back to his home base. So he went to the pay phone and called his dispatch, ordering him to find a heavy mover permitted to take a house down Highway 1 during the months of May and June.

Danny and Pam finished their breakfast and left the River View

Restaurant, Danny using a cane, as he was not accustomed to his new prosthetic leg. Stepping out, he saw the sheriff putting coins into the phone, so he and Pam sat down on the bench near the door, and Danny acted like his knee was hurting. They sat in earshot of the sheriff as he loudly made his demands to his dispatcher.

When the sheriff had left, Danny said to Pam, "Road trip!" Pam smiled in agreement.

18. BLINK ME!

As soon as the Wakefields arrived back at Danny's home, they called Annika and learned that she had left yesterday from Williamston, North Carolina, in hopes of meeting me in Racepond tonight.

Danny sat back in his chair and looked at the ceiling for a minute then looked at Pam and asked for her thoughts first, as he was uncertain what to do.

Pam said, "We've been through that area many times. It's only forty-five minutes away, and there's a motel there called Racepond Rooms. I think we should go."

Danny agreed and confessed, "I'm walking on eggs here. I don't want to interfere with the law, but this sheriff is doing work way out of his jurisdiction—he should be asking our Sheriff to do the search. I know where Nick's heart is, and I want to warn him. Let's go!"

Dan expressed to Pam that she would take longer to pack than he would, so he wanted to talk to Pastor Roy and share the new potential problem. Pam agreed, and Dan dialed. On the third ring, Rose answered the phone with a sweet, "Hello." Danny explained who he was.

She remembered him and said, "Please give Mr. Walker a minute, I will get him."

After a moment, the pastor came on the phone and said, "I am guessing that this is probably important, how may I help?"

Danny added some detail about where I was in my plight, and Pastor Roy explained that I had called him last night, and he was up to speed on that. Then Danny explained to him what he had overheard from the Richmond County sheriff. Annika was most likely to be in Racepond by this afternoon, and they were in the process of packing to go there too.

Danny then asked the pastor if he had a notion to go along as well. If so, they would wait for him.

Pastor Roy explained that they needed to sit this one out, but he would be concentrating his prayers of success for all and then begged

Danny to keep him informed.

Danny ended the call, informing Pastor Roy that they all would need prayers, and he knew that they would be receiving the best prayers possible from him.

After packing the Chevelle, Pam took the wheel. As bad as Danny wanted to drive, he was unsure of his new leg. Waycross had at least fifty stop lights on the way south—too much clutching for him right now. Even though the business could be very serious, it was a beautiful day, and they traveled with the top down.

Annika was on I-95 heading for Brunswick, where she would take 82 to Nahunta, catching 301 south to Homeland. Then she would head north on Highway 1 to Racepond. It was a few miles longer, but if she went to Hoboken and south, she may not be able to get around my moving house. Her plan worked, and she was able to book a room at Racepond Rooms in the early afternoon. She needed a nap and took it.

Shortly after that, the Wakefields arrived and booked their room, asking at the desk if a Miss Bjorn had arrived. They were given her room number, then went to settle in. After getting comfortable, Danny dialed Annika's room, but it was set to 'Do not disturb,' and he and Pam agreed that she probably needed some sleep. They turned on the TV and caught a weekly showing of *The Waltons*. After all the "goodnights" on the show, they tried Annika's room number again, and she answered with a very stern, "Who is this?"

Dan answered quickly, "It's Danny, its Danny, and we are here at Racepond Rooms too!"

Annika replied, "Oh my gosh, I am so happy that you are, so we can finally meet. But, but, why are you here? You are scaring me!"

Danny said, "Don't worry yet, I have information to share that may or may not be bad for Nick. We need to talk." Danny directed her to a mom-and-pop restaurant, just a block south, where they could walk. They left their rooms, which were only two doors apart, and met face to face for the first time. There were hugs and some tears, then more hugs, and they headed off to Nettie's Café. Once seated, three sweet teas were brought to the table, and Danny explained all that he had heard from the sheriff. He also proposed a few scenarios of what could happen.

Annika listened and replied that for tonight she didn't care, as she knew it would take at least a day to get an answer from the state in regard to the permits, even if the request came from a sheriff.

Danny laughed, as he knew she was right. He proposed they order something to eat, but Annika said, "No, I want to wait for Nick."

As she said that, a sheriff's patrol car went slowly past Nettie's with its lights flashing but no siren. Then a crew truck passed by with a sign on the door that said, "Trues Heavy Movers." Their hearts were pounding as they watched a Mack tandem-axle truck tractor, with a huge block of concrete up above its axles, pulling a house on many wheels past the restaurant.

Annika cried as Pam moved so quickly around the table to hold her. Annika was acting like she wanted to leave the booth and go.

But Pam held her and just said, "Wait girl, wait!"

Sobbing, Annika sputtered out, "The pecan farm where the house would be parked for the night is only a half mile south!" Recovering some, she added, "Nick told me the crew takes about a half hour to shut down and move out!"

Danny said, "OK then, let's wait about thirty minutes then start walking."

* * *

Sheriff Stump, having nothing else to do, decided to take the thirty-minute drive on down to Waycross, as he had never been there before. As he drove, he pondered the house on a barge—was it headed for the Atlantic coast or inland? Who would bear such an expense? If Finn was riding along, what was his plan? This would be the stupidest escape anyone ever attempted.

He slowed the patrol car as he entered the suburbs, as the traffic obviously yielded to the patrol car as fish might yield to a shark. He came to a train viaduct with a low clearance warning above it as the road dipped dramatically under it. He continued his cruise, but it hit him that the house would never fit under that trestle! He thought about the fact that the move had taken place entirely on Highway 1, but that would end right here at this train trestle!

He found a place to turn around and headed back, looking for a gas station. He turned in at the first station he found, went in, and found and purchased a Georgia state map. He laid it out on the hood of his car and studied it. It seemed possible that if Highway 1 really was part of the route to the final destination, they could not get past Waycross. He could see on the map that 203 crossed the Satilla River southeast of Waycross at Hoboken, then 203 headed south directly to Highway 1 at Racepond. He could also see that Highway 1 headed straight into Florida. He thought if Finn got to Florida, that his own situation and control could change drastically. The gas station had a pay phone, and he called his dispatch to find that there was no new information on the permits.

The sheriff then headed back toward the city, as Highway 1 went all the way through Waycross and straight to Racepond, a forty minute drive. He had no idea how long it would take to barge a house any distance, how long it would take to load or unload, or how fast a moving house could go. He tried to organize these unknowns and eventually came up with a plan. He thought that when he arrived at 203 in Racepond, he would head north toward Hoboken and just look for a moving house. If he didn't see one, he would begin asking local folks about it.

He arrived at the intersection of 203 and Highway 1 at Racepond around 1800 hours. The sheriff made the turn heading north, passing by three people on his right, walking south, then spotted Nettie's Café. He needed a short break, a bathroom, and a burger. He placed an order to go.

While leaving the café a Brantley County deputy pulled up and got out of his patrol car and addressed the sheriff. He said "Sheriff, you're a long way from Richmond County, what gives?"

The sheriff said curtly, "I'm collecting evidence."

The deputy said, "Evidence on what? Brantley County could probably help with that."

The sheriff replied, "I like to do my own, and I need to be leaving now." He hopped in his patrol car and headed north.

Ironically, if Sheriff Stump had been earnest in his pursuit and asked the deputy if he had seen a house being moved, the deputy would have said, "Yes, I led it south through town forty-five minutes ago." But, the desperate sheriff began the thirty-minute drive north to Hoboken instead.

* * *

Back at the Pecan farm, I watched through the door as Dan, Pam, and Annika continued their walk to the house, now parked and with the movers long gone. The huge parking lot was behind the main building on the farm, where the entire rig had pulled in. The three of them approached the front porch of the house on the rear of the trailer.

They just stood there for a moment, then Annika broke out with a loud cry, "Nicolas, are you in there? My God, I cannot wait any longer!"

At that, I opened door and emerged, somewhat cowered, feeling shame. I stood above them on the porch, hunched over, my hands on my face, crying and sobbing loudly. I sputtered out, "I'm sorry, I'm sorry, so sorry!"

Danny said in a commanding voice, "Calm down, Nick."

I was just not successful at collecting myself, but I climbed down, leaning against the porch. Pam was perceptive about the meeting and had grabbed a handful of napkins from Nettie's Café and handed me several. She did the same for Annika, retaining a few for herself.

I used them, tried to stand straight, inhaled and exhaled several times, and said, "I feel like the luckiest man in America. I love you all, but Annika, my Annika, I need to hold you so badly."

Annika leaped into my arms as we hugged, squeezed, and hugged more, with tears of joy pouring down our faces. We whispered to each other and kissed several times.

Pam broke the ice, herself in tears, and blurted out, "I didn't bring enough napkins!"

I chuckled first, then Annika, but Danny started laughing in earnest. Pam, looking perturbed at first, realized the situation and then the great hugs started.

I finally said, "I think I am OK now. The Father of us all has provided me with the best people on earth, what's next?"

Annika said, "I'm hungry, how about you?" I nodded, along with Dan and Pam.

Dan said, "Just walk north to Nettie's Café."

*　*　*

Stump had been going over the speed limit on his way to Hoboken, passing the tiny town and crossing the Satilla River Bridge. He turned around in haste, crossed the bridge again, and spied the marina on the west side. He pulled in, parked, and got out of the car. As he walked down toward the moorings, he could see a large empty barge. He wondered if it could hold a house.

As he stood there, flexing his knees and thinking, a small aluminum fishing boat putted into a slip. A young black boy tied it off, grabbed a stringer of catfish, and headed toward Drake's Little Super.

Larry spotted the sheriff, but the narrow path forced Larry to walk past him. He did so in haste as the sheriff said, "Not so fast son, I have questions for you. You come here very often?"

Larry stayed put, just looking at the sheriff with squinted eyes.

Stump then said, "Was there a house on that barge over there?"

Larry responded, "I don't know nothin, and I don't know any G-Man neither, now leave me alone!" Larry then headed toward town in haste.

Sheriff Stump smiled from ear to ear as he heard the words G-Man again. "Third time's the charm," he thought, "Finn must be moving south in that house, and I am going to get him."

Sheriff Stump drove into Hoboken, passing Larry as he walked. He pulled up to Drake's, got out, and walked onto the porch, approaching the three tobacco chewers. "Any of you fellas see a house on a trailer move through here?"

One said, "Well yes I did." He turned his head to spit in the spittoon, saying, "We usually see big farm equipment coming off the river, but never a house." As he turned his head back, the sheriff was gone.

* * *

We all sat in a booth at Nettie's. Danny and I sat together facing the door and the windows viewing the street, and the girls sat side by side facing us. We had burgers, fries, and sweet tea while reminiscing on the recent past. I began to take control and shared what life was like on the river—fishing daily, cooking on the bucket, filling the bathtub, reading, and exercise. I told them about the three punk kids and how I ran them off. We all laughed.

Then I began telling the story of Catfish John as Annika's eyes began to focus hard on me. By the time I explained leaving him bound in duct tape at the River View, her jaw had dropped. When I said, "Now for the important part," Annika was about to hyperventilate. I reached over the table to hold her hands and said, "Hang on baby, as there is more."

She just stared at me saying quietly, "Ok."

I then replayed using Catfish's boat, finding his hideout, springing the traps, finding the money, and clubbing an alligator in order to leave. Annika was smiling ear to ear but shaking her head.

Then I pulled out the map to the Catfish hideout from my pocket. I said, "I know where it is, but I need someone else to hold the map if I go back to jail, or worse." I explained the potential value of the Catfish treasure, and my fear of a governmental theft of what belonged to the public and to individuals. I wanted to make sure they found the right agency to recover it.

We all agreed as Annika looked strangely at the map then laid it on the table, folding it in half top to bottom. She looked at me and tore the map in two at the fold and handed half to Danny.

She said "There, rest your mind. We will follow through, and no one will get the map in one piece."

As we sat, both Danny and I alerted at the same time, staring toward the road. We looked at each other, then at the girls, saying in harmony, "The sheriff just drove by." We need to watch him."

We bailed out from our seats and to the door, then out near the street. We watched as the sheriff pulled into the motel, got out, and went to the office. He emerged fifteen minutes later, then reparked his car at the far end of the chain of rooms. He got out and keyed his way into a room. We went back in and sat down.

I was trembling but needed to think. "If he gets hungry, this is the only place to eat."

Danny commented, "The sheriff is definitely an annoying bird dog!"

We prepared to leave. I produced a $100 bill for payment and said I would get the tip too. I then handed out three envelopes to them—one to Annika, addressed to her parents, and two to Danny, one addressed to him and Pam and the other to Pastor Roy Walker. I said, "My friends, we have been blessed. Open or deliver them at a later time."

Stepping out, Danny beckoned a waitress to take our picture. She obliged as he pulled an Instamatic from his shirt pocket. We gathered close for the photo. She had us pose twice, and then handed the camera back. We then walked toward the motel as the sheriff got back in his car and headed south with the pedal to the metal. We knew the house was out of sight and that he would drive on south looking for it.

We all made a nervous chuckle as Danny remarked, "He will drive to the Florida line before turning around!"

As we arrived at the motel, we rehearsed the strategic plans for the next two days. Annika kept silent about what she had learned in the days prior to heading to Racepond—and for good reason.

We gathered in the Wakefield's room for a short chat. Danny was not sure if they would stay tomorrow or not, but they had nothing else to do.

Annika said, "Nick, I want to see the house."

I agreed, said goodbye to my friends, and advised Annika to take us there in her car.

Annika drove us to the back parking lot of the processing plant and parked at a curb for an employee. We got out and walked to the porch. She stepped back, looking carefully at the design and character of the house. When she was satisfied, she approached the porch, where I was already onboard offering a hand up. Even though Annika was a full-figured woman, I lifted her with ease to the porch.

The sun was on its way to set, but light still existed in the house. I invited her in, bowing like a butler as she went through the leaded glass door, and then leading her to the living room. I said, "This is my chair and my sleeping sheet." I showed her the entire house, including the back porch, the highboy chair, and how the view of the river from that point was so wonderful, and it was from there that I spotted John's boat. I showed her my food supply and the bucket I used for a grill.

Now, as the tour went on, we were bumping one another, glancing at one another, then Annika stopped and said, "You know, Nick, this house is the most mundane, straight lined, simplest, most elegant house I have ever seen. Now, where do you sleep at night?"

So I showed her the guest bedroom, explaining that I had never slept on the sheets but had always slept wrapped up in the chair sheet.

She said, "Show me how you prepare it."

So I retrieved the sheet, spread it neatly on the bed, stood back holding my hand toward the entire display, and said, "Like that."

She said "Oh," and sat down on the bed. I did too.

It was starting to get dark in the house, so I picked up the flashlight and showed Annika how the blinking system worked and how well I'd mastered the technique. I demonstrated while walking around the room and sat down again.

By then it was truly dark, and Annika stood up and said, "Nick… blink me."

I did, and she was throwing me a kiss.

After a hesitation, she said, "Blink me again." Her blouse was unbuttoned. After a few more seconds, she said, "Blink me." Her blouse was off. Now I was getting uncomfortable, when she said, "Blink me." Her denim slacks were unbuckled and unzipped. I was having trouble holding the light perfectly still when she said, "Blink me." The denims were gone. I swallowed hard as she said, "Blink me." The bra was gone, and I groaned in pleasure and said, "No more baby, no more. That is the most erotic thing I will ever hope to see, but baby I have no facilities for you. I have a covered p-u bucket and some water for the sink—that's it. I have not been to a drugstore, you know, for protection."

Annika said, "Have you noticed the bag I have been carrying? Well, everything we need is in it. Blink me, Nick."

I woke suddenly at 0200 hours with my right arm under her pillow, my left over her body to the front, holding her warmth as she slept with her back to my chest. I could no longer sleep as I held guard for the remainder of the night. I listened to her breath, which reminded me of the sound of a feline purr. I, having never tried to rhyme two words, kept drumming different options through my thoughts to pass the time. It eventually came to this:

On the slow lam, hard for sure.
Blinking light, unreal delight.
A chance to hear her feline purr.

I had turned the radio on low, playing rock in the background all night. "Maybe I'm Amazed" by Paul McCartney, along with others like, "Signed, Sealed, Delivered," "Ain't No Mountain High Enough," and

"Turn Back the Hands of Time," all of which I could relate to. Then there was "Mr. Bojangles," and I thought of Catfish. At 0500 hours I began rubbing Annika's arm, until she awoke, then I was kissing her cheek. She rolled over toward me and we kissed a few times. I let her know that the moving crew would arrive in an hour and she should prepare to go. I explained that I had toothpaste.

Annika said, "I have my own, but could you put some water in the sink? Nick, can you blink me to the bathroom?"

I replied, "All the way baby, all the way."

I turned the light on full this time and helped her dress. Fastening a bra behind a girl's back is always tough you know, and I helped her with that. We gathered her things and went to the door as I realized that I never locked it. I jumped down first and helped her down, which put us face to face. For that moment, we both nearly went to tears as we hugged so tight. We kissed several times, looking at each other each time. Then Annika showed a glint in her eye and a smirk as she winked at me.

"What?"

She said, "You wouldn't tell me where you were or how you were moving, so you will simply need to wait."

I took the camera from my pocket, wound the film roll all the way, and removed it from the camera. I handed it to her, and asked her to develop it soon, make two copies of all the photos, but make them eight by ten—she would see why.

*   *   *

Annika drove back to the motel to take a nice hot shower and hit the sack, since she wanted to enjoy her favorite egg sandwich supreme at the café in the morning. After her breakfast she went back to the motel and knocked on the Wakefields' door. Danny answered and invited her in. She sat at a small table with two chairs as Danny talked about the night before. "I had great concern about the sheriff and watched his room carefully all evening. He returned to the motel at about 1000 hours, which would have given him enough time to travel all the way to the Florida line and back. It looks like the sheriff has a real hunch that Nick could be in the moving house, but he doesn't know where the house is. Pam and I are going to do some sightseeing around the area, then head south to Folkston late enough that the house won't be blocking the road."

Annika was thankful and told Danny, "The next stop for the house will be between the town of Homeland and Folkston. It will be at a peanut processing plant owned by the same outfit as the pecan company. It will also be on the east side of the road."

Danny looked at her with great confusion and said, "How do you know that in such detail?"

She just replied, "It's a woman thing, we have our sources."

*   *   *

I was dressed and ready, as I heard the crew trucks arrive. Shortly after, Tonto was hammering the tires in his rhythmic pattern. The Mack fired up and went into warm up, and the point crew and slack crew were unfolding their road blocking warning lights and flags. At 0631 hours the Mack made its first gentle but powerful pull, and the forward movement started.

When the house was once again moving south on Highway 1, I went back to bed, drawn to sleep by the rhythmic sound of the Mack diesel engine lugging under the hard pull. I jerked awake at about 0930 hours, throwing my feet to the floor and rubbing my eyes. I couldn't help reliving the night before. I knew that I already loved Annika, but now, there would be no other. I went for the boiled eggs and devoured four of them, then opened a can of pears and devoured them. I went into my calisthenics regimen, emerging three hours later. I finally put on clothes, sat in my chair, and turned the radio back on. It was on the rock station.

At somewhere around 1330 hours an explosion rattled the entire house. I found myself on the floor, crawling toward the door. The rig slowed and finally stopped. Another blown tire! My heart still pounding, I went to the peepholes. The Mack began forward movement. Instead of dealing with the tire there on the road, Old Sarge pulled the rig in behind a building nearly identical to the peanut processing plant we had parked behind in Racepond. With Tonto and Harold working in sync, the tire exchange began.

*   *   *

Sheriff Stump, who normally was up at 0530 hours, slept in until 0600 hours. He bailed out of bed and dressed in his three-day-old uniform as fast as he could. He hopped into the patrol car, fired it up, and left the motel heading south at 0630 hours.

At 0632 hours the sheriff passed the Pecan Farm heading south. All the lights on the crew trucks were flashing as a little speed was building toward the right-hand turn from behind the processing plant and onto Highway 1. Stump accelerated past the plant, completely blind to the location of the house. He was convinced that he would come upon the moving house this time and would stop it. But he just couldn't figure out how he could have missed it last night—it was driving him crazy.

Once again, the sheriff drove all the way to the bridge at the St. Mary's River, turned around in disbelief, and turned back north. Highway 1 was the path! Florida was the destination! He knew it! He accelerated.

The sheriff drove all the way to Hoboken before turning around, the frustration enough to make him vapor lock. He went to the pay phone and dialed his dispatch in hopes of getting information on the permits. The dispatcher answered and confirmed that the packet was on his desk. He advised the sheriff that two of the county commissioners had just left the post and were wondering where he had been.

Stump told him not to worry, and that he would be back tomorrow with a prisoner. He thought of himself as 'Bird Dog Supreme,' but he had just lost his prey for the third time. He tried to reason with himself about what he had missed—his conclusion was correct, but he didn't know it. He thought the rig must have been out of sight on a side road while taking a break, but he didn't know where. He vowed to scan left and right down every pig path he saw. He drove back south, scanning every nook and cranny along the way.

*   *   *

Annika was taking her time, as she had planned, but found herself behind the moving house as it took a sudden left-hand turn in behind the processing plant. She slowed, wondering if she should stop and wait, but this afforded her a chance to move forward and get to Folkston ahead of time. It was probably a lunch break for the crew. As she accelerated her car south, she saw the Richmond County sheriff's patrol car heading north toward Racepond. The sheriff, well above the speed limit, passed by the plant without a thought. Annika pulled over long enough to see the patrol car disappear to the north. She sighed in relief, which quickly led to a smile, then a laugh, as she made her way to Folkston.

*　*　*

While the blown tire was being replaced, I settled back in my chair with the good book, opening to 2 Kings. King David had already subdued all the enemies of Israel, built most of the cities, and collected all the materials and supplies to build a temple for their God. It was now time for his son Solomon to take over as king. The only thing that Solomon prayed to God for was wisdom, and God granted it to him. He saw to it that the temple was built. It was the zenith of the Israelites' Empire in the Promised Land. Solomon was famous throughout the known world.

It was about 1730 hours, and I was getting hungry, so I opened a can of pineapple chunks—oh so good. I didn't want to overeat since there could be a chance of dinner with Annika, even if she brought in fast food.

Was I hearing a siren? Yes! And it was getting louder. I went to the door, looking through one of the leaded glass panes that was not a prism. It was Sheriff Stump trying to get Harold to stop the rear-guard truck. He finally found a driveway that added enough width to power the squad car into a side-slide and pass the truck, pulling in front to block Harold's path.

The sheriff jumped from his car, running to the truck driver's door, pointing toward the house. We were pulling farther away when I saw Harold's hand bringing his radio mike to his mouth. The house slowed to a stop; I was paralyzed. The sheriff tried to run to the house, but his paunch was getting the best of him. He tried to climb onto the porch, but couldn't. He was only eight feet away from me, screaming at Harold to get him something to climb up on. Harold ran up with a four-foot ladder and placed it, while stepping back some distance.

The sheriff climbed up on the porch and pulled his .38 from its holster as Harold backed up farther yet. The other crew members were joining him, as vehicles were starting to back up bumper to bumper on the road. I was still completely paralyzed, as Stump began yelling.

"COME OUT FINN, COME OUT NOW!" He then pulled a baton in preparation to bust the leaded glass door.

"YOU'VE BEEN CAUGHT, FINN! COME OUT!"

Was I hearing another siren? Yes, I was, and it was getting louder fast. I stepped back toward the hatch, but if I dropped through, it would be a miracle if I wasn't spotted, since now he had backup! What else could I do?

Stump screamed out, "I WILL COUNT TO THREE!"

Stump was so focused that he paid no attention to the siren or the Charlton County sheriff running from his car to the back of the house. Stump shouted, "ONE!"

The Charlton sheriff screamed at him, "SHERIFF, WHAT ARE YOU DOING?"

Stump shouted, "TWO."

The Charlton sheriff pulled his baton and started hammering the porch deck, then screamed again, "SHERIFF, WHAT ARE YOU DOING IN MY COUNTY?"

Stump finally turned to see the sheriff addressing him, and he really looked pissed. Stump said, "I AM IN PURSUIT!"

Then, the sheriff said, "I am Don Adams of Charlton County. I know this case, as we have heard your radio traffic. You lost your pursuit back on May 14 with failed hounds. Now GET DOWN OFF THAT HOUSE!"

Stump begged the sheriff, saying, "I know he is in there! He is a crazy Vietnam veteran, and he is armed and dangerous!"

Out of desperation, Stump added, "And Pea Picker confirmed that the G-Man was in the house!"

Sheriff Adams looked at him and must have been thinking his statement sounded nuts. He said, "What did you say? You had better holster that weapon and the baton now!" He pounded the deck hard with his baton again, shouting, "GET DOWN NOW!"

Stump finally complied in a fit of emotions. Sheriff Adams looked at Harold and the crew and said, "Is there anyone in that house?"

They replied, "Not that we know of, sir."

Adams said, "Well open the door and I will do a search."

I had moved back to the door and was listening, with the hatch door still open and ready.

The crew replied, "We do not have a key."

Adams climbed the ladder and went to the door to find it was locked. He climbed back down and directed the crew to get the house moving again. He looked at Stump and said, "You have traffic backed up ten miles, now get in your vehicle and leave our county NOW."

Stump got back into his squad car, turned around, and headed north as he weaved through stalled traffic.

*   *   *

Sheriff Stump drove toward Racepond. He was in a mental mess, but he had one more option. The Richmond County judge, Honorable Richard Stump, was a cousin, and he knew his home phone, so he stopped at Nettie's Café and used the pay phone to call the judge. He finally had one thing go right for the day, as the judge answered the phone. Stump explained the situation—that he was out of his jurisdiction, and it would take a call to the governor of Georgia to appeal to the Charlton County sheriff to stop the house before it crossed the bridge into Florida. Stump pleaded with the judge, saying, "I want my prisoner back. It's a personal thing now."

The judge said, "I'd rather call Florida and have them pick him up as soon as he crosses, then extradite him."

"That could take a year."

"I will see what I can do in the morning. The governor is a friend of mine."

Sheriff Stump crossed the road and booked in at the motel, too tired to go any farther.

*   *   *

After the delay with the sheriff, it was only a forty-five-minute ride to the final overnight stop. The buildings were nearly a quarter of a mile long, with the only car parking space between the building and the road. There was an access drive to the rear at each end, with an expanse of parking space behind the building. The crew did their thing and left, so I was alone again, my nerves still in questionable shape. Since it was a peanut processing plant, I thought about going on a scrounging mission, but I guess those days were over. I sat in my chair wondering, "What next?"

A car horn tooted twice at the back of the rig. I walked to the leaded glass door to see Annika getting out. I wondered how on earth I could have ever found a woman that I could love so completely. I keyed the door shut, jumped from the porch, and climbed into the passenger's seat. I said "Baby, what's the plan?"

Annika said, "Well first, we are going to a barber, who I needed to bribe to stay open another hour, then we are going to the motel to meet with Danny and Pam. Then you are going to take a shower. Then we are going to a real restaurant where I have made reservations. Don't worry about your clothes, I have a nice set for you. Then you are staying at the motel with me."

What could I say but, "That sounds like a plan to me! However, I have one request: I need to take everything I have accumulated from the house and load it into your car."

"Barber first. It's only ten minutes away."

It just didn't seem that long since my haircut and shave in Lyons, but I was looking unkempt. This barber cut my hair only, no shave, then we headed back to the house, where Annika loaded the car as I brought everything to the porch.

When I sat the tackle boxes on the porch, I said, "Please keep these covered up and find a very safe place for them when you get home."

She looked at me funny and said, "OK."

I left the hard hat and vest, and a few snacks for the short remainder of the house ride. After arriving at the motel, I truly enjoyed a most delicious shower. Annika had a razor and blades, shaving cream, after shave, and a can of antiperspirant ready.

While I was enjoying the shower, Annika called the Wakefields' room with the final arrangements. Pam would be driving the Chevelle. I put on the new outfit, including new brief underwear, tan slacks, and a nice loose-fit short sleeve shirt one might wear in Hawaii. The horn on the Chevelle beeped, and we went out to greet them. Danny needed to exit the passenger door of this two-door car to allow us to climb in the back seat. Annika had switched clothing while I was showering—a sleek burgundy skirt, white silky blouse with a large collar, a tight pearl necklace, and black short heeled shoes. She was stunning.

Annika directed Pam to the Black Swan restaurant in downtown Folkston, where reservations were already set. The four of us took our time, chatting as we went. I noticed how well these two women interacted.

Annika said, "What you did, Nick, was wrong, but it has—apparently—exposed other wrongdoings. The boat and the Jeep should never have been at the VFW. But there is more."

She continued, "I found that the sheriff and the commander of the VFW are brothers, and even worse, the Honorable Judge Richard Stump is a first cousin to them.

Turning to the others, she added, "I should never have been denied the right to visit Nick at the prison."

"And something else," she said, "I just recently learned that two Vietnam veterans are bringing suit on the commander of that VFW post. Apparently, the commander got physical with them while escorting them to the door. Nick never had a chance to voice his complaint with the commander, so it may constitute new evidence."

Danny added, "I talked with my dispatcher friend, and news travels through the county sheriff's post quickly sometimes. He had heard that Sheriff Stump was in some kind of reprimand for being out of his jurisdiction."

We all laughed about the sheriff and agreed that they were certainly correct about that. I was sitting back in the chair enjoying the chatter, mesmerized by how thorough Annika truly was, what a true friend Danny was, and how fortunate I was. My mind drifted to the final move tomorrow, when I questioned myself.

"Nick," I thought, "what day is this?" I had lost track as I attempted to count days. I said to the group, "This is June 8, correct?"

Pam replied, "Yes?"

I replied, "Good grief, it's Friday! The house will not make the final run until Monday!"

Annika, looking a little sheepish, said, "That's correct."

I suggested that we meet for breakfast at 0900 hours and decide what we might do for the weekend. We also needed to find a church for Sunday. The waiter arrived with a bill for $84, and I sent him away with a $100 bill. Pam drove us back to the motel, then we all traded hugs and went to our rooms.

I, in my crude way, was thinking:

Room 21, the number of our suite,
A queen bed made so very neat,
Tear it up, we don't give a damn,
I could not expect, with life on the lam.

At 0745 hours I was rubbing Annika's arm again. I knew she would want shower time, and I did too. I sorted a few clothes from Annika's car, more suitable for the day, and we were ready for breakfast. Pam drove, and we just cruised until we found a mom-and-pop restaurant with plenty of cars around it, usually a sign of local approval.

With just a ten-minute wait, we were seated and served hot coffee. I was hungry and ordered a seafood, spinach, Swiss cheese omelet. Oh, to die for. Annika had an egg croissant, and the Wakefields split an order of biscuits and gravy, southern style, with two extra sausage patties.

We went into all sorts of small talk; it was so enjoyable. Then I went a little deeper into the capture of Catfish John, adding details I thought they should know. I explained that the poor man had no idea who I was, since I didn't let him see me, and I never spoke to him. Before I left him, he proclaimed that I was a G-Man since no one else could have caught him!

Danny said, "Ah that makes sense now. My dispatcher friend said that the county jailers were having great difficulty with him. He would not cooperate with anything they wanted until he could talk to the G-Man that brought him in. He kept claiming that the county sheriff had to know who he was."

I said, "That's interesting."

The women changed the topic. "What should we do today?" They asked. As we traded ideas, someone mentioned Cumberland Isle National Sea Shore, just north of St. Mary's. It was a beautiful day for a walk on an Atlantic beach, and it was only forty-five minutes away. We all said, "Let's go!"

We first went back to the motel to freshen up and to pack a few different bits of clothing we might need. Pam 'Wheel girl' was behind the wheel of the Chevelle once again, and we headed west on Highway 40 toward St. Mary's.

On arrival, we needed to ask for information about the island and found that the only access was by ferry. We all thought that was cool and looked forward to the ride over on a boat. Myself, well, I had had my share of boats for a while, but I suppose this was different, and it was. Georgia has its share of mountains and high country, but it all goes flat. Crossing the intercoastal waterway to the island was beautiful, the wind coming inland from the Atlantic, carrying the smell of the sea. Seagulls were cruising the skies everywhere, and the pelicans, flying in small groups of choreographed hunters in search of food, only several feet above the water.

It reminded me of a poem my grandmother once shared:
Poor old pelican, his beak holds more than his belly can.

A road circumvented the entire island, with many stops along the way. Historical sites with interpretive signs and museum buildings. Beaches that had never been developed. We stopped at several to walk the beach, and Danny was doing amazingly well with his new leg, almost a normal gate, but unwilling to let go of the cane. I watched Annika approach the shore with her shoes off, trying to get close to the sandpipers grazing the beach as each wave receded. The wind blew through her hair and ruffled her blouse as she challenged the incoming waves. I was at her mercy; she was truly a beautiful woman.

At the far north end of the island, we exited the car one more time to view the Atlantic from a spectacular beach. We all gathered arm and arm as Danny delivered a wonderful prayer of thanks for the day and a request for safe delivery in the days to come. Making our way back to the ferry and back through St. Mary's, we were starting to feel hungry. We all agreed on an early supper before the ride back to Folkston. And with all of us scanning the sign boards along the highway, we found a restaurant. It was a mom-and-pop, with a bit of a high-end air.

Alcoholic drinks were on the menu, but it was time for sweet tea. Everyone placed their order. Mine was Cajun catfish, and I was not unhappy with that decision. I wanted to fish for cats, catch cats, and cook cats, and this provided a new recipe. The suggestion came from one of us that we make the cruise back to Folkston and find a church for Sunday. We all agreed, and I paid the bill—including a generous tip—as we left.

During the ride back to Folkston, Annika settled in next to me, my arm around her neck, and nearly went to sleep, and I did too, but Pam had the radio playing on rock and roll, and we both were mouthing the words to each song. Arriving in Folkston, we found a Church of God, only a few blocks from the motel, and agreed to attend their 0930 hours meeting. Wheel girl Pam drove us back to the motel, where we all exchanged hugs before going to our rooms.

Both of us felt we needed showers again and took turns. There were times that my old room temperature bathtub filled with river water felt really good, but nothing beats a hot shower. We turned on the TV, climbed into bed, and watched an *Andy Griffith* show then the *Twilight Zone*, YES! Then we turned off the TV, as other business needed attending.

Around 0300 hours I awoke from a bad dream, and Annika was then awake too. I explained that it was nothing and that it happened fairly often. "I have a spot on my back that is bugging me. Would you look at it?"

We turned a light on, and she examined the spot I tried to point to. She reported that something was going on at that spot and asked what she should do. I asked her to cover it with a tissue and squeeze as hard as she could. Annika was not timid and did what I asked, and the small festering wound gave up what it was holding.

She said, "What is this?"

I explained that it was probably a tiny piece of shrapnel, covered with a small piece of the jungle fatigue shirt I was wearing when I was hit. There were many scars on my back from that blast.

I took a minute to explain that bullets travel so fast, and because of their shape, they do not take much clothing with them, but they usually go straight through and out the other side. But shrapnel is ragged in shape and in all sizes, and it travels much slower too. Whenever you are hit, it almost always takes clothing in with it. Even if the fragment is buried into the flesh, the clothing may still be attached, making it difficult to get a shirt, pants, or even boots off.

"Ok, no romance after that, let's just try to get back to sleep," I said.

We did find sleep and awoke in time for church. The horn on the Chevelle sounded at 0900, and we were ready to climb in. Without enough time to get comfortable in the seat, we arrived at the Church of God and got back out. We were greeted very nicely while entering the church. Dan had some difficulty, as there were ten concrete steps to scale on the way in, but he did just fine. Announcements were made, then the familiar gospel songs, backed up by a very good choir. The pastor was an energetic young man with a great message, keeping us on the edge of our seats. When the offering was passed, I found yet another $100 for the plate.

"Breakfast, yes, breakfast, where should we go?" Pam said. "I'm driving, and I am going to Hilliard, Florida, you all can come along if ya like." She turned onto Highway 1 and headed south. In fifteen minutes, we were at Hilliard, but there was not much for a restaurant. She continued south, and in another fifteen minutes we entered Callahan. We had our choice of two restaurants, and the women voiced their preference. Danny and I looked at each other, thinking that Gators Landing had some appeal, but Clementine's at the Glade won out.

We enjoyed breakfast on an open deck at a round table with an umbrella. We chatted and laughed over and over. What a perfect morning.

Then Danny said, "Well dude, are you ready for the last ride?"

I pursed my lips after taking in a full lung of air and blew out slowly. "Yes, I am ready. If this is what I have to look forward to in the future, I will do the time and enjoy it."

Annika added, "Nick, I have been thinking."

By now, I knew that if Annika said she had been thinking, it would be something undeniable.

"What if you just turn yourself in here in Florida tonight, or early tomorrow morning, and skip the ride in the house?"

I said, "You know, Annika, great minds think alike, and I have also thought deeply about that. It certainly makes more sense. Why on earth would I feel an obligation to this house that basically saved me? Oh, perhaps I just answered my own question. It did save me! I suppose that I would be cheating myself, and cheating the house, if I didn't finish the ride. What if the house still needs me?"

My love and my two best friends were silent for an extended period of time. Then Danny said, "I understand, and I will support you to the end."

Annika and Pam, now fighting tears, agreed and said, "Ok, you do this."

Annika interceded again, saying, "Would it be prudent to call the Nassau County Sheriff's office and advise them that you will be turning yourself in tomorrow morning when you cross the St. Mary's River Bridge?"

We all thought about that and discussed the possible outcomes, and we all agreed it would be the right thing to do. A pay phone stood at the entrance to the restaurant, and we all migrated over to it. Flipping the pages in the tethered phone book gave me the number to call. "Anyone have a few quarters?" I asked. "I'm broke." Danny handed me two, and I made the call. I announced to a dispatcher who I was, and he took careful notes and asked pertinent questions.

He asked, "How will we know you?"

"Just keep a squad car posted on the south side of the bridge around 1100 hours. I will probably be wearing an orange hard hat and vest. I would also be obliged if your sheriff were among those that I surrender to." I hung up the phone.

It was a beautiful sunny day in Florida, so we put the top down for a slow cruise back to Folkston. On arrival, Pam took the first side street to the east and did a slow zigzag on every street in the city. We all pointed and wondered about some of the grand old homes. We went back to the motel, which had a nice veranda, with several sheltered tables. We gathered at a table and talked more. On the table was a flier advertising Roma Pizza and free delivery. None of us had ever tried ordering pizza to go, so we needed to make a list of what we all liked. Annika commanded that task, and in a short minute we had a pizza designed that we all could enjoy. Annika went to the room and made the call, ordering four more sweet teas to go as well. Thirty minutes later, our pizza arrived in an appropriately designed cardboard box. I paid for the pizza, and when the driver looked at his tip, his eyes got very big. He stuttered, "Th-Th-Thank you!"

After finishing that loaded pizza, the sun finally left us, and we went to our rooms. Annika forced herself to become very businesslike, asking me what I intended to wear tomorrow.

I didn't know, I hadn't thought about that, but laying out my clothes would probably be a good idea. So, I chose a pair of denim pants, a cotton button up shirt with western designs, and my prison shoes, polished with grease. For good measure, I added the hard hat and vest.

At 0500 hours I could hear Annika moving about, as I was already up and in the shower. Yes—one more hot shower before facing prison once again!

* * *

Back in Richmond County, Judge Stump had contacted the Georgia governor and asked him, as a friend, to apply some pressure on the Charlton County sheriff to stop the house being moved to Florida, as it was believed that a known felon was trying to escape Georgia, riding in the house. The judge exaggerated the situation, saying, "The suspect is a deranged Vietnam veteran, probably armed and dangerous. He escaped from one of our facilities on May 14, and we have been hunting him ever since. We want him back."

The governor said he would make some calls.

*   *   *

Annika drove me to the house, where we both got out and walked to the porch and held one another very tight. Annika said, "You know that we will be at the bridge, and we will support in any way that we can—we will cheer if it is appropriate!"

I said, "Once we cross the halfway point of the bridge, I would like to step out onto the porch and wave at anyone looking my way!" We kissed a few more times, and Annika sped off to the motel.

We had nearly waited too long, as I barely had time to key into the house before the crew arrived. They all exited the point crew truck, all stretched and yawned for a few minutes, then started the regimen for the day's final pull. There was that rhythmic testing of the tires, the firing up of the Mack diesel, and the going into a warm-up idle. The bridge over the St. Mary's River seemed to me to be a challenge itself, as it had an extremely high arch to allow sailing ships and large barges to pass underneath. The Mack would earn its keep on that bridge today.

The pull started as normal, with that first commanding tug then forward movement. Down to the end of the peanut facility, a right-hand turn toward Highway 1, then a slow left onto the tarmac of the highway. It wasn't long before car horns could be heard, fighting to get a better place in line. People were trying to get to work—you couldn't blame them—but there were plenty of postings in the local papers warning motorists of the temporary blockade.

I knew it would take several hours to navigate the city, so I settled into my chair with the Bible to finish 2 Kings. Solomon was an amazing man of God. He basically made every single Israelite rich during his reign. But even Solomon in all his wisdom and all his God given success, far beyond any other king, began to sin while honoring false gods. I was forced to quit reading as the house kept stopping. I didn't know when I could continue my read, but I would look forward to that day.

The house was stopping more often than in the past, as all the stoplights in the city were too low and needed to be lifted by crane. There must have been six or seven of them. I marched from peephole to peephole, trying to see something new. Then it appeared that we were leaving Folkston and went directly into the farming district. I had looked at this real estate yesterday as we passed, but I didn't pay much attention. There were vast orchards of peach trees, all so green. I thought, as Americans, we are so blessed with the fortitude of the farmers, who risk everything every year to produce a crop worthy of harvest. Then, they must hope for a market.

As I rode, I opened my last can of peaches and devoured them, providing for myself. Looking at the label on the can, it said "Georgia Peaches." There were programs working tirelessly to provide food and shelter for people less fortunate, especially for children. But with all the programs available to feed the little ones, it was simply impossible to get past a bad parent. I grumbled to myself about these facts, but then thought of Pea Picker, a very young man, making his way as an adult. He had good parents, who let him go as he asked, and trusted his judgment. They couldn't provide anything else for him. He was as poor as poor could be, but he was not hungry, or unhappy, and he was self-reliant.

I tried to think of more positive things, as Old Sarge now accelerated the Mack across open land toward the bridge. I smelled onions again, and it reminded me of passing through Vidalia and gathering young onions to eat. I was so desperate and so thankful at the same time. I was provided for, but I needed to get up and go after it every time.

A hundred thoughts of the last thirty-two days kept flashing before me, as the rumble of the road kept sounding in my ears. I wondered about Catfish John, living free as a bird, now a jail bird. He must be going crazy. I thought about his treasure, and how on earth I could get a government agency to do the correct thing with it. Would I have the power to make suggestions in advance in trade for its location? How long or short would the extradition time be? Would my case once again go before Judge Stump? Annika may have time to finish law school before I was released.

I got up and went to the back porch, opened the door, and stepped into the room, I stood back just far enough so Old Sarge could not see me. I was hoping to see the bridge rising up out of the countryside ahead. Another mile and there it was, and I was wondering if the old Mack would have the power to pull this rig up and over. Then I wondered about its braking ability.

As we began the approach to the bridge, there were cars and boats parked near the river at a boat landing. I closed and locked the door and headed to the front door to look back down the road behind us. On my way, the house slowed and came to a stop with only about five hundred yards to go.

Don't be alarmed Nick, it's probably normal stuff. I looked back through a small clear glass in the leaded glass door and decided that being alarmed would be an understatement. As what I was witnessing was the army, and it looked like all of it! Jeeps were pulling around on both sides, troop trucks unloading armed men everywhere. They were surrounding the house, hundreds of them.

I thought, "Lordy, help me now!" I was pinching myself, "Am I dreaming? This can't be for real. Is there a bounty on my head now? Why didn't I just turn myself in yesterday?"

Then came a pounding on the deck, followed by a command. "Nicholas Finn, come out of that house now. I am the commander of the Georgia National Guard, and I know you are in there!"

I opened the door, shaking from head to foot. My head hung low, my shoulders and arms hung so low, my knuckles nearly dragging as I trudged slowly to the edge of the porch.

A very commanding voice said, "NICHOLAS FINN GET DOWN FROM THAT PORCH!"

I climbed down, nearly falling, and just stood there in raw shame, not looking up. All I could see was more and more boots around my position. Then I heard, "Finn, get down and give me ten."

I thought, "What?"

"That ten is for stealing a ride in my mother's house! Give me another 10!"

Now I was thinking I had lost my mind; I was sure I wasn't dreaming.

"That ten is for not recognizing me!"

I finally looked up, and to my total shock, it was Colonel Hal Moore, now a general! He was dressed exactly as I had seen him in Vietnam. Camo uniform and helmet, with his chin strap tight. He was grinning at me from ear to ear. I was speechless, as I looked to his right to see Mr. Khaki Man, and it was Joe Galloway.

I finally said something I thought was profound, "I think I need to sit down." Two GIs grabbed my arms and helped me to the fender of a Jeep.

Then the general said in his commanding voice, "Men, listen up, THIS MAN IS ONE OF YOUR BROTHERS! He served under me in Vietnam back in '65. He was with my unit in the battle of the Ia Drang Valley. He was the lone survivor of a squad under ambush. The last time I saw him was in a field hospital, as he was recovering from a scratch on his backside."

The general looked at me and smiled again. "We are here under the request of Miss Annika Bjorn to make sure Nicholas gets over that bridge. I need a HURRAH on that!"

And at that, all in earshot responded with a very loud and powerful, "HURRAH!"

* * *

By order of the governor, the Brantley County sheriff arrived at the bridge, but he was behind the army convoy, and could not get around, even with the sirens going. The army was in control of this section of road. The sheriff knew the radio channel that the heavy movers were using, as it was state law for the movers to stay in contact with local authorities. He radioed the heavy movers, and Old Sarge picked up the mike and answered. The sheriff advised him not to pull the house over the bridge, and if he did, charges would be filed against him and his men, and the heavy movers would be fined.

Annika had driven to the opposite side of the bridge an hour earlier, knowing the police in Florida would block the bridge prior to the house being moved over. Sensing that it was taking longer than it should have, she walked back north across the bridge toward the house.

* * *

Old Sarge gathered up Harold and Tonto and went to the back of the house where the general was talking to me and the company of soldiers. Old Sarge informed the general that he, his crew, and his company would be in legal trouble if they drove the rig over the bridge. He and his crew had to stand down.

Generals need to be decisive, and so General Moore said to Old Sarge, "Are the keys in the Mack?"

Sarge replied, "Yes."

General Moore said, "Take your crew trucks on over. We will deal with the house, as the US Army has just taken command of it."

Old Sarge made a proper and well-trained salute to the general and followed his command.

Then the general shouted out, "Drivers, we need a driver for this Mack, do we have one?" There were many drivers present, trained from Jeeps up to 2.5-ton military trucks, but none of them felt qualified to volunteer to drive the Mack.

The general said, "We may have a problem here men, we need a quick solution."

I finally spoke out for the first time and said, "Sir, I can drive that thing." The general paid close attention when I said, "It's a Mack Model B, 4X5. It has a 490-horsepower Allison diesel, bolted to a Fuller four speed transmission. This one has a split differential, which gives it five lower gears, for a total of twenty forward gears. I have been watching and listening to a very professional driver operate this truck tractor for over a month. And it is just like the concrete trucks I drove in Atlanta. I can do it, sir."

General Moore looked at me in near disbelief and laughed in earnest. He said, "Well you will not be the first criminal to drive his own getaway vehicle, just don't do any stunt driving!" Then he shouted, "Mount your packs men, we're moving out!"

Then Annika stepped out from around the house, dropping the jaws on most of the men. The general said to her, "Hi, I'm Hal Moore, it's nice to finally meet you."

Annika returned many thanks to him, then asked if she could ride over the bridge with me.

The general shrugged his shoulders and said, "What do I know?"

I said, "Yes, but I will need one of your Jeeps to pull alongside the passenger door, so I can unload the passenger seat."

The general just pointed, and his men in earshot moved quickly. Then the general said, "Finn, we will see you on the other side."

I climbed into the Mack, set the key to heat the glow plugs, and then fired it up. As it idled, I cleared all the accumulated junk from the seat and floorboard so Annika could sit in the passenger seat. She climbed in, and we made a quick kiss. The split differential was already in the low range position, so I put Fuller in low and eased out on the clutch while adding just enough accelerator. That gentle, but first hard tug took place as I quickly shifted to second gear, laboring the engine a bit more, then third, then forth. At tenth gear, we were at a fast walking speed, headed for the base of the bridge.

The grade began gently at first, then took to the dramatic uphill grade, I needed to down shift from tenth to ninth quickly. Then eighth to seventh, feeding even more fuel to the engine. In short order, as we went into the long upward pull, I had shifted back into first gear, my foot holding the accelerator nearly to the floor. The engine was barking very loud but steady as a determined bull. Annika was looking at me from time to time, and I just smiled in confidence. The Mack took us on the 'granny slow lam' to the top of the bridge. I knew without a doubt that I was impressing my girlfriend.

At the neutral gravity point of the bridge, the Nassau County Florida sheriff was standing in the center on the road and waved us to a stop. I applied the air brakes and waited for him to come to the driver's door. I really wanted to cuss, "What the blank-blank now?" I held it.

The sheriff boldly jumped up on the running board and looked into the open window. He said, "You are welcome to come into the state of Florida, but you must have a valid driver's license to do so."

I was hanging my head again, when Annika produced a small purse and said, "Oh by the way, Nick, this came in the mail the day before I met you here." Mom had plowed through with my license! I handed it to the sheriff.

He noted the CDL on the license and said, "We will see you when you have the house in place at the address we have on record. Do not stop driving until the house is on that property. Then you must turn yourself in."

PART III:
REDEMPTION

20. PIKE POISONING

I HANDED ANNIKA the ledger and said, "While you are finding the final delivery address for the house, would you like to have an oatmeal cookie?" I opened Old Sarge's bag of cookies, took one out for myself, and handed one to Annika saying, "Long story."

We started the downhill run, with the Allison remaining in low gear. The weight of the house, the truck, and all the moving framing, axles, and tires showed their love for gravity. In less than a hundred feet, I applied the Jake brake, and the diesel barked even louder than on the uphill pull. I began applying the brakes with a hard hold for a few seconds to scrub speed, then let off to cool the brakes. I stabbed them hard again for a few seconds, then let off for some cool time. After about ten iterations we arrived safely at the bottom, tapering off onto the flat land.

Annika found the last page in the journal, scanning quickly, and said, "Slow down, the corner is just ahead."

I answered, "Does that mean stop?"

She said, "No, just turn left on Lake Hampton Road, it's just up ahead. Turn left again, on St. Mary's Circle. The site is at the end where the road turns to the left."

I advised Annika that the turns may get interesting, since so far we had been going straight ahead. The truck tractor was equipped with a pintle hook hitch, connected to a drawbar with a pintle ring. It did not use a fifth wheel on the truck, but the moving framework and the first four sets of axles were all fixed to a sub framework, which had a fifth wheel under its center, enabling the first four axles to turn at the will of the draw bar. All the remaining trail axles needed to side slide to make a turn, and that required power from the truck.

So, I understood what was required to make a turn with this rig but had never done it. I stopped in advance, got out of the Mack, ran to the back, gauged all the distances, got back in the cab, and shifted to low gear. My first left turn put the house off the road a little, but I made the second spot on. I needed to make another left, prior to backing up alongside a new poured concrete foundation for the house. I had to leave the cab of the truck several times to put the house into the proper position to be moved onto the foundation. The crew for that job was already on site, directing me to place the house at the optimal spot.

I said, "Ok Annika, it's done. Where do we find the sheriff—I am so ready to turn myself in." Leaving the keys in the ignition, we walked back toward the Highway 1 intersection. The army convoy was using the intersection to make the U-turn back over the bridge to Georgia. General Moore was talking to the Nassau County sheriff as we walked up. We stood back and allowed them to finish their conversation.

In minutes, we were beckoned to join, and the general shook my hand, saying, "Well done, son, well done." Then he stretched his arms around Annika, pulled her in, and said, "Thank you so much for believing in one of our brothers. We will be seeing you both soon." He tried to hop into his Jeep, but it was full of junk from the Mack. He pointed in the direction of St. Mary's Circle, and his driver followed orders.

Now, it was the sheriff, Annika, and me. The sheriff said, "Climb in the back of the patrol car, we need to talk."

Once we were inside the car he continued, "I am Nassau County Sheriff Marty Welker, and for a felon who has escaped from prison, you come with very good credentials, and powerful friends. When you called yesterday, I took the time to look a little at your case, and from the perspective of Sheriff Stump, you appear to be a big risk. But the general made it very clear that you are not, and he guarantees that you will follow through with the procedures required back at our post."

I replied, "I will, sir. I really do not want to go back to Richmond County because Sheriff Stump and Judge Stump have some sort of vendetta against me, but I must and will go."

Annika asked if she could speak on the matter, and the sheriff was very obliging. She said, "I have been doing research on Nick's case for the last month, and I have found the possibility of some misconduct on the part of the sheriff. What Nick did was wrong, but it caused a problem for the sheriff, hence, the extended prison sentence and all the extra work details he endured. I have many FOIA requests at the sheriff's office, but none have been answered. I can only hope that before the extradition time runs out I can amass a case before we sit before the judge."

The sheriff said, "Plan for about a month. Do you have a car here?"

Annika said, "Yes, it's a block south."

Then he said, "This is what we are going to do: I will take you to your car, then you are to find a motel for the night and report to my Sheriff's Post in Callahan at 0900 hours tomorrow. I will be there to meet you, and we will go through the process of turning yourself in, which technically, you already have. I am sure I will have more questions for you then as well." He added, "Don't go back to Georgia."

I said, "Don't worry, sir!"

He took us to Annika's car, and just like that, we were free to go. So we drove on down to Callahan and found a Howard Johnson's Hotel and restaurant. We booked our room, moved in what clothing we needed, freshened up, and went to the lounge. We both ordered cocktails and went outside to a gated garden area with canopy covered tables. Annika blurted out, "Nick, I would so love to take that truck over that bridge again, what a rush!"

I said, "I know, I loved it too, but glancing at you when I had the chance, seeing the look on your face, was priceless."

We decided to walk downtown, slowly meandering hand in hand. We window shopped for an hour or so and slowly made our way back. We had a first-floor room and needed to pass the concierge's desk on the way. There was General Moore checking in. Annika received another hug from the general, and I received one from his wife. General Moore said, "We were hoping you would show up here. We need to catch up, and I have a proposal for you." We agreed to meet at the hotel restaurant at 1830 hours and went to our rooms.

Annika wanted to just soak in the tub for a while, so I just stopped and sat down. I bowed my head and gave thanks for yet another delivery. Annika emerged from her bath, wrapped in towels, and said, "I am so happy that you are Christian. You know we need to make this both legal and right in the Father's view."

I said, "I know, and I am fully convinced that I want to be married to you too, but should we wait until I am out of jail?"

Annika said, "I just don't know, we will need to pray about that as well."

I mentioned to Annika that I was past due in calling my parents, and Danny, but perhaps I should wait until I finished turning myself in tomorrow morning. She agreed.

Before meeting the Moores, Annika made suggestions for my clothing, which I followed. That woman could wrap up in a curtain and look like a movie star. So I was stepping high as we entered the restaurant, finding that the general and his wife were already seated. We joined, and a wonderful conversation came forth. I nearly went to tears as we rehashed a few events from our tour in Vietnam. I felt that I was at home again, just being around him. My closest military friends had all been killed, but my ties to the 1st Cavalry as a unit were still very strong. I observed once again that veterans' wives and even girlfriends respond with the camaraderie that their veterans have. Social comparisons go out the window, all are equal.

Military leaders do not have the luxury of taking their time about much of anything, so General Moore said, "How much time do you have?"

I said, "It looks like thirty days, sir, but I cannot be certain."

He said, "Well that is enough for a start. I need a foreman on this job of placing my mother's house on this new property. Most of the work for the next month will be the concrete, driveways, sidewalks, patio, and the like. Can you do it?"

"Yes, and I have a month of back rent to pay you, so that may make us even."

The general said, "Deal."

I exclaimed, "I have a job!"

The restaurant stocked St. Julian's Ruby Red wine, and two bottles between the four of us didn't last long, so we went for a third. The conversation moved to the general's mother, as we were told about the family and that the Moores had become fairly wealthy. General Moore's father had passed away a few years earlier and his mother always wanted to live on the St. Mary's River. They decided to make it happen, acquired property, and Joe Galloway agreed to hunt down a reliable mover and help plan all the logistics for the trip. I told the general that I had seen Joe several times while hiding in the house, but his back was always to me, so I had not recognized him. He was documenting and photographing all the major events.

General Moore talked about his mother, saying that she was doing well in her upper eighties and loved the whodunit books and mysteries. But above all, she loved adventure books, and the moving of the house was to be one of her own adventures. He said, "Can you imagine her thoughts when I tell her that there was a stowaway prison escapee hiding in the house for the entire journey?" He analyzed that he had better tell her the rest of the story, in bits and pieces. The prisoner driving the house over the bridge, delivering it to the building site, then being a foreman on the job.

"Now, how will you explain that the prisoner served under you in Vietnam?" I asked.

The general said he would need to think about that one for a while.

I looked at Annika, and she looked at me. I looked at the table in silence for a short time, enough so that it was noticeable to the general. I turned my head toward him and said, "Sir, there is more to the story, a lot more. So much so, you may not believe me at this time. Many things happened on the road south, but on the Satilla River, it all changed."

General Moore looked at me with one eye fully open and the other partially closed and said, "More? Then tell me more!"

I replied, "I am very sorry, sir, but at this time, I cannot. But it is important that you know that there is more, since we will be using it before the judge back in Augusta." Then I said, "Trust me, sir, your mother is going to approve of this one."

The general said, "Well, if I could bust your ass to private I would, but seeing as I can't, I will accept your wishes, bid you goodnight, and see you after you turn yourself in tomorrow."

I agreed as I picked up the bill left on the table and counted out the cash as we headed for the checkout counter, the general in the trail sputtering that he would get the bill. I said, "Don't worry, sir, your mom has got this one." General Moore looked at me with a perplexed look on his face. I said, "You may want to start reading her Bible." We all hugged and shook hands and went to our rooms.

We got ready for bed, and Annika had one more surprise for me, a nice pair of pajama bottoms. YES! We turned on the TV and watched *Ironside, The FBI,* and *The Waltons.* As the Walton family finished their goodnights, we turned the lights out as well. Sleep could very well be hard to obtain that night, as thoughts of turning myself in were weighing heavy. But, I did sleep fairly well and was awake at 0600 hours, realizing I could not follow through with my regular routine. As Annika slept, I went through what calisthenics I could, topping that off with various stretches. I closed myself in the bathroom and took a good hot shower.

I was nearly dressed before Annika awoke, so I laid down beside her, just cuddling for a while, as I whispered into her ear.

Annika said, "At this rate I'll never want to get up."

So, I laid the covers back for her exit and asked if she would care for a cup of coffee, and she did. As she closed herself in the bathroom, I followed the hallway to the lobby to get two cups of coffee. While there, I learned that the motel offered a continental breakfast every morning. I took my two cups to the lobby desk and inquired about extended stay rates and was handed a flier with all the options.

Back in the room, I quietly opened the bathroom door and placed the coffee on the countertop. Then I sat down to sip slowly, thinking about how I had so missed these simple pleasures. When Annika emerged, I explained the daily continental breakfast and that we had plenty of time to enjoy it prior to going to the County Sheriff's office. I had scrambled eggs, sausage, and toast, while Annika had oatmeal and a bagel with cream cheese. Then we split a banana, sipped coffee, and tried to guess what the day might bring. I tried to apologize to Annika again for making such ridiculous decisions.

But she just said, "Oh stop it Nick, this is the best adventure I could ever have hoped for. It has already changed my college major, and I am so looking forward to studying law."

I said, "You know, you're right, I don't really have any regrets either. I am actually looking forward to the new trials of life ahead. I can only thank you, Annika."

We drove to the sheriff's office, arriving a few minutes early, and sat in the car holding hands and whispered a prayer together for guidance through the day. We walked into the sheriff's office, advising the dispatcher who we were and that we had an appointment with Sheriff Welker.

He said with a smile, "We have been expecting you. The sheriff will be here in short order, please have a seat."

We did, but not for long, as the sheriff emerged from behind the counter and said, "Please follow me."

We were seated in the sheriff's office, when he announced that they had already received a request from Richmond County for the extradition of Nicholas Finn. It was requested and signed by Sheriff Stump. Sheriff Welker chuckled as he said, "This guy really wants to get his hands on you." He chuckled again, "I think we will make him wait the full time. Finn, you can plan on thirty days."

"Oh, thank the Maker because General Moore has given me a job as a foreman over the concrete work to be done at the house site. I am sure it will take the next thirty days to complete that work."

Sheriff Welker guided me through a series of signatures needed to turn oneself in, and as he showed us to the door, he asked where we were staying. I explained that Howard Johnsons had a great extended stay program, and he could contact us there. Annika then asked him if she could ask questions relative to county law, even if Georgia law and Florida law might be different.

He said, "Call me any time, and I will try." We were free again, at least for the next thirty days.

We drove back to the motel, but on a good day we could walk it in thirty minutes. Callahan was a small town with larger aspirations. It could feel the draw of people from the north looking for a warmer place to stay in winter. Going to our room, I mentioned to Annika, "It is far too early in the day to make calls, so why don't we go back to the house and see what is happening at the job site."

She thought it would be a good idea, as she would love to see the house with more daylight. As we were heading back to the house, she advised me that she really needed to go back home on the weekend. She had not only needed to check in with her parents and share the details of the ride into Florida, but she was also anxious to see if any of her FOIA requests had been answered and touch base with the college law professor.

Seeing the house backed in alongside a new foundation, and men working to move it onto that foundation almost gave me chills—it was wonderful. General Moore was there with his wife, watching the progress. We joined them and exchanged pleasantries. I then explained that Sheriff Welker had provided me with a free pass for about thirty days, prior to extradition, and I could start the job on the 14th. General Moore explained that the heavy movers should have the house on the foundation by end of day on the 14th, and after that, the job would be mine. He gave me all the documentation for the concrete contractors, the blueprints and plans for the work. I smiled, after looking at the prints, and said, "Sir, this is a piece of cake, I will make you proud."

We watched for several hours as these professionals worked stacking cribbing timbers like small log cabins in strategic places and adding steel 'H' beams from the house to the foundation. Then many hydraulic jacks, plumbed together for coordinated lifting of the house. I needed to apologize to Annika, as it was not a good time to view the interior. The general asked how I had been getting into the house. And to his surprise, I pulled the brass key from my pocket, holding it up. He looked with great question, asking, "How did you get that?"

I said, "It was in the desk drawer in the dining room." He continued his look of question. Then I chuckled a bit and said, "I made my first access to the house through a hatch in the floor, it was my savior."

He said, "Hatch?"

So, I explained the hatch in the floor, as he had no idea that it existed.

He laughed in earnest and said, "Thank our Maker for that one."

As we were getting ready to leave, General Moore said, "Dinner is on me tonight, let's be seated at 1800 hours."

Back at the Howard Johnson's, I was enjoying simply adding the cost of phone calls to the room bill. I called my parents first, and thankfully Dad answered the phone. I explained the entire situation, and that I was in Florida awaiting extradition. But many things, good things, had happened in between, and I was looking forward to the time I could tell the entire story. I told him that Annika was with me for a few days and asked him to thank Mom for the driver's license—I owed her for that one. Then I asked if she could renew the plates on the Caprice.

I called Pastor Roy but had no answer. I called Danny, and Pam picked up on ring two. She relinquished the phone to Danny and he exclaimed, "It's about time!"

I said, "Sorry, I have been busy." He forgave me as I filled him in on all the events that had taken place since we were last together.

"Batz, I wish I had been with you."

"Me too, but Annika was there." We went into other thoughts, and I asked Danny if they had any plans for marriage, now that he had his prosthetic leg.

He replied, "Not really."

Before we hung up, I briefed him on an idea I had been thinking about, and he told me about Catfish John. The guards at the prison were having a bad time with him, and he just wouldn't cooperate with anything until he met the G-Man.

Danny said, "You may need to try and remedy that one day soon."

I said, "One day soon I may be in the next cell beside him!" We both laughed, but only for a second.

I dialed the pastor's number again, and Mrs. Walker answered. She said, "Is that you Mr. Finn?"

I replied, "Yes."

"I will put Mr. Walker on the phone for you."

The pastor came on and said, "It doesn't surprise me that it has taken so long for you to call, as slow as you move." He chuckled.

I informed him that everything was going well, and I had a great many stories for him. I knew he had been praying for my success, as there were times I thought I could feel them.

He said, "I have been, son, I have been."

I explained the extradition time and that I was free to come and go in Florida, but that one of us would call him when they put me in jail back in Richmond County, which would be in about a month. I explained another proposition I would need help with in the future, and he agreed.

At 1800 hours we met the Moores in the lobby of the restaurant. Once again we enjoyed good conversation over another three bottles of St. Julian's wine. The Moores would be leaving on the weekend also but returning after the 4th of July celebration. Annika would stay in Williamston with her parents until the extradition, then move to the apartment in Augusta until sentencing.

We wrapped it up with business about the house, meeting the contractors for the concrete work, carpenters and bricklayers for the fireplace, the electricians returning power to the house, and plumbers for the water and septic systems. Oh yes, and the state building inspectors.

On Wednesday, Annika dropped me off at the job site in Boulogne at 0700 hours, then making the twenty minute drive to the motel to begin her regimen of phone calls. General Moore was already there, and we sipped coffees acquired from the lobby of the motel. The day went quickly, without much progress aside from the heavy movers actually placing the house on the foundation. All the other contractors spent most of their time prepping and unloading for their part of the work.

We met with the Moores each night, reviewing the day's work and Annika's reports from her legal hunt. The week went by so quickly. I shared goodbyes with the Moores, and with Annika, in the parking lot. But between embraces, Annika spun her head toward the road, holding still for a few seconds. Then she laughed and said, "I thought I saw Sheriff Stump driving by in a tan car without his uniform."

We both laughed, and just like that, I was alone again. One of the brick layers, Mr. Howard Goens, a black man with extended experience in his profession, agreed to pick me up from the hotel whenever I needed a ride, and I would need them.

By Wednesday, June 20, the following week, the temporary walls blocking the original fireplace opening needed to be taken down, leaving the house wide open in that area. I packed everything I thought I may need to spend several nights in the house until it was closed back up. The first night was like déjà vu. The Howard Johnson's had a coin operated washer and dryer, and along with my regular laundry, I had washed the chair sheet again. I had a supply of snacks, my flashlight, and the radio. We had a portable toilet at the site, so I didn't need the p-u bucket. There was a small mom-and-pop restaurant in Boulogne that was open all day every day.

During the second night, I heard noises outside and eased out of my bed. We had taken down all the paper blinding the windows, so only the interior shutters were closed. I grabbed my flashlight, still equipped with the pinhole lens. I slipped on denims, a T-shirt, and, you guessed it, my old prison shoes. I blinked my way to the back porch where I glimpsed the red flash of a brake light up the driveway. I took the pike from behind the door and brought it with me to the fireplace opening, climbing down from the scaffolding as quietly as I could. I moved around the house from the opposite side of the driveway leading to the house, blinking only when necessary. With a blink, I identified a 1970 Ford Galaxy but did not see a driver. I turned toward the porch and blinked again. A man with a very tiny flashlight was making his way up the temporary steps to the door.

For cripes cakes this was really happening again, and I even had the pike. I moved ever so quietly into position, holding the pike between the legs of the intruder, who had no idea I was there. I waited, aided by the trickle of light coming from his tiny flashlight. He too, held his tiny light in his mouth. He didn't have a heavy tool, but as he went for the doorknob, I heaved the pike with great snapping strength toward his crotch.

21. BIG GAME

THE SCREAM WAS bloodcurdling. I could hear the scream as it started at the height of his head, descending to the porch deck, and ending with a loud thud. Then more howling and deep guttural cuss words. I flashed the scene to see Sheriff Stump in street clothing, a brown boonie style fishing hat pulled tight over his head. Both his hands held his crotch. (One pike, two groins.) Beside him on the deck lay a leather blackjack, a pair of handcuffs, what looked like a set of lock picks, and a tiny flashlight, bent in the center but still working. If I were a hunter, I'd call this one big game.

Now, I knew who he was, but he had no real idea who just put him down, and I needed to keep it that way. It would take him a few minutes to recuperate enough to move, so I blinked my way to his car and opened the passenger door. I opened the glove box, found the registration, and took it with me as I blinked my way to the back side of the house. I took to one knee and patiently waited for him to hobble his way back to his car. He was coughing, cursing, and crying at the same time. He waved his little light to the rear, to the sides, and ahead repeatedly, looking for his assailant. He climbed slowly into the driver's seat and started his car, turning the headlights on and slowly zigzagging the car as he backed out, the lights scanning the area from side to side. I held fast, just out of sight.

I watched as he drove haphazardly out of St. Mary's Circle, and as his lights went out of sight, I began to shake out of control, I suppose from the adrenaline pulsing through my veins but also from knowing that I had just fully assaulted a county sheriff. It took a half hour for the shaking to subside as I made my way back through the fireplace opening and back into the house. I failed at finding much sleep the remainder of the night, even though I was sure I had seen the last of the sheriff, for now. However, from that time on, I balanced a glass bottle on the doorknob of both doors on the house, and later, on the motel door as well.

I put full concentration into the work, wearing the orange vest and hard hat every day. The crews learned early that even though I was younger than most, I knew what was going on and would have all the preparation ready for their work every day. Before that first week was finished, I had full respect from the crews. I also sported for lunch at the restaurant on Fridays.

We were to begin pouring the concrete driveway one day, when the old rear dump mixer arrived, but the driver needed to use the port-a-potty first. I looked at that truck, hopped into the cab, gripped the steering wheel, and wished I had the nerve to drive it all the way to Augusta. I knew of a 1970 Ford Galaxy that was just waiting for a yard or two of nice creamy delicious concrete! I got back out before the driver saw me.

Mr. Howard Goens proved his worth over and over as he built a perfect replica of the original fireplace in the house, shown to him in photos and original blueprints. He also built the front and rear steps. The next three weeks flew by so fast, ten to twelve hours a day on the site, trying to keep up with the Bible reading, and phone calls, mostly to Annika. My thirty days were coming to an end, and all the contractors had finished their work several days ahead of time. I was able to go out on my own and hire a landscape company to put the entire lot into appropriate shape, backfilled with topsoil and planted with grass seed. In those last days, I purchased plenty of hose and a good sprinkler, and watered the grass seed constantly, since it was nearing July.

I was living mostly at the house, since it now had running water, including hot water, and sewage. YES! Sheriff Welker stopped by quite often. I suppose at first he was making sure his trust in me was being met, but then he simply had interest in the construction process. It helped me during that last week, as I needed transportation back to the Howard Johnson's in Callahan several times, and the sheriff always obliged. I hardly noticed the 4th of July as it passed, and by the 14th the sheriff advised me while traveling back that the extradition would take place on the 17th. I asked Sheriff Welker about the logistics of being transported back to Augusta. He said typically, the authority asking for the extradition would send transportation.

I laughed and said, "Shucks, if Sheriff Stump comes to pick me up, I may not make it back alive!"

At that point I shared with Sheriff Welker what happened at the house—that it was I who put Stump down, but I had no idea it was him until he lay on the porch deck struggling in pain.

He stopped the patrol car, held his head on the steering wheel for a minute, and said, "Finn, you are truly a pain in the ass! The county having the prisoner in custody can volunteer to make the delivery to the county making the request." Then he chuckled and said, "We can also subcontract that job as well. In this case, do you think Annika would be willing to drive you back to Augusta? We pay for the fuel and $6.00 per road hour."

I called Annika as soon as I could, begging her to fulfill the wishes of the sheriff. She said, "Take it easy, I will be there tomorrow."

I was so happy to hear those words, but that meant she needed to travel 250 miles during the night to pick me up. Now, I made the call at about 1200 hours, and she was at the apartment in Augusta. She must have been ready to go because she arrived at the motel at 1830 hours. I was so thankful for no night driving. She was tired of driving of course, so I drove back to Boulogne to show her the progress on the house. She was shocked at the transformation and finally had a proper opportunity to see the interior. It made it so much better, as all the lighting was working, and the fireplace was a powerful focal point in the living room.

We walked the grounds and followed the meandering brick path to the river—it was a beautiful view. As we walked back to leave, I could see that the grass seed was sprouting and the lawn would be like a carpet in a matter of weeks. I had made arrangements with the landscape company to do the watering as needed, and informed Hal of what I had done, which met his approval. He wished me the best in regard to facing the judge back in Augusta and that he had my six.

I drove us back to the Howard Johnson's, where we enjoyed a light supper. I had alluded to an encounter with Sheriff Stump during our phone conversations, but I told Annika the rest of the Stump story after our supper. She was totally nauseous with the thought, especially having just eaten a nice meal. So, me being me, I told her how I subdued Catfish John.

Annika blurted out, "Finn that is enough, that's enough." But then she began to laugh and shake her head, saying, "I believe it, I believe it!" We meandered back to the room.

We packed the car with all the clothes and junk I had remaining, keeping only what we needed to make our exit in the morning. Then

Annika said, "The flashlight, do you know where it is packed?"

"Yes."

"Would you care to go get it?"

"No problem."

She winked. I blinked.

At 0600 hours, I was up, shaved, and showered, and then I rubbed Annika's arm softly until she awoke. She showered quickly and dressed for the road trip, then we took advantage of the continental breakfast. Back to the room for a quick check, and we were ready to travel. On the way down the hall, we passed the woman who had been cleaning the rooms daily. I stopped, thanked her for her work, and put a $100 bill in the palm of her hand, closing her fingers around it, and smiled.

I shared a thought with Annika that we should stop at the sheriff's office and ask if we could have one or two days of travel time to Augusta, as we had several items of business to take care of. She looked at me in question, then I said, "The plates for the Caprice and the Atlanta bank account."

She said, "Go for it."

Arriving at the Sheriff's Post, we were fortunate Sheriff Welker was already there. We made the request for an arrival of June 22 at the Richmond County Sheriff's Post. Sheriff Welker dialed the phone while we were standing at the dispatcher's counter, informed the Richmond County Post that their prisoner would be delivered on Monday the 25th, and hung up the phone. Then he just grinned as we made our exit.

Highway 1 was the obvious way back to Augusta, but we stopped first at Waycross, Georgia, to locate the Pierce County Sheriff's Post. We wanted to meet the sheriff and share with him the fact that it was I who captured Catfish and called in his location at the Riverview Restaurant. It caused us a two-hour delay, but we did meet Sheriff Joe Leary. At first he didn't believe me, putting me through a series of questions that only a law man could know. After passing his test, I shared the critical parts of my story with him. I asked him to call Sheriff Marty Welker in Nassau County, Florida, to verify what I was telling him, and he did so right then. He asked us to leave the room for a minute while they talked and waved us back in when the call ended. Sheriff Leary sat down and smiled at us, chuckled, and said, "What can I help you with, as I need help with something too?"

I asked him for several things, which he noted and agreed to, then asked what I could do for him.

He answered, "It's your prisoner Catfish. He has been a great problem for us, and it will be some time before he goes to trial. He says that he will not cooperate until he talks to his captor, the G-Man, and that must be you."

I said, "Wow, let me think about that for a moment." I got up and walked out of his office, up and down the hall, then went back to take my seat. "Sheriff, I think I can play along with this. I need to go to the car for a few things first, then you can take me to his cell." Sheriff Leary obliged, and within a few minutes we were entering the cell block. I put on my old baseball cap and tied a handkerchief around my face like a bandit in a western movie. I asked Annika and Sheriff Leary to remain out of sight as I presented myself in front of Catfish's cell unannounced. I quietly sat backward on a folding metal chair, resting my arms on the back, and made a loud cough.

Catfish had been sleeping but snapped awake, sat upright on his bunk, and looked my way. He said, "Who da hell is you?"

I said in a deep but loud voice, "John, I am the G-Man who put you in this place. I am sorry I cannot reveal my face, but not even these police know who I am. I am posing as a distant relative of yours, just to check up on you. You were my toughest case."

John said, "Yo lying to me, just so I'll cooperate."

I said, "No John, I am not lying." I pulled his tiny broken flashlight from a paper sack and showed it to him.

He stared intently at the tiny light, nearly giving in, but stiffened up and said, "That don't mean nothin."

I said, "Well John, maybe this will." I pulled his old family Bible from the sack and held it up. John was standing but fell back on his bunk when he saw it.

His eyes grew big, as he breathed in and out hard. He stuttered, "Yo—yo—yo—been to my place!" He hung his head and burst into tears. He sobbed out, "That Bible is the onlyest thing I wanted! It's the onlyest thing that holds me to my kin, wees Cajuns, but I can'ts read a word of it." He sobbed more, saying, "No one has ever been to my place."

I said, "John, I know what you have at your place, and it's safe with me now, but in time I will need to reveal it. For now, I want you to cooperate with the county police. It could be some time before I can return to see you, but when I do, I will read everything you want from that Bible. Please accept my word on it."

He nodded as I rose from the chair and exited the cell block. I told the sheriff that John should be much more cooperative for a while. We shook hands, and I shared with him that I was in the process of being extradited for walking out of the Richmond County Correctional Facility over two months ago. Sheriff Leary staggered back a step, looking at us both, raised both hands, palms facing us, and said, "This entire thing is completely strange and without protocol!"

I said, "Please call Sheriff Welker one more time. He will explain this detail as well."

Sheriff Leary shook his head and said, "Just be on your way."

Then we went to Danny and Pam's there in Dixie Union. It was too early for lunch, but Pam had fresh-baked gingersnap cookies and coffee. We spent another two hours bringing them up to speed on all that had happened. We made promises to call them as soon as we knew what the hearing date would be and to reunite as soon as my prison time was over. It was really hard for me to leave Danny this time. Danny my comrade, my friend.

Another three hours up the road put us in Blythe, the home of Pastor Roy. We found his house and were received in Christian grace. I did my best to fill in the blanks for Pastor Roy as he worked to digest what happened on the river and crossing the St. Mary's into Florida. I told him about turning myself in on arriving in Florida and everything that happened after that. Mrs. Walker, sitting at the end of the table, was privy to the conversation. She sat, rocking back and forth in her chair, saying, "Oh my, Oh my." Cooling her face with a paper fan on a wooden stick.

Pastor Roy said, "Finn, I have learned more about shell shock, and I will share it with you at a future time. Possibly while you are back at Richmond County Correctional Facility."

We exchanged handshakes and hugs, and Annika handed him the envelope I gave her weeks earlier, and he slipped it into his inside vest pocket. Then, as we all held hands, Pastor Walker took a knee and prayed for our safety and delivery from this curse. We left the pastor knowing that we would call when we knew the hearing date and when the sentencing would occur.

As we traveled north, I pondered his words and what had brought me to this place in my life. To me, Vietnam was not a curse, but a solemn lesson in life. Freedom is truly not free—it must be earned if we are to keep it. The curse is only what is imparted on the veteran when he returns home, how he is received. We ultimately choose to react positively or negatively to that reception. But, the veil of darkness absorbed in the stark fear of battle can and does overrule our common sense sometimes.

It was late afternoon when we arrived at the apartment in Augusta, the Caprice sitting exactly as I had left it. I put my hand over on Annika, signaling her to sit for a minute as my thoughts dove back into the last time I was here giving myself up for destroying the boat and Jeep.

She took my hand, kissed it several times, and said, "I know, I know. Let's go in."

She keyed us in, and I turned on the lights even though it was midday. The place was in immaculate condition, with many changes to the decor. Hanging pictures, tablecloths, and doilies on all the furniture—Annika had put her hand to it. It was such a nice surprise, so nice and homey.

The things I accumulated while traveling on the lam were stacked neatly at the side of the kitchen area, the fishing pole included. I asked Annika about the two tackle boxes, and she gestured toward a storage closet. I smiled and thanked her, then proceeded to unload the car. I called my bank in Atlanta to find that they were open on Saturdays until 1400 hours. I told Annika that we had another road trip tomorrow and hoped she was up to it. I explained that I wanted my account to be put in her name as well and activated. She replied that Atlanta would be a six-hour turnaround, so if we left by 0800 hours, we would be back to Augusta mid-afternoon.

We made the trip on Saturday, arriving at the bank around 1100 hours. The clerk that waited on us took the time to show us four letters from Sheriff Stump demanding that the bank turn the Nicholas Finn account over to the evidence department in Richmond County. She said the letters looked convincing, but the bank manager said that they just didn't have the correct legal standing. The bank had recently installed a copying machine, which was new technology. The clerk made a copy of each of the letters for us. They were somewhat blurry, but legible. We ordered new checks with both our names on them. If my jail sentence were to become a long one, Annika could take care of any financial business that may occur.

When we arrived back at the apartment, I wanted to take a nap in the worst way, however, I needed to revive the Caprice. But first I called the restaurant downtown that I had taken Annika to for our first real date and made reservations for 1800 hours. Then I used jumper cables from Annika's car to start my car, but the battery was completely dead. I drove to the nearest auto parts store and purchased a top-of-the-line Delco battery and installed it. That did it, the 396 engine fired up but refused to run smoothly on the year-old fuel, so I drove it to the local Shell station and filled it with their highest octane gas. On the way home, it slowly began running better and better, until its tire burning power finally returned.

We had Sunday to ourselves. I expressed to Annika how I would so love to see her parents, but the round trip to Williamston would just be too much. She agreed and suggested that we call them that night and spend time on the phone. I agreed. We both freshened up, and I put on the outfit I purchased in Baxley, including the Panama hat. Annika loved it, but I couldn't compare to her, she was such a gorgeous woman. I wanted to take the Caprice, but I had already risked driving with the illegal plates. We drove Annika's car and enjoyed a beautiful Augusta summer night out, having dinner outside on the restaurant veranda. Annika would be turning twenty-one years old in a few weeks, but she presented herself as such an adult that the waiters never asked her age—which saved me a lot of extra tip money.

While driving home I asked Annika if she would care to stop by the VFW and have a cocktail. I was grinning toward her, as she spun her ahead toward me, ready for a few expletives, but saw that I was kidding with her. She punched me in the arm, then expressed her desire to return to the apartment and make calls. So that was what we did.

Annika knew the habits of her parents and was able to catch them at home on the first call. We handed the receiver back and forth between us while talking with her parents. We left them fairly well-informed about crossing the St. Mary's River, turning myself in to the Florida sheriff, working at the house, and finally heading back to Augusta. At this point, they knew nothing of the capture of Catfish John or his treasure. It was impossible to share any of that yet. Annika's parents were trusting me, and us, on merit earned. They obviously knew their daughter and had learned to trust her judgment. I wanted so badly to put the full proof of my integrity in front of them, but that simply had to wait.

Annika was happy with the call, so we dialed my parents as well, making a connection. Both Mom and Dad were at home, and we brought them up to speed with all that had occurred since we had talked last. We shared with them, as we did with the Bjorns, that the extradition would put me back in the hands of the Richmond County Judicial system tomorrow, July 24. Annika agreed that she would keep everyone informed as the new sentencing came forth. I finally had a chance to thank Mom for providing the driver's license, as it became a deal maker. I also asked her if the license plates were in her purview as well. She said she would try to get them.

At 2100 hours, we gave it up, both content that we did all that we could do for the ones that we loved. We spent an hour or so discussing the Catfish treasure, how to deal with it and how to expose it, but there was no clear answer for us. The legal problem would be in trying to introduce new evidence into the resentencing hearing. We could only hope that the judge would allow for new evidence, since that could be our only chance. Annika took my hands in prayer, asking for guidance and safety in the task that I was duty bound to follow through with. We vowed to simply give it up to Jesus, and we both slept for the entire night.

On Monday, June 25th, we had breakfast at the local Waffle House, then traveled to the Richmond County Sheriff's Post. I was wearing denim pants, a button-down short-sleeve shirt, and the well-worn but comfortable prison shoes, which were now polished and shined as best as possible. Carrying my Bible, I walked in with Annika. A dispatcher asked how he could help us.

I said, "My name is Nicholas Finn, and I turned myself in down in Florida for leaving the Richmond County Correctional Facility ahead of my sentence time. Now, I have been extradited back here. I am reporting in."

The dispatcher looked at me with some alarm, standing up and saying, "Why are you not in handcuffs? Who is she? Where is the deputy?"

I said, "Did you not hear me? I turned myself in! I am here voluntarily! If you think I need handcuffs, you will just have to do it yourself, as we are going over here to have a seat until you do whatever you are supposed to do."

After sitting for a few minutes, I returned to the desk and advised the dispatcher that he should contact Sheriff Stump at his earliest convenience. The embarrassed dispatcher agreed but added that the sheriff had been in an accident while fishing a few weeks ago and had not been in the office much since.

I said, "If you tell him Nicholas Finn is waiting for him, I will bet he will be here posthaste."

That did it, as in only a few minutes we could hear the breaking tires squealing as Sheriff Stump's squad car stopped in front of the post. The Sheriff entered the dispatch area in an effort of full command, but his bloodshot eyes and pale look gave his weakened condition away. He entered the room looking like an old bow-legged cowboy, and I felt sorry that I had struck him so hard. We were face to face for the first time in a long time. He looked at me, his face turning very red as he focused. He twitched a glance toward Annika, then back at me. Now any man that looked at Annika once was bound to look again. I grinned and privately forgave him, as in his present condition, he may not have regained his natural human lust.

He focused on me but began yelling questions as if his staff were all around him. "Why isn't this prisoner in handcuffs? Where is his guard? Has Finn been processed? Get him into a cell now! Get this woman out of here! Get me a chair! I don't feel so good."

The dispatcher was standing helpless behind the counter, so Annika and I quickly slid our chairs under the sheriff as he started to go down, catching him in a heap. He continued waving his hands and mumbling orders as we went through the extradition paperwork with the dispatcher. Annika and I held one another and vowed with positive smiles that we would get through this.

This time, only clothing went into the evidence and personal belongings bags. Annika had all my personal items. I donned my original prison clothing and was taken to my cell. I chuckled to myself along the way, as I knew the place fairly well, recognizing the faces of a few officers as we went and nodding hellos along the way. I could only hope that the judge wouldn't be as anxious to see me back in prison as the sheriff was. The hearing to re-sentence would be our only hope. The state had certain protocol to follow in these procedures, and we may have a chance to plead leniency.

For me, it was to sit out the time, reading my Bible, which took me through the books of Poetry and Songs, then through the five Major Prophets and the twelve Minor Prophets. The gospels of the New Testament were next. For Annika, it was a double task. She needed to switch her junior year major to law, get herself enrolled, and get ready for classes. She was also working to be fully prepared for my hearing. The apartment was not only the perfect tool for her task, but it was also in a near perfect location. She didn't sleep much during the two weeks it took for the judge to set the date—Monday, August 5. Then she had to call Sheriff Marty Welker, Sheriff Joe Leary, Pastor Roy Walker, and Danny Wakefield, hoping for witnesses. Then she needed to call both of our parents with the date but encouraged them not to be present.

For me, those last days and the weekend passed in slow motion. However, it provided ample time for our witnesses to arrive. Annika also provided hotel locations and phone numbers for all but the pastor, as he could drive home at any time. My case was the second scheduled to be heard that morning and didn't commence until 1100 hours. I was brought into the courtroom through a side door. I was in shackles, which were also chained to my handcuffs, so I needed to shuffle to my seat. Annika was already seated at our table, looking absolutely stunning in a dark business suit. I needed to pinch myself hard, as a reality check, just to see her. Then I looked behind to see seven people that I either loved or had full respect for. Two county sheriffs, General Hal Moore, Danny and Pam, and Pastor and Rose Walker. Farther back was what looked like a student reporter. On the opposite side of the isle sat Sheriff Stump.

I made an effort to thank them, while trying to maintain composure. Happy to tears, if you will, for their support. At that we all heard the bailiff report, "All rise, Judge Richard Stump Presiding." The judge entered the courtroom, just as I had seen him a year earlier. The bailiff handed him a folder as he sat behind his podium, and he opened it. It looked like he was reading, but I think not. His face was slowly turning red, as I remembered from my trial last year. I withdrew, forgetting about everyone around me, knowing he had the power, and the reason, to carry out a maximum sentence. I knew that I was going to be in jail for a very long time.

The judge looked up to see the audience behind me, looking longer at the three uniformed men, then at Annika. He pondered in silence for a few seconds, then recited the reason that I had been jailed in the first place, the willful destruction of personal property. Then he recited how I had escaped his prison, causing thousands of man hours in trying to apprehend me. He recited all the work Sheriff Stump went through in orchestrating his search, which went on for weeks. He then looked at his watch and declared a recess until 1300 hours. Our entire side of the aisle was shocked, as Sheriff Stump looked our way grinning ear to ear. I was escorted back to a holding cell and given a glass of water. I do not know what the rest of my friends did.

At 1300 hours we were all seated as the bailiff introduced the judge once again. The judge recited nearly word for word what he had said earlier, then declared that he was giving a new sentence for Nicholas Finn to include the remainder of his first year, from the date of escape to the current date. The sentence was a second year, as was called for in the first sentence, and one additional year as punishment for escaping.

Judge Stump raised his arm flamboyantly, clenching his gavel and looking across the courtroom, and started the downward swing.

22. DEFEND YOURSELF!

Annika bolted to a standing position and shouted, "JUDGE STUMP, STOP!"

He held the pose, looking at her with daggers coming from his eyes.

She shouted again, "ARE YOU GOING TO PERJURE YOURSELF IN FRONT OF THESE OFFICERS?" She lowered her voice but said very sternly, "You know well that Georgia law states that resentencing cases must allow for any new evidence, and there are four people here with new evidence. I believe you had better hear them!"

The judge continued his swing, slamming his fist on the bench, not the gavel.

Sheriff Stump turned our way, a hard look of disgruntlement on his face, believing his brother, the judge, would quickly put Annika in her place.

The judge looked piercingly at Annika, silent for too long. He said, "Who are you? Are you a lawyer, and what is your name?"

She said, "Annika Bjorn. I am not a lawyer, YET, but I know the law fully in regard to this case. You should know me and my name, as it was your name on the paperwork denying me the legal visiting rights to Nicholas when he was in prison." The judge turned his head toward Sheriff Stump, holding his gaze for too long.

Then the judge looked back, gritting his teeth, "Miss Bjorn, how would you like to continue?"

She promptly said, "I would like to introduce each one of the four men as physical or character witnesses, have each one stand and give five minutes to state his case—then I will present mine."

As he breathed hard through his nose, thinking almost too long, he said, "Permission granted; you may begin." Sheriff Stump turned toward the judge, his jaw dropping a bit, a little less confidence on his face, as Annika presented General Hal Moore to stand.

The general was in full dress greens, his garrison hat under his left arm. He cleared his throat and began to speak, holding his right hand toward me, "Judge. We were soldiers once—and young. I would trust my very life to him, and I did, in the Ia Drang Valley, South Vietnam, just a few years ago. Judge, do you know that he was a lone survivor in a horrible battle? Did you know that he was shot in that battle, and carries many shrapnel wounds as well? Now, I swear that by an act of our Father above, he found my mother's house as it was being moved and used it to make his escape. I can only be thankful that it was there for him."

Then he mentioned, "Oh yes, Sergeant Finn has two years remaining in his six-year commitment to the inactive reserves, perhaps I will need to re-activate him back into the service and out of your control?"

Annika then introduced Sheriff Marty Welker from Nassau County, Florida. Sheriff Welker stood up and began his address, "Judge Stump, I met your escapee, Nicholas Finn, on the Georgia side of the St. Mary's River Bridge as the house movers were legally attempting to cross. We intercepted radio traffic from Georgia Sheriff Stump threatening to arrest the moving crew if they took the house over the bridge. It was fortunate that the army was on convoy that day, which prevented the Georgia sheriff's posse from reaching the house.

"With the driver of the moving crew held by Georgia law, Mr. Finn, knowing all aspects of the Mack heavy mover, volunteered to drive the rig over the bridge. His actions cleared a traffic backup that had gone out of control, all caused by Sheriff Stump.

"After he parked the house at its new site, he walked back to the bridge and gave himself up to me. General Moore vouched for him, saying that he would take full responsibility, as he wanted him to be the foreman in charge of placing the house on its new foundation and all the infrastructure involved with it. I not only allowed it, but I also carried Mr. Finn back and forth to the construction site many times. Your Honor, he did this while awaiting extradition—no cell, no handcuffs, and no guards. As General Moore trusts him, I too trust him." He sat down.

Annika stood again and introduced Ware County, Georgia, Sheriff Joe Leary, who stood. He started by saying, "Your Honor, have you heard of the recent capture of a bank robber who goes by the name of 'Catfish John'?"

The judge nodded, while twisting his face in question.

"Well, it was Mr. Finn that captured him and advised us where to pick him up. He is now in the Charlton County Jail awaiting trial. Mr. Finn stopped at our post on his extradition trip to you, which he did purely on his own merit. He wanted to check up on the man he captured. The prisoner was and had been out of control, wanting to talk to the G-Man that captured him. Nicholas then posed as a G-Man, talked to the prisoner, and returned his personal Bible to him. The prisoner is now cooperative. I too have full faith and trust in Mr. Finn."

Annika then introduced Pastor Roy Walker, who stood to address the judge. Pastor Roy began by telling the judge, "I was involved in prison ministries and visited the Richmond Facility on a regular basis. I had seen Mr. Finn at many of my sermons. I didn't know Mr. Finn at the time but recognized his face. I had seen him while he was on the lam, and on the second occasion, I confronted him. Mr. Finn confessed that he was indeed on the lam and that he was traveling in the house."

Pastor Roy went on to explain my reasons for escaping the prison. "His goal was to turn himself in to the authorities in Florida. His hope was to gain time for Miss Bjorn to gather more information."

Pastor Roy told him that in his profession he was duty bound to inform the authorities, but he would use discretion in doing so. He told the judge, "Your Honor, I did send a letter to Sheriff Stump advising him that I knew where his prisoner was hiding. However, I used an alpha-cipher based on the King James Version of the Bible. It was actually simple to decipher, but I think Sheriff Stump ignored it. Now as you can see, Mr. Finn has done exactly what he said he would do. I too have full faith in Nicholas."

Then the pastor said, "Your Honor, in my work, I deal with many people with many problems, and I take many courses of study on human behavior. I more recently have studied the effects of an old problem called 'shell shock,' a syndrome caused by traumatic exposure. It sometimes happens to people exposed to terrible experiences, especially soldiers exposed to many battles. It can manifest itself in many ways—fits of rage, suicide, or simply doing something one would normally never do. I believe Mr. Finn has this syndrome, and I recommend that he seek help through the VA health system. It is now recognized by the federal government as a health problem. Studies are now being made in this regard, and volunteers are being sought for participation in the research." Pastor Roy sat down.

Annika, already standing, said, "Nicholas Finn, defend yourself."

I stood, but the chains prevented me from being totally upright. I prepared to speak, when the judge interrupted, "So, you claim to have captured the infamous Catfish John. I read the brief on this case, and it stated that the Sheriff's Department had no idea who captured him or who made the call. At this point anyone could pose as the captor. I want proof."

I said, "Your Honor, I anticipated that. Sheriff Leary, did you bring the item I requested from John's evidence file?"

Sheriff Leary nodded and pulled a very tattered wallet from the evidence bag.

I said, "In that old wallet you will find a fairly new $100 bill. Would you pull it out, please?"

The sheriff did so, exposing the bill.

I said, "In the chaos of the moment, I couldn't take time to retain the entire serial number, but I can give you the last five digits." Sheriff Leary examined the bill as I recited, "2501B."

He said, "Correct," and offered to show it to the judge, who waved a decline.

I spoke to the judge, "Your Honor, I am very sorry for destroying the VFW commander's vehicles, and even more so, for walking out of his prison. I really don't know what would cause me to do either. But I knew that in your prison, I was being singled out and worked harder than any of the other inmates. Then I was denied visitations. I just didn't know why, and I still don't.

"There is one more thing, Your Honor." I said, "While General Moore's house was being restored on the new site, the fireplace was being rebuilt, causing a large opening in the house. I decided to spend the nights in the house until it was fully closed in again. On the second night, I awoke to subtle noises outside and snuck out through the fireplace opening to see for myself what was going on. I found a 1970 Ford Galaxy parked a distance back down the driveway.

"I then worked my way back behind the house and around to the front door. As I approached the front door with great stealth, I saw a figure of a man hunched over the doorknob, holding a very tiny flashlight in his mouth. It looked like he was trying to pick the door lock. Using a pike, I eased it between his legs and smacked his hind parts rather hard. The dark figure fell to the deck, and I saw that it was Sheriff Stump in civilian clothes. At his side were lock picking tools, a pair of handcuffs, and a leather blackjack. I think he was trying to capture me, even though I had turned myself in and even though my extradition papers had been filed."

The judge looked at me, and said, "That could also be a tall tale as well. I will need proof of that, so good luck!"

I said, "Judge, I believe I can furnish proof."

At that, Sheriff Stump stood up shouting, "I was never down in Florida!"

Judge Stump pointed his finger at him and said, "Sit down and shut up!"

I turned to Annika and asked her for the envelope I had given her earlier, and she handed it to me. I opened it and retrieved the contents, beckoning the bailiff to show it to the judge, which he did.

The judge looked at the paper and said, "Sheriff Stump, do you own a 1970 Ford Galaxy?"

Stump sheepishly replied, "Yes."

The judge then said, "Sheriff Stump, how did Mr. Finn get possession of your car's registration if you were not in Florida?"

The sheriff, hanging his head, remained silent. I sat down.

Annika stood back up and said, "Your Honor, did Mr. Finn show any resistance to the Augusta City Police when they came to arrest him? Did Mr. Finn plead guilty to the crime he was charged with, saving the county the expense of a trial? Did Mr. Finn offer full restitution for the Jeep and the boat he destroyed? Why was the boat and Jeep supposed to be in the sheriff's evidence compound, but instead was behind the VFW?

"Why have all my FOIA requests to the Richmond County Sheriff's Office been ignored? Why was Mr. Finn worked harder than any of his fellow inmates? Why was I denied visitation rights? Why was all our mail opened and redacted? Do you know that the VFW commander is being sued for laying hands on a Vietnam veteran who wanted to join his post? Do you know he tried again to lay hands on a 101st Airborne Ranger, who put him in a very painful pretzel hold until he said 'Uncle?'

And finally, why were you willing to perjure yourself in this courthouse today?" Annika sat down and just looked at the judge.

The judge slowly turned his head toward his brother, the daggers headed his way now.

He picked up his gavel again, raised it high, and struck the bench, announcing that the court was recessed until 1000 hours tomorrow.

We all stood as the judge left the courtroom for his private chambers. I took the opportunity to address these wonderful people, whom I considered my very best friends. I told them how much I appreciated them being there, and that I was sorry that it would take one more day to come to a conclusion. I said I hoped that I could one day repay them with equal honor.

Pastor Roy, speaking for the group, said, "You already have, Nick, you already have."

The deputies quickly came and ushered me out of the courtroom, unchained me, and escorted me to a regular cell. What my friends did for the night, I do not know. For me, it wasn't much more than solitary confinement—no one else was on the cell block. I laid on the cot for an extended period of time, then realized I needed to pray, to be thankful for the good things coming to me despite my wrongdoing. I laid on the bunk, trying to make sense of the day, and went to sleep.

The jailer pounded on my cell bars at 0600 hours, advising me to get ready because the judge was anxious to get this case settled. They gave me a plate of SOS for breakfast, then took me to the courtroom. The judge was there, but no one else—not the bailiff or the stenographer, only armed guards.

The judge said, "Finn, I am charging you exactly as I described yesterday. You will be going back to the correctional facility today, and pray I do not hear another word from you."

Just like that, I was back at the Richmond Facility doing time. I wasn't allowed visitors, mail, or calls. Life was just several months of road work every day, nonstop. One evening, I was the last inmate behind the bus, preparing to have the leg-irons removed. I noticed once again that the gate was unlocked as before. I knew I couldn't survive another escape, but I pushed the gate open in defiance. I looked at that old maple tree across the road, but this time there was a shadowy figure kneeling beside the tree. I thought I could see a sheriff's patch on the right shoulder, then I realized the figure was in the firing position with a scoped rifle aiming right at me. I saw the bright muzzle flash, as I instantly went limp, falling to the ground. Gasping in pain, I found myself doubled up on the floor beside the cell cot.

Sitting back on the cot shaking, I shouted out, "I HATE THESE DREAMS."

I may have slept off and on the rest of the night, but my final verdict was haunting me badly. The jailer came by at 0800 hours, asking me if I wanted something for breakfast. I said, "Can I order?"

"It depends."

"I would love to have about three eggs scrambled, salt and pepper, and coffee, water, or juice, I don't care."

The jailer said, "That is doable." Then went on his way. Twenty minutes later he returned with a hot cup of coffee, and two minutes later he returned with a plate full of scrambled eggs and buttered rye toast. This was not a dream, and I enjoyed the meal.

At about 0945 hours, I was ushered back through a private hallway to a side door in the courthouse. I was chained hand and foot again, walked into the courtroom, and put into a chair. Annika was already sitting there and gave me a kiss as soon as I sat down. Turning back to look, I saw all my friends were there too. Regardless of what the judge may decide, I knew I was in good hands. I whispered to Annika that we needed help from the Father above as well, and she agreed, reaching over to hold my chained hand. We gave quiet thanks and asked for freedom if it was in his will.

At 1000 hours sharp, the judge entered the courtroom, and the bailiff shouted for all to rise. After the protocol, we all sat to hear what the judge had to say. Sheriff Stump was there, but he was sitting as far to the left of the bench as he could.

The judge sat, making himself comfortable, then turned his chair toward us. He started by saying, "I have not had sufficient time to verify every question that Mrs. Bjorn presented to me yesterday, but I have verified the ones that count the most. I have heard all your statements, and now I have something to share with you.

"I have been on this bench for thirty years, believing that I have been delivering judgments with the blindfold on. This case has revealed to me that I have failed in that regard. When I first heard this case, my judgment was that a one-year sentence would be sufficient, but I allowed my brother to convince me that his prisoner was an out-of-control Vietnam veteran that needed a very harsh lesson. I went along with his suggestion, without taking one minute to look at the other side. I swear to you now that I will never look at another case brought before me without looking fully into the opposite side of the story. I will never take one side of any case ever again.

"So, I am reducing your sentence to the original one year that I had in mind in the first place, of which you have served eight months. I am waving the four months remaining on your sentence, as I believe that Catfish John is a fair exchange. I am not going to call for the one-year extension for your escape either, but, Mr. Finn, more importantly, I want you to realize this! I am reducing your sentence from a felony to a misdemeanor. I will also expunge all records of the felony."

At that, he raised his gavel and cracked it against the bench.

The courtroom was dead silent, Annika and I looked at each other, tears welling from our eyes, but exploding into full sobbing. We were trying to hug one another, but the chains were getting in the way. The guard came quickly, unlocked and removed them. We just held one another for a while. Pam was at the rescue with tissues for everyone that needed them. The guard handed me a bag that had all my possessions and clothing, from the first day they jailed me.

The judge was preparing to leave the room, and I needed to break away from Annika to ask him if he would please stay for a minute longer. Annika and I went to the two officers, thanking them and asking them to stay longer as well. Gathering Danny, Pam, and Pastor Roy, we took a few steps toward the rear of the room and huddled in discussion for a few minutes.

Then I turned and addressed the group loudly, "Officers, Judge Stump, THERE IS MORE! Judge, could we all convene in your private chambers? We have something important to share with you."

The judge nodded, turning in that direction.

Then Sheriff Leary said, "Yes, there is more from me as well!"

Our group looked at one another with question on our faces, then turned toward the officer. Sheriff Leary continued, "We do not need the private chambers for what I will tell you. I thought it best to keep this information out of the court proceedings. Mr. Finn, did you know that all the banks in several of our local counties had posted a reward for the apprehension of the bank robber and river pirate, Catfish John?"

"Reward? No, sir."

"Mr. Finn, there is no question that it was you that captured Catfish John, and I will be filing that fact with the banking association that put up the reward for $50,000."

My knees went weak as Annika and my friends held me up. We were all in awe. I was speechless, and I almost wished he had waited to tell us, but what amazing news. Everyone in the courtroom had eyes as big as dinner plates and smiles just as big too. I said, "Judge Stump, can we still meet in your chambers?"

He answered, "Please do."

Everyone present began to move through the door that the judge was holding open, including Sheriff Stump. The judge stopped him cold, advising him to go home and be available for him to contact tomorrow. At that, the judge closed the door and immediately took command of his room. He said, "Finn, you have earned my respect, but this had better be good, or you will lose it. Make it quick."

I cleared my throat and said, "My friends and I have agreed that this particular group of individuals is exactly what we need to form a nonprofit organization. We believe we can fully trust every one of you."

The judge snapped, "A nonprofit for what?"

"For a vast amount of money and artifacts that Catfish John had in his secret hideout. I discovered it by accident, but I explored it and took photos of it, which I will share with you now."

Annika pulled the packet of photos from her attaché and spread them on the judge's table. I continued, "Our biggest fear has been revealing the whereabouts of this treasure to the authorities—any of them. We fear that it would end in graft and thievery. But, we believe that this group will do the right thing with this treasure."

Then I said, "Are you interested?" This small group was stuck in amazement, but General Moore spoke first.

He said, "Nicholas, I will need to decline the offer, as my profession takes me away for years at a time. I would very much like to help with this, but to be fair, I cannot." One at a time, all the others stepped forward agreeing to be an active member of a charitable group that did not yet exist.

I also explained that I was the sole holder of the location of the Catfish treasure, and that I would not reveal it until a 501(C)(3) nonprofit was fully established. Then all of us would need to visit the secret site together. "Meanwhile, not one word of this can be uttered for any reason, do we all agree?"

There was a unanimous "YES."

I continued, "It is my belief that once this treasure, mostly of cash, is accounted for and secured, then we can break it to the news."

The conversation broke into all sorts of positive thoughts, with the judge agreeing that he would be the best source for cutting red tape in nonprofit paperwork. A challenge went to the pastor to ponder possible recipients. Annika was willing to work on bylaws, but law school was now her top priority. I decided to wait until the spring semester to return to college and would do all the legwork for Annika in developing bylaws. I would also act as a secretary and liaison between all in the group. Danny would begin the logistics for the expedition to extract the treasure. Sheriff Leary would provide safe transport of the treasure from the hideout to a secure location. Sheriff Welker would find not only a secure location for a deposit, but he knew several very good investors. My original inside group, Annika, Danny, Pam, and Pastor Roy, had agreed earlier not to reveal to anyone that the treasure was on the river.

As we were summarizing this wonderful business, the judge asked Annika if she had a sponsor for entering law school. Annika answered, "Actually I do not."

The judge said, "May I do that for you?"

Annika needed a tissue as she said, "Yes!"

Danny and I then moved to the pastor, asking for a minute of his time. He agreed, with question on his face, and waited for us to speak. Danny and I both spoke at the same time saying, "Pastor Roy, will you marry us?"

Pastor Roy looked at us completely mortified and stepped back. Danny and I looked at one another, realizing our blunder, and tried to correct, saying, "Not us, but us—both of us—at the same time, you know, Annika and Pam?"

The pastor held his hand to his chest for a moment, made his wonderful chuckle, and said, "Yes."

The entire group had paid attention to our blunder but realized the significance, breaking out in clapping and cheers. I was so happy that I was numb. Annika and Pam were exchanging hugs as they both sobbed in happiness, exchanging tissues. The pastor, a little wet eyed himself, then took both Danny and I by the arm, saying, "When and where would you care to have this happen?"

I said, "At your church, this coming Saturday?"

Pastor Roy, his eyes growing large, swallowed hard and said, "DONE! Let's have the ceremony at 11:00 a.m."

Again, all our new friends clapped and cheered as we extended the invitation to them all.

The judge, who always kept his personal gavel in his quarters, picked it up, held it high, and announced, "The old case is closed, we are now challenged for the new!" The gavel cracked on top of his desk, and we all clapped and cheered.

It was time to leave. The judge, ahead of me, ushered us out through his private entrance and exit. I was the last to leave the room, and I turned one last time to look at the room where so many wonderful things had just happened. I turned out the light, darkening the room, and saw shadows of someone stepping away from the gap at the bottom of the judge's courtroom door. My instincts begged me to walk point and investigate, but the thrill of the moment overrode, and I moved out with the others. In the parking lot, we gave thanks and praise to everyone and shared goodbyes. I advised everyone that a newsletter forming the nonprofit would be forthcoming.

Danny, Pam, Annika, and I drove to the apartment where we celebrated on our own. We stayed up half the night planning for our weddings in just four more days. We knew that we wouldn't need to entertain many people, but we hoped our parents could drop what they were doing to travel to Georgia. The apartment had a fold-out sofa, which we deployed and made up as best we could for Dan and Pam. They had planned for an overnight stay and were prepared for another. We kept up the chatter until we just couldn't go any more and turned in.

Wednesday morning we lounged as long as possible before rotating through the shower one at a time. While waiting, I opened the bag that held my pre-prison clothes, wallet, and my dog tags. YES! When we were all ready, we climbed into Danny's Chevelle and drove a short distance to the local Waffle House for breakfast. We chatted in near bliss, as so many things had changed so quickly, and all for the good. We were going to have work to do, in calling our parents, and agreed to return to the apartment and get started. There was only one motel in the pastor's town of Blythe, so we needed to reserve several rooms as quickly as possible, which we did.

Mom was beside herself, as we anticipated, but she and Dad committed to travel south the next day. Annika's parents said they had hoped for this news and were already prepared for travel. We provided all with the address of the motel and the church, then packed what we needed and traveled to the motel to stay until Saturday. The Wakefields went home, passing the church at the halfway point to Dixie Union. They, too, packed for their wedding and traveled back north to Blythe to stay at the motel for the remaining two days.

By Friday evening all our families had arrived at the motel. We had arranged a meet and greet at the church, where all our parents finally met, and also met Pastor Roy. After an hour or so, Pastor Roy took command and coached everyone through what he had planned for the wedding day. We were all in agreement and then agreed to return to the motel. Dan and Pam were ahead of us all and invited all of us to the tiny patio in front of the motel where they presented a fairly nice bar, with enough libations for everyone. We then went to the only restaurant in town, a mom-and-pop diner, where we nearly filled every seat. Prior to being served, the pastor stood, blessed the food in advance, and blessed the reason that we were there. The food was quite good and very cheap. I tipped the waitress and the cook with a $100 bill each. The waitress was in tears.

Saturday was a little chaotic, but it all worked, and we all traveled to the little white church. All I had to wear was the Panama outfit. Annika's mother supplied her with a few extras, but I remain dumbstruck at how beautiful she could be with the tiniest amount of effort. As it worked out, all of our parents were dressed far more appropriately than we were, and that brought some chuckles. Danny and Pam were dressed a little more conventional, but when Danny saw my getup, he removed his tie.

We gathered in front of the podium as Pastor Roy had instructed, and at 1100 hours, the pastor stepped up. He put his hands on each side of the podium, first bowing his head in noticeable hesitation, then he looked at me and shook his head. He then turned to Annika, nodding and smiling all the while. He then turned to Danny and Pam and said, "You have chosen friends wisely." After taking us all into very meaningful prayer, he started the marriage process.

Danny was my best man, and I was his. Annika was Pam's maid of honor, and Pam was hers. Danny thought it best that Annika and I go first, so we did.

The pastor went through the entire process with both couples but held the best for last, proclaiming, "Gentlemen, you may now kiss your brides!" An ovation proceeded! Even our dads were sobbing and in need of tissues.

The pastor took the podium one more time, slowly bringing everyone to silence. He said, "Mr. Finn now has something to share with you. Good luck, Nicholas, in explaining your adventure in twenty-five words or less!"

As he moved to be part of the audience, I stepped in front of the podium and then moved down to the first row of pews. I gave a very brief explanation of my escape from jail and an even briefer story of the house. I nearly needed to lie, making the story of capturing Catfish John even shorter. But it all ended with being completely exonerated by Judge Stump and the announcement from Sheriff Joe Leary of a $50,000 reward. Our family had been listening more intently than I had realized, and my last statement must have been like a punchline. Everyone gasped at the same time. I heard "Oh my God" from ten different voices at the same time, then laughter and hands slapping their knees!

We so wanted to share the development of the nonprofit, but it could not be revealed yet, and besides, I do not think their hearts could take it at this time.

We broke camp after joining Pastor Roy at his church for Sunday services. What the pastor found in his collection plate later that day may keep him operating for another year. But, we wanted him on our decision-making team.

Mom and Dad were upset when I told them that I would not be going back to college until the second semester, but I gave them my best smirk of assurance, saying, "Don't worry, you will be amazed at my reason."

Back at the motel, we remained with the Wakefields until everyone left. We made vows to get together as soon as possible. For Annika, that wouldn't be until Christmas break. For me, I would be traveling to Dixie Union soon. Then Dan and Pam headed south, and we headed north. We needed to make a fuel stop before leaving Blythe, and I was standing at the rear of Annika's car when I had one of those episodes of my sixth sense. Even though my neck had recently been shaved, it felt like the hair was standing up. I stepped away from the pump attendant and did a slow circle, looking for anything, but saw nothing. It was as though we were being watched.

23. STILTS VILLE

SOMETIMES WHEN I become the recipient of feelings of vulnerability, that something is wrong, something I cannot see or touch, it can actually make me feel sick. Every time I pass it off as nothing, it seems to materialize into something. It can leave me confused. I wondered, could this be part of that syndrome? I just didn't know, and I vowed to myself to contact the VA and set up a consultation.

I paid the station attendant who filled the car and gave him a tip as well. Climbing back into the car, I shared with Annika the weird feeling I had of being watched. She gave it some thought and said, "You are clear with the law now, and I even feel that with our marriage, we have satisfied a debt with our Savior Jesus and our Father in heaven above. Let it go, Nick, and get us back to Augusta."

She was right, so we relaxed and enjoyed the drive north through some very rural Georgia countryside. As we traveled, I recited as many things that I could remember that happened while I was traveling the same route running from the dogs. Annika was mesmerized by the stories, and I did my best to embellish the events to impress her even more. She was too smart for that and would punch me in the arm if she thought I was fibbing.

The hour drive evaporated as we pulled into the apartment driveway. We unloaded the car, put everything away, loaded the washing machine, and sat outside at the tiny table on the tiny concrete porch. I asked Annika if she would mind if I smoked a good cigar, and she just smiled. I retrieved the only cigar I had in the apartment—it was a year old and not kept in a humidor. I added a bottle of Johnnie Walker Blue Label scotch and two glasses filled with ice. After pouring each with a triple shot over the ice, I lit the cigar. We sipped, and I puffed.

It was a very good cigar and was in very good smokable condition, as the ash clung to the cigar through the first third of the burn. I had enjoyed good cigars in the past, but this was a true celebration, just the two of us. Annika added slices of pungent cheese, rice crackers, and slices of aged summer sausage. As the daylight was beginning to dim, we filled our glasses one more time, mostly reminiscing, but then also focusing on the future. Annika's first class would start on Monday, tomorrow. I tucked Annika in bed and finished the chores as quietly as I could. Climbing into that familiar old bed, I turned the lights out.

I woke up at 0600 hours. I so didn't want to, but I got up, paving the way for Annika. Fresh towels in the shower, her day bag opened and ready. I brewed a pot of her favorite coffee and had a pot of oatmeal ready to boil. I was also ready to add raisins, pecans, and walnuts. I went to the bedroom, sitting down slowly on the edge of the bed, and rubbed her arm, "It's your show, baby, I am here to support you."

Annika responded positively, accepting the challenges of the day. She accepted the wholesome breakfast I prepared for her, then I drove her to school, where she went headlong into her law classes. I became her nursemaid for the next four months, except for those times when she naturally needed a man. I was always ready for those times!

There was no reason for me to produce an income at this time, since Annika was my principal job.

House cleaning and grocery getting took only a few hours a week, leaving me with plenty of time to work on the nonprofit. I talked with Judge Stump weekly, and the 501(C)(3) moved through the gauntlet provided by the state and federal government in near record time. One of my biggest concerns was that our organization would not have the freedom to invest our moneys as we saw fit. But as the process moved forward, we found that there were few boundaries for an organization designed to simply give away money.

I created a newsletter that went out to all the board members every month, summarizing the progress. In return I received many thoughts and ideas, as we were slowly becoming a very tight organization.

It may have been late September when Judge Stump himself shared with me that his brother, Sheriff Stump, was suspended from duty. He was under investigation for certain problems regarding the inventory of the Richmond County evidence compound under his supervision. He was not only out of work, but in this case, he could lose his retirement benefits. I accepted the information that the judge shared with as much grace as a country boy could muster, but inside I was jumping for joy!

I called Danny every week, though our conversations had very little to do with our organization. We did discuss the various aspects of shell shock syndrome and what we should do about it. He shared that he too was having problems trying to be "normal," but as normal as his life was leading him, he couldn't let go of the horrible things that happened to him during the war. He too wanted to seek counsel. He was in touch with the VA counseling department and encouraged me to join him as he made appointments with them. Traveling to Jacksonville was out of the question for me, but I could make a round trip to Atlanta in a day. I requested my primary VA doctor in Atlanta and scheduled a routine annual checkup. The doctor prescribed an appointment for mental health, and then that phase was started.

Some of the early tasks in forming the 501(C)(3) was to create a name for our organization, write a mission statement, and then create bylaws. This was not the sort of thing that was in my purview, but I was determined to do the right thing with Catfish John's treasure, so I persevered.

Thinking about Catfish John, I called Sheriff Leary to check up on him. The sheriff explained that he had remained in their custody, as his trial had been set for January. He had been cooperative but asked if we had heard from the G-Man because he wanted to see him again. I shared with the sheriff that I had made a promise to him, and that I would make a surprise visit soon.

As always, I shared my thoughts of Catfish John with Annika, and as always, she understood and urged me to make the trip. Within a few days, after seeing Annika drive herself to classes, I headed south. I knew that I could make the round trip in one day and be back in time to make her supper. I was actually looking forward to traveling back down Highway 1 all the way to Dixie Union. I contacted the Wakefields and planned a visit with them as well. Arriving before 1100 hours, I stopped at Danny's first for a brief hello. Then I went to the River View Restaurant and ordered a large bowl of their fresh catch gumbo to go. It contained mostly blue crab from the river, catfish, river mussels, crawdad tails, and gulf shrimp all in a Cajun tomato sauce. It was to die for.

Then I drove to the Charlton County jail to meet with Sheriff Joe Leary. I carried in the bag of gumbo, setting it on his desk, and let the aroma drift through his office as we reconnected. I brought him up to speed regarding our organization and my suffering with the paperwork, but also the positive progress. He alluded to the treasure and that he understood my persistence in keeping the location a secret, but wondered how safe it was. I assured him that I had full faith that it was absolutely safe. I jested that if anyone somehow discovered it, then they deserved it, and that would be that.

He said, "Is it near here?"

"No." His questions were actually legitimate, but I was not about to allow anyone on our team the slightest advantage over any of the others.

He smiled in understanding and gestured that we make our way to John's cell. The guard inspected the contents of the bag as I tied the handkerchief back over my face. John was once again sleeping on his bunk as I quietly sat the folding chair in the reverse position and sat down holding the bag in front. I made a coughing sound again, and John raised his head. Seeing me, he nearly jumped to his feet, exclaiming, "G-Man, oh, G-Man." The aroma had time to float into the cell by then, and John, with his lower lip quivering, said, "What chew got in dat tote?"

I replied, "It's lunch time, you interested?"

He closed his eyes, drawing a long sniff through his nose, then exhaled slowly. While almost tearing up, he said, "Yo knows me G-Man, yo knows me good, yes. I knows dat is my kinda food, and I is so hungry fo' it!"

I sat the bag where he could reach it, plastic-ware and napkins inside, and he ever so gently removed the contents from the bag and placed it all on the bunk. He finally removed the lid from the paper bowl, set it in his lap, bowed his head, and mumbled a few words. He said, "G-Man, I don'ts really know how to pray, I can only do what I remembers my daddy did."

I said, "John, you did exactly the right thing. If our Father in heaven stays with me, I will teach you the rest, or I will see to it someone else does." After John savored several scoops of the gumbo, I interrupted, "John, hand me your Bible, and we will read some of it while you have your lunch."

He got up, retrieved the Bible, and handed it to me, sitting back down and positioning himself toward me. As he sat, slowly savoring every spoon full of his gumbo, I told him I wanted to read what his kinfolk had written in the first pages. It was a genealogy, starting back in the

1800s. It told of his grandfather, John DePierre, born in 1844. His parents had migrated to the United States from France in 1839. The ink was smudged in that line, but it looked as though they were escaping from Napoleon. Once here, they found their way into southern Georgia. They were fishermen and lived off the water.

It looked like his granddad married in 1849, and John II was born in 1877. His wife's name was Kris. John was listening intently as I half read to him and myself at the same time. I read that John III. "That's you John," was born in 1907. His mother's name was Kelly. I said, "John, do you know how old you are?"

He replied, "I don'ts rightly knows, but I recons I must be sixty years or so?"

"John DePierre III, you are sixty-five years old, and your birthday is June 18. Which happens to be the same date that Napoleon was defeated at Waterloo. You are definitely of French descent—and a Cajun."

John, having finished his gumbo along with a side of buttered Johnny cake, stood up. He puffed out his chest, walking around the cell. He repeated, "I knowed it, I knowed it. My blood is Cajun through and through. Mr. G-Man, how can I thank ya?"

"By being good. You will be going to trial soon. You will receive a long sentence in a state prison, but I will find you, and we will continue reading."

As I handed his Bible back, I leaned in close to the bars, urging him to do the same, and whispered, "John, all that you worked, stole, and robbed for is still in the tackle boxes at your place, but we will be retrieving them soon. Six other honorable people and I are building a charitable organization where we will use your money for people and causes we deem truly worthy."

I said, "John, I will contact you when we have acquired, deposited, and invested your savings. I will also advise you when we make the first gift."

Before leaving, I asked John if he knew a young boy called Pea Picker. John first shook his head, saying, "Yo is a G-Man, yo is! Yes, I loves dat boy."

I left the jail with the idea of heading back to Augusta, but I had stayed too long. I drove to Dixie Union and begged Danny and Pam for a room and use of a phone. I was obliged and began making calls to Annika, again wishing that I could just leave a message for her. I sported for supper at the River View Restaurant, where we discussed the encounter with Catfish and the logistics of going after his treasure. Danny had a nearly endless source of friends and equipment, but after careful thought, we agreed that we should approach this business with as much discretion as possible. Our hope was that no one would know.

Back at Danny's, I finally connected with Annika, sharing the day with her and that I wouldn't be home until late tomorrow.

She ended the call with, "I'm with you baby, I understand!"

Southern Georgia usually experiences some cool nights in late December, and this was no exception. We sat in easy chairs in Danny's living room swapping stories and a good Manhattan until bedtime. The next morning, Pam had onion bagels, toasted to perfection and spread with cream cheese, served with coffee and papaya juice. We talked and laughed for another hour, then I pointed the car toward Hoboken. I wanted to try and see Larry Harris before going back to Augusta.

This time I drove into that strange little town, thinking that I was correct in relating it to the *Twilight Zone*. I parked on the opposite side from Drake's Little Supper and guided my steps carefully across the dirt street as the same old men spat tobacco over the handrail. I walked in and asked the counter attendant if she had seen little Larry Harris.

She replied, "You mean Pea Picker?" Smiling and nodding she said, "He is walking back down to the dock right now, but hurry. Since he got that dang speed boat, he is always gone."

I followed my own tracks back across the road, fired up the Caprice, and did a U-ey and a quick left turn toward the dock. I caught up with Larry just as he was turning off the road into the marina. I skidded to a stop and tooted the horn at the same time and obviously scared the bejesus out of him.

He stared at me until he made the recognition, then squealed, "G-Man! I was going to give up on you."

I said, "But Larry, we are just getting started. Would you hop in the car and go with me to your folk's house?"

His eyes got big as he said, "I ain't never rode in a car before!"

"Hop in, you'll love it."

He did, and I backed up, accelerating more than needed, and

cut the wheel so the front of the car slid round to the opposite direction, then I hit the gas. Larry's eyes continued to get bigger as I accelerated the powerful 396 toward the main intersection. He leaned farther and farther forward, his hands gripping the edge of the seat as hard as he could. I put the car into a left-hand side slide, putting the accelerator to the floor and throwing dirt all the way back to the Little Super.

It only took seconds to reach sixty miles an hour, but the road to Larry's house was very rough and full of mud holes. I applied the brakes and turned to Larry, who was laughing as he turned to me, his eyes still so big, and said, "Can I get me one of these?"

"Yes you can Larry, but you will need to go to school and grow up learning a great many things."

Larry crossed his arms, saying that he didn't like school at all, and that he would just live his days in his boat. I just smiled at him as we came up to his squalid house. His mother was there and recognized me, showing joy for the earlier cash gift I had shared with them. I expressed to her that I was hoping Larry would go back to school because he was a very smart young man.

She explained that he was his own man now and that with his new boat, he was providing for the household right along with his daddy. I understood—I actually did. I could only hope that I could find an honorable way to break the chain for Larry.

I explained to Larry that I would be back during the spring months and may need his help with a few things on the river.

I could just see his smart mind working out the words, "What you talking about, help on the river?"

I just smiled and hopped in the Caprice to begin the day's cruise back to Augusta and to Annika.

I stopped at the only filling station in Dixie Union to top off the tank prior to the long drive. I stood outside the car as the filling station attendant added the fuel, checked the air pressure in each tire, and checked the oil. The young man doing the work commented about the size of the engine. As I nodded, I once again had that weird feeling of being watched. This time I bullishly looked at the entire perimeter of the station, then beyond. I didn't see anything, and it almost angered me.

I finally just let it go and continued to retrace my house getaway run in the opposite direction. I arrived at the apartment prior to Annika and was able to eliminate my mess. Annika arrived, and I realized that in only one day's absence, I was already behind the curve. She was intent, pointing and saying, "Put that there, put that here."

I just did as I was told. She finally collapsed on the sofa, saying, "I am so glad you are home! Tomorrow is Friday the 22nd, my last day of school until January 8. What should we do? I am exhausted." She said, "It's your show."

Batz, I needed to come up with something good. Friday would be my only day, my only opportunity to plan a total escape. I slept that night, but not well. I took Annika to her first class, then returned to the phone at the apartment, giving it no rest the remainder of the day. Short notice on a major holiday season. In desperation I called Danny with my problem—I had no idea what to surprise Annika with. It could be like a honeymoon if I planned it correctly. Danny talked about a cruise ship he and Pam went on just prior to his going to Vietnam. He said that it went to the Bahamas and was all inclusive, you just go along for the ride and party as much as you want. He gave me the name of the cruise line in Miami, noting that the food was fantastic.

I made the required calls and found that the cruise line had a ship leaving Miami on December 29 and returning on January 4, a seven-day trip to many stops in the Bahamas. What was better, they had cabins yet to fill, along with one honeymoon suite. I confirmed a honeymoon suite but needed to wire the money on Saturday. I really wanted to keep the cruise a secret as long as possible, but advising Annika as to proper clothing could be very hard. I also looked for vacation oddities in the Miami area by calling the Miami Chamber of Commerce. I wasn't sure if I had gotten lucky or not when a chamber secretary gave me the name and number of a private house owner who did overnight stays at a place called Stilts Ville. She described it as man-made islands that were built in the 1930s out in the shallow international waters of Biscayne Bay. They were originally for gambling and booze during the prohibition days. I called and made a reservation there too.

Ok, I believed that I had a plan, with just enough time remaining to pick up Annika after her last class. On the way home, I said, "Baby, I didn't have time to prepare a meal, so what would be your desire for supper?"

She said, "Let's stop at the China-A-Go-Go. I love their fresh hot food directly from those big woks." It was on the way home, so we ordered peapod and shrimp, which came with rice and condiments. We continued on to the apartment, moving into the house quickly since the December air was getting cold.

It was a joy telling Annika that I had an escape plan, along with the thought of traveling to Williamston to spend Christmas with her parents. She was elated with the idea. Then I explained that she would need to pack for two weeks, with about ten days of those two weeks in very warm weather. She would have Saturday to pack, as Sunday would be needed to travel to her parents. I looked at her, my face with a smirky-questioning look, my right eyebrow peeked up, waiting for an answer.

She said, "So, it's your show, let's go."

This required dipping deeper into tackle box number one, since there wasn't time to write checks. I put one thousand bucks into an envelope and asked Annika to place it deep in her purse. I wished I had a money belt but settled for just having a wad of folded $100 bills in my left pocket, and that worked nicely. I took both tackle boxes and placed them into the clothes dryer, along with my principal notes and documents of the charitable organization. Then I wadded a couple of clean towels over them and shut the door.

Sunday morning, we were packed and ready to head north. Just prior to walking out, I placed a toothpick on top of both the bedroom and laundry room doors, closing them carefully. Doing so could either prove or disprove my feelings of being shadowed. I had promised Annika that I would drive the entire trip, and if she wanted to recline the seat and sleep as we traveled, she could just do it.

We arrived at Annika's parents' house in Williamston late afternoon, and their welcome was more than what we needed. After greeting Mr. Bjorn, I pulled him aside, explaining the busy travel plans in days to come. Smiling, he agreed to simplify the remainder of our stay. We had nothing to offer her family as Christmas gifts other than ourselves as a married couple. The Bjorns were still saddened by the hasty wedding, and then Annika's mom pulled us aside and asked, with her head down, if Annika was pregnant. We both laughed at the same time, answering, "No, Mom."

Mrs. Bjorn expressed a heartfelt desire to have a reception for us in the summer. We not only agreed, but we also committed to recite our vows again at their family church. We could tell that Mrs. Bjorn was finally at ease, and we all enjoyed a relaxed Christmas Eve, indulging in a very large spread of snack favorites. Mrs. Bjorn reinforced the plan for us all to attend the Christmas Eve church program at 2300 hours. Annika had three older brothers, the youngest of which arrived with his wife and baby at 2200 hours. They were also spending the night but were ready for the church event. Mr. Bjorn drove the four of us as Annika's younger brother Jim followed with his family. The service was an exciting and reverent remembrance of the birth of our savior, Jesus Christ.

We awoke somewhat late Christmas Day, so we showered, dressed, and went downstairs to the kitchen. Annika's two other brothers, Les and Larry, had already arrived. They were all enjoying coffee and dipping into a pile of Christmas cookies. We were introduced as Mr. and Mrs. Nicholas Finn, and I was so proud.

Shortly after, the family gathered in the living room where a nicely decorated tree stood, with colorfully wrapped boxes stored under the bows. The family swapped gifts for at least an hour, with no contribution from us. How Annika had time for what she did, I do not know, but she produced a stack of Christmas cards with the names of all her siblings, their children, and her parents. She passed them out and sat back down. Annika winked at me, as each one opened their envelope to find a crisp $100 bill.

Now, there was a great question in the eye of her parents and the older brothers, which was understandable. Annika stood up and closed her eyes, her arms at her side with her fists clenched, and said, "My family, it has been a very strange and wonderful year, which you will learn about soon enough. Meanwhile, please accept my husband Nick into our family. It is he who has put me on my new course of study, law." Then she went on to release her parents of any obligation to help her financially in finishing her studies. At that, there were some large eyes in the room, along with silence.

Then I stood up, agreed with Annika's description of the year, and begged for their patience and their silence regarding their gifts. I suggested that in the new year, 1973, there could and likely would be some very interesting stories to share with them.

I think everyone wrestled with some questions in their minds, but not enough to keep them from totally enjoying the remainder of the day. Plus, the Bjorn's had catered in an amazing luncheon. We all dove into the cleanup afterward, then lounged in conversation as each older brother packed up their families and left for their homes. Annika and I retired early, knowing tomorrow's trip would be a long one.

Mrs. Bjorn must have gotten up very early, as she had a continental breakfast ready for us as we came down the stairway with our bags. We munched on toasted onion bagels spread with cream cheese, boiled eggs, and strawberry yogurt. Mr. Bjorn arrived last in his night robe. We exchanged many hugs, loaded the Caprice, buckled the lap belts, and headed south.

I was now traveling for the first time, not only with someone else, but with someone I loved. I followed I-17 and I-95 down through Jacksonville and St. Augustine down through Cape Canaveral all the way to Miami. We stopped to change into short pants and short sleeved shirts, as the temperature began to rise. We traveled to Cutler Bay and found a motel. In the morning we would report to the boating dock for the ride to the mysterious Stilts Ville.

Sleep, we needed sleep! We picked up some take-out food, ate it at the motel, and crashed. The next morning we traveled directly to the marina and made contact with the boat captain. He explained that his boat would leave the dock at noon and supplied us with a list of dos and don'ts for an overnight stay in the Stilts Ville island house. He said we would have twenty-four hours in the house, and then he would arrive at noon the next day to bring us back to the dock.

We read the list and were glad we did, as we would not have been properly prepared to fully enjoy the stay. We went back to the motel and took showers, since water was rationed in the house. We scurried about getting food and drinks, and packed clothing appropriately. We reserved the motel for the following day and returned to the dock.

The boat was actually a small yacht with inboard engines. After the captain maneuvered out of the marina and several man-made canals, the view opened up to the Atlantic. The captain followed small buoys the entire distance, since Biscayne Bay is fairly shallow, even though it is huge. The captain warned us again about the use of water, as all of the freshwater was hauled out in tanks, and the black water hauled back to shore in the same way. Arriving on time, we marveled at these houses on stilts so far out in the water. They were all hundreds of yards apart, all different sizes and shapes. Some were occupied, some not.

The captain wasted no time, shouting that he'd see us tomorrow at noon. The entire underside of the house was a deck, with an occasional pier jutting out twenty to thirty feet. This lower deck had picnic tables, lawn chairs, and at random, hammocks between the poles that supported the structure. A stairway near the center led up to the house. We were given a key to the door at the top and let ourselves in. For the most part, it was one big open room, with beds and seating arrangements wherever you may want them. It had a plywood ceiling that was painted white, a few light fixtures, and Casablanca fans. If you wanted to operate them, you needed to run the generator. The bathrooms were on an outer deck, separated by gender, one labeled "Inboards" and the other "Outboards."

It was a beautiful clear day, so we threw our bags on one of several beds we thought we would want to use and got into bathing suits. We opened all the windows and let the breeze move through. We placed our liquid refreshments in a gas-powered refrigerator that had already been running, popped the tops of a couple of PBRs, and casually walked the entire place. It took sitting in the sun for an hour for the feeling of this solitude to even start to sink in. We were alone, really alone. We might wave at a passing boat a distance away, but that was it.

We found hammocks side by side, climbed into them, and swaying in the Atlantic breeze, we both succumbed to sleep. I woke up first, playfully bumping Annika until she revived. We went back to the main floor, where I made myself a Manhattan and poured Annika a glass of white zinfandel, a tall one. Our package deal included one staple meal for supper and a breakfast, both included recipes.

We chose to use the gas grill on the lower deck to prepare our one-inch-thick rib-eye steaks, with grilled veggies on the side. We had our supper on a table that we moved to view the sunset. We laughed and talked until it was time to start the generator. Going back up, we prepared our bed of choice and made use of the bathrooms. There were flashlights placed everywhere, so I took one with me and went to the lower deck to shut down the generator. Moonlight flooded the place, and it was easy to find my way back to Annika. Oh, Annika! She was ready for Mr. Finn.

I have had some sound sleep in my day, but this was different—never-ending waves telegraphing through the timbers holding this place secure, a nonstop Atlantic breeze constantly changing the air we breathed. This was addictively different. We relaxed in bed longer than necessary, then used our supplied breakfast, altering their recipe to suit ourselves, and ate it all. We spent more time in the morning sun and were ready when the boat arrived at noon. It's amazing, if you can just shut down your body and mind for twenty-four hours, how your internal batteries are recharged.

The captain smiled all the way back to the marina because he knew we fully enjoyed that unusual stay.

Back at the motel, we made the final plans to board the cruise liner and even drove to the docks to make sure nothing would go wrong. We knew where to park and where to board. Again we got take-out food and retired to the motel. We watched the local news, then some national news. President Nixon was talking about a peace treaty with North Vietnam. I thought it was about time the politicians gave that war up.

We arrived early at the boarding platform, carrying what we thought we needed. We were welcomed on board and easily found an escort to our room.

What we experienced over the next seven days would take too many words to express, but foremost, we relaxed, completely relaxed, and Stilts Ville was the primer.

On the journey back to Augusta, we decided to stay in the ancient town of St. Augustine Florida, for a night then make our way home. It made the trip much more tolerable, except Annika would need to start her first class the next day.

We unlocked the apartment, hauling out travel baggage and tossing it on any available surface. I went to the laundry room door, where the toothpick was on the floor, but the boxes in the dryer were untouched. I went to our bedroom door and the toothpick was not visible anywhere. I was shaken deeply but held my cool and decided not to tell Annika until tomorrow. When I knew Annika was sleeping, I balanced a pop bottle on the doorknob and went on with my chores.

24. FORTY-SEVEN WORDS

I SORTED OUT THE clothing from the trip, most of which needed washing, and loaded the machine. I uncovered and extracted the boxes from the dryer to see if the hiding place had worked, and it had. I breathed a sigh of relief and opened both boxes to check the contents anyway, and it was all there. I looked very carefully for anything else out of place but found nothing.

I was very tired and went to bed at 2100 hours. I slept for a couple of hours but needed to get up and sit in the living room. At least I knew that my feelings were not just paranoia. My first thought was Sheriff Stump, as he would have an axe to grind, but if anyone had gotten a whiff of an idea that there may be treasure involved, it could be anyone. I began to make defensive plans. I would go to a locksmith as soon as I delivered Annika to college. I would get a couple of safety deposit boxes. I would call Sheriff Joe Leary to make inquiries regarding Stump and ask about possible spying devices that could have been put in the apartment. The movies always show bugs inserted into telephones, but he would know if that were true or possible.

In looking at the entry door, an intruder could cause the balanced bottle to drop and break, warning me, but he could be inside the house before I could get out of bed. I took a kitchen chair and propped it under the doorknob, then rebalanced the bottle. I thought about having no self-defense tools in the apartment either. I would purchase a baseball bat tomorrow, and if I called Judge Stump to share my findings, he may provide special permission to carry a concealed sidearm. I would be totally comfortable with a concealed carry pistol, but I had never talked to Annika about such things. I could not bear to make her uncomfortable if I did.

I laid out on the sofa, pulling a light blanket over myself, and managed another hour of sleep. It was enough when I woke again at 0600 hours. I moved clothing from the washer to the dryer and set the table for breakfast. Thankfully, eggs last forever in the fridge, and I prepared everything required for French toast supreme. Annika was up on her own and in the shower before 0700 hours, and I snuck a cup of coffee into the bathroom, placing it on the counter, while she was showering. I so love providing for her.

My queen emerged from her private chambers, ready to face her royal day, but not until I fed her. She sat at the prepared table, looking like a million bucks. After giving her a good morning kiss, I began placing slices of battered bread into a fry pan. I placed a finished slice on a plate, then spread a thick layer of cream cheese on it, topping it with the next slice. I placed it in front of her as I presented a bottle of Michigan pure maple syrup. I did the same for myself, which only took a few minutes. In a small fry pan on the side, I also prepared four link sausages, putting two on her plate and two on mine. We then thanked the Lord for everything.

After delivering Annika to school, I went on the hunt for a good locksmith. I found Augusta Lock and Key, operated by Doug Rosenbach. I caught him on a good day, and he followed me to the apartment. I explained to him that I wanted a door lock that could not be picked, even by a professional.

He said, "No problem, I have what you need here in the truck, so I will install it right now." He freed one item from my list.

I went to a sporting goods store and purchased a Louisville Slugger made of hickory. I called Sheriff Leary, catching him before he left his office. I shared with him the apartment findings and asked if he could do a check up on the whereabouts of Sheriff Stump and possible bugs in the apartment or our phone. He said he would call me after hours, if that would work for me. I agreed.

Then I took the long shot and called Judge Stump. A secretary answered, so I gave her my name, and waited. These people are not only busy, but they also need serious time in solitude for making their most serious decisions.

After a minute the judge came on the phone. He was elated to hear from me and made it known, asking what he may do to help. I explained last night's experience and that I wanted a permit for a concealed weapon. He didn't hesitate, knowing what all was at stake. He explained exactly what to do and where to go, and that by tomorrow the permit would be in my hands.

"Thank you, Your Honor, thank you," was all I could say.

I took one more step for security by going to the post office and having all our mail delivered to a PO box. Then I put the cash from the two tackle boxes in grocery bags and drove to a Wells Fargo bank. In order to acquire the safety deposit boxes, I needed to have an account with the bank. Having plenty of cash with me, I opened a savings account with $1,000. With that I could rent two safety deposit boxes, dividing the cash into both and locking them up for storage. I was given a key for each box, and I added them to my dog tag chain. On the way home I stopped at a Salvation Army store and found a used telephone. I replaced the one in the apartment, as I knew nothing about how phone bugs might work. It was just a gut hunch. I spent the afternoon making calls on the new old phone and changing our address to the PO box. After finishing up with a quick nap on the sofa, I went to pick up Annika.

I pulled up in front of building five on the campus and waited a few minutes for Annika to walk out.

She said, "Dang, I feel like I have jetlag, can we just go home?"

I smiled and headed straight to the apartment, as I felt the same way myself. On the way, I explained that I had something she needed to know about, but it could wait until we were home and comfortable. It was a cool day, and I had purchased a half gallon of apple cider. While Annika was flopping on the sofa and throwing her feet on the coffee table, I heated two large cups of cider, adding a cinnamon stick in each. I served her a cup then sat down beside her and put my feet up too.

I first asked her about her day. She elaborated, then said, "Ok, what do you need to tell me?"

I explained the precautions I had taken just prior to leaving on our trip and the toothpick test that failed. Annika just looked at me without saying a word. I explained the precautions I had taken during the day—the PO box, the safety deposit box, and the key on my dog tags. I explained the new push button combination lock on the door and the call to Sheriff Leary, who should be returning a call soon. Then I told her of the call to Judge Stump and the possibility of carrying a concealed pistol. I told her I wanted to seek the advice of Sheriff Leary on packing a sidearm as well.

Annika continued staring at me, but she was not smiling. Things like this may be tough for her, as her analytical mind must process to a conclusion. Finally, she said, "It sounds like you have covered all the bases. I will be content with that."

Then she continued, "But let's think about this for a minute, should we have anticipated something like this? I will be giving thanks for your gut intuition, or we would not have known." After a little more hesitation, she said, "You know Nick, the perpetrator does not yet know that we know he infiltrated our home. He will not know until he finds the lock changed and no more mail in the box. Perhaps we should move?"

We both jumped when the phone rang, and I chuckled as I got up to answer. It was Sheriff Joe Leary. We swapped short pleasantries and got down to business. Joe said that Sheriff Stump was off the grid, and he had resigned before the city council could fire him. He was not answering his phone.

I said, "Well, I don't know what sort of news that is, but now I have a different question for you." I explained my request to the judge and the fast track for a personal concealed carry pistol permit. (Annika had not commented on that subject yet.)

Knowing my military background, Joe didn't advise me as to whether I should carry or not, instead he went directly into what his personal weapon of choice would be. His advice was a smaller automatic pistol, six or seven shot 9mm, a Beretta or a Kel-tec, which was made in Cocoa, Florida. He advised an inside the belt holster, which was easily concealed. He added, "If you want real comfort, order yourself an Adams Holster. You may need to wait a while to get one, but his holsters are worth it."

He continued, "The illegal entry of your apartment was no doubt done by someone with trained skills, and yes, there could be bugs either in your apartment or in your phone." He explained what to look for. I explained all the precautions I had taken that day, and he agreed that they were all good moves. Then he said, "Let's think about this for a minute. The only outward change that you have made was changing the lock. If he returns and sees the new lock, he will know you are wise to him. Can you put the original lock back on?"

I said, "Yes."

"How hard would it be for you to move to a new apartment, a high-rise if possible, where mail is delivered to postal boxes inside the lobby area and there is private parking?"

"Sheriff, I smell what you are stepping in. We could be living elsewhere for a very long time before our intruder would know."

"Yes, keep me informed. I will find Stump."

Annika asked, "What!?"

I didn't hesitate, "Stump is off the grid, but Sheriff Leary will continue trying to locate him. I want to carry a pistol—do you agree or not?"

She looked at me with very stern eyes and said, "Are you shitting me, Finn? I'd go with you if you wanted to carry a machine gun."

I was quite relieved, but then needed to say, "Oh, and we will go with your idea and move to a new apartment." She looked at me with her best disgruntled and stern look as I said, "What would you like for supper?" That was just enough to disarm her. We had little remaining in the fridge, so it was China-a-Go-Go again.

I woke up at 0530 hours, unable to sleep any longer. I went to the kitchen table and sat and wondered what had happened. I had been diligently reading the Bible and had gotten to the New Testament, and I was doing calisthenics every day. I missed all that. It was freedom of time, but how could I get that back? I faced reality—everything that's happening now simply had to be worth it.

I started to read the Gospel of Matthew, then hearing Annika begin to stir in the bedroom, I started preparing breakfast for both of us. We had five eggs remaining, three slices of American cheese, and three slices of whole wheat bread that did not seem to have any fungus growing on it. Ah, cheesy eggs with toast was very good.

I washed the dishes, making the kitchen neat, while Annika made ready for her day at school. Early January in Georgia can be very cool, sometimes cold. It was getting colder every day, so I would go to the car a few minutes early, fire it up, and let it warm the interior. Annika loved that, and I did too.

After dropping her off at school, I drove back to the apartment, made a pot of coffee, and opened the phone book to the yellow pages. Apartments, apartments. Yes, a great many were listed, and now to find a high-rise. With a little observation, I found each page had larger block ads for the larger complexes. There were two near the college, so I called them first. Only one had an open apartment, and I immediately drove there. On arrival, I was impressed. There was a small parking area for guests, and the rest of the parking was inside the building on the lower floors. Entering the lobby was more like a hotel because there was a maître d'.

I went to the desk to ask about the last remaining apartment they had, wanting to secure it. The clerk, or maître d', at the desk explained that the only apartment remaining was a suite on the top floor.

She looked at me from head to toe, scanning slowly. I was wearing my comfortable prison shoes, denims from the church yard sale, and an old Pendleton long sleeve shirt. She said, "I am sorry, sir, but the suite is very expensive and reserved for folks of good standing."

I swung down both arms, planting both fists on the desk, and said, "What do you consider expensive?"

She cowered for just a second, then boldly said, "$450 per month, and $550 if you want reserved parking."

"Deal, do you want cash or a check, and would you also like the following month in advance?"

Her jaw dropped when I slapped my checkbook on the desk, followed by a bundle of cash larger than anything she had seen prior. In somewhat of a nervous state, she found the contracts in her file drawer, and placing them in front of me, she pointed out the important aspects. I filled out the contract and handed it back. Again I asked, "Check or cash?"

"A check will work nicely, sir."

I told her I expected a porter to show me the apartment and how to negotiate the private parking ramp. She said she was calling the porter at that moment. Soon enough, a gentleman emerged in a suit and tie, asking if I was Mr. Finn. I nodded, and he gestured to follow.

The elevator took us to the fifth floor, the top floor. Exiting, we walked out into another foyer with five doors; four were marked with apartment numbers and the fifth with laundry, ice, and soda machine. I was shown apartment number four. For me, this was opulence. Fully furnished and a view facing the city, with large windows even in the master bedroom. It had a guest bedroom and guest bath. I knew Annika would approve of this. The man took me back to the elevator and down to the parking ramp, showing me how to insert my key into the gate and where parking lots four and five were located. We were blessed with two parking spaces.

Fully content with my business for the day, I went back to the apartment. I filled the Caprice to the roof with mostly clothing, but also the few things we had collected along the way. In two trips I managed to move everything we had, including my fishing pole and tackle boxes. I made one more trip just to box up the food in the fridge as well as the canned and dry foods. I spent the afternoon putting everything away carefully in the new apartment. Then it was time to go pick up Annika.

I waited outside her building for her to exit along with other students, and she did. I was at the passenger door to see her seated and closed the door. Once in the driver's seat, I insisted on the seat belt, and she obliged as we headed out on a different route. She alerted immediately, throwing her hand onto my right arm and squeezing lightly.

I turned to her smiling and said, "Baby, we are moving. No, we have already moved, and I'm driving to our new digs."

I first got the, "I am pissed at you" look, then the "OK" look when we pulled into the parking ramp of City View Place. I carded my way into the parking ramp and to our private parking spaces. She was snuggling in a little closer when we entered the elevator at the parking garage and I pushed the fifth-floor button.

The elevator door opened to the foyer leading to the four apartments but also had a large window facing east toward the city. The view was just enough to cause a person to take in a bigger breath. Annika stopped, holding tight to my arm and holding a fixed gaze on the view. Then she turned to me with a very satisfied smile and looked at the four different entryways. I held up our key, exposing the tag marked 501, and she walked to the door. I opened it then turned to Annika, lifting her off her feet and carrying her over the threshold. She was thrilled with that age-old tradition. The east view was many times larger than the elevator view, and she was stuck in place again.

Soon enough she turned to me as a tiny tear came from the corner of her eye. She choked up just a little as she said, "Nicholas, I do love you." I showed her the remainder of the apartment, with the second bedroom and bath. She almost shouted, "We can have guests!"

The bedroom had a walk-in closet attached to the master bath. My clothes were already hanging or stored in the drawers. I put all of Annika's clothing and personal things on the queen bed and gestured that she had a job to do.

As my love was putting her things neatly into the rather large closet, I began making something to eat for supper. Believe it or not, I had two cans of ravioli remaining from days on the lam. The labels were worn, but the contents were great. I made a double portion of toast and concocted a garlic butter spread for it. The table was set, complete with a glass of Annika's favorite port, as she came to the dining space. She enjoyed the meal, then I shared with her the source of ravioli. While laughing in earnest, Annika said, "Is there a second helping?"

Then I laughed and said, "Yes."

As we sipped the wine, we shared our day. Annika revealed that the law classes were really hard but that drove her interest even more. I announced that I too was signed up to take two core classes for the spring semester and would start that next Monday.

She knew that the old apartment was paid for until sometime in June and asked what the plan was for it. Then she said, "Nick, can we really afford all this?"

I said, "Well, if you allow me to drive cement trucks on the weekends, we will do just fine." That punch to the arm actually hurt. So, I gave her a resounding "YES." Then I told her that I intended to return to the old apartment just enough to keep our infiltrator believing it was occupied. It would be good if her voice came on that phone sometimes too.

I told her that I had taken the phone apart at the mouthpiece and found a tiny device soldered in place that matched the description given to me by Sheriff Joe Leary. I just put it back together and left it. My intent was to make bogus or useless calls and to leave bogus papers laying around in the apartment. My thought was that any decent detective would eventually see that we were performing a ruse and try to find us again. A good detective would find us, but trying to infiltrate the new apartment complex would be all but impossible. He would also know that we had been suckering him for a long time.

We went headlong into 1973. Annika studying law, and I was taking pre-reqs for engineering. We played out the game with the old apartment, not knowing if we were shitting any one or not. Judge Stump had kept his promise to me and to our group; I received my personal right to carry a concealed pistol, and the nonprofit was poised to receive its 501(C)(3) status. After a dozen possible names, I really liked Satilla Benevolence to use as the name of the nonprofit. I had time daily to read and study the good book, and I did.

As soon as I received the papers for my right to carry, I stopped at the sporting goods store where I had already picked out a Kel-Tec 9mm six shot automatic. It's a compact, somewhat slim profile, with enough grip for my big hands. It lacks the knockdown power of a .45 ACP but is still a formidable sidearm. The inside of the belt holster, worn just above the right-hand back pocket, caused me to alter my dress code permanently. If I tucked my shirt in, I needed to also wear a vest, a jacket, or a shirt-jacket to hide the butt of the gun. As the weather warmed, I wore many more shirts designed to be worn out of the pants, which concealed the 9mm.

In April, the Wakefields were able to plan a weekend with us the first week of May. Our nonprofit application was complete, and it was time to begin the planning for the first business and organizational meeting, along with the expedition to Catfish John's hideout.

One of the two parking spaces that came with the suite was always open, as we kept one car or the other parked at the old apartment. There was a pullout parking spot just prior to the gate where a visitor could simply open the driver's window to pick up a courtesy phone and dial the correct suite number. When the Wakefields arrived on Friday, May 3, we just went to the gate and carded them in.

We had not been together since the wedding, but they knew of the apartment intrusion and the subsequent move to the suite. We helped them in with their luggage, and I noted that Danny was walking so normally that I nearly forgot his prosthetic. We opened the door to the suite and set everything down in the foyer.

As we walked toward the windows, Danny blurted out, "This is what I am talking about, YES."

We gave them a fifty-cent tour of the suite, including their room, then moved their luggage in. We suggested that they prepare their things in their room, freshen up a bit, and then we could explain our plan for the evening.

Knowing their arrival date and time, I made reservations at Luigi's downtown and had advised them of the dress code. Dan and Pam had arrived at 1600 hours, and our reservation was not until 1900 hours, so we had time to just sit and talk. Danny had started monthly sessions with the VA in Jacksonville, the same as I had done in Atlanta. We both had volunteered for a group study of mental trauma caused by war experiences. We shared our own experiences with each, noting similarities in the way we act in public and the quirks that can drive us to do unusual things. The sometimes hyper-awareness of our surroundings, resistance to crowds, and aversion to sitting facing away from a door. The very bad dreams. We would share more about that topic after dinner.

Arriving at Luigi's, which used valet parking, we made our way to the concierge and were shown to our seats. Both Dan and I wore dress shirts and a sport jacket with dress slacks. The jacket kept the 9mm concealed nicely since Danny didn't even notice that I was packing. The women—well let's just say that as we made our way to the table, heads were turning. Relative to good looking women, Danny and I had both fared extremely well. We ordered wine for starters and again went with a choice from home, St. Julian's from Paw Paw, Michigan. We enjoyed a bottle of sweet Concord wine. Reading the label, I saw the grapes were from Hunt Farms in Mattawan, Michigan. So close to my hometown.

We were served our entrées, which had proportions sized appropriate to the capacity of an average human being. We were recommended the tiramisu, which Annika and I split, and Danny and Pam did the same. There were open tables and no emergency to leave our table, so we shared another bottle of Concord. It was fun catching up on all the silly and meaningful things that we all experienced day to day, week to week. Pam, however had something more interesting to add—she had missed two menstrual periods and had an appointment with her doctor scheduled for the following week. It was likely she was pregnant. Oh, we all rejoiced with that news, and Annika added a few tears.

Back at the suite, we all put on pajamas and converged at the sofas facing the view of the city. We made small talk as the entire eastern view twinkled with thousands of lights. I asked Danny if he would care to have a cigar on the patio.

He said, "Sure, if we can add a beer to the menu."

I handed him a Kilian's Red in a Koozie, and we retired to the balcony. I handed Danny a Quorum Maduro Nicaragua cigar. We spent a few minutes opening the wrappers of these very good cigars, then properly clipping the draw ends. When ready, I had a box of wooden kitchen matches ready for the light. We chuckled as it took several matches each to secure a good burn.

Danny and I went into deep conversation for the time it took to burn down those cigars to a finger width of the end. That required two more Kilian's. Part of the conversation went to the VA study, as we both had our first several sessions with the VA psychology department and were scheduled for the next.

Danny said that from what he gathered from the first session, he could see things now that he couldn't previously. I agreed completely, confessing that I was affected too.

At 2300 hours we decided to give it up, but our wives were still chattering with several different bags of snacks sitting on the coffee table. I stood with Danny, and when we finally drew their attention, we made the time out sign and gestured toward the bedroom. Our beautiful women complied.

We all slept in the next morning, but I was ahead of the others and had a full pot of coffee brewing. The aroma brought everyone out to the dining room. As we all sipped and chatted, I suggested we walk to the new Waffle House just around the corner. By 0900 hours we were on foot. After breakfast, we returned to the suite, where Danny and I returned to the balcony to talk. I explained everything I understood about the 501(C)(3) charitable organization. I shared my thoughts about naming it Satilla Benevolence and that we needed to write a mission statement and bylaws. We would also need to formalize our first meeting of the entire group to ratify these documents and plan the extraction of the Catfish treasure.

Danny just said, "Where do we start?"

"With the women. This will take all of us."

So we gathered at the table, where Annika provided note paper and pencils for all four of us. Pam noted that she had a lot of experience taking notes, so she volunteered to act as secretary.

I said, "Well then, I will bring the first meeting of Satilla Benevolence to order, please note the time and date. The first order: is Satilla Benevolence an appropriate name?"

"Yes" was unanimous, so the first order was complete with one exception. The title needed to end in Inc.

"Second, what is our mission statement? In twenty-five words or less. We will call a recess for one hour while we brainstorm our mission, then resume the meeting. But first the remainder of items for today's meeting. We will need a date, location, and an agenda for the second meeting, which all members should attend We will need to develop by-laws, and Judge Stump has provided samples for us. Then we will need a proposal for the third meeting, which should be at Dixie Union. At that gathering we will go to John's hideout and move his treasure to a location of our choosing."

We went into a brainstorming session for one hour, throwing every possible thought out and listing them. Danny had the most, as he had spent the most time on the river. Pollution in its many forms was at the top of the list, as well as poaching, forest clear cuts to the banks of the river, oversized barges, speed boats at the narrower headwaters eroding the banks, and the housing at Ragman Point, where Larry Harris lived. Danny also commented that the river had been originally named for a Spanish officer named Saint Illa, but time changed it to Satilla. Our hour was up, and that was enough. We began our mission statement, which read:

Satilla Benevolent, Inc. A nonprofit entity, accepting gifts or grants for the preservation, conservation, and protection of the Satilla River and its tributaries. For the good and proper growth of all who live, work, or visit this southern Georgia river.

Well, it took forty-one words, but it was still constructed in brevity. We needed to stretch, so we took another recess, but this time for two hours. We walked from the apartment building around several new residential areas. Augusta was a growing city. That warm Georgia fresh air in the spring was enough to invigorate all of us. Back at the suite, Annika set out snacks and water glasses. We munched for a minute and got back to work, bringing the meeting to order.

Next on the agenda was the bylaws and the required articles. The judge had provided three different but very similar samples for us to read and choose, reminding us that amendments could be made every year. We went into a thirty-minute recess, allowing the four of us to read each submittal carefully. We opened the meeting again, looking at various requirements:

Names of all the founders.
Purpose or mission statement (which we now had).
Names of the board of directors.
Names of officers; President, Vice President,
        Executive Director.
Committee chairs.
Asset allocations director.
Compensation and benefits for employees.
Gift processing.

It was a little intimidating until Pam said, "This is exactly the sort of legal documents I am accustomed to working with. A few phone calls during the next week, and I will have this typed up and ready for all to inspect, along with a complete agenda ready to mail out."

The last item on the agenda was the next two meetings. We needed something positive on the next meeting, so we gave a choice of three weekends, June 1, 8, or 15. I would make the calls until we had a date all members could attend. We added a tentative date of July 12 for the extraction of the Catfish loot.

Annika had made reservations for Luigi's, and we had several hours to relax prior. We were all a little brain fried. The suite had a built-in radio system, and I found that it would pick up WLS out of Chicago. Larry Loujack was a DJ at the time and was pushing the rockers that afternoon. We heard driving rock from Lynyrd Skynyrd, Motown from Gladys Knight, easy rock from Billy Joel, and the ballads from the Eagles. The music was so good, we nearly missed our reservation.

We all dressed appropriately then took the elevator down to the parking garage and walked to the Caprice. As I leaned to unlock the driver's door, I bolted up, looking back toward the elevator. Danny had sensed the same thing, moving to join me back to back, as we slowly turned a 180 and back again.

I said, "Do you see anything?"

Danny replied, "No, but I feel it. We're being watched."

25. IGGIT!

As Danny and I stood facing opposite directions, determined to unveil something, Annika whispered in my ear, "You packin'?" I nodded. She said, "Then screw the SOB, let's go have some fun!" So we did.

Luigi's once again proved its worth, providing us with a wonderful dinner and two rounds of good wine. When we walked out there was music in the air, so we rolled down the windows and followed it to a city park set up for concerts. Parking was nearby, and seating was available, so we walked in and sat down. It was a free concert, featuring a new bluegrass group calling themselves the Red Clay Ramblers.

Now Danny and Pam were bluegrass music fans and said, "We may be in for a treat." They were correct—every musician played multiple instruments, and all were vocalists accustomed to tight harmony. The music varied from near rock to country, but when they performed an Italian sounding song called "One Meatball," we were in stitches.

Arriving back at the high-rise, we carded into the elevator, but just as the doors were going to close, a gentleman quickly walked up wanting in. Danny and I both blocked the entry, pushing him back.

I said, "You had better use your own card if you have a right to use this elevator, otherwise, go to the office." I knew I had better watch myself, as my neck heated up in an instant. I didn't need to do anything that may put me back behind bars, but it sure felt good to exercise a little defense.

Back in the suite, the women were very thankful for what we did. Danny and I discussed what may have triggered our instincts at the same time earlier. It was apparently subliminal, something small. Your eye sees it, but in the constant chaos, doesn't fully alert. The same with a smell or what you hear. It may be a combination of subliminal things, but it tickles a sixth sense. We both wondered what the observer may have thought when he watched both of us alert and go into defense mode. He would know he was nearly caught. I commented that one good thing came of it—we could close out the old apartment. Any cat and mouse game we played may have caused a delay, but that was over now. We were marked again.

We all migrated to the porch for iced teas. The Wakefields would be going back to Dixie Union and wanted to leave at a reasonable time in the morning. We talked about the objective of our stalker, and after a great deal of discussion, we concluded someone must have had more than a hunch about the Catfish cash. Physical risk would be unlikely, but we needed to pay attention to storing or disposing of any paperwork or anything that could provide clues.

As we sat, Danny had pulled off his prosthetic lower leg, leaning it against his chair, while Pam put his stump on her lap then worked through a series of massages on it. When it was time for bed, he just hopped where he wanted to go, using his fake leg like a balance beam.

After seeing Dan and Pam to their car and out of the parking ramp Monday morning, we went to work. We both had obligations at the college first, then we went to the local library to use their public typewriters to create proper documents requesting confirmation of the second board meeting. Annika rattled the typewriter keys as I arranged all the notes and recited them for dictation. It worked. I was not worried about a spy, as our action was unpredictable. However, I found myself scanning the aisles anyway. The library had a copier, and we made eight copies of our document. The copies were crude, but legible.

We found a Stationers Store on the way home and purchased a hand-held file box, file folders, and a box of envelopes. We also bought a portable electric typewriter and a box of typing paper. Moving from the car to the elevator, I concealed the typewriter box with a jacket—anything to prevent a clue for a spy. We set up the machine and addressed seven letters for the members, filing our own copy. We would do the mailing directly at the post office the next day.

On the way to do the mailing, we stopped at Waffle House for breakfast, where we talked about a visit to Annika's parents prior to the second meeting. Classes ended at Augusta State on May 24, so we could plan the trip directly after that. As the next few weeks passed, I made repeated phone calls to back up our letter for confirming a date for the full board meeting. During which time, Pam made delivery of the minutes, mission statement, and bylaws. It was concluded that June 8 would work for all, and Sheriff Leary volunteered his conference room at the

Waycross Post for the meeting.

We could actually relax at Annika's parents' place and did so for over a week. I made rounds to their stores with Mr. Bjorn, really getting to know him and his business. We were bound now to be friends for life. I shared with him what I did to the three stooges and why I did it. He laughed so hard that I volunteered to drive. It was even hard for me to leave when the time came, but we did, and we found ourselves back at our digs in Augusta.

We were both chomping at the bit to get the nonprofit legal beagle crap out of the way so we could extract the Catfish treasure and get started putting it to good use. But we had no choice but to follow the protocol. With nearly a week to go and nothing to do, I followed a hunch. I slipped the maintenance man a C-note to allow me access to the roof of our building. I had the binoculars from John's house, and Annika started making bogus runs to the college, grocery store, park, bank, etc. I put a folding chair on the roof, with a view of the parking lot. In only two days, I watched a light-colored Ford POS follow Annika out from the lot. The car followed her two more times in the next two days.

I marked the plate and called Sheriff Leary with the plate numbers and the story. Meanwhile, Annika had been using the Caprice for her divisive trips. While the spy was following her on his third mission, I put a few tools in Annika's car and parked far back in the outer parking lot. I slumped down behind the wheel and waited, wearing my old baseball cap. If I could wait all night in an ambush in Vietnam, I could wait an hour here. In time Annika returned in the Caprice, but it took several minutes for the Ford to return and park. I had water and snacks, and as the hours passed, the spy finally gave up and drove out of the lot. Waiting as long as I thought I dared and looking very carefully at the details of the Ford's taillights, I drove out to follow.

I held back as far as I dared and could still identify the taillights. Quite strange to me, the car made its way west on Highway 1 toward Wrens, turning off into a fleabag motel. I was so far back I couldn't begin to identify the driver as he keyed his way into a room. I parked the car a quarter mile back on a farm trail. I walked slowly to the motel, letting time pass until the light went out in his room. I sat on a concrete column near the entrance for another hour, then walked to his car, bathed with light from a tall pole near the center of the campus. I knelt down at each tire, letting the air out with a tool on the Boy Scout knife. Then I went back around and used the bradawl tool on the knife and punched a hole in the sidewall of each tire. I knelt down behind the car, waiting to see if I had raised any eyebrows. As all was quiet, I circled around front, opened the hood, and removed the ignition wire from the distributor. Fords were easy, as the distributor is at the front of their V-8 engines.

I walked back to my car, drove to the high-rise, and got back to Annika, who was worried sick. When I told her what I had done, she laughed then hesitated, saying, "You know, this may be the best time to move again."

I thought she was brilliant. We stayed up part of the night discussing options for a new home and settled on Jacksonville. Annika's professor had advised her to look for a bigger school for finishing her law degree, and we were certain that Jacksonville University would offer whatever we needed. We packed both cars full, and they held everything we had, including food. We gave up a month's rent, but that would not pose a problem.

Highway 1 was the best path to Jacksonville, so we stopped at Pastor Roy's house in Blythe, but they were gone, so we left a note on the door that we would call soon. At about 1400 hours we stopped at the Wakefields' in Dixie Union and spent just enough time to freshen up and tell them about our little drama the previous night. The Wakefields thought the quick move was warranted and were elated since it put us much closer to them and the Satilla River. As we crossed the St. Mary's River Bridge into Florida, I put my arm out of the window and waved at Annika as she followed. Around 1630 hours, we were on the northern outskirts of Jacksonville. After finding a motel for the night, we rested.

I was up first and got cleaned up and dressed. Shorts and sneakers were in order, and as Annika was doing the same, I unloaded the passenger side of the Caprice so Annika could ride along. We drove to a nearby Waffle House and had a quick breakfast, then drove back to the motel to use the phone. We called the chamber of commerce for greater Jacksonville and found them to be a great resource. They gave us the address and phone for Jacksonville University and several high-rise apartment buildings in the area of Pickenville, northwest of the city. We started our mission to find a new home first, calling all the complexes on the list for rates and availability. We found a good possibility at the

Atlantic View Suites, only a mile away, and drove to it for an inspection.

Approaching the parking lot, we saw it all looked somewhat of a cookie-cutter replica of the Augusta high-rise. But, once you have a good thing, there is not much reason to change it. Once again we secured a suite on the fifth floor, facing east, and although it was a great distance, you could see the Atlantic. We were able to take immediate possession, so we emptied the vehicles and took the time to put everything away. Back at the motel we loaded the Caprice with our travel bags and checked out. The lady at the counter said we were checking out an hour too late and owed for another night. I flipped up a $20 bill and asked if that would cover the problem. We were on our way.

Annika drove her car to the new suite, as I drove mine. We unpacked all that remained, again taking the time to find proper homes for everything. We had food and created a supper for ourselves, opening our last bottle of St. Julian's, and relaxing to watch a little TV. We watched the *Carol Burnett Show, Gunsmoke* (as I needed to know better how to draw my 9mm, ha!), and *The Waltons*. It was goodnight for us as well.

After getting the phone transferred to our name, we had unfinished business of the same nature back in Augusta. We struggled with it until it was all resolved, everything closed out or canceled. We ordered our transcripts from Augusta State to be sent to our new address, and we would pursue college after the transcripts arrived. We were now gifted with some free time, with nearly a week remaining prior to the full board meeting, and we were already prepared for that. We just vegetated. The high-rise had a sun deck on the roof, and we used it. We also did a lot of cruising around Jacksonville, getting the general lay of the city.

We made preparations with the Wakefields for several nights' stay at their home starting on June 7. We had added all the hotel and motel contact information on the meeting invitations to the board members and hoped that all of them had found their accommodations.

Arriving at Danny's mid-afternoon on the 7th, we were shown our room and went to the porch. I asked Danny if he had kept the bicycle, and he said, "Yes, I ride it most days, thank you." We needed to share with Annika about my purchase and use of the bike while I was on the slow lam. Annika just looked in question for a moment then said, "We do what we need to do at the time, don't we? I understand." Pam arranged a nice light supper, and we chatted for a while, as Annika and

Pam made a ham, cheese, and mushroom quiche for breakfast. Then we all went to our quarters for the night.

The morning of the 8th, we enjoyed the work the ladies put into the quiche, with plenty of time to drive to the Charlton County Sheriff's Office. The conference room was ready, complete with donuts, cookies, coffee, and iced tea. The sheriff even had notepads and paper at each seat. NICE! Prior to the meeting, I had a chance to ask Sheriff Leary about the plate number I called in to him.

He replied, "Stolen, a week earlier." CRAP!

When all our members had arrived and were seated, I gave great thanks to all, then asked everyone to bow their heads in prayer as Pastor Roy Walker blessed the meeting. All our subsequent meetings would begin and end in that way. I called the meeting to order at 1000 hours.

All members were armed with everything they needed to review prior to the meeting and all were energized for their role in this organization, so the proceedings, checks, and balances went quickly and smoothly. We brought the portable typewriter, and Pam typed everything needed for the judge to submit to the state and feds to put us in business. The judge said that the submittal was all that was remaining. If we wanted changes in the future, we just needed to re-submit them.

We chose officers, and they were submitted with the other documents. That was the first time I had been chosen as president of anything, and I couldn't have been prouder. After lunch we re-convened to discuss details of our expedition to acquire the Catfish treasure, which was to take place on July 12. Danny would have two small four-passenger boats at the marina in Hoboken, ready to transport us all to the site, with no uniforms and no unnecessary attractions. I added one more request to the meeting: my proposal for a certain expenditure. It involved Larry Harris, and I promised I would provide details after the deposits were complete. Our newly elected chaplain, Pastor Roy led the closing prayer.

We sat about for a while just looking at one another. Everyone was energized at what had been accomplished based on the promise of a source of money to fund our dream. I was taken aback with it all, as it was all based on faith in what I had told them. Not one had seen for themselves a treasure of cash, accumulated by a pirate, a thief, a robber. Only I had actually seen it. I had photos for it, yet they were only photos. Jesus says he has a treasure for us, and all we need to do is have faith in him to acquire it. His photos are the Bible.

There were many handshakes and hugs as we parted in anticipation of our gathering on July 12. Before leaving, I asked Sheriff Leary if I could pay a quick visit to Catfish John, and he agreed, making provisions. I entered the cell block carrying the folding chair. Catfish was laying on his cot humming a tune to himself. I ever so quietly sat on the reversed chair and made the now traditional cough. John spun to his feet, squealing, "Yo got gumbo?"

"Not now, but soon." Then I asked, "Are the jail ministries coming to see you now, are they reading to you?"

"Yes."

"John, I will do more for you in time, even when you go to a state prison. That is, if our Maker allows it, I will be there." Then I thanked him for being cooperative with the sheriff. Going back to the others, I learned most were on their way home, so we went back to Danny's for the night.

We finished the remainder of that delicious quiche while Annika asked Pam about the progress of her pregnancy. Pam explained that aside from the lack of her monthly, which she was thankful for, everything was quite normal, as she chewed away incessantly on a sack of pralines. Danny talked about the burden of not having regular work, and now that he could walk and drive with complete confidence, it was time to start hunting for a job. He went on about his boat and motor being the best he ever had—but just how much can a man fish?

I asked him, "Do you have enough fuel capacity to sail all the way to the Hoboken Marina?"

"Yes, but dude, we will be trailering the boat if we need to go that far."

I explained that Hoboken would be our destination July 12 and reviewed our need for two boats the size of his but no bigger. I also explained that he should plan for about two hours of fuel for both boats to make the Catfish Run from the marina and back again.

He said, "I'll have two trucks with trailers and boats ready to go."

Danny was nearly giddy at the idea of finally getting down to the action. I stressed again for absolute silence since the spy knew who he was also and told him to plan the trip with Sheriff Leary. We talked about other supplies like an axe, machete, limb loppers, and food and water for an all-day venture. That task was now in the best hands possible, so I could just forget it and work on other things. It was time for me and my love to depart, so we tossed our travel bags in the trunk, did the hugs and handshakes, and drove south.

Having plenty of time, I asked Annika if she would mind if I stopped in Hoboken so she could see the marina, which was not much more than a mooring dock, and to see if we could find little Larry Harris. She was good with the stops, so we motored in that direction. Hoboken had not changed. It was still stuck in the *Twilight Zone*. We went down to the dock, where the same two old fishermen were out on the dock with their lines in the water. I walked out to them and said, "Right nice day, y'all catching any today?"

They said, "You sure look like that G-Man."

"Well, I'm just looking for Pea Picker, y'all seen him?"

One of them said, "Well, sir, I do believe that boy may be at home about now."

I tipped my old baseball cap and went back to the car. I had been to Larry's house by boat and once by car, but I needed to remember exactly where the driveway was. It should be on the left, just east of the town intersection. We passed several old homes first, then found a trail with several mailboxes on posts at the entrance. We turned down the two-lane path as brush rubbed the side of the car, and did I say potholes—big ones, full of water and mud!

The path eventually led to an opening of several acres, with eight shotgun houses along the river and garden plots everywhere. The first one to the west was Larry's parents' home, so we pulled up in front. A small dog alerted the residents that we were intruding in his space, and just like that, Larry emerged.

When I stepped out of the car, Larry started jumping up and down, and shouting "G-Man, G-Man, I knowed you would come back!"

I went to a knee as he came running, and we threw arms around each other. I introduced him to Annika, and of course he was as bashful as any young man being introduced to a beautiful woman.

Annika just said, "Come on over here Larry. I'll feel bad if I don't get a hug too." Not sure who wrapped who around who's finger, but they were now buddies.

By then Larry's parents had stepped out, humbly giving thanks for the gifts they received earlier. We chatted, and I asked them many details about how and why they came to live there, along with the other families that lived out there on Rag Man Point. I heard what I needed to hear. Then I asked Larry about school and if he planned to attend this fall.

He twisted his toe in the dirt while looking down and said, "I don't know, I'm doin' dang good now with that boat you gave me. We's gettin' all the things we need now, sides, I'm too far behind, them teachers gunna think I'm some kinda iggit."

We both wished that we could debate with Larry about that but now was not the time. I wanted to tell Larry that we would be back in July, but withheld details, saying that we would be seeing him soon. We said goodbyes, turned the car around, and headed back down that nasty half-mile path leading to the road.

I asked Annika if she was in for a stop at the house we put on the St. Mary's River. She said she would love to. So, in another half hour we arrived at St. Mary's Circle and pulled up to the house. We sat, reminiscing for a while, when an elderly woman stepped out from the back porch and began shaking out a rug. She froze when she saw the car, and as I stepped out, I waved and said, "Hello, I'm Nicholas Finn."

Her eyes got big as she said, "I have heard about you and what you have done with my house. I prayed I would meet you one day, please come in."

Annika emerged from the car to meet Mrs. Moore, and we went into the house. The woman was probably in her mid-eighties, five feet four inches tall, maybe one hundred fifty pounds. She was a high school teacher most of her life and was tough as nails, very smart, and quick witted. She drilled me with questions about the prison escape and how I used her house to elude the law. She was happy that the charges were dropped for me. She was wonderful and both of us loved her right off. I explained that we could stop from time to time if she liked and share more details of my living in her moving house. I noted that Frank Lloyd Wright was now my favorite designer.

She quickly quipped, "Not if you would have known him. He was horribly demanding after we hired him and such a nuisance to the contractors that it took an extra six months to complete the job. A lot more money too. Why that fussy old fart would be rolling over in his grave if he knew I had this house moved. That's part of the reason I moved it, just to spite him.

"He also made me so mad one day, long after we moved in. He stopped by and presented us with a vase that was to be put on the fireplace mantle. He pronounced it 'voz.' He cleared our things off the mantel and placed his green vase at the center. After he left, I threw the thing into the backyard and broke it. However, it really did go perfectly with the house, and I have regretted doing what I did. He named the house Rosa Laevigata, the botanical name for our Georgia state flower, the Cherokee rose. The lead glass window in the front door and the patterns in the rugs depict it, and I do thank him for that."

We needed to laugh some with that. After receiving hugs and more hugs, we went on our way. In less than an hour we arrived at our complex, hauling everything up to our home and putting it all away, with most going to the washing machine. It was late afternoon, but it was nap time anyway.

As usual, I awoke first as daylight was fading and went to the balcony to watch the effects of the sun set as I faced east. In time Annika joined me, and we just sat, then sat some more. We knew we had a month before the Catfish expedition would take place, and we would need to register at Jacksonville U, but that would only take a few hours. We decided to just lay low—no vacations, no excursions—find some beach time, find a local hangout we both liked, dance, and have a few cocktails.

That's exactly what we did, and I also divided time out to keep up my regular reading of my new NIV bible. As we approached our July date, I thought it would be a good idea to have a few of the right clothes. We went shopping for hiking shoes since we had nothing of that nature. We wouldn't need them very long at the Catfish hideout, but with soggy ground, water in the boats, bugs, and other critters, they would be worth it. We also bought loose fitting hiking cargo pants and vented shirts with long sleeves. Danny and the two sheriffs would be prepared, but the judge and the pastor would probably not, so we called them with suggestions for footwear and clothing.

Phone calls flourished in those last few days. We finalized a gathering point on Highway 82 east of Waycross, where a casual group of fisherman would meet to caravan us on to Hoboken and to the boat landing. A sheriff's patrol car would arrive at the dock, two hours after our boats were in the river, in anticipation of moving the treasure to the jail.

Annika and I arrived at the Wakefields on the 11th, giving us time to have everything ready. However, my friend Dan was ahead of the game in a very professional way. All I needed were the keys to his buddy's GMC, parked alongside his Chevrolet pickup, both with fishing boats trailered in tow. The ladies retreated quickly to the house, and we followed. Pam was a host-of-hosts for the evening, and after Dan and I volunteered to do the dishes, we relaxed on the porch, talking about our excursion tomorrow.

July 12, 1973, we converged at the meeting point on Highway 82, then caravanned to the Hoboken docks on the Satilla River. Our truck radio played, "Rock the Boat Baby," "For the Love of Money," and "You ain't Seen Nothin Yet." I sang along to myself, smiling, as we drove to the Satilla.

We launched the boats and parked the trucks. Both Sheriff Welker and Sheriff Leary were in casual fishing clothing. Pastor Roy needed a hat, which we provided, and we were ready to depart. When all were seated, four in one boat at my command and four in the other boat at Dan's command, we made our way out from the docks as I pointed west upriver.

Before I opened the throttle, I scanned the dock, seeing no one, and shouted, "This will be an hour ride."

The engine spun the prop, pushing our boat up to its top speed. Danny followed fifty yards behind as we maneuvered our small vessels through every bend in the river.

In about fifty minutes, I marked the old sunken yacht and backed off the throttle, idling slowly to the opposite side. Enough time had passed since I had been there, and the river itself was in constant change, so it took several failed attempts before finding the path. Sheriff Welker went knees down in the bow and used the limb loppers to open the path just enough for the boat and passengers to move through easily. We entered the dock opening, where there was just enough room for both boats, but we still needed to take turns unloading.

Walking off the plank dock, I was amazed at how much undergrowth had grown up in just one year. With no foot traffic, the trail was disappearing, except for the area at the water's edge that was covered in chicken feathers. I was thankful for the tools as we cleaned our way back to the Catfish hideout. We passed through the rough iron traps, camouflaged so well most didn't know what they were; however, Danny did and groaned, "Holy Batz," when he saw them. We broke out into the opening under that mammoth live oak, slowly filing into a row, with all eyes locked on this very strange hobbit house.

I felt pain increasing in my left upper arm and found Annika was unknowingly sinking her fingers into my arm. I could hear various noises, grunts, and groans coming from the group.

Annika began to sob, and the pastor went to one knee and began to pray, thanking the Lord for the Holy Spirit within him that said, "Trust Nicholas, and as outlandish as his story was Father, I did. Now I see it's all true. In the name of Jesus Amen."

Annika released her grip, and pulling me up close, she laid her head on my shoulder while sobbing out, "Pastor is so right. I had doubts too, thought I would go nuts sometimes, but I just had to believe."

All the rest bore wet eyes as well, then Sheriff Welker said, "OK, OK, what do we need to do next?"

Just then, the old red rooster came running from the rear of the hut, dozens of chicks along with all the hens following just behind him. He ran straight to me, stopped, and crowed, then marched back and forth in front of all of us crowing with delight! The rooster was the only one hollering, "Eureka!"

I finally laughed and said, "It's a long story. Prepare your flashlights and follow me."

I walked past the large bench and anvil and ducked under the opening into the dark of the hobbit's den, instructing, "Lights on." The silence continued, as everyone walked inside and dispersed, shining their lights on many things.

I moved to the stairway and said, "There is not much room up there, so I will go up, then each of you take turns coming up. I would like Annika to go first, then each of you in turn."

I went up, with Annika behind me. We both needed to slouch with the low ceiling. I knelt and began to set the tackle boxes on the bunk, asking Annika to open each one. She finished with number five. We stood together holding hands, looking at a large amount of cash.

She inhaled and exhaled for a while, finally saying, "You're right. I love you, you're right—a nonprofit. YES!"

She went back down the narrow stairway, sending the next member up. It was the pastor. I had shoved a prop under a thatch window blind by then, which let a lot more light into the room. The pastor all but vapor locked when he took full view of the cash.

He said, "Finn, did the large donations at my church come from this?"

"No, it first came from the Bible in the escape house, but I paid that back with my own money."

"My brother, I love you, and Jesus loves you." He went down the stairs to send the next member.

One at a time the remainder of our members became witnesses, Pam documenting everything with her 35mm camera and taking many notes. I closed and latched each box, handing one to each man as he went down to put it on the table. I carried the last box down, trying to feel what Catfish would feel, knowing his life's work was being taken away, but for the good of the very place that he lived. As I made the last step to the floor, flashlights were waving everywhere as our members were dazzled by thousands of indigenous artifacts. I too was taken in again at the bizarre quantity. However, I did zero in on what looked like a jade vase, about eight inches tall. I was drawn like a moth to a light and wanted to take it with me.

The plan was to have a patrol car show up at the marina, then wait for our return. We would put the cash in the trunk and take it back to the Charlton County Jail, then put it in the cell next to Catfish John. Sheriff Leary carried a handheld radio with him and received a report that there had been a serious car accident on the south side of Waycross. Our designated patrol car was needed for the emergency and had no guarantee of return. So we elected to take one of the five boxes with us, then return the next day for the remainder. It gave us a lot more time to search the house, where we discovered many small treasures. It was amazing what Catfish managed to collect in forty plus years of pilfering from the rich folks' yachts and homes.

Small items were kept in mason jars with lids, preserving them perfectly. We were finding things like Rolex watches, Tiffany jewelry, and spectacles made with silver frames. We concluded that it could take days, possibly even weeks, to sort through so much stuff, and then how would we deal with it? We decided to call it a day at 1600 hours, taking only the one tackle box. We would all go back to the motels and then meet at the Plant Café for supper and planning at 1900 hours.

We all got back into the boats, made our way out through the tangle, and motored eastward toward the landing.

*　*　*

We didn't notice the barely visible fishing boat far off to the west, nor the man with a pulled-down fishing hat watching carefully through very powerful binoculars. We were long gone when he idled his way to the path leading through the water to the small dock.

The man wasted no time finding his way back to Catfish's house and going in. Even less time in discovering what was in the tackle boxes. Sweat poured from his forehead as he hustled back and forth, putting everything including several of the mason jars near the plank walkway.

On his final trip to the dock, he stopped suddenly at the opening covered with chicken feathers, as there was a very large alligator, partially hauled out onto the land. This big guy had a patch of hide missing from the side of his head and the end of his nose, showing bone that could not heal over. He pulled a snub nose .38 special revolver from a belt holster, aimed, and fired twice.

26. PICAROON

WE CARAVANNED BACK TO the Charlton County Sheriff's Office and the county jail, where we carried in the tackle box and placed it in the cell next to Catfish John. He alerted to shuffling in the cell bay and crowded up to the bars to try and see what was going on. I had carried the folding chair in with me and sat it backward in front of his cell again.

He stepped back and gasped, sputtering, "Yo da G-Man, yo showin' yo face. I is in trouble now!"

I laughed and said, "No, John, I retired from the agency. I nearly got killed on my last mission, and my new wife said that was it, I had to quit. But, that has finally allowed me time to form a group of very honest men and women to retrieve your money and collections. We have formed a legal entity, which will invest your treasure for you and use the earnings to promote the health and welfare of your home, the Satilla River."

Catfish John sat back on his bunk when I told him that part of his money was in the cell next to him. He said, "I don't knows if I is better or worse cuzza dis."

"John, now your name will be recognized for the good that came because of you, not for the bad things that you did. Every correspondence made by Satilla Benevolence Inc. will have your name on it as being sponsored by the C.J. DePierre Foundation."

"Dat sounds dang highfalutin to me. I's not sure what you said."

"Don't worry John, I will be telling you about the good things your money will help accomplish."

He sat back on his bunk smiling and said, "Well I reckon that will be rite good then."

We all gathered back in the sheriff's conference room and talked about what we saw and what we needed to do tomorrow. We agreed to extract what we could see on the surface along with the four remaining tackle boxes, but what about the remainder left there after that?

Danny spoke up saying that there was a storefront available in

Dixie Union, and it may take him several months to sort all the stuff with resale value, but he could do it. Then he said, "I could operate the store until it was all sold, but what about all the useless junk remaining on that state land?" We all agreed that just may be the first job Satilla Benevolence tackles.

Judge Stump added, "What if I were to petition the state to purchase that land in the name of Satilla Benevolence Inc.?" That idea was met with unanimous approval. We all agreed to meet in the morning with a replay of this morning, then we dispersed to our own chores and digs.

With more anticipation in the air, everyone arrived at the rendezvous area early. We chatted together for a few minutes, and all drove on to the Hoboken Marina. We unloaded the boats and prepared to leave as Pea Picker idled into the dock and hopped out with his biggest gas tank.

He said, "Why you all here again?"

We all replied that the fishing was good. He looked at us with a question on his face, "Really?"

I said, "You like some help carrying that tank when it's full?"

He smiled and headed up toward the gas pumps. As the others finished loading up, I walked with Larry. I asked him again if he had considered going back to school and told him that we could provide special help for him to catch up.

He filled the tank, adding the proper amount of oil mix, and I carried the five-gallon tank back to his boat. He said "Naw, I ain't goin' back." He continued, "My bidness is doin' pretty good, and today I'm explorin' a new fishin' and froggin' part of the river. It's an old canal that goes south, all the way to the Okefenokee Swamp. I knows that they's big frogs in there, and I can sell a boat full."

"Ok, but you be dang careful all by yourself."

I put his tank in his boat as he said, "You knows me misser G-Man, I'll be fine. 'Sides, I got pappie's picaroon, and he showed me how to kill a 'gator with it."

My knowledge of a picaroon was from Michigan, using it to move firewood from pile to stack. It looked like a small version of a miner's pick but with only one spike, a very pointed and sharp one.

I hopped into the lead boat, and we motored west toward our

own destination as Larry motored off in the opposite direction. The gang knew what the run would be and hunkered down for the one-hour trip as the small boats got up to speed. They also knew to look for the sunken yacht, and some pointed as we drew near. I cut the engine to a near drift as I poked the bow into the path. We idled our way back to the docking lagoon and were completely taken aback when we saw another small aluminum boat already there!

Sheriff Leary, again in the bow of my boat, pulled a concealed .38 Special and pointed it forward. He was on the dock first and untied the intruder's boat, pulling it along the walking planks to the shoreline, constantly looking back into the thicket toward the Catfish lodge.

He pulled it to the open area with the chicken feathers and on shore enough that the rest of us could unload. Sheriff Welker was next, and he too had pulled a concealed .38 and moved quickly to the side of Sheriff Leary. The two of them began a systematic move up the trail one to the left, one to the right, checking their flanks as they boldly pushed toward John's place. I was next, motioning the others to stay back as I too pulled out my concealed 9mm and moved onto the soggy land and through the feather patch, where I came to a very abrupt halt. The officers were concentrating on the open trail and didn't notice the tackle boxes and mason jars sitting off to the side. Nor did they notice the floppy brown fishing hat alongside a police model snub nose .38 Special.

I stared at them for a moment, realizing that there was a lot of blood and torn bits of clothing around the site. It also looked like a lot of thrashing took place, with drag marks in the ground heading out and under the intruder's boat. It was a foregone conclusion to me that the same old gator I confronted must have heard the motor noises, and after such a long absence, came back in hopes of some fresh chicken snacks. I thought this intruder must not have fared as well as I did with his encounter.

I shouted, "Stand down, stand down," to the officers, who had already cleared John's place and were heading back down the trail. I just pointed down as they walked up, allowing them to deduce for themselves what likely happened.

Sheriff Welker bent down, picked up the hat, and used it to pick up the bloody gun. He wiped the side of the pistol, revealing the serial numbers, and said, "Let's call this in right now."

So Welker read off the numbers, and noted that there were two rounds fired, as Leary made radio contact with his Charlton County dispatcher. They relayed the numbers, then added a request to try and locate Sheriff Stump up in Richmond County.

I then jogged up to the house with Danny at my six and found an old garden rake with the handle broke off halfway and returned to clear a path through the bloody leaves and feathers. That would hopefully relieve the gross-out problem for the girls, but they and the pastor and judge were climbing back in the boat, insisting that they would wait right there in the boats. The four of us huddled to discuss our exit plan.

*　*　*

Little Larry was making his way down the very old cypress tree logging canal, which was seriously overgrown but navigable with such a small boat. He had made his way deep into the swamp, which became the far northern reaches of the Okefenokee Swamp. With only one way in and one way out, he wasn't afraid of getting lost, but he wondered where all the frogs were. He wasn't seeing any. He did see gators along the way, hauled out onto rotted stumps and such. They didn't like the sound of the motor, and he would give a quick snap of the throttle from time to time so they would hang back.

He came to an area much wider, creating a pond area, covered with green algae. He looked around to see really large gators around on the edges, one bigger than the rest. He noticed also that there were no smaller alligators. The big one turned toward him slowly, and he gave the throttle a snap, but when he did, the propeller hit something down under the water, chewing on it until the motor stalled out.

At that instant, a huge Burmese python lunged out of the water, right beside Larry's small boat. It jetted upward ten feet, twelve feet, then crashed down on top of poor Larry before he could do anything. The huge snake's body held Larry down, as it quickly began to wrap coils around him. Larry fought and fought hard. He still had one hand free and grabbed the picaroon. The snake had him good and began to constrict.

Now these snakes have a very caustic and corrosive acid in their guts, which they can control, and the snake began its preparation of vomiting it onto its prey. When this biological potion gushes over its prey, it not only causes instant burning death for the victim, but it makes them slippery for easier gorging of large meals.

Larry was starting to fade, as he could feel the ball of acid working its way up through the coils toward the snake's mouth. The viper was unlocking its jaw, making its mouth huge. Its head arched over the top of Larry's. He made one last try to shove the picaroon handle into the snake's mouth when all went black for him.

The snake had been concentrating on a meal that would last him for weeks, as his tail splashed and slapped the water, spewing blood from the many cuts chopped into it by the propeller. As the snake prepared the vomit to ooze over Larry's head, the big gator had moved in and snapped down on the snake's tail above the gunnel of the boat and went directly into a death roll, tearing the last six feet of the snake completely off.

In a snap, the monster snake raised and spun its head, spewing its acid toward the alligator, and as it hit the algae covering the pond, it caused an instant chemical reaction. Fine acid spray, hitting the alkali, burst into a smoking gas. The python uncoiled from Larry even faster than his attack, again stretching high into the air and diving deep into the lagoon. By then all the other gators had converged on the scene and grabbed the snake before it could get away. The lagoon erupted in alligator death rolls. The alligators were shredding the python to bits as they swallowed whole chunks of snake meat. Larry's boat was being tossed about violently in the process, helping to force air back into his lungs.

Larry lay on the floor of the boat gasping, and as the tumult subsided, slowly he righted himself and sat at the pilot's seat board. He was still in a daze as the gators began circling his boat. The big one raised his head out of the water, laying its jaw on the gunnel of the boat and tipping it to the point of bringing the motor out of the water. Then its front leg came up over the edge, pulling the boat deep enough to take on water. Larry began to gain his wits, and he jumped to the picaroon. With both hands Larry raised it high, then slammed the pick straight into the gator's skull, right between the eyes. Then he reefed up on the handle, goring the gator's brain. The pressure of the gator's gushing blood pushed the pick out of the hole like a pop gun.

The quivering reptile agitated the water like a vibratory, and its blood sprayed out like Old Faithful. All the other alligators reacted violently to this new meal, turning the lagoon into a frenzy of splashing water and smoke from the snake's acid spray. Larry fell back to the pilot's board, grabbing for the starter rope. Upon finding it, he pulled hard and fast several times to bring the engine back to life. He backed away in an arch, swinging the bow toward the canal opening, and traveled as fast as he dared to go back toward the Satilla River.

*   *   *

We finished our huddle, concluding that our gator-bait intruder had done most of the heavy lifting for us. All we needed to do was load it into the boats and take one last look in and around the house. We were about to head back to the boats when I remembered the jade green vase, so I ran back into the house and grabbed it.

Back at the docking lagoon, Sheriff Leary motored out first, then I pushed the intruder's boat out and tied it off to our boat. Fifteen minutes later we were back on the river headed east toward the marina. Sheriff Leary radioed the dispatcher again to have a patrol car leave to meet us earlier than expected.

Even though the weather was fantastic and we were bringing back the motherload of the treasure, the mood of our group was solemn. I was not sure if it was driven by such a gruesome death of another human or that the other human nearly made off with what we were to use to start a great humanitarian effort. But the intruding spy did meet his just demise for his treachery.

On arriving back at the docks, we tailored up our boats and tied off the intruder's boat to the dock. The patrol car arrived, and we loaded the tackle boxes, the jars wrapped with shipping cloth, and my vase into the trunk. Sheriff Leary then sat in the passenger seat and escorted his deputy back to the jail, where they were to put the day's load in the same cell as yesterday. The remainder of us were climbing into the pickups and the judge's car when little Larry came putting into the marina and tied off his boat. As he came around the truck, I thought he looked really tattered, with tiny red dots all over his body. I thought measles, but the dots were on his clothes too.

I said, "Larry, what happened to you son?"

Larry just looked up at me, an expression on his face I couldn't figure out, and stuttering, he said, "M-M-M-Mr. G-Man, t-t-t-tell me m-m-m-ore a-b-b-bout that sch-sch-sch-hool."

We asked Larry if he would tend to the boat parked near his and told him if we couldn't find an owner, it would be his too. In time, we not only told him more about school, but we also provided him with private tutors. Larry was a very intelligent kid, and once he learned how to read, there was no stopping his appetite for books and learning.

We all convened at the sheriff's office to use his conference room. Everyone sat around the table in silence unsure of what to do next. I chuckled, then said in a serious business tone, "The next thing on our agenda is to—COUNT THE MONEY!"

Cheers went up in the room, "Yeah! Hurray, yes! Yeah!"

Then the judge stood up and made several loud coughing sounds, bringing us all to order. He shouted a resilient, "YES," followed by, "BUT, this will be a daunting task, since it needs to be done with extreme accuracy. The bank we take this to will charge us high rates to do it for us." Then he said, "Sheriff Leary, what do you call the room that accesses your cell block?"

The sheriff answered, "We call it the Green Mile, since it has a green and white high polished asphalt tile floor."

The judge, accustomed to having command, continued, "We will need two eight-foot portable tables and eight folding chairs set up in the Green Mile by tomorrow. We will need money wrappers from one of the local banks, lots of them, and we will need notepads and a good calculator, and Finn, bring that new typewriter." He continued with the list, and we all knew that this was important.

We broke the meeting, and all headed for their quarters, wherever they were. It was only 1300 hours as Annika, the Wakefields, and I pulled the boats back to their house. We had all afternoon, so we washed Danny's friend's boat from bow to stern, washed the trailer, and spit shined the rims. Then we washed his friend's truck inside and out and brought it back to him full of gas. Danny lived by the rules of LIBTY-FI—the same as I did and the same as the bylaws set for Satilla Benevolence—leave it better than you found it.

Pam, who was showing her pregnancy fully, had braved the boat rides, the meetings, and travel, and she not only had a meatloaf ready for us in the oven but a quiche ready to bake for the morning.

When all was ready, we joined hands at the table, and Danny began the prayer, asking all of us in turn to add our personal thanksgiving to the prayer before asking Jesus to pass it on to the Father. We did. After supper we got comfortable, then lounging in the living room, we watched the *Carol Burnett Show* and the first feature showing of *Gilligan's Island.*

During the night, I awoke to what sounded like a mumbling voice. At first, I thought Danny was having some kind of problem. I put my feet on the floor, scanning the very dark room. My peripheral vision noticed the faintest movement to my right, and as I turned my head slowly in that direction, chills went down through my spine as a very old man approached me, saying softly at first, then in a louder crescendo, "Put the voz on the hearth. Put the voz on the hearth, PUT THE VOZ ON THE HEARTH!"

Annika grabbed me, saying, "Finn, what is wrong! Oh, baby, it's a dream, isn't it?"

Her magic snapped me back into reality, and I said, "Yes, but there will be something I will need to do soon." Then we slept well.

Our reveille was Pam, pounding a wooden spoon on the bottom of an aluminum stock pot. As in the military, she shouted, "Shit, shave, and shower! Get moving, the chow will be served at 0600 hours."

We knew that Pam was doing us right by waking us up, but it was already 0700 hours. We all took quick showers as the quiche baked. After a quick and delicious breakfast, we left for the Charlton County Sheriff's Office. When we were all assembled at the tables in the Green Mile room, I called the meeting to order at 1000 hours, thanked all attendees, and asked the judge if he would take it from there.

The judge asked that all five boxes be put on the table first, then we would open them all and try to determine the age of each by the dates on the bills. We would return all the boxes to the cell except the oldest box and continue until we were finished counting each one. We separated the boxes some distance apart along the length of the two tables, opened them, and began jotting down dates from various stacks of bills from the top, middle, and bottom of each box. Several minutes passed as each box was closed and the list of dates laid on top. The judge mentioned that this exercise may not have any bearing on anything, but if it did, we would have it documented correctly.

The dates came out with overlapping but quite accurate time frames. The oldest was from 1915, and the newest was from 1962. Everyone looked at each other, knowing that it was 1973, and it had only been a year since the local banks had been robbed.

The judge wondered, "We must have a box missing?"

I said, "Yes, and I have it. Depending on if we go public with our find, the insurance company covering the stolen money from the banks could seek restitution, so I will hold it in escrow until we decide."

Then I added, "If not, I will consider it property of the Finns. Does anyone have a problem with that?"

Everyone started laughing, then the judge said, "Nick, we would all be wondering why you didn't just take all of it in the first place, except we all know who you are now." Then the judge said, "Show of hands, should this find go public? Yes, or no? I see all hands voting no. Then we remain a silent entity."

We marked the dates on the boxes, putting all the oldest in the back of the cell. We then divided the pile roughly into quarters, with two members to a team. The judge had us sort denominations first, which showed the smallest bill was $20 and the largest $100. We counted and bundled, then traded piles and counted again. In the process, someone noticed a bill marked "Silver Certificate." Everything stopped until we went back through all the bundles looking for bills marked the same way. The certificates had a higher value than the face of the bill, so we would need a collector to verify the values. Once those were separated, the count continued.

We gained speed as we gained practice but needed to break for lunch between box three and four. During that break, I went to Catfish John's cell to see how he was doing. He was talkative even though he had been completely silent during the work.

He said, "G-Man, I can't always understand what is going on here today, but I could tell that you have my last tackle boxes. That's good, it makes me happy. I can tell that you were not lying to me about these people with you, they is good people."

I said, "John, I wish you good health long enough to see the good your work will accomplish, and our good Lord willing, I will be showing it to you."

At 1400 hours, we re-convened and the counting continued, noting any bill that had any unusual labeling. We counted, bundled, and labeled the boxes one at a time until we finished the last box just prior to 1700 hours. Trust us, you can truly become tired of counting money. The final face value was $1,167,900.00. The antique value of the silver certificates would need to be added at a later date, but tomorrow we would bring in renowned antique experts for watches, jewelry, and artifacts. We were awestruck at the final cash count and looked forward to the future findings. Before we broke for the day, Sheriff Welker notified us that he had an investor representing Raymond James scheduled to present a financial growth proposal for us tomorrow.

We all went home to whatever digs we had for the night, having a fair idea that we truly could do good for the Satilla River. For the four of us, we decided to save a little work for Pam and stop for a pizza to go on the way home. Danny and I had a beer or two while we dined. We all daydreamed while sitting on the porch as to what may be the first major project for Satilla Benevolence. I shared a vision with them of something I wanted to do for little Larry Harris, his family, and the seven other families living on that peninsula. They were intrigued by the idea, seeing a little deeper into the good that our organization could do.

We met for the third and last morning at the county jail. The judge had called in a favor from a friend of his who was an expert in antique jewelry. Sheriff Welker had called the Tiffany Museum in Winter Haven, Florida, and it was sending its antiquities expert. We had nearly one hundred silver and gold certificates set aside from the older cash. We had counted the face value but had not yet found a collector of paper money to estimate the actual value. The last item for the day would be the financial investor. We sat at the tables and went through the formal start of the board meeting, then while waiting for the first estimator to arrive, we opened all the jars and placed the items on the table. We marveled at what the rich folks left lying around their yachts and other accessible places in their homes.

We had called the meeting to order at 1000 hours, and the first expert, the Tiffany jeweler, arrived at 1100 hours. There were seventeen Rolex and Waltham watches, and forty-seven pieces of gold and silver jewelry, most of which had precious stones. The jeweler started with the watches. Pam took notes as he recited information from each one, taking off the watch backs with special tools and reading information from mechanisms. The process took until 1230 hours, so we broke for a quick lunch and were back at work by 1315 hours. Each piece was photographed as it was placed in a plastic bag along with Pam's notes. The jeweler placed an estimated auction value on each one, and Pam noted each on a separate page.

When he finished, he smiled at all of us in turn, then shook his head while holding the last watch. He looked at it again with his monocle and said, "Tiffany began trademarking wrist watches in 1915, and this watch is marked with the serial number of 0004, 1915. The others are worth $2500 to $5500 each, so in total that's an average of $56,000 for all the watches. This watch, however, is very likely worth $500,000. If it were number 0001, it would be worth $1,000,000.00."

He said, "Sorry for the bad news," then he laughed. And we did too.

The jewelry expert had arrived by then, so we laid out all the jewelry, photographing each piece carefully. Another hour and thirty minutes of the jeweler working with his monocle while Pam again did the dictation. He also produced a small beam scale from his valise and took the weights of each piece. We were all tagging and bagging as the process went on. When he finished, he made an appraisal as Pam noted each.

He said, "Folks, jewelry is much tougher to estimate since style enters into the equation for collectors, but in gold and jewels, you have about $500,000 in value. Only at auction will you know the final value."

Both the jewelers were preparing to leave, when I asked them if they had any particular interest in any of the items, aside from the 0004 Rolex. I said, "If it pleases the board, I suggest we offer each of these gentlemen a piece worth around $5,000. After all, it is likely that Danny will discover more and need more appraisals." The board agreed, and we made fair payment for their work.

As they were leaving, one of them said, "So where did you acquire all this stuff?"

From his cell, Catfish John shouted out, "FROM ME!" The men looked at us in question as we all just nodded.

Sheriff Welker's friend from Raymond James arrived just as the others were leaving. His timing was great, and we sat him down. Our next order of business was to add the proposed value of everything to the cash amount. At that point we would have a better financial profile for the investor to look at. When we added the cash value to that of the watches and jewelry, we presented to the investor, Mr. Larry Anderson, $2,223,000 as the basis for the initial deposit.

He then explained that Raymond James had no way to actually deal with cash or antiques, but they partnered with Chase Bank for that sort of transaction. He went on, saying that the Chase Bank in Jacksonville could handle the cash and the silver certificates. They also had deposit boxes large enough for antiques, and he suggested that we take it all there. But he added, "If I were you, I would hire a Brinks truck for the transport."

Then he said, "For the investments, please open your folders, and I will review options in something we call risk tolerance." He covered the subject well and asked us to think carefully about the subject matter, read the pamphlet, and then plan a meeting in about a month to conclude our decision. Meanwhile, he would pave the way with the Chase Bank in Jacksonville and plan to move the money during the next week.

Then he said, "Keep this in mind. With a low risk of 2.5 percent, the yield will be about $60,000 annually, at medium risk about $190,000 annually, and at high risk about $360,000." He added, "I will give council at whatever level you choose." Then he too went on his way.

It was time to close the meeting. We agreed to receive and transfer all the banking information and set the date for the next meeting one month from now. Sheriff Welker would arrange for the Brinks truck and share that date with me. We were all tired, but before closing the meeting, Pastor Roy said a prayer. As his prayer ended, we all heard a distinctive 'amen' come from Catfish John's cell. After that, opening and closing prayers would also be included in the minutes of every meeting.

As we all traded hugs and goodbyes, I mentioned that I would be available for Danny's recovery missions to John's hideout for the remainder of the summer and hoped for a chance to go with him. I ventured over to John's cell to say goodbye and let him know I would be stopping to see Danny when the chance arrived and would visit him too.

We were all ready to walk out when the dispatcher ran into the room and went to huddle with Sheriff Leary. They mumbled for a short minute, then the sheriff said, "Listen up folks. We have a report back from Richmond County in regard to the .38 police revolver we recovered at John's boat dock. It did in fact belong to Sheriff Edward Stump." We looked at each other trying to figure out just how to feel about his demise when Pastor Roy went to a knee, praying for his soul.

Then the sheriff added, "However..."

27. ATOLL, ATOLL, ATOLL!

WE ALL FACED THE sheriff with questioning looks on our faces. He cleared his throat and repeated, "However, Sheriff Edward Stump turned in his service revolver the day he resigned, and it was placed back in the arsenal. However, he has not yet been located."

Pastor Roy finished his prayer and said, "Well isn't that just a pig in a poke. You know, there is more money here than what I could have guessed was in the whole state of Georgia. I would like to meet this man, Catfish John."

The sheriff said, "Then I will see if Mr. DePierre is willing to meet guests." He walked to the cell, spoke to John for a minute, then said, "Yes, he would very much like to meet you all. Please come over one at a time." The pastor went first.

The sheriff made the introduction, saying handshakes would be authorized. Pastor Roy shook his hand and maintained his grip on John's while asking him if he cared to join him in prayer. John just nodded and bowed his head, and the pastor prayed quietly between the two of them.

Then Danny stepped up, followed by Pam, then Annika, the judge, and Sheriff Welker. The general message to John from the group was of thankfulness and that they were determined to use the money for good purposes.

I went last because I had a question for him. A year earlier I had made a sizable contribution to the Sheriff's Posse, with the stipulation that they provide a bowl of hot seafood gumbo with oyster crackers to John every Sunday. I said to John, "Are you getting your gumbo on Sundays?"

With a tear forming in his eye, he stuttered out, "Yes, I—thanks ya."

I told him that I would be back to check on him, but his trial was scheduled soon and he may be in a state prison by then.

We all moved to the parking lot for final goodbyes, and Annika and I headed back to Jacksonville. We needed to locate the Chase Bank and make preparations for the Benevolence account and the arrival of the Brinks truck. In the following two days that part of the business was complete, and we could concentrate on the financial investment decisions we would need to make at a meeting scheduled for mid-August. On day three, we received a call from Judge Stump, saying that they had located his brother Sheriff Stump, who was still alive, but barely.

The judge had quite a story. He began by saying, "The deputies had noted one of their men had been missing for a week, but no one got excited at first because the guy caused the department various troubles and was constantly absent. They had taken him off road duty and were using him only as a guard during court. I got a call yesterday from Sheriff Joe Leary, who was investigating a car with a boat trailer that appeared to be abandoned at the Dixie Union Marina. Sheriff Leary ran the plate and found the car, a 1965 Ford, was registered to Mr. James Bachi, a.k.a. Deputy James Bachi, the missing man.

"I sent a patrol car to my brother's house. Officers found the door unlocked and went in to look around. Their footsteps on the floor were heard by Sheriff Stump, who was in the basement but could no longer holler out. All he could do was jerk the chains that had him bound.

"The deputies went down with guns drawn but found Stump helplessly chained to an old cot. One of them ran back to the patrol car and called for first responders and an ambulance. The other found a way to free the chains.

"My brother is in the hospital recuperating now. I talked briefly to him this morning, and he told me he had caught Deputy Bachi listening at the door of my private chambers after the Nicholas Finn hearing. After that he kept an eye on Bachi, and eventually figured out what he was up to. My brother said he had confronted Bachi the day before we all went to Waycross, but that Bachi had knocked him out with a blackjack, and he woke up chained in his basement. I told my brother I wanted him to rest for a few days before he shared the rest of the story."

I thanked the judge profusely for sharing that information. I then shared the story with Annika, and we made calls to all the others, sharing our guilt for misjudging the sheriff.

As there were two county sheriffs at the scene where we all believed that Deputy Bachi had been killed, hauled off, and eaten by an alligator, there was no further investigation by the coroner's office. They issued the death certificate to the sheriff's office, which in turn located the nearest of kin. Bachi was married but had been separated for some time. His wife accepted the death certificate and agreed to arrange a funeral gathering with the sheriff's office in the near future. When the date arrived, several of us traveled to the service, where officers provided a gun salute, even though there were no physical remains and even though he was not a model deputy. There was only a half dozen family members in attendance, one, a young grandson, was the only one to shed tears.

Summer went quickly as Annika planned for her senior year, and I planned for my sophomore year and a full load. At the mid-August board meeting, we chose to invest the money at a moderately high risk level in hopes of gaining some principal for our first project, which was the subject matter of the remainder of the meeting. Danny would be the principal lead, working with the Department of Natural Resources, or DNR, to find appropriate projects to tackle, with a list of possibilities for this time next year. I had a project of my own in mind, and with my charge-forward personality, began its planning shortly after the meeting. I shared it with Annika, and even though it didn't fully fit our mission statement, she really liked it.

We plowed headlong into the fall semester, not coming up for air until Christmas break. Our new digs had a few amenities we quickly took advantage of—an exercise and weight room, as well as a small pool and hot tub. I ran a 5K on the campus track three evenings each week and worked out in the weight room three mornings each week. Annika didn't care much about running but took out any frustrations in the exercise room.

We drove to Williamston to spend Christmas with the Bjorns, and my parents stopped by for a couple days while on their way to Florida for the remainder of the winter. On the way home we stopped to see Larry Harris. We had bought a wardrobe of new clothing for him, with several pairs of shoes. We had hoped it would help him feel more comfortable in school. It did.

While there, we inquired about the landowner of the eight homes. The tenants, Larry's parents included, had some sort of sharecropper arrangement going on. It was obviously stacked against the tenants, and there was no maintenance or upkeep of the property. However, with a little vision, the property could be a stunning setting on the river.

We plowed back into the spring semester and the celebration after graduation provided by the Bjorns. We spent a week doing almost nothing. Annika was getting excited about finding a graduate law school close to home, and I was getting excited too. Annika and I wanted to follow through with our idea of turning Rag Man Point into Harris Peninsula, but we would need to try and acquire the property first. We decided to make something happen.

Hoboken was only two hours away, but regardless, it always took a little trip planning. Larry ran out to meet us as soon as we pulled up to the house. We were very happy that he was there, as the family had no phone. None of the homes had phones, as the phone company had simply neglected to supply the lines to get to them.

We needed to travel back and forth for two days, but we secured an appointment with a Mr. Bernard Shurburn, who had a storefront office in Blackshear, just north of Hoboken. Mr. Shurburn was primarily a farmer but had other business interests as well. We spent time talking with many local folks in regard to Mr. Shurburn and developed a biography on him that would help us devise a plan. We then spent some time coaching Larry for his risky task, which he was surprisingly eager to perform, and made an appointment for him totally separate from ours.

We were just outside the open door when Larry walked in to Mr. Shurburn's office. Mr. Shurburn was smoking an Old Dutchman cigar, the fifty-cent variety. He wrinkled up his forehead, looked at Larry, and said, "What the hell are you doing here, get yourself back home!"

Larry stood his ground saying, "I think you better listen to what I gots to say. I wants to buy that ten-acre parcel of land just off Highway 15, where it crosses the Satilla River, right by Big Creek. Now how much money do you want for it?"

Mr. Shurburn was dumbfounded for a few seconds, then said, "Today's your lucky day son, I'll take $35,000 for the whole damn thing," believing he would scare the kid off.

Larry snapped back, "That's too dang much, but I'll give you $30,000 cash right now."

Mr. Shurburn, looked at Larry, his face twisted in disbelief. Figuring he would call his bluff again, he said, "Sold."

Larry reached into the paper bag he was carrying and pulled out three bundles of bills equaling $30,000 and slapped each one on the table. By the time Larry slapped the last bundle on the table, Mr. Shurburn was leaning over his desk, and the cigar had fallen out of his mouth to the floor.

He looked in wonderment at Larry, but that only lasted for a second as he snatched the three stacks as fast as a viper's strike. Then he started yelling at Larry, "Get the hell out of my office now!"

That's when I stepped around the open door and calmly asked Larry if the gentleman was giving him any problem. I was dressed in a way that showed that I was no slouch and that for paunchy Bernie to get tough would not be a good idea.

Mr. Shurburn said, "What is this, some kind of shake down?"

I said, "No, Mr. Shurburn, it was an honest deal that you just accepted."

His face was turning beet red when he said, "You're going to need a lawyer to prove that."

"That's no problem. Let me introduce you to Mrs. Finn, Larry's personal lawyer." I did a full about-face from Bernie, purposely allowing the grip of my 9mm to show, as I invited Annika in. She was holding a portable reel-to-reel recorder and said, "Do I need to play this back for you? If not, we can get down to business."

Annika was not a lawyer yet, and it would be another two years before she would qualify for the bar exam, but she pulled off a wonderful act, having all the paperwork necessary to complete the sale of the property to Satilla Benevolence.

We drove to Larry's parents' house and asked them if they could gather a representative from each of the other seven homes and meet here, and they did. We made an announcement that the property they lived on had been purchased by a certain organization, and that they would no longer need to make rent payments. We told them that it could take up to four years, but they would all have the property deeded over to them, and they could expect other good things to happen as well. There was probably a party that night on what we now called the Harris Peninsula.

We Finns made the initial purchase of the land on behalf of Satilla Benevolence and planned to fund the infrastructure changes later that summer. As we awaited our August board meeting to choose projects for the corporation, we had gone forward with our own money. If the board thought it worthy to compensate us, then good, if not, that would be good as well. We first hired an excavating company to build a road back to Harris Peninsula that would meet county specifications, and therefore, regular county maintenance. Annika pursued the legal process to force the phone company to provide phone lines to all eight homes. After that came an appropriate electrical power system.

I had been pursuing mechanical design and engineering in college while three of my school buds were pursuing architecture, so I challenged them that summer to a contest. They had to individually, or as a group entry, survey the Harris Peninsula and make a grand design for the entire ten acres. They had to divide it into eight privately owned properties that included community space for all. I offered $10,000 for the best plan. They chose to join forces, ensuring a win for all. My only mandate was that my three buds be finished by August 15th, the scheduled date of our next board meeting. The challenge was met even beyond what I could envision.

Just days before the meeting, they told me that they had traveled to Harris Peninsula and spent many days there talking to the residents. They looked at every aspect of their lives, what they liked about their current homes, and what they didn't like. They came up with three different designs, each with complete buildable plans and elevation drawings that showed how each house would look from the outside and inside. All of these drawings were in color. I was totally humbled at their talents and the effort they put into their designs. Annika provided them with their check, but the lawyer in her had them vow to do future work with Satilla Benevolence. They agreed.

On August 15, 1975, our meeting came as scheduled in Waycross, since it remained central to our cause. Sheriff Leary provided us with his conference room, where we opened the meeting with prayer from Pastor Roy and got down to business. After several things of the clerical nature that needed to be resolved, we moved to the potential projects for the year. Annika and I wowed the group with prints and plans for the Harris Peninsula, and we got accolades for the advanced work. Danny had additional ideas, as that was his job. We would continue with the Harris project, with complete infrastructure updates and heavy landscaping for this year. Then we would build two new homes each year until all eight were complete. As the property was in a flood plain, all the homes would be set on pilings four feet above the natural grade.

Before Danny laid out five possible projects, he gave a report on operating the antique store on weekends in Dixie Union. He explained that the store was getting good traffic and that the old boat motors were very popular. His biggest problem was being discreet about going back to the Catfish Lodge to collect more items to sell. He added that at the current rate, supply and demand could last for another year or two. As he handed over a check for $10,000 made from his sales, we cheered!

Then he said, "Now for the guns." He explained that all but one were not much more than junk, but one was a Henry Repeating Arms, a hex barreled, sixteen shot, lever action .44 caliber rifle. He continued, "This gun was built around 1864, when the Civil War was still raging, and these rifles were exclusive to the Union. There were possibly about two thousand of them built. How on earth he had one of these, the Father only knows. We will need to auction it and expect to get between $100,000 and $250,000."

We were all dumb struck.

Danny then laid out the list of five projects for judging, and we narrowed them down, ending with two major projects for the year and keeping the others for consideration the following year.

The project that caught the most attention was the Woodbine Recycling and Scrap Company. Recommendations coming from the DNR and Danny's observations, cited the company as being a major polluter to the river. It happened to be the very place that Catfish John did most of his scrap business. This project would be a drawn out affair, which would require a great deal of legal work—first through the state, then the company. It would take that first year just to gain their serious attention. Then we would hold the legal club over their heads to make substantial changes. However, all of our correspondence was not aimed at stopping the business, since recycling is tremendously important to every aspect of life on the planet. We urged them to work with us, as we could provide state-of-the-art technology through Jacksonville University, and we were poised to become formidable grant writers. Woodbine could very well be a recipient.

The second thing on Danny's list that took interest was the non-recyclable junk piles at the Catfish hideout, as it would take manpower and equipment to remove and transport them to the Hoboken dock. Danny explained that as soon as he was satisfied that all the sellable items were removed, he would take bids for the work.

Before the meeting closed, I proposed a motion to pay Danny an annual stipend of $12,000 for his work. It passed unanimously. During that year, all the jewelry and the silver certificates had been sold at auction and netted an additional $280,000 above estimate and face value. This put the initial investment at around three million dollars. Then we added the interest for the year, which added another quarter of a million, for a total of three and one quarter million.

During my senior year at Jacksonville University, I met two new buds who were finishing with electronics degrees. They also ran 5Ks the same evenings I did, and during one of those runs, I proposed a collaborative effort to build a simple phone message recorder. One that anyone could purchase at a Sears & Roebuck or electronics store. Between my skills at mechanical design and engineering, theirs in advanced electronics, and the use of the campus labs, we produced three working models. We chose what we thought was the best model and pursued a patent. The initial search showed other devices as early as 1903 and others later, but none using magnetic tape or small enough for home use.

Late in that fall semester, we had the most wonderful news that Annika had become pregnant. We elected to keep it to ourselves until Christmas, when our families would meet at the Bjorns. We needed to sneak the news to the Wakefields, whose son was approaching his first year. Pam and Annika made frequent calls after that. We learned that a trial for Catfish John had been held, and he was convicted and sentenced to twenty years at Ware State Prison, about thirty miles north of Waycross. He would remain in traveling distance for me, and I would visit him from time to time.

After graduating in 1975, I wanted to find work, and there was plenty around. However, Annika was working in her spare time for Satilla Benevolence during her first year in law school. Most of her work was done from an office created in the spare bedroom of our apartment. To make room for the baby, we either needed to move the office to some other building, or we needed a larger place to live. I consulted the board members with the problem, both by phone and letter. The consensus was that we could afford a storefront for the Benevolence, and I should go find one. I did, about fifty miles north, in St. Mary's, Georgia. I also found a nice ranch house on a tributary of the St. Mary's River, only a ten-minute drive to nearly anything we might want. I would miss the monthly group meetings at the VA and my volunteer participation in the shell shock study, which I had been attending since moving to Jacksonville, but at this point I had learned a great deal about the syndrome, now called post-traumatic stress disorder, and felt confident in controlling it. So, we moved to St. Mary's.

In June 1975, our first of two sons was born. We named him Joseph Larry Finn, and home life took a drastic change. We loved it. I spent time at the new storefront, turning it into a furnished office. At that time we only had one file cabinet and still needed a desk and chairs. We needed a phone for the office and with it, a new number. We needed to change some letterhead paper and notify all the members, so the switch was fairly easy.

I looked for work, but there was very little manufacturing in the area, so it allowed me time to travel to the Harris Peninsula. I wanted to keep an eye on the progress and to stay in touch with Larry. I was surprised when I saw him. He had apparently begun his growing stage and seemed to be a foot taller, outgrowing all the clothes we gave him. I had to laugh and tease him about it, but I promised to outfit him again as soon as possible. I asked him about all the disruption around their home and if the family's were tolerating it alright.

He said, "With no rent, no one is complaining. Besides, that Mr Sherburn stopped to see what was happening here. He was so impressed that he throwed a big ol' party for all of us. He had a big tent full of food."

I also had time to have a very nice visit with Mrs. Moore. Now in her eighties, she was slowing down noticeably, but still as sharp as a tack. She had the house looking so comfortable, but it was time to leave when I found myself gazing at the fireplace mantle.

"Mrs. Moore, would you like to have another green vase?"

"Oh my! May I see it?"

I retrieved it from the car, and as I handed it to her, she teared up. "Yes," she said, "It's just like the one I broke!"

* * *

In November of that year I received the amazing news that our telephone message recorder had won its patent. Annika took charge as we put it up for bid with the major electronics manufacturers. An international mega-corporation won the bid at three million dollars but also agreed to a royalty of .06 percent for each unit produced. My colleagues and I split the spoils equally, and I dedicated my .02 percent to the Satilla Benevolence. In coming years that small percentage would gain the organization nearly a half million each year. We really didn't need to work any longer, but Annika loved what she was doing and could adjust her time to be completely comfortable.

While scheduling so many meetings with our organization and with my electronics friends, I developed another idea. This one would not require my mechanical abilities, only those of the electronics engineers. My friends had faith when I told them I had another winner, so they signed agreements for intellectual trust. I shared the idea that we needed to develop a device that would permit multiple phone calls to a central device, allowing a conference involving several people to be conducted by phone at just one location. Annika was becoming an old hand at this end of the business, she applied for the patent—which was granted within a year—and put it up for bids straight away. The bidding was won by a major Japanese electronics company, and once again, we donated a portion of the royalties to the Benevolence.

In 1976 Annika announced that she was pregnant again, and the news went out to everyone. I was happy that our house had four bedrooms, as the grandparents and the Wakefields made regular visits. Danny Jr. was already walking, and we had so much fun with him. Satilla Benevolence had several successes that year, and we chose to add projects on the St. Mary's River as well. We managed to stop the mega barges from using the river when the manatee were making their winter migration, which was a win that gained us some notoriety. The phone was ringing more and more with inquiries from humanitarian and natural resource groups. Some had projects worthy of note for our objectives. We had finished two of the Harris Peninsula homes, and construction was moving forward on the next two. Larry was in the top three of his class.

1977 was another year of successes, including the birth of our second son, Hal Joseph Finn. On the downside, we lost Pastor Roy, who we believe went to the Father as a happy man. Before he left us, he managed many things for Catfish John and other inmates at Ware Prison. Aside from his ministries, he started reading classes, employing other inmates as teachers. Catfish was able to learn to read his own Bible. Four houses were now complete on the Harris Peninsula, and the next two were in progress. The grand plan for the entire ten acres was now really taking shape, and everyone there could plainly see that the end result would be beautiful. Danny had completely finished everything at the Catfish Lodge, with the exception of the house itself, which had become a rather large chicken house. It would be left to nature. The store was closed when the collectibles ran out, and Danny was adopted by DNR and given a commission as a special agent. The Wakefield's second child was a girl, and they named her Annika.

Wonderful years passed, with occasional sadness mixed in. We lost Mrs. Rose Walker in 1980, and Sheriff Stump and Judge Richard Stump in 1982. We all attended their funerals. Larry Harris had graduated from high school *summa cum laude*. He had already joined junior DNR officers' cadet school and was active in it. He also went for a degree at Jacksonville University, where he graduated with a degree in law enforcement in 1986. Larry was accepted into the Georgia State DNR as an officer. He proved his worth, not only in his ability to administer the law with fairness, but also with his tough stance on invasive species introduced into the Georgia environment. By 1990, he was chosen as the chief DNR officer for Georgia.

We watched the completion of the Harris Peninsula, transforming the land and the people from a simple existence to one with an ambitious future. The people needed to provide for their own future, but they had been released of any debt or rent.

Even though Satilla Benevolence had not pursued any public presence, recipients of our wrath, and our grace, spread the word. Through grant writing and donations of various kinds, the organization grew. In the early 1980s, the Benevolence had five full-time employees and began work in Florida and the waterways farther north in Georgia. Annika fully enjoyed the work, and I became somewhat of a stay-at-home dad, tending to the boys and the house. I worked mostly as an inspector for the board and approved prints and plans submitted by private and public engineers, like the Army Corps of Engineers.

We lost Mrs. Moore in 1985, and we conducted a memorial for her. Around 1989, I received a call from Joe Galloway, who was organizing a small group of veterans to help General Hal Moore in writing his memoirs and the true story of the battle of the Ia Drang Valley. They were meeting at Hal's mother's house on the St. Mary's River, which was a very good setting for that work.

Whether my recollections helped or not, I don't really know, but they interviewed a great many of the GIs involved in the battle at LZ X-Ray. In 1992, Hal and Joe published *We Were Soldiers Once, and Young*, which quickly became a bestseller. Not long after that they sold the movie rights to Paramount Pictures.

1992 was also the year I was contacted by the University of Florida at Gainesville. They found out that I was a principal with Satilla Benevolence and was skilled with mechanical engineering involving things associated with water and the river. Their biology department was investing in exploration of the Amazon River and were looking for a team of engineers to create an amphibious craft for extended exploration of an aquatic jungle. I joined the team and traveled to the university several times a month for the next three years.

I had made visits to Ware Prison to check on Catfish John two or three times each year, reporting the amazing things that had happened because of him. I always brought plenty of before and after photos. I told him that all the stuff he had piled up that was not recyclable had been cleaned up, but the house was left alone, as the chickens had taken it over. I told him that I had opened up all the cages the first time I was there, and Big Red was so appreciative. John had a laugh over that one. I told him we went through great trouble keeping the location quiet and all intruders kept away.

One day in 1993, Sheriff Joe Leary, who was retiring, called with a message from the prison that John was not doing well and was begging to see his G-Man. I didn't hesitate, as the man had never asked me for anything. On arrival, I learned he had been put into the prison infirmary. The warden knew me well and cut the red tape, taking me directly to his bed. I pulled up a chair, sitting in it backward. I called to John, and as he turned his head toward me, I could see he was struggling, but I asked what he wanted of me.

He worked at his thoughts for a few moments and said, "Just to talk, I knows I ain't got much time." I urged him to continue, that I was listening.

He spoke mostly with his eyes closed as he said, "I thanks you for all that you have done for me, even if it was you that caused me to be here. I knows now that I was a bad man, and one day I may have hurt somebody. I can read now, and I read that Bible you brought back to me."

As he coughed, he chuckled and said, "It took me five years, but I knows I have a friend in Jesus." I expressed my thanks and praise for that. He went on and said, "G-Man, you know that place of mine where you found my house? Well we Cajuns call a piece of land like that an atoll. It's not really an island, but almost. They's two more atolls behind mine—the next was my pappy's hideout, and the one all the way back was my granddaddy's hideout.

John needed to work to catch his breath and think, but he did and continued, "My granddaddy built his hideout at the start of the Civil War. He knew General Lee and General McLean. My daddy told me that he hid all sorts of things for the Southern Army before the war ended, including chests of gold coins. He claimed the North had passed a law called the Legal Tender Act, which made men want to hide coins. After the war, came Jesse James, who hid money from his bank robberies. Jesse stole guns from the Union Army too, and I had me one of them, a Henry. Pappy also said that Granddaddy had relics back there, ancient ones."

John rested for a while, struggling for air. He came around again and said, "My daddy built his place on the second atoll and seemed to know lots of people who needed a place to hide. I was young, but I could see that most of these folks was totin' guns and always had satchels full of money. There was a woman Daddy called Ma Barker, who had two sons with her—seemed like big dummies to me. Then there was Clyde Barrow. He and his girlfriend came to hide several times, but that woman complained about the place the whole time. One day Daddy took some unsavory folks out to do a job, and he never came back. I was stranded and had to build me a raft to float down the river. That's when I stole me a boat, started my own business, and built my own house."

As John struggled, I told him how much I appreciated knowing his past and asked if I could do anything else for him.

He struggled to say, "No, but you better go find my pappy and my granddaddy's places." At that his eyes closed tight, and he quit breathing. Just like that he died. I prayed for his soul and thanked God for my experience with John. The warden expected it and assured me he would receive a proper burial.

I needed to drive through Dixie Union to get home, so I hoped to see the Wakefields. However, I first drove to the marina where the house had sat waiting to be loaded onto the barge. I parked the car where the house had sat for that long weekend. I went to the dock, found a place to sit for a while, and thought deeply about my life path at that time. I went to my God in prayer, thanking him for every path he had sent me down. I thanked him for my survival in Vietnam and that I had been given the opportunity to do many humanitarian things for my fellow Americans. I felt as if I needed to do these things, as my brothers who lost their lives at my side needed me to carry on for them. I confessed my unwillingness to listen to his Holy Spirit at times, but I knew that his guidance had never given up on me. I ended my prayer of thanksgiving.

Going then to the Wakefields, I shared the last dying words of Catfish John with Danny. He shook his head and said, "Holy batz, Finn, here we go again!"

Leo Flory served as a Combat Medic with the famed 101st Airborne "Screaming Eagles," B-Company, 2nd Battalion, 501st Infantry Regiment in Vietnam from 1968-1969. He wrote about his time in Vietnam in the critically acclaimed *101st Airborne Combat Medic: Transition to Duty* (Elm Grove Publishing, 2023).

He lives in Michigan with his wife, Ann.

On The Slow Lam is Leo's first novel.